The Courteous Cad

The
Courteous
Cad

CATHERINE PALMER

Tyndale House Publishers
Carol Stream, Illinois

Visit Tyndale online at tyndale.com.

Tyndale and Tyndale's quill logo are registered trademarks of Tyndale House Ministries.

The Courteous Cad

Designed by Sarah Susan Richardson

Edited by Kathryn S. Olson

Scripture quotations are taken from *The Holy Bible*, King James Version.

Scripture quotations in Miss Pickworth's Ponderings are taken from the *Holy Bible*, New Living Translation, copyright © 1996, 2004, 2007 by Tyndale House Foundation. Used by permission of Tyndale House Publishers, Inc., Carol Stream, Illinois 60188. All rights reserved.

The Courteous Cad is a work of fiction. Where real people, events, establishments, organizations, or locales appear, they are used fictitiously. All other elements of the novel are drawn from the author's imagination.

For information about special discounts for bulk purchases, please contact Tyndale House Publishers at csresponse@tyndale.com, or call 1-855-277-9400.

Library of Congress Cataloging-in-Publication Data

A catalog record for this book is available from the Library of Congress.

Repackage first published in 2023 under ISBN 978-1-4964-7394-3

Printed in the United States of America

29	28	27	26	25	24	23
7	6	5	4	3	2	1

For my husband. I love you.

For God so loved the world, that he gave his only begotten Son, that whosoever believeth in him should not perish, but have everlasting life. For God sent not his Son into the world to condemn the world; but that the world through him might be saved.

JOHN 3:16-17

One

"I shall never marry," Prudence Watson declared to her sister as they crossed a busy Yorkshire street. "Men are cads, all of them. They toy with our hearts. Then they brush us aside as if we were no more than a crumb of cake at teatime. A passing fancy. A sweet morsel enjoyed for a moment and soon forgotten."

"Enough, Prudence," her sister pleaded. "You make me quite hungry, and you know we are late to tea."

"Hungry?" A glance revealed the twitch of mirth on Mary's lips. Prudence frowned. "You think me silly."

"Dearest Pru, you *are* silly." Mary raised her wool collar against the cold, misty drizzle. "One look at you announces it

1

to all the world. You're far too curly-haired, pink-cheeked, and blue-eyed to be taken seriously."

"I cannot help my cheeks and curls, nor have they anything to do with my resolve to remain unmarried."

"But they have everything to do with the throng of eligible men clamoring to fill your dance card at every ball. Your suitors send flowers and ask you to walk in the gardens. On the days you take callers, they stand elbow to elbow in the foyer. It is really too much. Surely one of them must be rewarded with your hand."

"No," Prudence vowed. "I shall not marry. I intend to follow the example of my friend Betsy."

"Elizabeth Fry is long wed and the mother of too many children to count."

"But she obeys a calling far higher than matrimony."

"Rushing in and out of prisons with blankets and porridge? Is that your friend's high calling?"

"Indeed it is, Mary. Betsy is a crusader. With God's help, she intends to better the lives of the poor women in Newgate."

"Better the lives of soiled doves, pickpockets, and tavern maids?" Mary scoffed. "I should like to see that."

"And so you will, for I have no doubt of Betsy's success. I shall succeed, too, when God reveals my mission. I mean to be an advocate for the downtrodden. I shall champion those less fortunate than I."

"You are hardly fortunate yourself, Pru. You would do better to marry a rich man and redeem the world by bringing up moral, godly, well-behaved children."

"Do not continue to press me on that issue, Mary, I beg you.

My mind is set. I have loved and lost. I cannot bear another agony so great."

"Do you refer to that man more than twice your age? the Tiverton blacksmith? Mr. . . . Mr. Walker?"

Prudence tried to ignore the disdain in Mary's voice. They were nearing the inn at which they had taken lodging in the town of Otley. Their eldest sister, Sarah, had prescribed a tour of the north country, declaring Yorkshire's wild beauty the perfect antidote to downtrodden spirits. Thus far, Prudence reflected, the journey had not achieved its aim.

Now, Mary had raised again the subject of great torment to Prudence. It was almost as though she enjoyed mocking her younger sister's passion for a man she could never wed. Whatever anyone thought of him, Prudence decided, she would defend her love with valor and tenacity.

"Mr. Walker is a gentleman," she insisted. "A gentleman of the first order."

"Nonsense," Mary retorted. "He has no title, no land, no home, no education, nothing. How can you call him a gentleman?"

"Of course he has no title—he is an American!" Annoyed, Prudence lifted her skirts as she approached a large puddle in the street. "Americans have no peerage. By law, they are all equal."

"Equally common. Equally ordinary. Equally low." Mary rolled her eyes. "Honestly, Pru, you can do far better than Mr. Walker. Sarah and I hold the opinion that her nephew, Henry Carlyle, Lord Delacroix, would suit you very well indeed. She writes that he is returned from India much improved from their last acquaintance. Delacroix owns a fine home in London and another in the country. He is wealthy, handsome, and titled. In short, the perfect catch. Leave everything to your sisters, Pru. We shall make it all come about."

"You will do nothing of the sort! Delacroix is a foolish, reckless cad. I would not marry him if he were the last man in England."

Annoyed, Prudence stepped onto a narrow plank, a makeshift bridge someone had laid across the puddle. Attempting to steady herself, she did not notice a ragged boy dart from an alleyway. He splashed into the muddy water, snatched the velvet reticule at her waist, and fled.

"Oh!" she cried out.

The plank tilted. Prudence tipped. Her balance shifted.

In a pouf of white petticoats, she tottered backward until she could do nothing but unceremoniously seat herself in the center of the dirty pool. Mud splattered across her blue cape and pink skirt as she sprawled out, legs askew and one slipper floating in the muck.

"Dear lady!" A man knelt beside her. "Are you injured? Please allow me to assist you."

She looked into eyes the color of warm treacle. A tumble of dark curls fell over his brow. Angled cheekbones were echoed in the squared jut of his jaw. It was the face of an angel. Her guardian angel.

"My bag," she sputtered. "The boy took it."

"My man has gone after him. Have no fear on that account. But what of you? Can you stand? May I not help you?"

He held out a hand sheathed in a brown kid glove. Prudence reached for it, but Mary intervened.

"You are mud from head to toe, Pru!" She blocked the

stranger's hand. "You must try to get up on your own. We are near the inn, and we shall find you a clean gown at once."

"Hang my gown!" Prudence retorted. "Give me your hand, sister, or allow this gentleman to aid me. My entire . . . under-carriage is wet."

At this, the man's lips curved into a grin. "Do accept my offer of assistance, dear lady, and I shall wrap my cloak about you . . . you *and* your damp undercarriage."

The motley crowd gathered on the street were laughing and elbowing one another at the sight of a fine lady seated in a puddle. Prudence had endured quite enough derision and mockery for one day. She set her muddy hand in the gentle-man's palm. He slipped his free hand under her arm and helped her rise. Before she could bemoan her disheveled state, he swept the thick wool cloak from his shoulders and laid it across her own.

"My name is Sherbourne," he said as he led her toward the inn. "William Sherbourne of Otley."

"I am Prudence Watson. Of London."

Utterly miserable, she realized a truth far worse than a muddy gown, a missing slipper, and a tender undercarriage. She was crying. Crying first because she had been assaulted. Second because her bag was stolen away. Third because she was covered in cold, sticky mud. Fourth and every other number because Mr. Walker had abandoned her.

He had declared he loved Prudence too much to make her his wife. He kissed her hand. He bade her farewell. And she had neither seen nor heard from him since.

"You will catch pneumonia," Mary cried as she hastened ahead of them to open the inn's door. "Oh, Pru, you will have a fever by sunset and we shall bleed you and care for you and you will die anyway, just like my dear Mr. Heathhill, who left me a widow."

"Upon my word, madam," William spoke up. "I would never lay out such a fate for a woman so young and lovely. Miss Watson is hardly bound for an early grave. Do refrain from such predictions, I beg you."

"Oh, Mary, his rose was in my reticule," Prudence moaned. "The rose Mr. Walker gave me. I pressed it and vowed to keep it forever. And now it is lost."

"Your husband?" William asked. He helped her ascend the stairs and escorted her into the inn. "Give me his name, and I shall alert him to your distress."

"She has no husband," Mary informed him. "We are both unmarried, for I am recently a widow."

"Do accept my sincere condolences."

"Thank you, sir. But we have not been properly introduced. I am Mrs. John Heathhill of Cranleigh Crescent in London."

"William Sherbourne of Otley, at your service." He made a crisp bow. "You are Miss Watson's sister?"

"Yes," Prudence cut in, "and if she will stop chattering for once, I shall welcome her attention. Mary, come with me, for I am shivering."

"Heavens! That is exactly how the influenza began with my dear late husband!" Mary took her sister's arm and stepped toward the narrow staircase. "Thank you, Mr. Sherbourne. We are in your debt."

"Think nothing of it," he replied. "I wish you a speedy recovery and excellent health, Miss Watson. Good afternoon, ladies."

"Such a gentleman!" Mary exclaimed as she accompanied

her sister up the stairs and into their suite. "So very chival-rous. I wager he is married. Even so, I should be happy to see him again. You have his cloak still, and on that account we are compelled to call on him. What good fortune! He is well mannered indeed. And you must agree he is terribly handsome."

Prudence was in no humor to discuss anyone's merits. "Find my blue gown, Mary. The one with roses. And ask the maids to bring hot water. Hot, mind you. I cannot bear another drop of cold water. I am quite chilled to the bone."

While Mary gave instructions to the inn's staff, Prudence began removing her sodden gown. She shuddered at the memory of that boy snatching her reticule. Thank heaven for Mr. Sherbourne's kindness. But Mr. Walker's rose was gone now, just as the man himself had disappeared from her life.

"Did you like him?" Mary asked as she sorted through the gowns in her sister's trunk. "I thought he had nice eyes. Very brown. His smile delighted me, too. He was uncommonly tall, yet his bearing could not have been more regal. If he is yet unmarried, I think him just the sort of man to make you a good husband."

"A husband?" Prudence could hardly believe it. "You were matchmaking while I sat in the mud? Honestly, Mary, you should wed Mr. Sherbourne yourself."

"Now you tease me. You know my mourning is not com-plete. Even if it were, I am certain I shall never find another man as good to me as my dear late Mr. Heathhill."

"If you will not marry, why must you make such valiant efforts to force me into that state? I have declared my intention never to wed. You and Sarah must respect that decision."

"Our duty to you supersedes all your ridiculous notions, Pru. You have no home and no money. Society accepts you only because of your excellent connections."

"You refer to yourself, of course. And Sarah. With such superior sisters to guide me, I can never go wrong."

When the maids entered the room with pitchers of steaming water, Prudence gladly escaped her hovering sister. She loved Mary well enough, but the death of Mr. Heathhill had cast the poor woman into a misery that nothing could erase. Mary's baby daughter resided in the eager arms of doting grandparents while she was away, but she missed the child dreadfully. With both sisters mourning lost love, their holiday in the north had proven as melancholy as the misty moors, glassy lakes, and windswept dells of Yorkshire.

Not even a warm bath and clean, dry garments could stop Prudence from shivering. Mary had gone to the inn's gathering room with the hope of ordering tea. The thought of a cup of tea and a crackling blaze on the hearth sent Prudence hurrying down after her sister.

Amid clusters of chatting guests, she spotted Mary at a table near the fire. Two maids were laying out a hearty tea—a spread of currant cake, warm scones, cold meats, jams, and marmalade. A round-bellied brown teapot sent up a curl of steam.

Prudence chose a chair while Mary gloomily cut the cake and served it. "Not enough currants," she decreed. "And very crumbly."

"I have been thinking about your observations on my situation in life," Prudence said. "I see you cannot help but compare my lot to that of my siblings. Thanks to our late father, Sarah has more money than she wants. You inherited your husband's estate and thus have no worry about the future. But I? I am to be pitied. You think me poor."

"You *are* poor," Mary corrected her. "Sarah is not only rich, but her place in society was secured forever by her marriage into the Delacroix family. She is terribly well connected. Surely you read Miss Pickworth's column in last week's issue of *The Tattler*. She reported that Sarah's new husband is likely to be awarded a title."

"Miss Pickworth, Miss Pickworth. Do you read *The Tattler* day and night, Mary? One might suppose Miss Pickworth to be your dearest friend—and not some anonymous gossip whose reports keep society in a flutter."

"Miss Pickworth keeps society abreast of important news." Mary poured two cups of tea. "I value her advice, and I welcome her information."

"Unfounded rumors and hints of scandal," Prudence retorted. "Nothing but tittle-tattle."

"Oh, stir your tea, Pru."

For a moment, both sisters tended to their cups. But Prudence at last broached a subject she had been considering for some time.

"I am ready to go home," she told her sister. "I want to see Sarah. I miss my friends, Betsy most of all. Anne, you know, is dearer still to me, but she is rarely at home. I do not mind, really, for the thought of Anne only reminds me of Mr. Walker."

"Please forgive my interruption."

A man's deep voice startled Prudence. She looked up to find William Sherbourne standing at their table. He was all she had remembered, and more. His shoulders were impossibly broad, his hair the exact color of strong tea, his hands so large they would circle a woman's waist without difficulty. She had not noticed how fine he looked in his tall black riding boots and coat. But now she did, and she sat up straighter.

"May I trouble you ladies for a moment?" he asked.

"Mr. Sherbourne, how delightful to see you again." Mary's words dripped honey. "Do join us for tea, won't you?"

"Thank you, but I fear I cannot. Duty calls." He turned his deep brown eyes on Prudence. "Miss Watson, my man retrieved your bag. I trust nothing is amiss."

He held out the velvet reticule she had been carrying. So delighted she could not speak, Prudence took it and loosened the silk drawstrings. After a moment's search, she located her small leather-bound journal and opened it. From its pages, the dried blossom fluttered onto her lap.

"Sister, have you nothing to say to Mr. Sherbourne?" Mary asked. "Perhaps you would like to thank him for his kindness?"

"Yes, of course," Prudence said, tucking the rose and notebook back into her reticule and rising from her chair. "I am grateful to you, Mr. Sherbourne. First you rescued me from the street, and now you have returned my bag. You are very gallant."

He laughed. "Gallant, am I? I fear there are many who would disagree with you. But perhaps you would honor me with the favor of your company for a moment. There is someone I wish you to meet."

Prudence glanced at her sister, who was pretending not to notice anything but the few currants in her tea cake.

"Do run along, Pru," Mary said. "I am quite content to take my tea and await your return."

William held out his arm, and Prudence slipped her hand around it. "I hope you do not think me forward in my request," he remarked. "You know nothing of my character, yet you accompany me willingly."

"I have called you gallant," she replied. "Was I mistaken?"

"Greatly." His brown eyes twinkled as he escorted her toward the door of the inn. "I am so far from gallant that you would do well never to speak to me again. But it is too late, for I have taken you captive. You are under my spell, and I may do with you as I wish."

Uncertain, Prudence studied his face. "What is it you wish, sir?"

"Ah, but if I reveal my dark schemes, the spell will be broken. I would have you think me courteous. Noble. Kind."

"You tease me now. Are you not a gentleman?"

"Quite the opposite. I am, in fact, a rogue. A rogue of the worst sort, and never to be trusted. I rescue ladies from puddles only on Tuesdays. The remainder of the week, I am contemptible. But look, here is my man with the scalawag who stole your bag. And with them stands a true gentleman, one who wishes to know you."

Feeling slightly off-kilter, Prudence turned her attention to a liveried footman just inside the inn, near the door. In his right hand, he clasped the ragged collar of a young boy whose dirty face wore a sneer. Beside them stood a man so like William Sherbourne in appearance that she thought they must be twins.

"Randolph Sherbourne, eldest of three brothers," William announced. "Randolph, may I introduce Miss Prudence Watson?"

"I am delighted to make your acquaintance, madam." He made her a genteel bow.

She returned a somewhat wobbly curtsy. It was one thing to

meet one man of stature, elegance, and wit, but quite another to find herself in the presence of two such men.

"Miss Watson, you are as lovely as my brother reported," Randolph said. "His accounts are so often exaggerated that I give them little notice. But in your case, he perhaps did not do you justice."

"I believe I called her an angel, Randolph. There can be no superlative more flattering. Yet I confess I did struggle to give an adequate account of Miss Watson's charms."

"Please, gentlemen," Prudence spoke up at last. She had heard too much already. These brothers were men like all the rest, stumbling over themselves to impress and flatter. "My tea awaits, and I must hasten to thank your footman for retrieving my reticule."

"But of course," William agreed. "Harris, do relate to Miss Watson your adventures of the afternoon."

The footman bowed. "I pursued this boy down an alley and over a fence, madam. In short order, I captured him and retrieved your bag."

"Thank you, Harris." Prudence favored him with a smile. "I am most grateful."

"What shall we do with the vile offender?" William asked her. "I have considered the gallows, but his neck is too thin to serve that purpose. The rack might be useful, but he has already surrendered your reticule, and we need no further information from him. Gaol, do you think? Or should we feed him to wild hogs?"

Prudence pursed her lips to keep her expression stern. "I favor bears," she declared. "They are larger than hogs and make quick work of their prey."

The boy let out a strangled squawk. "Please, ma'am, I'm sorry for what I done. I'll never do it again, I swear."

She bent to study his face and noted freckles beneath the dirt. "What is your name, young man? And how old are you?"

"I'm ten," he said. "My name is Tom Smith."

"Tom Smith," she repeated. "Does your father own a smithy?"

"No, ma'am. My father be dead these three years together."

"I am sorry to hear it. Tell me, Tom, do you believe your father would be pleased that you have taken to stealing?"

"He would know why I done it, for he would see Davy's sufferin' and wish to ease it—same as all of us."

"And who is Davy?" she asked.

"My brother. We're piecers, ma'am. And all our sisters be scavengers. Davy was crippled in the mill." Tom's large gray eyes fastened on William Sherbourne as he pointed a thin finger. "*His* mill."

"Impossible," William said. "My family built our mill, in fact, with the express purpose of providing honest and humane labor for the villagers of Otley."

"Take this, Tom." Prudence pressed a coin into the boy's grimy hand. "Please use it for your brother's care."

"A shillin'?" He gaped at her.

"Yes. But you must promise to turn from crime and always be a good boy."

"I promise, ma'am. With all my heart."

"Run along, then." She smiled as he pushed the shilling deep into the pocket of his trousers.

"You *are* an angel," Tom said. "Truly, you are."

With a final look back at her, he slipped out of the footman's grasp and flew through the doorway and down the street.

"Now that is an interesting approach to deterring misbehavior," William addressed his brother. "Catch a thief, then pay him. What do you think, Randolph? Shall you recommend it to Parliament on your next appointment in the House of Lords? Perhaps it might be made a law."

Prudence bristled. "I gave the shilling to aid Tom Smith's injured brother. Perhaps you should recommend *that* to Parliament. I have heard much about the abhorrent treatment of children who work in the mills."

Randolph Sherbourne spoke up. "My family's worsted mill, Miss Watson, is nothing like those factories of ill repute."

"I believe young Davy Smith might argue the point. His brother blames your mill for the injury."

"Do you take the word of a pickpocket over that of a gentleman?" William asked her.

"I see you call yourself a gentleman when the situation requires one, Mr. Sherbourne. Only moments ago, you were a rogue."

"I fear William's first account of his character was accurate," Randolph told her. "We have done our best to redeem him, but alas, our efforts always come to naught. He is bad through and through, a villain with a black heart and no soul whatever."

"As wicked as that, is he?" Prudence suddenly found it difficult to fan her flame of moral outrage. "Then I am glad our acquaintance will be of short duration. My sister and I soon end our tour of the north country. Perhaps as early as tomorrow morning we shall set off for London."

"But I have hardly begun to abuse William," Randolph

protested. "My brother deserves much worse, and you must know the whole truth about him. My wife and I should enjoy the honor of your company at dinner today. You and your sister are welcome at Thorne Lodge."

"You will never persuade Miss Watson to linger in Yorkshire," William assured his brother. "Her heart hastens her toward a gentleman who has been so fortunate as to win the love of an angel."

"Ah, you are engaged, Miss Watson," Randolph said. "I should very much like to congratulate the man who prevailed over all other suitors."

"His name is Walker," William informed him. "With a single red rose, he secured his triumph."

"You assume too much, sir. I am not engaged." Prudence looked away, afraid the men might see her distress and mock it. "Marriage is not the object of my heart's desire."

"Yet your pain upon losing Mr. Walker's rose was great indeed," William observed. "What can have parted you from him?"

"Upon my honor, Mr. Sherbourne," Prudence snapped, "I think you very rude to intrude on my privacy with such a question."

"Yes, but rudeness is the hallmark of my character. I give offense wherever I go."

"Indeed," Randolph agreed. "William is always impolite and discourteous. I should urge you to ignore him, Miss Watson. But in this case, I am as curious as he. How dare anyone object to a gentleman of whom you approve so heartily?"

"Mr. Walker is an American," she told the brothers. "He is a blacksmith. And poor. With so many disadvantages, society decreed a match between us unconscionable. We were parted, and I do not know where he has gone."

"An American, did you say?" William asked. "Is he an older man? rather tall with a stocky build? black hair?"

"Mr. Walker's ancestors were native to America," Prudence said. "Of the Osage tribe. He is more than twice my age. Sir, do you know him?"

"I hired the man three months ago. He is the blacksmith at my mill."

Prudence gasped. "Mr. Walker is here? in Otley?"

"Perhaps she will not be leaving Yorkshire quite so soon," Randolph commented. "I believe Miss Watson has found a reason to stay."

"She may find reason to go when she learns that Mr. Walker is soon to be married." William's brown eyes softened. "I am sorry to bear unhappy tidings. Dear lady, you look quite pale. May I bring you a chair?"

"No," she said, holding up a hand. "I am unmoved by your news. It is right and proper that Mr. Walker has found a wife. I am very happy for him. And now if you will both excuse me, my sister has long been wishing for my company."

After giving the briefest of curtsies, she turned away and made for the fire as swiftly as her feet would fly. She would not cry. She would not reveal the slightest emotion. No one must guess she felt anything but contentment and perfect ease.

"Whatever is the matter with you?" Mary asked as Prudence sank into her chair. "You look as if you might faint dead away!"

"Mr. Walker is here," Prudence choked out. "In Yorkshire. In this very town. And he is engaged to be married."

Mary offered her handkerchief. "Shocking," she whispered.

"Shocking and sad. But dry your eyes before you make a scene, Pru, for I have just had the most wonderful news from the lady at the next table. Do you not wish to hear it?"

Prudence could barely form words. "No, Mary. I am quite undone."

"You must hear it anyway, for this news concerns you." Mary leaned across the table and lowered her voice. "Mr. William Sherbourne, who rescued you from the puddle and has paid you such extraordinary attention, is a proper gentleman with excellent connections. His eldest brother is a baron and owns a great estate in Yorkshire. His second brother is a clergyman who lives in India. He himself is a most distinguished officer in the Royal Navy, and he has just returned from sea after many months fighting the Americans . . . or was it the French? I can never recall."

"Nor can I," Prudence murmured.

"Never mind, because he has quit the Navy and is now settled in Otley for good. He owns a large worsted mill and is worth five thousand pounds a year. Think of it—five thousand a year! And best of all—he is unmarried. Quite unattached. How wonderful for you!"

Prudence swallowed against the growing lump in her throat. "I do not care if he is worth ten thousand a year and owns five worsted mills, Mary. I do not want him. I do not want him at all."

"Quick, dry your eyes, Pru, for here he comes. And his brother. You may win his heart yet, and what happiness awaits you then. Oh, heavens, why did I not wear my good bonnet?"

Two

"Mrs. Heathhill, forgive me. I have been thoughtless indeed."
William kept his focus on the elder of the two sisters. She was
pretty enough—bright eyes, lustrous brown hair, sweet smile.
But Mary Heathhill could hardly compare to the beauty he had
lifted from a mud puddle that afternoon.

"Thoughtless?" Mary echoed. "Dear sir, you rescued my
sister and returned her stolen reticule. How can I think you
anything but chivalrous?"

"Easily done, once you know him better." Randolph stepped
up to the ladies' tea table. "I fear William is the black sheep
among us."

"Among three brothers," William clarified. "Mrs. Heathhill,
I should like you to meet the eldest, Randolph Sherbourne, Lord
Thorne. Randolph, I am pleased to present Mrs. John Heathhill."

She rose from her chair and gave the most elegant curtsy William had seen in a very long time. Certainly better than her sister's had been. While Mary and Randolph made polite conversation, he ventured a glance at Prudence. Reddened cheeks and a handkerchief knotted in her hand told him she had been weeping.

How in the name of all things right and proper had a common blacksmith won the heart of Miss Prudence Watson? Walker never spoke, and he rarely ventured beyond his cottage near the mill. The man had nothing to recommend him save his skill with a bellows and forge, while Prudence surely was the ripest, juiciest plum in the pudding of London society.

Perhaps she had neither money nor title, but how could such trivialities detract from the mounds of golden hair coiled high above a creamy neck and soft shoulders? Her figure alone—sumptuously curved in all the right places—would garner droves of admirers.

But Prudence had more than beauty in her favor. She had proved herself both intelligent and witty in their short conversation. William had enjoyed the spark of indignation that lit her green eyes when he chided her about rewarding the little thief who had taken her bag. More intriguing, she had declared herself untouchable. No man could steal her heart, for she intended to remain unwed forever. Exactly the sort of challenge he found irresistible.

"My wife is calling at the linen draper's across from the inn," Randolph was saying. "She must have a new ball gown with sleeves, she informs me, for we anticipate a large party of friends from London, and the women will all wear sleeves."

"A lady cannot be happy at a ball unless she is well dressed."

Mary turned her attention to her sister. "Is that not so, Prudence? Indeed it is, for my sisters and I are very partial to balls. Prudence takes particular delight in filling her dance card. Do you not, Prudence?"

Mary touched her sister's shoulder, and the younger woman looked up from the fire in surprise. "What is it, Mary?"

"Lord Thorne and I have just been discussing sleeves, Prudence, for he and his wife are to host a ball in two weeks. Sleeves, as you well know, are indispensable these days."

Without responding, Prudence lifted her teacup and took a sip.

Mary gave a nervous laugh. "We are out of sorts today, you see," she explained. "My poor sister met with a great calamity in the street. Your brother's kind assistance was most welcome, I assure you."

"I am glad William came to your aid today. But do excuse me, Mrs. Heathhill, for I see that my wife has just entered the inn."

As always, William felt a mixture of envy and admiration in the presence of Olivia Sherbourne. Randolph had somehow managed to capture the heart of the woman most forbidden to him. The peace they shared radiated through the room even now. Their love shone as they came together, her deep brown eyes meeting Randolph's blue eyes. Olivia whispered to her husband before turning to the tea table for introductions. Randolph saw that they were quickly made.

"Miss Watson," Olivia said as Prudence attempted to rise. "I am pleased to meet the lady who is all the talk of Otley. Your misadventure in the street has turned wagging tongues from speculation about my choice of silks at the linen draper's, trimmings at the haberdasher's, and designs at the dressmaker. How can I thank you enough? But of course! You and your sister must join us at dinner this very evening. Please say yes, for I cannot bear to think of your dining alone."

When Prudence said nothing, her sister was quick to speak up. "How kind, Lady Thorne. We should be delighted to accept your invitation. I can think of nothing more enjoyable."

"Very good. And, Miss Watson, if you are willing, I am eager to hear a true account of today's events. That William plays the hero in the drama is most astonishing. He has been termed a cad—albeit a charming one."

"I may have been a cad yesterday, dear Olivia," William spoke up. "But perhaps this morning I turned over a new leaf and am now eager to redeem my character. My actions in the street may have been the beginning of a pristine chapter in my life."

Olivia chuckled as she spoke to Mary. "My husband and I hold high hopes for William's reformation, for he is very amiable."

"As we can attest." Mary beamed at him. "Make yourself easy, Mr. Sherbourne. Prudence and I shall delay our judgment of your temperament until we know you better."

"You are kind, Mrs. Heathhill," Olivia said. "And how better to continue such acquaintance than with dinner? With great anticipation we shall await you at Thorne Lodge this evening."

William joined in the general bidding of farewells and adieus, but he could not resist an aside to Prudence.

"Miss Watson," he murmured in all seriousness, "your happiness is my desire. If I may assist you in some way . . . that is, if you should like to meet with any person in my employ . . . if such a meeting might ease your heart, I shall be glad to—"

"No, please," she cut in. "Never mention me to anyone, I beg you. I must not speak to that person. I cannot . . . see him . . . Oh, excuse me!"

With a muffled cry, she rushed from the room.

Mary started after her but then apparently thought better of it. "Prudence is not given to hysterics, I assure you," she informed the gathering. "I fear the distress of my sister's mishap has unsettled her."

"Please comfort Miss Watson with the assurance that we shall never speak of it again," Olivia said. "This evening we shall solicit William's tales of naval exploits. He usually can be coaxed to relate his adventures."

"Though we rarely believe half of what he tells us," Randolph added. "But forgive me, brother—I discredit you again. We affirm your reputed transformation from rogue to gentleman, and we are keen to witness it."

"And so you shall," William pledged. "Mrs. Heathhill, please give your sister my regards."

On that note, they departed the inn and moved down the street toward their carriage. Olivia declared Mrs. Heathhill to be the very picture of a lady, though her younger sibling, she feared, might be the nervous sort. Randolph defended Miss Watson's tender nerves and remarked upon her loveliness.

William kept his thoughts to himself. If Prudence Watson was half the woman he supposed, she was far above him in integrity and virtue.

He had not turned over a new leaf.

Even if he had, she would be beyond him. The secrets of

his past would haunt him forever. He had no doubt of that. Nothing he might do now or in the future could absolve him.

Miss Watson must be left alone. Despite her protests to the contrary, she would find another man to love. In time, memories of her fondness for a certain poor blacksmith would fade. As would any recollection of a man who had helped her from a puddle somewhere in Yorkshire.

❖

"I believe an unmarried woman must do good wherever she goes." Prudence spoke with fervor before the assembled friends and family of Lord and Lady Thorne.

After a sumptuous dinner, they had gathered around the fire in the great drawing room. The meal had warmed Prudence's spirits, and her hosts' kindness had eased her heartache. The subject of eager discussion was Prudence's future, with every participant—except William Sherbourne—advocating matrimony. Several possible husbands were suggested, their merits and shortcomings the theme of heated debate.

"I shall never wed," Prudence declared before they could begin to set a wedding date and select a gown. "Therefore, I await the call of God. When I am certain of the cause He wishes me to champion, I shall march into the fray and do battle to the end."

"Does God often require such violence of His followers?" William Sherbourne asked. "I confess I was blissfully unaware."

He stood with one arm on the mantel, the image of idleness and indifference. The man had said little all evening, and when he did speak, it was to trivialize every topic of conversation. Making jests at the expense of others and bandying with his brother humored him no end. Prudence had decided to despise him.

"Miss Watson, I am of a mind to inspect the armory here at Thorne Lodge," William went on. "You will need a strong shield and a sharp sword if you are to combat the evils of this world."

"Are you *blissfully unaware* of the shield of faith and the sword of the Spirit, sir?" She made little effort to conceal her disdain. "They are described in St. Paul's epistle to the Ephesians. The full armor of God is all I require in my quest."

"Ah, I begin to suspect a Joan of Arc in our midst. Indeed, I feel flames burning about me even now. Or perhaps it is merely the blaze on your hearth, brother, that warms my . . ." He paused and winked at Prudence. "My *undercarriage*."

She looked away, determined not to smile. "Have you a copy of Fordyce's Sermons, Lord Thorne? I believe the nourishment of Scripture may sustain me even more than the fine gooseberry pudding we just enjoyed."

"Certainly," he said. "My forefathers amassed a grand collection of books of which we are exceedingly proud. William, will you be so good as to show Miss Watson to the library?"

Before Prudence could protest, the younger man stepped to her side and offered his arm. Lest the others sense her loathing, she slipped her hand around it.

Unfortunately for Prudence, William possessed a remarkable musculature. She tried not to notice how her fingers formed around his biceps. Had his many sojourns at sea hardened him in both body and soul? He was cynical, mocking, and contemptuous. But his dark eyes beckoned her.

"Miss Watson," he began as they strolled down a corridor

lined with portraits of his ancestors and laid with thick carpets. "I must say how delighted I am to learn you plan to remain forever unwed. I, too, am bound for such a future. As fellow partakers in uncorrupted innocence, we shall be great friends forever. Chums, in fact."

"Chums . . ." She barely mouthed the word.

"When we are together," he continued, "we shall always be at ease. As comfortable as a pair of old shoes. Can you disagree?"

"No," Prudence said, hardly knowing whether to laugh at his preposterous remarks or to consider him quite as mad as poor King George.

But he persisted. "I find I am perfectly content with my lot. The solitary life is unmatched for those of us who prefer piety to a household with a spouse and children."

"Piety?"

"Of course. I do hope you mean to keep yourself chaste."

At his careless use of such a term, a wash of heat flooded Prudence's cheeks. She prayed he would not notice.

"Certainly," she mumbled. Spotting the library a short distance away, she detached from her escort. "Excuse me, Mr. Sherbourne, but I am capable of walking the rest of the way alone."

She picked up her skirts and hurried toward the library, now a veritable haven into which she might escape this man who was at once both disarming and annoying.

"I am glad of your resolve," he said, easily keeping pace. "As King Solomon the wise asserted, a virtuous woman is more valuable than gold."

While still speaking, William reached around Prudence to open the door. Unaware, she took another step and glided into his arms. Catching her breath, she hung there for a moment, conscious that he too had paused in surprise.

Whose fault? Which of them could be blamed for this accidental intimacy?

Neither moved.

"Rubies," she whispered, looking up into warm treacle eyes, soft and luminous in the lamplit hallway.

"Rubies?" he asked.

"Proverbs 31."

At the touch of his hand on her shoulder, the air went out of her, and she sagged against him. His lips brushed her cheek, lit a fire on her mouth.

"Forgive me, Miss Watson." He spoke against her ear, his voice low. "I believe we have arrived at the library."

"Indeed we have," she acknowledged, ducking under his arm.

She stepped through the open door and made for the fireplace on a far wall. William Sherbourne had kissed her! She had allowed it! Worse, she had welcomed it. An instant in another man's arms, and she had betrayed her greatest and only true love.

And for whom? A naval officer so wicked that his own family could not speak of him without scorn. But was she any better?

Prudence had not been faultless in her conduct with Mr. Walker. Her friend Anne had been compelled to reproach her more than once for secret tête-à-têtes and hushed avowals of passion. If her sisters knew what she had done now, they would reprimand her with fervor. Rightly so.

Her pulse thrummed as she stepped up to a bookcase and laid her hand on the nearest volume. Was William still in the room? Or had he gone away in shock? Oh, she could hardly guess what he must think of her. Would he tell his brother about the strumpet in the family library?

"Are you quite sure it was rubies?"

His voice from behind shattered her nerves like a pane of glass breaking. Wrapping her arms around the book and holding it tight against her chest, she turned. He stood less than a pace away. Too close.

"Rubies," she said. "'Who can find a virtuous woman? for her price is far above rubies.' Proverbs 31:10."

When he made no response, she hastened on. "But I do not find Fordyce's Sermons, and so I must return to the drawing room. My sister will be anxious to depart for the inn before the roads are dark. Pardon me."

She made an attempt to start for the door.

"The books on religious matters are shelved near that window," he told her, his outstretched arm blocking her way. "As you see, it is too late to hope for light. Even the moon hides behind a cloud. But you have no cause for alarm, Miss Watson. My brother's torchbearers will run ahead of your carriage."

"All the same, Mary will worry if I am away long."

"Will she?" He touched a tendril of her hair that had escaped its knot. "Mrs. Heathhill was content when we left her. I believe she and Lady Thorne had agreed to exhibit their talents on the pianoforte. In fact, I hear them now. My brother will be entertained. He is a great aficionado of music. We are not missed."

"I love music too. I should enjoy a recital."

She started to move away again, but his fingers on the lock of her hair prevented it.

"Sir," she said, "please release me."

"I beg your pardon." He lowered his hand. "I am bemused at such a curl. In the whole of my life, I have never seen another like it."

"You jest, of course. Many woman have curly hair. Mine gives me no end of trouble. It is willful."

"Much like the lady who possesses it."

"On the contrary, I am most compliant, Mr. Sherbourne. I assure you of that. Now if you will excuse me, I have selected a book which I am eager to read, and I must return to my sister."

"Of course. I should not want to prevent you from your perusal of . . ." He took the book from her arms. "*Two Treatises: in the One of Which, the Nature of Bodies; in the Other, the Nature of Mans Soule; Is Looked Into.* Ah, an enlightened tome. Do you wish to study bodies, Miss Watson, or souls? Mr. Kenelm Digby will allow either or both."

Prudence looked down at the title. How could she have chosen such an ill-befitting subject? Now Mr. Sherbourne had found a new way to tease and embarrass her. But she did not have to endure it.

"Man's soul is well worth study," she told him. "I have met many gentlemen, sir, and few can boast any redeeming qualities. You, for example, are determined to make a mockery of everything and everyone. In the short time we have known each other, I daresay I have not heard a single admiring comment about you. Your entire family enjoys goading you to your face. The poor children employed at your mill speak openly of your heartlessness and cruelty. Indeed, I am sure Mr. Kenelm Digby, whose treatise I hope to read momentarily, would have enjoyed making a study of your soul. Perhaps he concludes that some men have no soul at all."

"You are correct in every wickedness you surmise about me, Miss Watson." He looked down, a frown furrowing his brow, as if he saw his failings written out across the carpet. "I am not a good man. I have committed such evil, in fact, that I cannot hope to be forgiven. I do have a soul, but it is blacker than the night outside that window. I might as well have sold it to the devil for all the good it will do me in the life to come. And now you know all there is to understand about me."

He lifted his head. She expected to see the smirk that would tell her he once again made light of what she had said. But his expression was sober, his dark eyes shadowed.

"Take Mr. Digby to the drawing room," he said, handing back the book. "Read what he has to say about men's souls, Miss Watson. Tell me if, upon my death, I may anticipate anything but the flames and torment of a fiery lake. But I shall seal my fate with a comment I cannot resist: Mr. Walker the blacksmith was lucky to win the love of a woman like you. And he is the greatest fool alive to have let it go. Should I ever be so blessed as to win your good opinion, be assured that nothing in the world could induce me to sacrifice it."

His serious tone could not be mistaken.

"It is not my good opinion you should seek, Mr. Sherbourne," she told him. "It is God's. You will find Him more forgiving than I and certainly more merciful. But I shall endeavor to like you. We are, after all, chums."

With a little curtsy, she ended their conversation and left the room as swiftly as she could without breaking into an all-out run.

William sat at the end of a settee, as far as he politely could from the jolly gathering in the drawing room. After much pleading from the other guests, Mrs. Heathhill and Miss Watson had condescended to sing. Their voices were melodious and sweet as they blended in perfect harmony. Standing at the pianoforte, they gazed at one another with such fondness that William could scarcely endure it. Such genuine happiness. Such sisterly affection. Such innocence and wholesome beauty. He felt ill.

The life he had tried to leave behind held nothing in common with the genteel accord of these friends assembled at Thorne Lodge. An evening of dining, music, polite conversation. There had been some mention of whist. Perhaps they would even dance. Heaven forbid.

"Your humor, brother, is as black as the coals on our grate." Randolph, who had approached from behind, now seated himself in an ornate chair beside William. "Surely Miss Watson's pretty smile has little to do with your dark disposition."

"She is nothing to me," William returned. "I have known women ten times as pretty who could not disturb the rhythm of my heartbeat. She is a city lady who cannot cross a country street without tumbling into a mud puddle. Forgive me, but I have no more to say about her."

Randolph chuckled. "I shall take this discourse as proof that Cupid's arrow has struck true. Methinks you do protest too much."

"Now you quote Shakespeare. Miss Watson took delight in reciting the Bible. Has no one in this room an original thought?"

"William, your scorn fatigues me, and I know its source. I shall not mince words. The boy we met this afternoon most certainly works at Quince's Mill. He cannot be one of our laborers, and you are not to blame for his brother's injury."

"How like you to meddle until you have discovered the source of my unease." William watched as the women rearranged themselves at the pianoforte—colorful butterflies hovering around a drop of honey. Now Mrs. Heathhill played while her sister treated the company to a solo.

"I did not like the look of Tom Smith's wagging finger," William went on. "For all I know, he and his siblings do work at Thorne Mill. Injuries are common, Randolph. The piecers and scavengers move about in the midst of such a tangle of looms, carding engines, and scouring machines it is a wonder we don't behead several a day."

"William!" With a wry laugh, Randolph leaned back on the settee. "The things you say never cease to astonish me. You know we built the mill to the specifications of the best architect in Yorkshire. Our looms are as safe as any such mammoth apparatus can be."

"They were safe when we installed them. But I have been away at sea these many months. I do not know how well my overlookers tend the machinery or supervise the laborers. I confess the mill was not my primary concern while my men engaged the French navy in battle."

"Yet I have been here all the time, and I have heard no complaints."

"You were engaged in wooing and wedding Olivia Hewes, as I recall. Not to mention producing your heir and spare."

"The spare is only just under way, brother," Randolph said in a low voice. "Keep that information to yourself, if you will."

"Am I not the paragon of discretion?"

"Hardly." Randolph studied the gathered ladies. "She is a beauty, William. I assure you I have never known a woman so lovely or so good."

"Her hair is too curly, don't you think? Bits and pieces keep escaping her knot." He paused and smiled. "You were talking of Miss Watson, were you not?"

"My *wife*," Randolph growled. "You know very well who I meant."

"Your wife is perfect. Miss Watson is silly. A woman of such surpassing beauty can have nothing in her head but gowns, balls, receptions, intrigues, and gossip. I ought to cast my lot with her sister. A widow might make a tranquil diversion."

"William, can you never be serious? Mrs. Heathhill is in mourning, and her temperament is unsuited to yours. But observe Miss Watson now. She sings well. Her manners are impeccable, and her family is well connected. You really should marry. It would do you good to gain the steadying influence of a wife."

"Hmm . . . yes, I suppose so." He mused on the curve of her shoulder as she turned a sheet of music for her sister. "If you must know, Randolph, Miss Watson and I have an agreement."

"What?" His brother sat up straight. "Already?"

"In the library just now. We spoke; we kissed; we confessed our true feelings. In short, we are in perfect accord. Our future union is settled."

"Can you mean this? William, speak plainly. You hardly know the woman. Are you engaged already?"

"Engaged? Oh no. Our agreement is of another sort. Until death do us part, we are to be the best of chums."

"You agreed to be friends? You and Miss Watson? William, you astonish me."

"It is my single aim to astonish my eldest brother three times each day. If Edmund were not busy scuttling about in India, I should enjoy dumbfounding him as well."

"I shall not give way to your impudence, William. You need a wife, and Miss Watson is suitable in every way. Can you not set aside your melancholy air and dark wit long enough to win her heart?"

"Win her and then grow glum and miserable again? She would not like that, I think. No, we are not well matched. She loves London, and I prefer the country. She is pious, and I am irreverent. She is happy and charming, while I am always tedious. Leave me in peace, Randolph. My future is laid out. I intend to maim as many children as possible in my mill, develop a wicked case of gout, and die a bitter old man."

"How lovely you sing, Miss Watson," Randolph exclaimed, drowning the end of William's remarks as the young lady approached. He stood to welcome her. "I have rarely heard that tune sung with such animation. Do you not agree, William?"

"You might be mistaken for a nightingale, Miss Watson."

She seated herself on the settee, though at a distance from him. It was all William could do not to stare at her. Singing had heightened the color in her cheeks and brought a bright fire to her eyes. She was—he could no longer deny it—the most beautiful woman he had ever met. Their kiss in the library played at the edges of his mind, taunting and mesmerizing him with possibilities. Yet there were no possibilities. He knew that too well.

With a genuine smile of pleasure, she took a fan from her bag. "You have a marvelous pianoforte, sir," she addressed Randolph. "I am delighted with the purity of its sound. Indeed, this has been a lovely evening—a great boost to my spirits after my earlier mishap."

"My wife and I are pleased to welcome you at Thorne Lodge as often as you like, Miss Watson. But I fear you are eager to return to London and deprive us of your company."

"I abhor the city. Balls and receptions fatigue me, and I take little joy in shopping for bonnets or ribbons. My sisters find my indifference dreary. Mary adores being always in society, and Sarah has learned to like it well enough. But I should much prefer riding across the moorland over carriage rides in Hyde Park. While I do enjoy dancing, I would rather spend an evening walking along a country lane. Can you disagree with my preference?"

"Not at all. Indeed, William was just saying how much he enjoys the country. Like you, he prefers it to town. Were we not discussing that, William?"

"With zeal. I daresay we could have gone on about it for another hour at least."

At this comment, Randolph shot his brother a glare. But when Prudence turned to him again, he brightened.

"My brothers and I all fancy the out-of-doors, Miss Watson. William is a particularly skilled rider. Everyone admires his form. Nor does he object to shooting and foxhunting in season. I have known him to swim often in pools and streams on our estate. There is little in the way of sport and exercise that he does not enjoy. I cannot think of anything you dislike, brother."

"I am not fond of idle chitchat."

"Oh, come now. Verbal jousting is one of your greatest talents."

"I will not argue that. Were there a contest in irritating and infuriating one's family and friends, I should win first place."

"Champion of the world, no doubt." Randolph addressed Prudence again. "Miss Watson, I fear you know little of our beloved Otley save a mud puddle and a vexing rogue. My wife and I wish to welcome you and your sister to stay here at Thorne Lodge for as long as you like. Have you any fixed engagements in town?"

"Well, we . . . we . . . ," she began, clearly fumbling about for excuses. "We have been very long away from my sister's young daughter. I am sure she misses her mother. And our eldest sister has sent several letters to inquire when we shall return to London. Sarah is anxious to see us again."

"But you asked about fixed engagements, Lord Thorne," Mary Heathhill pointed out as she and Olivia joined the others near the fire. "Prudence has none. Her family and friends can do without her very well for at least a fortnight. Perhaps even a month."

"Dispensable, is she?" William muttered, perhaps a little too loudly.

"Prudence is dearly loved, I assure you, Mr. Sherbourne." Mary favored him with a forced smile.

She did not like him. William saw the aversion plainly written on her face. Yet somehow he had become the object of her matchmaking endeavors. Mary must have decided that Prudence should marry William, though she herself could hardly endure him.

"Our dear sister brings us such pleasure," Mary continued, "that we are quite gloomy when she is away. Yet her contentment is always our aim. We gladly surrender her company on the many occasions when she is invited to stay in the country."

"Then you must join us here for another month, Miss Watson," Olivia offered. "Spring is nearly upon us, and summer will follow very soon after. You will take great joy in exploring the moors as the heather blossoms and the birds begin to nest. Many of our closest friends stay in the country all year, and they would love to know you. Perhaps we shall give a ball to introduce you."

"I adore a ball," Mary spoke up. "There is nothing I like better than dancing."

"Then you must stay too, Mrs. Heathhill," Olivia insisted. "We keep a stable of many fine riding horses. As you enjoy the exercise so much, Miss Watson, I am sure William can take you out for several short excursions."

"My goodness . . . such generosity." Prudence glanced at William, then quickly looked away. "You are all so kind. Were circumstances different, I should eagerly agree to your invitation. But I fear our long journey has fatigued me no end."

She stood abruptly. "Indeed, I am so tired, I fear I shall become as irritating and infuriating as Mr. Sherbourne claims to be."

"We cannot have two irksome characters in one house," William agreed. He rose and made her a little bow. "You and I are forced to remain apart forever, Miss Watson, lest we exasperate our loved ones. Good evening, then. And, Mrs. Heathhill, how very congenial you are. Thank you so much for deigning to trespass upon us this evening."

"Trespass!" Mary gasped out the word, but Randolph, Olivia, and Prudence were swift to surround her, covering the awkward moment with the general hubbub of farewells and thank-yous. In a veritable tempest of chatter, the entire company made for the drawing room door. Randolph called for a carriage. Olivia ordered cloaks and bonnets returned to their owners. Servants bustled about.

As the sounds faded down the hall, William stepped to the fire. He leaned one arm on the mantel and gazed at the flickering blaze. He felt content. Prudence Watson was beautiful, accomplished, and kind. A better man than he would make her happy one day. No matter what William might wish, he had spurned her for all the right reasons.

One stolen kiss and his heart had begun to ache. He longed for a life he could never have. He hungered for a happiness that could not be his. Yet once again, he had succeeded in resisting urges and desires that would only make him—and everyone else—miserable.

The woman had gone. Temptation had been eluded. He was alone again.

William closed his eyes, leaned his forehead on his arm, and offered up a prayer to a God who long ago had stopped listening. "Thank You," he mouthed. "Thank You."

Three

"*Trespass!*" Mary turned from the mirror where she had been admiring the jet brooch at her throat. "Did you hear him, Pru?"

"I heard him. Every word." Prudence had opened a diamond-paned window to let in the cool, misty air. It was early, and the two women had breakfasted and packed their trunks before dressing for the day. The coach would arrive at the inn soon to whisk them back to London for yet another round of balls and receptions.

Leaning against the sill, Prudence observed the market vendors pushing their carts along the cobbled street below. The puddle—site of the previous day's humiliation—had dried. No one would need William Sherbourne's rescuing arms today.

"Horrid man! I detest him." Mary was adjusting her brooch

as she spoke. "He comes from a fine family, but he besmirches their good name with his insolent speech and unmannered behavior. I should be ashamed to call him brother."

"You will never have that obligation, I assure you."

"No, for Sarah and I would never permit you to become his wife. I liked Mr. Sherbourne at first, I confess. He is uncommonly handsome, and some might call him a wit. But it was not long before his contemptuous and odious character came to light. Your sisters shall settle on a better husband for you, Pru. Have no fear."

"I have great fear of your meddling, Mary!" Prudence spoke to her sister in alarm. "How often must I tell you that I shall never marry? How loudly must I shout it until you hear me? It is really too much. You ignore me time and again."

"What is that dreadful clatter?" Mary frowned at her sister. "It sounds as if the whole town is falling down."

Prudence looked into the street to discover a stream of people pouring out of their homes. Garbed in patched, faded clothing, they carried baskets under their arms and wore wooden shoes on their feet.

"I believe it is the mill workers," she told Mary. "They wear pattens."

"How many can they be? Is it an entire army?"

"Enough for Mr. Sherbourne to injure several a week, I should think. Someone ought to—oh!"

The sudden realization that Mr. Walker might be among the throng brought a gasp to Prudence's lips. She set her hands on the sill and leaned out, searching for a man who would stand head and shoulders above the others. His dark hair would be threaded with silver. His massive shoulders would—

There! She covered her mouth with her hand to keep from crying out again.

Mr. Walker, who had held her in his arms, kissed her lips, whispered his love . . . now walked beside a small woman in a mobcap and cotton apron. He smiled at the woman, saying something Prudence could not make out. His companion laughed. A thin girl held her hand. A taller boy followed close behind.

"What is it, Pru?" Mary stepped to her side. "I heard your gasp of shock. Let me see."

"It's nothing." Prudence straightened, blocking the window. "Your brooch is crooked, Mary. You should return to the mirror and try again."

"Stand aside, sister. You're quite pale, and I must have a look at what has distressed you." Shouldering Prudence aside, Mary peered out the window. "Just as I thought! It's that boy again. The one who knocked you into the puddle. It appears he does work at the mill, after all. It must be his brother they carry along. Poor child."

Relieved and confused all at once, Prudence joined her sister. In the distance, Mr. Walker and his companions were just rounding a corner, nearly indistinguishable in the flood of other laborers. Pulse pounding, Prudence gripped the sill as he vanished from sight.

How could he have found another woman so quickly? It was not a year since their sad parting. Prudence had danced with many men and received countless callers since that day, but none could fill the empty place Mr. Walker had left in her heart. No man ever would.

"You should give him the leavings from our breakfast, Pru."

Mary shook out her skirt as she left the window. "We have two kippers, several buns, a nice cheese, and plenty of fresh butter. Wrap it in a napkin and take it down to him. Make haste, or he will soon be out of sight."

Give Mr. Walker their breakfast scraps? Bewildered, Prudence could hardly fathom such an act. Would he not be offended? But Mary was gathering up the remaining items on the table and tying them into a white cloth. She pushed the bundle at her sister and bade her fly.

"Tom Smith! Tom Smith!"

Mary's voice rang out as Prudence left their chamber and hurried down the steps. She burst into the street and came to a halt. At the inn's front door, Tom stood looking at Mary. He and a little girl supported a frail boy by his arms.

Seeing Prudence, he tugged off his cap and attempted a bow. "Mornin', ma'am. If you please, we must hurry to the mill, for if we are late again, the overlooker will beat us."

"Beat you?" Shaking off her preoccupation with Mr. Walker, Prudence shifted her attention to the three children. "Here, Tom, take this. It is fish and bread for your dinner."

"Thank you. We are much obliged." He tucked the package under his free arm and was turning away when Prudence stopped him.

"Is this your sister, Tom? and your brother?"

"Aye, she be Martha, and here be Davy what I told you about yesterday. The other sisters are gone ahead of us already, five of them."

Each arm draped around a sibling's shoulders to bear his weight, the younger boy was gaunt and pasty white. His great gray eyes, identical to those of his brother and sister, regarded

Prudence from under a fringe of long black lashes. Like their brother, Davy and Martha sported a sprinkling of freckles beneath the dirt and grime on their cheeks.

Prudence gathered her skirts and crouched to face the boy. "Davy, were you truly injured at Thorne Mill?"

"Aye, ma'am." He bent and drew his pant leg up to the knee.

At the shocking sight of twisted bone and scarred flesh, she gasped. "Was Davy taken to the doctor, Tom?"

"Not yet, ma'am. Until your shillin' yesterday, we had no money for it." He returned his cap to his head. "Davy's leg were caught in a machine, you see, and the skin and flesh peeled off. The bone weren't broke so much as bent. It happened six months ago, and we all prayed that God would put his leg right again. But our hope is gone now. So we help Davy back and forth to the mill between two of us. I always hold him up on the right side and our sisters trade out for the left."

"But how can your brother work when he is in such poor health? He must be in pain every moment."

"If Davy don't work, ma'am, there ain't enough for us all to eat. As I said yesterday, our father be dead these three years. With him went our garden and sheep, for none could tend them but he. Our mother be ill with mill fever a good bit of the time."

"Do you go to school?"

Tom cast a worried glance in the direction of the mill. "No, ma'am. We work till sundown, and the mill has no school. If these questions lead to wantin' your shillin' back, I'll give it to you, but truly we must go."

"The overlooker has a thong and a stick," Martha spoke up, her voice high and childlike. "I can bear the thong, but Dick the Devil kicked me from my stool last week. If he goes after me with the stick, I may perish."

"Dick the Devil? Is that what you call the overlooker?" A shiver of horror went down Prudence's spine. "Go quickly, then, children. I am sorry to have kept you."

"Good day, ma'am. God bless!" Tom called over his shoulder as he and his sister dragged their brother down the street.

Wrapping her arms around herself, Prudence watched the children until they and the other mill workers disappeared around a corner. Tom, Davy, and Martha Smith. Five more sisters besides these three. Eight children laboring from sunup to sundown under threat of a beating from Dick the Devil.

Prudence reflected on her own idyllic childhood—riding horses across meadows, swinging from the branch of a great oak tree, sitting on a flat green croquet lawn to study Latin verbs with her tutor. Her stomach had rarely groaned with hunger, for tea and scones were always at the ready. She wore colorful silk frocks and slippers especially crafted to fit her feet. Her bonnets were trimmed in ribbon and lace to match her gowns. Singing and painting lessons, evenings around a pianoforte, embroidery and beading—these had been her leisurely pursuits.

True, she had known hardship. Like the Smith children, Prudence had lost a parent too early. Her mother had died, and her father grew bitter and cold. Sarah was sent away to school, then married off to a man she did not love. Prudence and Mary mourned their losses. But sorrow had been eased by outings to the theater, expeditions to the lake country, sea bathing at Brighton, and a hundred other pleasures.

God had blessed her greatly. Until this moment, she had

never even known of any man so cruel as Dick the Devil. God's blessings . . . the devil's cruelty.

At the disturbing vision of a world divided cleanly in two—one side good and the other evil—Prudence trembled. A shiver coursed through her. Tears welled in her eyes.

"Is the coach late today?" Mary's voice rang out. She stepped into the street and looked it up and down. "I shall be quite put out if we do not reach our destination by teatime."

Pondering her revelation, Prudence did not respond. Instead, she began walking. At first, her steps were hesitant. But as determination took hold inside her, she gained speed.

"Pru, where are you going?" Mary called. "I expect the coach just now. What has come over you?"

She rushed forward and grasped Prudence's wrist. "Speak to me, sister! Oh, dear, you are very chill, indeed. So much like my poor late husband at the onset of his influenza. You must come out of the mist at once. Return to the inn with me, and we shall sit by the fire until the coach arrives."

"Stop pulling me, Mary." Prudence removed her sister's hand and began walking again in the direction of the worsted mill. "I am not ill. Not in the least."

"But where are you going? Truly, you are not well. Your cheeks are flushed. Your eyes are glazed. Oh, heaven help us!"

Prudence stopped. Excitement coursed through her as she took her sister's shoulders and gazed into concerned brown eyes. "Mary, I have just heard the voice of God. Not two minutes ago. In the street. He has revealed my mission."

"What nonsense are you talking, Pru? Did Tom Smith do something to you again? I knew he was not to be trusted!"

"No, Mary, listen to me. I know what I am to do with my

life. God has given me a crusade, a battle I must wage for Him." She lifted her chin and squared her shoulders. "I am to save England's children from the worsted mills."

Mary's eyes narrowed. "Did that boy offer you tea or a biscuit? Did you drink something?"

"I am perfectly fine, sister. Indeed, I am happier than I have been in many years. Can't you see? I have a purpose at last. I am going to save the mill children!"

"Ah, there is the coach—thank heaven. Return with me and take your seat while I order the trunks sent down. We shall depart this misty, dreary place at last, and you can tell me all about your little crusade on the way to London."

"I cannot go home, Mary," Prudence declared as she set her stride again. "I must stay in Otley. I must help these children— Tom Smith and the others. God has commissioned me to better their lives by giving up my own."

"Prudence Watson, you speak not two words of sense together!" Mary stumbled in an effort to match her sister's pace. Her voice was shrill. "Stop this foolishness, Pru! At once! Get into the coach before we are left behind!"

"I stay here, sister. Mr. William Sherbourne and his wicked overlookers will rue the day I set foot in their town. The children will have good food to eat, a school, clean clothes, time to play outside. I see it all now, Mary, as though a golden path has been laid out before me. I can do nothing but travel that path, for it is my destiny."

"Excuse me, ladies," the coachman called to them. "Do you mean to take your seats? I'm bound for Leeds and late as it is. I've no time to dawdle."

"We shall have our trunks sent down to you in a moment,"

Mary assured him. She lowered her voice to a growl. "Prudence, you are a silly girl who should be dancing at balls, flirting with men, and finding a suitable husband. Now get into the coach!"

"Go back to London, Mary." Joy filling her, Prudence lifted her hands over her head and spun about in a circle. "Tell everyone what I mean to do here in Yorkshire! Tell Betsy Fry most especially, and ask her to pray for me. If she can better the lot of England's poor prisoners, then I can rescue our nation's children from slavery."

"Slavery?" Mary caught Prudence around the waist and forced her to halt. "Those children are working at the mills just as their parents and grandparents before them. A single woman cannot hope to change that, nor should she. God Himself ordained the proper order of things—from kings in their palaces to the poorest paupers on the street. Elizabeth Fry has put this religious rubbish into your head, and I shall tell her what I think of it."

"Mrs. Heathhill, I believe the coach must depart Otley at once." A footman approached the sisters, addressing Mary in an urgent tone. "Shall I order your trunks brought down?"

"Oh, hang the trunks!" Mary exclaimed. "Tell the coachman to be off. We shall sort out this muddle and go to London on the next coach."

"Oh, Mary, thank you!" Prudence threw her arms around her sister. "I am so happy. So truly happy. How can anyone be as glad as I? At last God has spoken to me, and at last I see my future life. I must go to the mill at once. There is no time to lose. Even now, Dick the Devil may be beating poor Martha with his stick. I shall insist on being let inside, and there I shall see . . . I shall see . . ."

Her voice hung on the words as the truth seeped in. She would see none other than Mr. Walker.

◆

William Sherbourne took the proffered hat and gloves from a footman and stepped through the front door of Thorne Lodge. The morning mist curling up from the distant moors might have charmed him had he been in a better humor. At sea so many months, he had pined for the wild, barren beauty of Yorkshire. But his return to Portsmouth brought the crushing reality of a series of misfortunes and errors he had set in motion and could never undo. And Otley—so dearly loved throughout his childhood—had not proven a healing balm.

Randolph's bliss in marriage and fatherhood tormented William with longing for the same contented state. Edmund's felicitous match—a lovely woman his equal in religious ardor and intellect—made a mockery of William's fruitless efforts to better his own lot.

The latest in a string of encounters that had succeeded in humbling and humiliating William had culminated in words he could not forget.

"I have met many gentlemen," Prudence Watson had told him the previous night. Her bright green eyes sparked with disdain, and her pretty lips curled in scorn. *"Few can boast many redeeming qualities."*

She referred pointedly to him, of course.

"You," she had asserted, *"are determined to make a mockery of everything and everyone. In the short time we have known each other, I daresay I have not heard a single admiring comment about you. Your entire family enjoys goading you to your face. The poor*

*children employed at your mill speak openly of your heartlessness
and cruelty."*

How could he deny the truth in her accusations? Impossible.
She was accurate in every allegation.

"Your horse, sir." A stableman led the animal to the foot of
the stone staircase. William set his tall black hat on his head
and tugged on his gloves as he descended. He did not recognize
the horse, just as he did not know the man who held its bridle.
Everything had changed since his last sojourn in Otley . . . himself most of all.

"Thank you, my good man," William said, taking the reins.
"And your name?"

"Hedgley, sir."

"Hedgley, do you know Thorne Mill at Otley?"

"Aye, sir. My wife and children labor there."

The news surprised William. He had supposed the Thorne
estate employed entire families.

"What do they say about the mill?" he continued. "Does the
overlooker treat them well?"

The stableman cast a sideways glance. "They are pleased
to have work, sir. Very pleased."

"I am sure they are. But do they call the overlooker a fair man?"

"They . . . they work at several tasks at the mill. My wife
is a weaver. Some of the children are piecers, scavengers, wool
sorters. They work under different overlookers."

William would get nothing out of the man, he saw. He
would have to observe the condition of the mill for himself.
The sooner the better.

"Thank you, Hedgley." He mounted the horse, but before
setting out, he spoke again. "Have you sons?"

"Aye, sir. Five."

"I have noted that our maze is overgrown and the rose beds are sadly out of sorts. Would your sons like to work in the gardens at Thorne Lodge? Or do they prefer the mill?"

"The gardens." He answered quickly, his face brightening. "Indeed, sir, I should be most grateful to see my sons in the gardens."

"I shall speak to my brother. I am sure he can find places for them."

"Thank you, Mr. Sherbourne. Thank you very much. I am most obliged."

Before the man could abase himself further, William turned the horse and set off for Otley.

◆

As Prudence neared Thorne Mill, her elation flagged and her determination wavered. It did not help that Mary continued to add to the list of reasons why it was imprudent to take another step toward the large stone building.

"What if you are injured?" Mary threw out, a last gasp for some reason to hold her sister at bay. "You saw that boy, Pru. He was not at all well."

"A machine had peeled away most of his leg, Mary. Of course he was not well."

"And what is to say your leg will not be peeled, too? The workers have been told where to stand. They know how to look out for their safety, but you have never been inside a worsted mill in your life. You could be ground to bits! Mashed as flat as an oatcake! Torn to ribbons!"

"Honestly, Mary, do be sensible. I shan't be *working* in the mill. I mean to observe the laborers and their conditions. Then God will reveal the manner by which I am to ease their lot."

Arguing the whole way, the two women neared the imposing structure. The road took them alongside a wide brook that flowed toward the building. Workmen had dammed this stream to maintain a steady supply of water, and brown reeds encircled the resulting millpond. From the pond, a channel cut into the earth formed the millrace. The headrace brought water from the pond to the wheel, and the tailrace—which Prudence could barely see in the distance—carried it away. The great wooden wheel had been set inside the mill, but she heard it creak as each blade cut through the rushing water.

Though she and Mary were outside in the fresh air, the rumble of machinery grew deafening as they approached. Thick stone walls did little to muffle the sound. Black smoke belched from a tall brick chimney. Windows, few and small, appeared to be coated in soot. Tiny white particles of dust filled the air and sifted through the open front door.

"I'm sorry, ladies, but we don't sell worsted from the mill." A rangy fellow in a leather apron emerged from inside. "You'll find cloth at the two dressmakers' shops in the village. The better stuff we send to London. I'd advise you to stop at Messrs. Henry Howell & Co. in Cheapside for your finest Yorkshire worsted."

Prudence recognized the name of one of the choice linen drapers in London.

Mary brightened at the mention of this familiar dress shop, a favorite of hers for many years. "I am pleased to learn the source of the worsted I purchase in London," she told the man. "Thank you for this information. My sister and I are sorry to have troubled you. We shall retire to the inn now. We depart for London as soon as may be."

"I should like very much to see inside the mill, sir," Prudence spoke up. "I wish to observe the looms."

"Observe the looms?" He scratched the back of his head. "Why would you do that, if you don't mind my asking? Do you have a problem with the quality of our worsted?"

"I have a problem with the looms themselves. One of them harmed my friend—Mr. Smith by name. He has been crippled since the incident. Today I was shocked to learn that neither the owner nor the overlookers at this mill engaged a doctor to treat Mr. Smith's injuries. Equally bad, he was not given a better and safer position. He is still a piecer."

"A piecer?" The man's eyes widened. "Your friend . . . Mr. Smith . . . works here? As a piecer?"

"You are surprised?"

"There ain't no misters doing piecework in this mill. We've only children at that job, boys and girls both."

"Children? Do they go to school before or after their hours in the mill?"

He swallowed, growing discomfort written on his face. "You cannot hail from Yorkshire, madam, or you would know we've no school around these parts. Like everyone at the mill, the children labor from dawn to dusk."

"But when do they play?"

"Play?" His brow furrowed. "If you'll excuse me, ladies, I'll fetch the piecers' overlooker. Perhaps he knows your Mr. Smith. Who shall I say is calling?"

"I am Miss Prudence Watson. This is my sister, Mrs. Heathhill."

"Very good. The overlooker can answer your questions. My work is in the smithy."

The smithy. Her pulse quickening, Prudence watched the man reenter the mill. So . . . he worked with Mr. Walker. Somewhere inside these walls labored the man who had swept up her heart and would possess it always.

It mattered not if he married another woman, Prudence told herself. She would love Mr. Walker forever. His kindness, his bravery, his handsome face could never be forgotten.

But she had not come to the mill in search of Mr. Walker. She had walked this way in obedience to God, while following the path He had laid out. She stood at the door to Thorne Mill for one purpose alone: to rescue the children from slavery.

"Come, Mary," Prudence ordered. "We must see this vile edifice for ourselves."

"You mean to go inside? Upon my word, Prudence, I shall not take a single step into that mill. And neither will you! This mission of yours is utter nonsense."

"Then I shall meet you at the inn when I return," Prudence replied. Lifting her skirts, she climbed the steps and walked through the door into the mill.

Four

William reined in his horse and dismounted. He was more than a mile from Thorne Mill, but he enjoyed the walk. Too many months had passed since this route was his daily journey.

Once, he had fancied himself a man of exceeding ambition and renown. Prosperity, celebrity, comfort, and amusement were his destiny. The activities of his daily life confirmed this conviction. His connection to the great family of Thorne made him welcome at every society gathering. During the social season, he partook of each opportunity to enjoy the bounties of London—wine, women, cards, glove matches, bearbaiting, balls, assemblies, even the theater and the opera.

Out of season, he enjoyed country pleasures. His family welcomed him home to join his brothers and friends in shooting, foxhunting, riding, and hosting a regular parade of visitors—women, mostly, eager to win the hand of one of the three eligible Sherbourne men.

To please his father, William had taken a position in the Royal Navy. He liked the sea and the rigors of military life. His comrades became good friends, and their battles on behalf of the Crown increased their bond.

Now, as he strode the well-traveled pathway toward the mill, William ran his riding crop along the dried seed heads of grain that had been left standing after the last harvest. Everything in his life might have continued in such a satisfactory vein. If only he had not . . .

"Blast," he muttered aloud.

Regret would do no good. The hands of time could not be turned back. His recklessness in the games of chance that had stripped him of money and dignity would never be erased. Men to whom he owed great sums waited impatiently, wrote letters, threatened, complained. Women to whom he owed far more would never cease to haunt him.

The sight of Dawkins, the mill's assistant blacksmith, racing full tilt down the road toward him gave William a start. The man's skinny arms waved wildly and his knobby knees flew out in every direction as he ran.

"Sir!" the man cried out. "Sir, thank God you've come! She's going after the piecers' overlooker, and everything has gone amok!"

He sped a few more paces before shouting again. "The looms are stopped, sir! The overlooker will knock her down in two minutes! I'm sure of it!"

William halted as Dawkins skidded to a stop before him.

The blacksmith bent over, wheezing and gasping for air. Hands on his knees, he coughed until William began to fear the poor man might drop dead on the spot.

"Of whom do you speak, Dawkins?" he asked. "What calamity gives you such alarm?"

"Her!" He straightened and pointed a long finger at the mill. "That woman from London. She claims her friend was crushed by a loom, and she begins to give Warring the fault of it! He'll have none of that, and so he begins to say he'll toss the woman into a carding engine if she don't go away. Someone stopped the waterwheel so that the looms cease one by one, and we'll never meet the day's quota, not by a long shot!"

William had begun walking again as Dawkins poured out the tale. "Richard Warring? Is he the overlooker of whom you speak?"

"Indeed, sir, and if you know him at all, you'll increase your pace."

"Know him? I hired him." Recalling the tall, brawny man who once worked as an overlooker at Quince's Mill, William frowned. "Warring is a good man. He performs well. I studied the ledgers compiled while I was at sea. Under Warring and the other overlookers, the mill turns a reasonable profit."

"Aye, sir. But that lady means to be the undoing of it!"

"Of which lady do you speak? I must know her name."

"Miss Watson, sir. Miss Prudence Watson."

At that, William stiffened in surprise. He paused on the road and looked out across the moor. Prudence Watson. That pretty little creature had turned his mill topsy-turvy? To what end?

As he began walking again, William lifted up yet another entreaty to the God he felt sure had abandoned him. He envisioned his prayer wafting away in the breeze like a puff of mist that soon vanished into thin air.

Why—of all people—did Miss Watson have to involve herself in this row? He had successfully put her out of his mind, just as he had evicted every other pretty woman of his acquaintance. She, more than most, intrigued and tempted him. Now he had no choice but to encounter her again.

"Listen, sir!" Dawkins cried as they reached the mill's door. "Can you hear it?"

"How could I not?" The sounds of chaos echoing out from the building drowned the melody of rushing water and birdsong.

"Have all my looms and carding engines ceased?" William asked the blacksmith. "I hear nothing but shouting and shrieks."

"Lord save us all!" With a cry, Mary Heathhill burst through the doorway and lurched down the steps. "Help! Oh, heaven help us!"

"Mrs. Heathhill?" William caught her just as she began to sag. "Dawkins, bring a stool!"

"You must rescue my sister, Mr. Sherbourne," Mary sobbed. "That man will kill her!"

"Make yourself easy, madam." He settled her onto a low stool in the shade of the building. "No one will be murdered in my mill. I assure you of that."

Before the weeping woman could detain him further, William hurried into the mill. Just as Dawkins had described, every carding engine, scouring machine, spindle, and loom had come to a complete stop. Children wandered about, crying in confusion. Women shouted for help as they struggled to free themselves from suddenly frozen looms. Men had gathered in a mob at the far end of the building. Cursing and waving an assortment of tools and implements in the air, they pressed and pushed at each other.

The sight of William Sherbourne striding toward them down the mill's central aisle brought the commotion to an uneasy halt. Workmen, few of whom he recognized, parted to allow him entry. At the center of the knot of angry onlookers stood two people who could not appear more opposite.

Richard Warring, his arms beefy and his neck as thick as an ox's, faced his opponent. Miss Prudence Watson, her golden hair piled in curls beneath a sweeping, ostrich-plumed bonnet, glared at her adversary. He wore leather trousers, thick boots, and a sweat-stained shirt in some indistinguishable shade of brown. Her spotless blue gown set off a brown velvet pelisse, a pair of white gloves, and a small bag of pale blue silk.

Warring stood a good nine inches taller than Prudence. William surmised that with one swift blow, the overlooker could flatten her. But she was blind to her peril. Cheeks a vivid pink and eyes flashing green, she turned toward William.

"Mr. Sherbourne, how good of you to come," she spoke up as he neared. "I understand you have been living in the vicinity of the mill for almost two weeks without once setting foot inside this den of abomination."

Den of abomination? William struggled to suppress the grin her accusation elicited.

"Sir, this lady here be calling me a demon," Warring snarled, pointing a stubby finger at the woman.

"A *devil*," Prudence corrected. "You are a devil!"

"And you're a—"

"Miss Watson," William cut in, "you look lovely this morning. I am pleased to see you have chosen to pay us a visit. Perhaps you would like a tour of the mill? I shall be happy to oblige, but may I first speak to you in private? Your sister awaits us outside."

"No, Mr. Sherbourne," she replied. "Privacy is impossible in such a case as this. We must converse here, where all may hear us. As you see, I have taken up the cause of this great company of men, women, and children gathered inside your mill."

"Cause? What cause have my employees to cease their work and assemble themselves into such an unruly band?"

He took two steps closer to the woman. Her breath was shallow, her hands trembling. She was afraid, William saw, and he congratulated himself for having provoked at least a small measure of dread from one so bold and headstrong.

No matter that her heart might quake, however, Prudence addressed him without hesitation.

"It is my cause," she told him, "not theirs. Ending the mistreatment of those who labor in your mill is my mission, sir. I speak for the children in particular. I am their champion."

"Ah yes, we discussed this last evening after dinner at Thorne Lodge. Perhaps you recall our conversation in the library?"

His reference to their awkward moments alone together did not dissuade her. "Indeed I do, Mr. Sherbourne, and now you see for yourself how the children are compelled to labor in the most perilous circumstances. Some are crippled, yet they must carry on laboring in order to earn their pittance. These poor piecers creep beneath your dangerous looms to tie broken threads together again. Their backs are bent and broken. Their legs are twisted and lame. They have no schooling, no time for rest or play, nothing to look forward to in life but crawling about in the darkness from sunrise to sunset."

She stretched out her arm, finger pointed at him, and raised her voice as she concluded her tirade. "You, Mr. Sherbourne, are no better than a slaver!"

At the accusation, the crowd gave a collective gasp and began to murmur. William let out an audible sigh. Though tempted to pitch Miss Prudence Watson over his shoulder, carry her out of the mill, and drop her into the nearby pond, he refrained. Her allegations were serious, and her listeners awaited their master's response.

Should he fail to quash the woman's revolutionary ideas, she might foment a mutiny in the mill. He could ill afford to lose another hour of production, let alone days or months to rebellion.

"Miss Watson," he said, removing his hat and making her a bow somewhat too grand for the setting, "I submit to your admonishment, for I know from whence it comes. Your purpose is good. Your ambition, noble. You speak from a motive of the heart. Love, in fact, fuels your cause. Am I wrong?"

"Love?" For a moment, she appeared flustered. Uncertain where he intended to take his argument, she paled a little. But he was pleased to see her recover.

"You are correct, Mr. Sherbourne," she informed him. "My purpose is born of love. And that love is inspired by God Himself. Yesterday, as you will recall, an incident occurred which—"

"Forgive my interruption, dear lady, but I cannot deny you the object of your mission another moment." Looking toward a stairway that led to the mill's second floor, William bellowed a command. "Mr. Walker, come down! Mr. Walker, blacksmith of Thorne Mill, show yourself at once!"

Prudence let out a little cry as the man himself appeared

suddenly in full view. Eyes fixed on the woman, he descended step by step. William saw at once that his blacksmith was displeased. His hooded eyes darkened as he drew nearer. His mouth was a grim line. Miss Watson pressed both hands to her heart, no doubt likely to swoon at any moment.

Neither party would welcome a proclamation of their affections, past or present. William knew that, but he convinced himself this public exposure was for the best. Miss Watson, after all, had nearly incited a riot in his mill.

Despite her professions of religious zeal the night before, her attachment to the American must be the source of her actions today. Whether she had intended to impress Walker or truly to denounce the young piecers' working conditions, William could not say. It hardly mattered. The incident must end, and as Walker drew near, he saw that it would.

"Good morning, Miss Watson." Walker gave her a peremptory bow.

"You must imagine how surprised I am to see you," she replied.

Her attempt at a curtsy caused a definite wobble, and William reached out to steady her. She turned flashing green eyes on him.

"Thank you, but I am perfectly fine, Mr. Sherbourne," she snapped, brushing his hand from her arm. Her attention returned to the blacksmith. "I understand I am to congratulate you, sir. You will marry soon."

Walker gave a nod but made no response.

"I am told you have been employed at Thorne Mill these many months since the last occasion of our meeting," Prudence continued. "Mr. Walker, what is your opinion of the treatment given the children who labor here?"

"The smithy is upstairs," he said. "I have no children working in that place."

"Aha, you see?" William spoke up. "All is well, Miss Watson. Your fears come to naught."

For a moment, he believed the incident was ended. He stepped toward Prudence, determined to escort her from the building as swiftly as possible. But she turned on him.

"Whether your blacksmith or any other person in your employ dares to speak the truth, Mr. Sherbourne, I have only to look around me to see the unpardonable reality. Your mill is a death trap. You maim and cripple children every day, leaving them broken, ignorant, and without hope."

Now she drew herself up to her full height and unleashed the last of her venom. "You, sir, are the most contemptible man I have ever met. You may be certain that wherever I go from this moment on, I shall revile and condemn your name."

So saying, she turned and marched down the aisle between the rows of machines. William watched her go, the hem of her skirt dragging a little behind her and picking up bits of lint and dust. Without looking back, she stepped out the door and was gone.

He turned to speak to Walker, but the blacksmith was already halfway up the stairs to the second floor. Before William could take a single step, the great waterwheel came to life, machines began to crank and whine, spindles started to whirl and spit out reams of brightly colored yarn, and worsted cloth once again rolled from the looms.

The children, he noted, swiftly vanished to their posts. Invisible as they crept about the stone floor beneath the looms, the boys and girls worked in silence. William was glad. He crossed the mill to the door, making an effort to avoid meeting the eye of any in his employ. If he saw young Davy Smith, he would be unable to quell the rising tide of self-loathing that filled his chest. Of that he had no doubt.

◆

"Evil man!" Prudence splashed her face with cold water in a vain effort to wash away her tears. "I hate him, Mary. There can be no other feeling toward such a vile, hideous wretch of a human being. I despise him to the very depths of my heart."

Mary had ordered tea sent up to their room at the inn, and now she poured out two cups. "You may call me fickle, but I liked Mr. Sherbourne better today. I confess, Pru, I have reverted to my good opinion of him."

"Good opinion?" Prudence whirled around to face her sister. "You have a good opinion of that beast? You must be joking! He humiliated me in front of everyone."

"You humiliated him first, dearest."

"But *he* deserved it. Did you see those poor children? So frail and ill—all of them! I have no doubt he feeds them gruel and oatcake every day of the week. And that horrid Richard Warring! Dick the Devil, they call him. I can see why. He is a cruel taskmaster. Mr. Sherbourne hired him for the express purpose of beating his charges into submission."

"Mr. Sherbourne has not been in Yorkshire these many months, Pru. Perhaps he does not know about the abuses of his overlookers. I am sure he will put it all right tomorrow and your silly crusade must end."

Prudence dropped into a chair, picked up a pair of tongs, and tossed two lumps of sugar into her tea. Each gave a healthy splash, spilling the hot liquid down the sides of the cup to puddle in the saucer. She did not care.

"Oh, how well he looked today," she moaned as she stirred in a dollop of milk. "If you had seen him, Mary, you would understand exactly why my heart is broken."

"I did see him, and I thought him among the handsomest gentlemen of my acquaintance."

"You saw Mr. Walker?"

"I saw William Sherbourne." Mary took a sip of tea. "I shall never forget his kindness to me. He ordered a stool brought over, and he settled me onto it with the most tender and kindhearted concern."

"Then marry him yourself if you like him so well. He treated me abominably."

"Measure for measure," Mary intoned. "An eye for an eye and a tooth for a tooth."

"I would knock out all his teeth if I could. Horrid man."

A knock on the door brought Mary to her feet. A housekeeper stood in the hall bearing a tray that held a letter. In a moment, the door was closed again and Mary had broken the seal as she returned to her chair.

"It is from Lady Thorne," she exclaimed. "She invites us to dine with the family again tonight. She most particularly wishes us to play the pianoforte and sing, for she has rarely heard anything that gave her such pleasure. Several friends and neighbors will be in attendance, she writes, for everyone is eager to know us."

Mary set the letter on the tea table. "How honored we are by this invitation, Pru. What a fine beginning to our acquaintance with that good family."

"But we cannot go! *He* will be there and no doubt determined to gloat over his victory today."

"We most certainly shall go. The innkeeper informed me that the last coach to Nottingham departed while we were at the mill humiliating ourselves before the peasantry. We have nothing better to do this evening than visit Lord and Lady Thorne and their friends, and we must make what we can of it."

Prudence shook her head in misery. What would Betsy Fry say to her friend's sad attempts as a crusader? Every time the memory of Mr. Walker's grim expression crossed Prudence's mind, she winced. He surely hated her now, for she had exposed and shamed him before all his society. Why had she ever gone to the mill? If only she had thought her actions through to the end, she would have abandoned the idea at once.

"I believed God wanted me to better the lives of the children," she murmured. "How could I have been so mistaken?"

"You were not mistaken at all, dear heart. Those poor children ought to be taught to read and count. They should have fresh air and the chance to run about. Certainly they must be given tasks where they will be safe and cannot fall into the millworks. But I am sure there is a better way to help them than taking the mill by storm and shouting insults at their employer."

"There is no better way. Indeed, there is no way at all to help those little ones. If Mr. Sherbourne is making a tidy profit, why would he alter anything at the mill?"

"Perhaps because he has a good heart."

"His heart is black and cold."

"I am going to write to Sarah at once and ask her to find out everything she can about William Sherbourne. I believe our sister will tell us that our new friend is good and kind—just as he was to me this morning. He is a gentleman, Pru. His breeding and education are excellent. He served England in the Royal Navy. Perhaps the mill has not been at the forefront of his thoughts, but he will put it all right soon enough."

While Mary set about finding paper and ink, Prudence sipped her tea. How could she ever show her face to William Sherbourne this evening? He was just the sort of man to enjoy making a fool of her twice in one day. His mocking wit and his snide comments would surely cut her until she had not a shred of pride.

Perhaps that had been God's design after all, she mused. Perhaps she needed taking down a notch or two. If so, the plan had worked well, for she felt as low as a worm.

There was only one thing to do now. She must wear her pink silk gown, white gloves, and ruby necklace to dinner. If she could not shame William Sherbourne into helping the mill children, she would entice him to do it.

◆

"The deed is done, William. You can change nothing now." Randolph studied his younger brother across the tea table. "She will come here tonight, and you must be polite."

As was the custom since William's return to the Thorne-Chatham estate, he had joined his brother at tea that afternoon. Olivia sat with the men when she was at home, and quite often visitors came to the table as well.

William had learned to take pleasure in the congenial assembly of family and friends. True, it was not as hearty or raucous a gathering as some he had enjoyed, but he found the conversation stimulating, the advice sound, and the affection genuine.

Following the morning's incident at the mill, the mists had faded and the day had grown warm. An open window ushered in the sweet scents of early spring—fields newly turned by the plow, flowers unfurling petals one by one, a hint of rain in the breeze.

The table in the sitting room at Thorne Lodge fairly groaned beneath the load of delectable treats carried up from the kitchen. Fresh currant buns, a bowl of sugared strawberries, a plate piled with thinly sliced ham and savory cheeses, and a large pot of hot strong tea crowded the round tabletop. Unpleasant news had no place in such an amiable family scene, but William could not rest until he had disclosed the debacle that now occupied all his thoughts.

Randolph received the information and fell silent, but his wife appeared scandalized.

"Had I known Miss Watson's true character, I should never have invited her to dinner again." Olivia's warm eyes met William's. "But she must be all deceit. Her beauty and charm hide her defects. By outward appearance, she is witty, clever, and accomplished, and her family connections are more than satisfactory."

"Satisfactory? Have you forgotten that her father traded in opium?" William asked. "You informed us of his iniquities not ten minutes ago."

"I have not forgotten what I said about Mr. Gerald Watson. I do not repeat gossip, William, and you must know that every shred of information I have reported was either taken from Miss Pickworth's society news in *The Tattler* or given to me by our minister's wife."

"Making the information, of course, utterly and irrefutably true."

"Yes, indeed. Miss Pickworth rarely errs in her accounts, and Harriet is never wrong."

William could not resist teasing Olivia. He knew she enjoyed reading the society gossip in the London newspaper. He also knew she treasured her friendship with the Reverend Nigel Berridge's wife, Harriet. The young minister's growing family, now residing in the parsonage beside the church at Otley, brought a welcome warmth to the small town. As a boy, William had dreaded his family's Sunday obligation to attend church services, but of late he found them more palatable.

"Mr. Watson's superior connections in society were purchased," Olivia continued. "Trenton House, the family's home in London, belonged to a peer of the realm before Mr. Watson bought it. He procured his eldest daughter's first husband, the late Lord Delacroix, in the same way."

"He purchased a husband for his daughter?" William asked. "That is singular."

"Lord Delacroix had a title but no money," she explained. "The arrangement was easily made. Attachment to the Delacroix name gave Mr. Watson influence and prestige, yet I am told the marriage he made for his poor daughter was a disaster from first to last. Upon the husband's death, she was finally free of him. But I fear our Miss Watson's sister cannot be a sensible woman. She has taken a new husband who has no name at all and is a tea merchant in Cheapside—Charles Locke, I believe his name is."

"Dearest wife," Randolph said gently, "Mrs. Locke cannot help that her first husband died. Nor can we abuse her for choosing a more common man to replace him. We must grant the woman some kindness."

"You are quite right, my dear," Olivia agreed. "Mrs. Locke suffered a good deal before she met her new husband. Yet I wonder how much real pain she could have endured in such a case? Her father's demise left her wealthy, and her husband's left her titled."

"Ah, the joys of a convenient death," William observed. "All things considered, Miss Watson's sister has not done badly."

"Oh, William." Olivia shook her head at him. "You do not take these things seriously, but you should. Miss Watson benefits greatly from her elder sister's position in society."

"Does that give her the right to march into my mill and incite my laborers to revolt?"

"Of course not. What can she have been thinking?"

"She was thinking of her lost love—our very own blacksmith."

"Are you quite sure of this information, brother?" Randolph asked, leaning forward. "Has Miss Watson formed an attachment to a native of America? Is the man not twice her age at least?"

"Thereabouts, and he is to wed one of our weavers before the year's end. But I understand he first knew Miss Watson in quite a different circumstance. I questioned him today after the incident at the mill. He told me that the Marquess of Blackthorne has been his particular friend from childhood. It was through this connection that the acquaintance with Miss Watson was made and the attachment between them formed. He knew their mutual regard could never result in marriage, and so he ended the friendship, moved far away from the woman, and began anew."

Randolph shook his head. "William, do you really believe

Miss Watson went to the mill this morning with the express purpose of drawing the attention of our blacksmith?"

"A heart awash in love can lead a person to do many curious things," Olivia said. "As you, my darling husband, can attest."

Randolph smiled tenderly at his wife, yet he was not satisfied to drop the matter. "William, you report that Miss Watson actually shouted at the piecers' overlooker? And you say she vowed to rescue the mill's youngest laborers from their purported *slavery*? She seemed a sensible enough young lady yesterday. Why would she employ such extraordinary measures to draw the blacksmith's notice? No, indeed, I begin to think Miss Watson's true purpose was exactly as she stated."

"You believe she fancies herself a crusader and revolutionary?" William lifted his teacup. "Have you looked at her, brother? She is too pale and pretty, too well-bred, too . . . well, she is simply too *curly* to lead an uprising."

"Too curly?" Olivia laughed.

"The woman is nothing but curls and curves everywhere. She smells divine. Even when she is shouting, her voice is like honey. No, indeed, Miss Prudence Watson was created for one thing: love. It is her purpose, her design, her entire function in life."

"You are smitten with her, William!" Olivia exclaimed. "Now I see the truth."

"I am not smitten. I merely make my case: her actions result from a forbidden love and not from any righteous zeal to save children."

"I suppose we cannot argue," Randolph said. "You know the woman more intimately than we. You observed her behavior, and you interviewed the blacksmith. Now we have only to think of a way to revoke her invitation to dinner."

"We shall do no such thing," Olivia declared. "Miss Watson and Mrs. Heathhill are welcome to visit us upon any occasion. But as we speak with the younger of the sisters tonight, we shall bear in mind her unsettled temperament and her tendency toward hysteria. While in our home, she will be treated with kindness. But we shall bear with fortitude her eventual return to London and the solace and protection of her family."

Randolph gave a snort. "I shall find it difficult not to envision her shouting at our overlooker in a preposterous attempt to draw the attention of our blacksmith. It will be impossible to give credit to anything she says."

With that pronouncement from his brother, William took another sip of tea and studied a patch of daffodils blooming just outside the open window. He had convinced his family of Miss Watson's romantic purposes. They now thought her childish and a little mad. Their general pity would be felt by the young lady, and she would leave Yorkshire on the first coach tomorrow.

Once again, William had succeeded in accomplishing the task at hand. But as he sipped his tea, he could not deny his own great doubt. It was entirely possible, he had to admit, that his overlookers were cruel to the mill labor. It might be true, in fact, that the children suffered daily abuse and lived in a state of fear.

It might even be likely that Miss Watson had wished to aid those children this morning. That her attachment to the blacksmith might be entirely innocent. That her presence at dinner this evening would unsettle and disarm William.

He had made her an object of scorn and condolence to his family. But he was the one who deserved their scorn and not Miss Watson at all, curly though she was.

Five

"France is lovely in the spring," Prudence informed those gathered at the dinner table. She had gone to Thorne Lodge determined to capture the attention and admiration of everyone there, restore her good reputation, and squash William Sherbourne all in one evening. Thus far, she had succeeded admirably.

"Calais, you must understand," she continued her discourse, "is the very essence of all things beautiful and refined. But I cannot pronounce the former emperor of that nation to be as intriguing as most of my countrymen assert. I observed Napoleon's actions firsthand at Waterloo, and he was too cleverly outwitted by our forces."

"You were at Waterloo?" Randolph Sherbourne, Lord Thorne, all but gaped at her across the table. "You witnessed the battle itself?"

"Did I not, Mary?" Prudence turned to her sister. "You can attest to the truth of my account."

"Prudence was indeed at the battle," Mary confirmed. "It was a most unhappy accident, of course. Along with her traveling companions, my sister hid in a barn very near the center of combat. She had accompanied her dearest friend Anne, Lady Blackthorne, on a mission to transport lace into France."

"A lace *machine*," Prudence clarified. "As you all must know by now, I am never reluctant to fight for the greater good."

Lest anyone should mention her ill-advised visit to the worsted mill that morning, she drew in a deep breath and continued. "I believe that God expects us to spend our time on earth in worthy labors. A clear division exists between good and evil. The world is either black or white. There can be no gray."

"No gray?" William asked. "Madam, I see nothing *but* gray."

"Then you do not see clearly, sir. Honor, beauty, truth, justice—all these are good and right. When evil is discerned, it must be rooted out and destroyed."

"So, this lace machine of yours," he said. "Was it an evil contraption? Or was it good? I am mystified."

Prudence favored him with the most condescending smile she could summon. "A machine, sir, is neither good nor bad. What must be judged is its effect on mankind."

"You refer, by extension, to my worsted looms."

"Dear Mr. Sherbourne, let us not quarrel this evening. Lady Thorne's table is hardly the place for bickering and disagreement."

"You find the floor of my mill a more suitable arena?"

She opened her mouth with a retort at the ready, but Olivia spoke up quickly.

"At the mention of lace, Miss Watson, I must say I am entranced by the lace on your gown. Is it French?"

"This is Nottingham lace, madam. In fact, it was made by the friend I mentioned before. Anne gave it to me not long after her wedding."

"It is delicate and exquisite," Olivia murmured. "This lady's skill is greatly to be admired. Such workmanship is of great value."

"Indeed, and such a friendship is even more valuable." Prudence touched the scrap of bobbin lace at her throat and was gratified to discover William's attention already fixed there. She absently brushed at a curl that had escaped her chignon to dangle against her neck. His focus traveled to it and lingered.

Good, she thought. *If you cannot be tormented by the evils of your mill, Mr. Sherbourne, you shall be tormented by me instead.* Though Prudence feared she was not much of a crusader, she had no such doubts about her ability to conquer a man's heart.

"Dear friends are such a joy," she purred. "A warm fire, a delicious meal, a lively conversation . . . what could be more delightful?"

"Perhaps a turn at the pianoforte," William said. "We are beside ourselves with joy at the prospect of yet another of your performances."

"Thank you, Mr. Sherbourne. You are all politeness this evening. How very happy we are to be treated to this uncommon display of your good humor and wit."

"Oh yes," Mary spoke up at once, rising from the table and nearly upsetting her chair. "It is many a month since we have enjoyed such fine food and such congenial company. Come, Prudence. We must choose a song for our kind hosts."

As everyone made to stand, the footmen hurried to remove chairs and clear the table. Prudence regretted the hasty end to the dinner, but it seemed that William was quite determined to spar with her at every opportunity.

She did not mind. In fact, the man intrigued her to the extent that she had thought about little else all day. Her gown, her hair, even her scent were chosen with him in mind. She told herself that she intended to beguile and then discard him. He must become nothing more than another suitor to add to the growing list of men she had captivated and then abandoned to their misery.

"You must speak to Mr. Sherbourne with respect, Prudence!" Mary hissed as she took her sister's arm and hurried her down the corridor toward the drawing room. "After your demonstration this morning, the family easily might have withdrawn our invitation to dinner. But they have welcomed us, and you must be polite."

"I am as polite as he deserves," Prudence whispered back. "I hate him."

"Ah, Mr. Sherbourne!" Mary said as the man himself joined them. "I was just saying to my sister how much we have enjoyed the evening. Your family is all kindness. Indeed, sir, I should be happy to play a jig or two if you wish to dance."

"Dance? But partners are too few, I fear." He paused a moment. "However, I do recall that you praised your sister's skills on the dance floor. Perhaps you might teach me a step or two, Miss Watson."

"Dance? With you?" Prudence was about to reject him in no uncertain terms, but Mary elbowed her in the side.

"My sister would be delighted, I am sure," Mary said. "Would you not, Pru?"

"Of course, Mr. Sherbourne. I am always happy to come to the aid of a man who dances poorly. How bad are you?"

He laughed as they entered the large drawing room. Mary had only just seated herself at the pianoforte when he took Prudence's hand and turned her to face him.

"Will you play a waltz, please, Mrs. Heathhill?" he called across the room. "I can think of nothing that would please me more."

"A waltz? Oh! But of course." With a deep breath and a flutter of eyelashes, Mary hovered over the instrument for a moment. Her cheeks reddened as she searched through sheets of music, but she found a waltz at last and began to play.

William drew Prudence closer and danced her across the floor toward the fireplace. As it happened, they moved in perfect harmony with the swaying one-two-three rhythm. And with each other.

"I prefer the waltz," William said, his breath stirring the curls against her cheek. "Some may consider it a scandalous dance, but you, I think, must enjoy it."

"And why is that? I am as happy with a jig or a reel as any lady. I take great pleasure in a quadrille or a country dance."

"But unlike those, the waltz brings a man and a woman into an embrace as they accompany the music about the room. It requires a certain intimacy, and you like that."

She gave a little laugh. "You profess to know everything about me, sir."

"I know almost nothing. Yet this much is plain."

"But you are wrong. The waltz removes a woman's command over her own movements. She is left powerless in her partner's arms." Prudence glanced toward the pianoforte. "And you have made my sister blush."

"Do you blush, too, Miss Watson?" He drew back for a moment. His warm treacle eyes searched her face, lingered on her lips, and met her own gaze. "I see you are not as easily shocked as she. But you have been to France, of course. You must have danced the waltz many a time."

"And with many men," she added. "You, perhaps, rank among the most perplexing."

"Why is that? I have been forthright with you at our every meeting. Yet I see you are baffled by my character. I am, on the one hand, exceedingly charming—an officer of the Royal Navy, the son of a baron, the owner of a large worsted mill. On the other, I am a cruel taskmaster who thinks nothing of tearing children limb from limb. Have I assessed the source of your bewilderment correctly?"

"Not at all," she replied. By now he had danced her to the far end of the drawing room, near an alcove lit by candles. "I am perplexed by your skill at waltzing."

"Ah," he said with a laugh. "But I have traveled too, Miss Watson. France, Spain, Portugal, Belgium. Such places are perhaps more forward-thinking than our beloved misty isle. The waltz, in Paris, is quite a common dance, and no one blushes."

"Do you prefer Paris?"

"To Yorkshire? Never. I am country born and bred, and a countryman I shall always be. I believe we are alike in this. Yesterday, you professed a passion for riding."

"I do like riding."

"Good. Tomorrow I shall take you on a tour of the family estate. Now that you have finished abusing my overlookers and setting my weavers into an uproar, we may speak to each other as friends."

At this mention of the morning's calamity, Prudence stumbled a little. William checked her faltered step and set his hand more firmly at her waist. This had the effect of drawing them so closely together that she began to fear she might lose what little composure she had left.

All day, she had fretted over the evening's encounter with William Sherbourne. She had hoped that her pink gown, cascading curls, and lacy décolletage might soften the resentment she had created in him. Her air of confidence and her sharp wit, she had prayed, might elevate her in his estimation. And somewhere along the way, she might actually summon the courage to plead once again for fair treatment of the children at his mill.

But now she melted in his arms, set her cheek against his shoulder, and allowed the music to seep inside her. She was not a crusader, Prudence realized as William turned her into the shadows. She was not in love with Mr. Walker, she admitted as he lightly kissed her cheek. She was weak and imperfect and far too easily swayed.

"Have you reached a conclusion about me, Miss Watson?" William murmured against her ear. "Am I black, or am I white? Am I good? or evil?"

"Oh, dear." She realized suddenly that Mary was no longer playing. The waltz had ended, yet she hung suspended in this man's arms.

She tried to recall his question as she stepped away from him. "Good or evil? I cannot say."

"Perhaps you require more study. Will you ride with me tomorrow? I shall send my carriage for you at ten."

He bowed as he spoke the last words. Prudence dipped a curtsy and started to move away. But he caught her hand.

"I must have your answer," he said. "I shall not sleep tonight unless I know I may see you tomorrow."

Glancing across the room, Prudence saw that Olivia had taken Mary's place at the pianoforte. Mary stood beside the instrument to turn the pages of the concerto their hostess had selected. Randolph had taken a chair nearby, his attention centered on his wife as he sipped a cup of tea.

"I must join the other women," Prudence told William. "You must excuse me."

She stepped toward the fireplace, but he caught her again. "Ride with me tomorrow. You will see that I am not so evil as you suppose."

"You are good, then? A Christian. An honorable gentleman. You exist to make the lives of others easy and content. In all your choices you are moral, upright, honest—a man of good principle who is respected wherever he goes."

He looked away. For the first time, Prudence saw a darkness blot out the good cheer and mischief that usually lightened his face. Was it shame? or anger? Or was it something worse?

She waited for his answer, watching as he battled some unknown emotion. When he looked at her again, the treacle eyes were hooded by something she could not decipher.

"No man is as good as that," he said.

"No man is perfect, yet many make it their aim to take the high road."

"You will find, Miss Watson, that I am the exception to

your tidy view of life. I am neither wholly good nor wholly bad. Neither black nor white. I am, in fact, quite irredeemably gray."

"I do not believe that," she told him, lifting her chin. "If you have strayed from the straight and narrow path, you must acknowledge your misdeeds to God, turn away from evil, and let Him direct your path ever after."

"As easy as that, is it?"

"Mr. Sherbourne, a wholesome life is not so difficult as you make it. If you are truly baffled by my conviction in this matter, let me set you out an easy means to perfect understanding."

"I should be ever grateful for such instruction."

"Come, then." She slipped her arm through his and guided him toward a bookshelf near the fire. A moment of searching turned up what she had been seeking. She removed the volume and set it in his hands.

"The Bible?" he asked.

"Read the Gospel of St. John. It will not take long, and it is perfectly easy to comprehend. White, black. Good, evil. Heaven, hell."

He opened the book, turned through the pages, and then shut it again. "You are quite sure that in reading this I shall attain the level of perfection you require?"

"Perhaps not." She smiled at him. "The road you choose, sir, lies at your own feet. But—if you read St. John's Gospel tonight and give me a thoughtful review of it tomorrow, then you will attain something nearly as delightful."

"And what is that?"

"My company, of course. I shall be happy to ride out with you to survey your family's estate."

Leaving him with Bible in hand, Prudence hurried across

the room to the pianoforte. She joined her sister, but she made a less than earnest effort to sing with the other women.

She had arrived at Thorne Lodge this evening, she realized, with the aim of beguiling and bemusing the entire company with her beauty, wit, and charm. But she would depart it with her heart in grave danger of surrendering everything. Everything . . . for the affection of one man.

◆

William elected to stay inside while his brother, sister, and several footmen escorted Miss Watson and her sister to the door. Now he watched from a window as their carriage began to move down the graveled entryway, through the iron gates, and onto the main road toward Otley.

Only when he no longer could see the carriage did he look down at the book in his hand. Had Prudence Watson set him up to fail? She must expect he would find the task too onerous and give it up. He flipped the pages, located the Gospel of St. John, and scanned the text.

"I thought she was perfectly delightful," Olivia was saying to her husband as they entered the drawing room again. "You seemed to like Miss Watson better tonight, William."

Randolph gave a laugh. "By the look of that waltz, I should surmise my brother felt more than friendship for his sweet adversary."

"Do you call her sweet?" William tossed the Bible onto a small table near the settee. "You would not say that had you danced with her. She is anything but sweet."

"How would you describe her, then?" Olivia asked. "Is she a temptress? a tease?"

"She is a vixen."

"Oh, ho!" Randolph set his hands at his waist and assessed his brother. "A vixen, is she? Then you are in great peril."

"I am in no peril. Have I ever fancied a woman who would rather scratch my eyes out than submit to my will?"

"I can hardly say. I have not met half the women you liked. I do recall one particular fling, a Miss Caroline Bryse."

At the name, a wash of unease spilled down William's spine, and he quickly crossed from the window to the fireplace. But Randolph took no note as he continued to revive a memory his brother would give anything to erase.

"You accompanied Miss Caroline to Thorne Lodge in a party that included her brother and sister." Randolph turned to his wife. "She was a pretty enough girl, but I soon saw in her a most determined flirt. You met her once or twice, I believe, my dear."

"The two Miss Bryses were determined to wed you and your brother," she replied. "How could I forget them? Beatrice and Caroline were my rivals for a time."

"Never," Randolph assured her. "But I wonder what became of Miss Caroline. She seemed to please William well enough."

"No woman can please me," William retorted. His words were more curt than he intended, and now his brother took note.

"I believe we are no longer wanted," Randolph told his wife. "We must make our escape before William grows glum and boring."

She laughed, took her husband's arm, stood on tiptoe, and kissed his cheek. "Good night, William," she called over her shoulder as they left the drawing room.

"Yes, a delightful night," he muttered.

Alone at last, he walked the perimeter of the room, snuffing the candles one by one. He had no desire to think of Caroline Bryse ever again. And he could not stop thinking of Prudence Watson. Riding with her the following morning would only worsen his torment.

But as he paced, a simple solution presented itself. He would not read the pages she had assigned him. He would, in fact, make certain he could do no such thing.

Striding across the room, William grabbed the Bible from the table where it lay, walked to the fireplace, and cast it into the flames. The old paper kindled at once, bursting into a bright orange ball of fire. Tongues of blue flame danced above it. A loud crackling accompanied the blaze as it devoured the book.

It ended as quickly as it had begun. The flare died; dark ash sifted beneath the grate; coals gave off a gentle glow.

William leaned against the mantel. He felt sick. Sick inside and hollow. His chest ached. His heart thudded, so heavy he could hardly bear the weight. Tears filled his eyes and he angrily brushed them away.

He had caused his own pain. He had etched the jagged scars that marred his soul. Until his life ended, he would bear the emblem of his failure and guilt.

Prudence Watson with her bright green eyes, pert opinions, lively ways, and sweet . . . yes, her very sweet spirit . . . must never become part of that agony.

He straightened. She must be told. He would not rest until he ended what might have begun when he had held her close. Powerless in his arms, she had lamented of the waltz. Yes, she had been powerless. So had he.

Determined to spare the woman the contamination his life had become, William snuffed the final candles and left the darkened room. A footman in the foyer hurried to obey the order to bring his horse around from the stables. Another proffered his greatcoat, hat, and gloves.

After leaving a hastily scrawled message for his brother, William exited the house and mounted his horse. A full moon painted a silvery path as he spurred the steed to a gallop, through the gates and onto the road to town.

William knew the road to Otley well and could ride it blindfolded. In moments he was passing the mill. No longer drowned out by the rattle and clatter of machines, the sound of rushing water drifted across the moor. He much preferred the stream's quiet ripple, but he needed the mill. On leaving the Navy, he had viewed the mill as his only hope of salvation from the grinding debt and financial obligations that pursued him.

William's turn at sea had not resulted in the acquisition of gold and silver, as he and his shipmates had dreamed. Like many, he returned home burdened by debts too heavy to redeem. But the mill turned a tidy profit, and he could ill afford to jeopardize that revenue.

The mill would be his salvation in another way, William had realized. Work would divert his mind from memories and thoughts he could not abide. The daily effort of managing a successful operation surely must absorb the ever-welling tide of remorse that filled his heart.

Now he slowed his horse to a trot, rounding the stone public house and crossing the street toward the inn. As he neared, he saw the front door swing open and a woman in pink silks step out into the night. As she looked down the street in the opposite direction, William reined his mount and urged it into the shadows of an awning above a milliner's shop.

There could be no doubt. The woman was Prudence Watson.

Now she turned her golden head, looking directly toward him but finding instead a tall, well-built man who approached her in the moonlight. She spoke a few words and the man replied, but William could not distinguish what was said.

As her gentleman caller took Miss Watson's hand and bent to kiss it, she covered her mouth with the other. Straightening, he took a step that put him in profile.

William discerned his identity as easily as he had the woman's. It was Mr. Walker, his mill's blacksmith and the great love of Prudence Watson's life.

Six

"I received your message," Prudence gushed out, unable to keep from blurting out everything in her heart. "At first, I thought it must have been brought to me in error. Then I saw my name, and I thought perhaps Mr. Sherbourne had sent it in jest. But I knew your hand too well. I knew it was you who wanted me. I should not have come down, but Mary has retired and I could not sleep until I had answered your call."

"I need your help," Walker said. "You are English, one of them. Hear my plea, and do what you can."

"Your plea?" Gazing up at him now, Prudence studied the face she had loved so well. The mouth, the nose, the dark eyes, the black hair threaded with silver. This man had kissed her and made her believe there might be some hope for their future.

But he had gone away instead, vanishing into the night and

leaving her in miserable solitude. She had been bereft, certain her life was at an end without him.

Now, as she waited for his reply, she saw the man as others had described him so many times. *"Nearly twice your age, Prudence. . . . More than twice your age, dearest. . . . He is very old indeed. . . . He is foreign. . . . He can give you nothing. . . . He has no education, no wealth, no name. . . . Surely you must understand how unsuitable he is. . . ."*

"I heard what you said at the mill," he told her now. "Before I came down from the smithy, I recognized your voice and I listened to your words."

"I was unwise in my zeal. You have come to reprimand me."

"No, to warn you and to bring a plea. The piecers' overlooker is angry, but he cannot wreak open revenge on you. The hatred and rage of the people against him is too great. It is greater still for the lord of the mill, that man Sherbourne. They would kill him if they could."

"Kill him? The mill workers would murder William Sherbourne?"

"Perhaps, but they need him. They need the income his mill provides, meager though it is." Walker set his hand on her shoulder, his warm palm cupping her arm. "Prudence, I saw the way Sherbourne looked at you this morning. He admires your beauty. You have influence over him."

Her thoughts flew back to the moments she had spent in William's arms, and heat flooded her cheeks. But her sudden guilt was washed away by truth. She had not betrayed Mr. Walker, who stood before her now. He was the one who had ended their attachment.

The pleasure she had taken in the waltz could not be tainted by shame. Indeed, she had enjoyed dancing with William. She had delighted in their conversation. She had welcomed his attentions. The notion that anyone might want him dead mortified her.

"You said you bring a plea," she reminded the man who stood before her. "What is it?"

"Do all in your power to ease the working conditions at the mill. Do this for the sake of those who suffer so much. Do it, too, for the safety of the man, Sherbourne."

"But I am powerless. You saw me today—how ridiculous I looked. I made a fool of myself."

"You were brave."

For a moment, he fell silent. Prudence held her breath as his eyes tenderly appraised her. And then he shook his head, putting away the love they had known.

"You are a pretty young woman," Walker continued, his voice low. "You are wiser than your age. You have influence and strength—far more than you know. Do what you can to save the people, the children most of all. Do it before more are crippled or die."

"Can you mean this? Is it really true?"

"I have seen them crushed, broken, ruined by the looms and engines. The girls' hair is caught in the machinery and torn away. Lint in the air chokes them, and they fall ill to mill fever. In a single day, a child may walk twenty miles inside that building. I have calculated their steps. The children labor more than twelve hours each day and eat nothing but water porridge, potato pie, and oatcake. They have no tea or bread to warm them. Indeed, I believe many are even now starving."

At this account, at the image of poor fragile children

coughing and shivering as they labored beneath the looms, Prudence could not hold back tears. She drew a handkerchief from her sleeve and blotted her cheeks.

"But there are so many children," she told him, "and the overlookers are powerful and cruel. I can hardly believe I may rescue one child, let alone a mill filled with them."

"I have seen you do many things," he said. "I was with you at Waterloo, remember? I know your heart."

She nodded. "Yes, you do."

"The strength of God lives inside you. You have no need of me or any other man, Prudence."

She could not respond as she ought. Tears threatened again, and the lump in her throat ached. How she had needed this man! How she had longed to proclaim her love for him to all her friends and family. How earnestly she had desired to be his wife, live with him, bear his children.

But he was wiser than she. He knew their destinies did not follow the same path. Those who loved Prudence most had warned her against the American time and again. It was not until he abandoned her that she began to believe their cautions.

"I saw you walking to the mill this morning," she now said. "You were with a woman. Do you mean to marry her?"

"I do. She is good and gentle. I will make her children my own."

"Do you love her?"

"Yes. Very much." He paused. "Do you still cry for me, Prudence?"

"Not often. With much effort, I had given you up. I see I must do it again."

"God has a better plan for you."

"To shout at overlookers? To play the fool in front of everyone?"

"To save the children."

She bit her lower lip as she reached out and took his hand. Holding it, she studied the shape of those fingers she had loved. She lifted the hand and kissed it.

Releasing him, she nodded. "I shall try."

He smiled for the first time. "I knew you would."

Before she could speak again, he had slipped away into the night. She stood alone, reflecting on the past. Pondering the future. Mr. Walker was right, as always. She could save the children. And she would.

As she turned to enter the inn, she heard the thunder of hoofbeats. Mr. Walker, she thought as she looked in that direction. But at the sight of a dark rider in a greatcoat and hat, she was not so certain. Had it been the blacksmith . . . or someone else?

◆

"His carriage is here! Oh, Pru, such a wonderful beginning! You must make the most of every moment with him. Secure him if you can."

"Secure Mr. Sherbourne? As a husband?" Prudence laughed as she set a yellow bonnet on her head and tied the gossamer ribbons beneath her chin. She stepped to Mary's side and peered over her sister's shoulder at the street below. "I should rather marry that pig who is wallowing in my mud puddle."

"Nonsense! But indeed, your puddle is back again this morning. We must have had a little rain in the night. Do be careful, Pru. Your gown is lovely and I should hate to see it soiled."

"I shall be riding in this gown in an hour's time. It will return six inches deep in mud. I have little doubt of that."

"Will you be nice to him?" Mary caught Prudence's shoulders. "Mr. Sherbourne is a good match for you. Promise to be polite."

"I shall promise nothing of the sort. He kissed me last night, you know. He commanded you to play a waltz, and then he danced me into the shadows, where he kissed my cheek. Very ill-mannered of him. There can be no doubt William Sherbourne is a cad."

"What is a stolen kiss but evidence of a tender heart?" Mary followed Prudence to the door of their chambers. "Do try to be sensible for once in your life, sister. Mr. Sherbourne has completed his naval duties and returned home. He has a good income from the mill. And Lady Thorne told me last night that her husband has promised his brother a fine house on their estate. Chatham Hall, it is called—large and very grand. You might be mistress of it, Pru, if you can bite your tongue and give Mr. Sherbourne a pretty smile or two."

"You are quite sure he wants a wife?" Prudence shook her head as she gazed at her sister. "Oh, Mary, it is you who is in want of a husband. That is why you speak of little but matches and wedding dates."

"I cannot think of any man but my dear departed Mr. Heathhill. Do you know . . . I almost dread to return to my sweet baby. Her eyes will remind me of a true love with which none else can compare."

"No one will love you in the same way as Mr. Heathhill, but there may be many who can love you just as much."

"I cannot imagine it. Go down to the carriage, Pru, and try

to win Mr. Sherbourne. If you do not, I shall be forced to write to Sarah and bid her begin arranging your nuptials to Lord Delacroix."

"Heaven forbid!" Prudence hugged her sister and hurried down the narrow staircase.

A footman wearing the livery of the Thorne family stood at the door to the inn. He made her a bow and escorted her to the carriage. She half expected to find William waiting inside it, but he was not there. She would journey alone.

Just as well, she told herself as the horses set off in the direction of Thorne Lodge, for she had much to occupy her thoughts. Outside the inn last night, Mr. Walker had asked her to plead for a better life for the mill children. Not only were their lives in danger, but Mr. Sherbourne himself had become a target.

Were the laborers at the mill so ready to revolt? Prudence recalled the crowd that had gathered around her when she denounced Richard Warring. Dick the Devil had certainly made enemies. But his employer would bear the brunt of the antagonism that had built up while he was away at sea.

Prudence was determined to save herself the humiliation of returning to the mill for a second demonstration of her vocal powers. She would win this battle using the weapons she knew best. Feminine wiles could charm a man far more easily than any hotheaded oration.

But as the carriage neared the mill, she was startled to see a stream of workers begin to trickle outside, swelling quickly to a rush and finally into a cascade pouring through its doors. Ragged children and haggard adults lined the roadway. They waved, whistled, called to the carriage as it neared.

"We're Miss Watson's workers!" someone yelled. "Watson's workers! Watson's workers!"

The crowd took up the chant, clapping in unison to the rhythm of their cries. Stunned, Prudence leaned to the carriage window in disbelief. Instantly the throng surged toward her. Hands reached through the opening. Someone lifted a child and then another. The laborers began to beat on the carriage frame, startling the horses and forcing the footmen to prod the crowd back with their short whips.

The chaos lasted only moments before the carriage rolled through the horde onto clear roadway. Trembling, Prudence finally let out her breath. She looked behind to find several children running after her. One of them was young Tom Smith.

"Oh, Tom!" She clenched her fists in helplessness. "Go back! Go to the mill!"

Dick the Devil would surely beat the boy. And Tom's injuries would be her fault! She had roused this sentiment in the masses. *She* was to blame, but *they* would pay the price.

Sinking into a quagmire of dread and worry, she hardly noticed that the carriage had pulled to a stop in front of Thorne Lodge. A footman, cheeks still red from the effort of fending off the horde, opened the door. Prudence let out a breath, took his hand, and stepped down.

"Good on ye, Miss Watson," he said under his breath as she passed. "'Tis time the people had a champion."

She whirled around to face him, but he had turned away to lead the horses toward the stables. Had she heard right? Could it be that even the staff who served the great family were chafing under its rule?

Still quivering with shock and confusion, Prudence lifted

her skirts and ascended the steps to the door. She could hardly believe such undercurrents of mutiny existed everywhere—even within the family's household. Whether or not she liked William Sherbourne, she at least must warn him of the danger.

But when she stepped into the sunlit foyer, Prudence was met not by a liveried butler, but by Olivia Sherbourne herself.

"Lady Thorne," Prudence exclaimed. "How good of you to greet me in this way."

"Dear Miss Watson, I would not have you take another step until I had alerted you to some distressing news."

"What has happened?" Prudence blurted out. "Is he harmed?"

"Do you mean William?" Olivia shrank back a little in surprise. "Harmed? No, my husband's brother is in perfect health. But the steward of our estate has just arrived from London, and both men are compelled to meet with him on a matter of great financial import."

"I see. But of course." Stunned at this change of plan, Prudence tried to steady her breath. No matter what sort of engagement required William's participation, she could not rest until she had alerted him to the imminent danger in his path.

The silence in the foyer became awkward, and Olivia spoke up. "You will stay for tea, I hope, Miss Watson. We shall take it in the music room. It is far from the library and will not disturb the men. I should so much like to know more about your family. Did you say your sister has a home in Cranleigh Crescent?"

"Yes," Prudence managed as she accompanied Olivia down a carpeted corridor.

"And does your sister enjoy the city?"

"Very much. Sarah and Charles live but an easy walk from our family home, Trenton House."

"This is pleasant news indeed," Olivia observed as they entered a small, sunlit room. A pianoforte, violin, flute, and several other instruments had been set out, together with stacks of sheet music.

"And your sister's husband is in the tea trade?" Olivia continued.

"Recently. He and his father formed a partnership with Lord Delacroix and several other men. They import tea from China."

"How very nice. Will you sit?" Olivia motioned to a tufted damask chair.

Prudence all but collapsed into it. "Am I not to see Mr. Sherbourne at all, Lady Thorne?"

"I think not, for he is much occupied. Do you prefer cake with your tea? Or shall I ring for crumpets?"

"Cake is lovely, please." As she spoke the words, she recalled Mr. Walker telling her that the mill's children subsisted on water porridge.

"I am fond of hot crumpets," Olivia was saying as she rang for tea. "But I find that cake satisfies me more. I believe we shall have currant cake, for I ordered one yesterday."

She spoke briefly to the maid before returning to Prudence. "And how does Mrs. Heathhill fare this morning? I must tell you that her turn at the pianoforte last night delighted everyone. My husband declared he has rarely heard anything that pleased him more."

"My sister is well, but am I not to go riding? not at all?"

"Perhaps another time. Though I understand you do not plan to stay much longer in Yorkshire. Is that so?"

"We . . . we . . . Truly I must speak to Mr. Sherbourne, madam. It is a subject of much consequence, and I fear it cannot be delayed even one more hour."

"Oh?" Olivia's brown eyes darkened. "Well . . . if you will excuse me a moment . . . I shall just go and speak to my husband."

Prudence nodded. "Thank you very much."

Lady Thorne left the sitting room as the tea was being brought in. Envisioning mutinous schemes among Thorne Lodge's household staff, Prudence studied the expression of the kitchenmaid who set the tray on a table before her. The young woman's face was composed, her attention consumed by cutting slices of currant cake and pouring out cups of tea.

But just as Prudence relaxed into her chair, she heard the woman mumble something. Sitting up, she touched the maid's arm. "Excuse me? Did you say something?"

Blue eyes flashed in her direction for an instant. "Thank you, Miss Watson," she whispered. "My three little brothers are piecers and my sister is a scavenger at the mill. We are most grateful for what you done for 'em. You are the bravest lady I ever met."

Prudence opened her mouth to respond, but Olivia re-entered the sitting room followed by her husband. William was just behind them.

"Ah, Miss Watson," Lord Thorne greeted her, bowing as she stood to curtsy. "Delighted to see you again so soon. You are looking very well today."

"Thank you, sir." She looked at William, her mouth suddenly dry. "Mr. Sherbourne, are we not to go riding this morning? I very much wished to go riding."

One dark eyebrow arched. "I understand, of course . . . but my brother's steward—"

"He has come from London, yes, but you promised to take me out. I am very eager to ride, sir. Terribly eager."

"You are?" He looked at Randolph before facing her again. "But you see, Miss Watson, I have not completed the task you assigned."

"Task?"

"I was to read the Gospel of St. John."

With dismay she recalled the duty she had teasingly dispensed. "Indeed, but the most important part is in chapter three. Surely you read that far."

"I fear not. I was otherwise engaged last night."

"You were? After I left?" She studied the man, trying without success to read his expression. Was he angry? disinterested? troubled? She had always been good at discerning people's thoughts, but William was as inscrutable as ever.

"'For God so loved the world,'" Olivia spoke up, "'that he gave his only begotten Son, that whosoever believeth in him should not perish, but have everlasting life.' John 3:16."

"How well you recite Scripture, my dear," Randolph told her warmly. "Did you know, Miss Watson, that my wife and I first met inside Otley's little church?"

"Indeed, they are very religious. Both of them." William awarded his brother a smirk. "One cannot even think of wine, women, or cards in Randolph's presence. He sniffs out every hint of sin, compelling the offender to fall to his knees in repentance."

"And of all sinners, William, you are chief," Randolph

retorted. "Miss Watson, be very grateful my steward's arrival spared you the misery of my brother's company this morning."

"But I must speak to him privately. About the mill. About the labor." She divulged her mission with such frankness that even she was startled. William and his family absorbed the news with consternation.

"Miss Watson, you may say whatever you wish about the mill in the presence of my family," William assured her. "My brother constructed the building, and I established the worsted trade."

"Indeed," Olivia concurred, "and the better part of the mill stands on my family's ancestral land. The stream that powers the great waterwheel flows across our estate. There is nothing you have to say, Miss Watson, that should be kept secret from any of us."

"But my message has no bearing on you or your husband. Rather I seek privacy because I must protect the source of my information."

"Of course you must," William agreed.

Prudence looked for a sign of condescension, but his expression remained stoic. The thought that William's life might be in danger compelled her to persist.

"Then you will be pleased to take me riding, as you promised?" she asked.

The brothers eyed each other, sending unspoken messages. At last, Randolph spoke.

"Do as you wish, William. The steward has concluded any glad tidings about our affairs and is eager to launch into the gloomy forecasts of which he is so fond. Your day will be brighter in Miss Watson's company."

"Suffer the slings and arrows of outrageous fortune without me, then," William said. "Though I suspect Miss Watson may have a few darts up her sleeve as well."

"William, do be kind!" Olivia admonished with a laugh. "Miss Watson is our guest."

"And a lovely one at that." He held out an arm. "Shall we?"

Seven

The young woman in a yellow gown and matching bonnet gave William the surprise of his life. Prudence Watson, with her countless curls, pink lips, and sparkling green eyes, rode like a boy. Like a daring, reckless boy.

The moment they left the stable and set out across the moor, she urged her chestnut mare into a canter and then into a gallop that left her escort far behind. Despite the sidesaddle that encumbered her, she leaned into the horse and became a streak of gold across the horizon.

William held his breath as the mare leapt across a stream and made for a low rock wall. His own pace was impeded by a large wicker basket containing hot tea, cake, and a porcelain tea set—a burden insisted upon by Olivia, who would not hear of their missing tea—and he rode at too great a distance to avert disaster. Yet under Prudence's controlling hand, the mare effort-lessly surmounted the wall. Continuing on the other side, she thundered up a rocky outcrop and disappeared into a thicket of oak trees, her rider a yellow blur.

Stunned at the display of horsemanship, William pon-dered the woman as he followed her toward the grove. Perhaps Prudence Watson truly had wanted nothing more than an out-ing on horseback. She had told Randolph she liked riding. It was possible that her mention of secret information was a ruse to lure William away from the meeting in the library.

As he entered the copse, William spotted Prudence seated on a large, flat rock near a gurgling pool. She had removed her bonnet, placed it beside her, and lifted her face to the sunlight. The mare grazed along the water's edge.

"Aha, Miss Watson," William called out. He dismounted and unbuckled the tea basket, then led his horse toward her through the trees. "You wished to escape me, but I have tracked you down at last."

"Escape you?" She turned her head, and he saw that her glossy curls had come loose from their pins and now cascaded down her back. "How can you say such a thing? I am waiting for you that we may discuss in private a most dire circum-stance."

William had to bite his tongue to prevent an inappropri-ate comment about Prudence's fondness for secret tête-à-têtes. Surely she had to know how such clandestine encounters would be perceived by a suitor. Yet she appeared quite unaware. Did the woman have no idea how her appearance—such breathless, flushed beauty—might affect a man?

Pools of innocence, her green eyes followed William as he

stepped onto the slab of granite and sat beside her. She opened the basket, poured two cups of steaming tea, added milk and sugar, and placed slices of cake on two small china plates. Setting out the little picnic, she seemed as artless as a child, disarrayed from riding, eager to tell him her news, and utterly ignorant of the havoc she played in his heart.

"What is this dire circumstance?" he asked, removing his tall hat and leather gloves and setting them near her ostrich-plumed bonnet.

Her information had come from the blacksmith, of course. William thought again of the passionate exchange he had witnessed, a surreptitious tryst that had ended with Prudence kissing Walker's hand. She might appear naïve, but she had the wiles of a skilled seductress.

"I have had news about the mill," she announced as she offered a teacup and cake. "It is most important that you listen carefully to what I say, Mr. Sherbourne. I beg you to heed my advice and take action at once."

"Then speak, madam. I am ready 'to take arms against a sea of troubles, and by opposing end them.'"

"Do not tease me, sir. I know my Shakespeare, and you are no Hamlet."

He laughed at this. "How can you say such a thing? You may know your Shakespeare, Miss Watson, but you hardly know me. I assure you I have endured several tragedies worthy of Ophelia's tears."

"But I am not Ophelia. No man could make me weep or go mad. I can assure you without hesitation that lovelorn hysterics will never lead me to throw myself into a rushing stream and drown."

"No? What about your blacksmith? I daresay you would do anything for him."

Her eyes sparked. "Do not mention Mr. Walker to me again. He is a good man—indeed, he is the very best of men. You know nothing about the friendship between us. It was innocent and pure."

"Innocent?" William pictured again the ardent scene he had witnessed from the shadows. "Walker is well-intentioned, I suppose. But you? Perhaps you are not the angel you would have us all believe."

She was silent for a moment, her eyes fastened on him. After a sip of tea, she spoke again. "You are quite right, Mr. Sherbourne. You see me more clearly than most men do. My appearance is something I have learned to use to my advantage."

"Trapping us in our own folly. I confess, I succumbed as swiftly as any of your suitors."

"More swiftly than most."

Again, he laughed—this time in spite of himself. "So, you have toppled me, Miss Watson. I am your humble, groveling servant and will do anything you command."

"I am happy to hear that," she replied, "for I am asking you to improve the working conditions at your mill—at once. The children must labor no more than ten hours a day. You will engage the services of a teacher to ensure that every boy *and* every girl learns to read and write. You will feed them good warm meat and fresh bread every day. And cake . . . you must give them cake."

"Cake! School! A ten-hour day! Good heavens, dear lady, you will ruin me before the year is out."

"You have enough money to hire a teacher," she argued, setting her teacup aside. She held out her slice of uneaten currant cake. "You have more than enough to eat. An extra cake now and then cannot ruin you."

"My dear Miss Watson, you know nothing of my finances." He took the cake and set it aside with their teacups. "And as for your ten-hour day—if I release the children early, I must send the adults home too. Without scavengers and pickers, my looms will produce nothing but rags."

"But the children can scarcely hobble home after a day's work at your mill. They are crippled not only by your cruel machines but also by the beating of your wicked overlookers!"

"I employ the most efficient overlookers in England," he shot back.

"You have hired beasts!" She leaned toward him, prodding his chest with her index finger. "You allow those animals to pummel the children into submission! Your looms are death traps. Your fine worsted is woven with the pain and suffering of children. You are as cruel and pitiless as Dick the Devil!"

He caught her hand in his. "If I am a devil, be assured I never claimed to be anything better. But you? You tease and tempt men to their doom. I have seen your wiles, woman, and you will not get the better of me."

But even as he spoke, he took her in his arms and kissed her. He was rough, holding her close and searing her mouth with his. If he expected resistance, he got none. She slipped her arms around him, welcoming his embrace and eagerly meeting his kisses with her soft lips. A low moan escaped her throat, and she pulled back.

"Oh, what have I done?" she cried, covering her face with her hands. "I must go. I am no crusader. I am weak and pathetic in every way."

She reached for her bonnet, but he stopped her arm. "Stay," he ground out, drawing her close again. "Stay and let me try to make you as mad for me as poor Ophelia for her Danish prince."

"Do not torment me, sir." Her eyes searched his. "I am nearly undone as it is. I am not the unfeeling temptress you suppose. There are few men who could touch my heart, but I fear you may be one of them."

With that, she pushed away from him and stood. "They are going to kill you," she told him, her voice quavering with emotion. "The mill workers hate your thunderous machines and your polluted air and your wicked overlookers. I have seen and heard their agonies. If you do not make corrections, sir, they will kill you. Do you hear me? They will kill you!"

Lifting her skirts, she fled the granite stone. She mounted her horse with an elegance and speed unthinkable in one so encumbered by petticoats. Before William had digested her dire warnings, she was gone.

He let out a hot breath and raked his fingers through his hair. Kill him? He might have thought her cautions ridiculous had they not struck so close to home. His own beloved father had been slain not many years before. Shot through the heart. The death had been deemed an accident or a suicide until circumstances revealed the truth.

Reflecting on the mill, William felt again the terrible reality of his predicament. Even if he wished to shorten the workers' hours, he could not afford to risk the loss in production. Nor did he have funds to pay a teacher or feed the children meat and bread. As for cake . . .

No, William had decreed his lifelong sentence, crafted his

own prison, forged the bars that held him away from hope, from joy, from love.

He stood, picked up his hat, and saw where Prudence's bonnet had tumbled aside. Lifting it, he ran his fingers through the wispy plumes. Then he spotted a single strand of the woman's hair clinging to the bonnet's silken ribbon. He removed it and held it to the sunlight. Gilded and shimmering, the curl danced in the breeze that drifted off the moor.

This was all he would ever have of her, he realized. The woman herself could never be his. Even so, he released the strand and watched it dance and sway and waft away into the shadows of the glade.

⟡

Prudence flung open the door to her room at the inn, entered, and then slammed it shut. Mary looked up from her embroidery in surprise. Noting the expression on her sister's face, she stood.

"Oh, dear, this cannot be good." Mary sighed. "I hope the calamity was not of your making."

"My making? Do I own a mill and force children to labor sixteen hours a day? Do I quote Shakespeare and make a mockery of my family and friends? Do I kiss and then keep kissing a poor, innocent woman until she is utterly vanquished?"

"I should hope not." Mary tried to hide a smile. "I have not known you to kiss many women in your lifetime."

"But *he* has! William Sherbourne is a roué, I tell you. He is a cad of the very worst order. He woos and courts his prey until they are jelly and can do nothing to salvage their hearts."

"It is some time since I have seen you so overwrought, sister.

Do sit down and tell me what has happened. By your humor I can only expect the worst. But by your words, I wonder if true love may be in bloom."

"That man has never known true love in his life!" Prudence dropped into a soft chair near the window and drew back the curtain. "Oh, I wish I had never gone to see him! I wish I could undo a hundred errors I have made in these recent years. I should be terribly happy if I had never met Mr. Walker. I should be blissful if I had not passed through Otley. And I should be very, very . . . very . . ."

"Pru? Are you weeping?"

"No," she sniffled. "I am angry."

"Take my handkerchief, dearest." Mary held out the delicate scrap. "Now dry your eyes and tell me everything. Will you and William Sherbourne ride again tomorrow?"

"Never! I shall not see him again, I assure you. His charm and wit hide a black heart. Unfeeling man!"

"Why, because he will not ruin his worsted trade to please you? You would have him reduce the mill to rubble, Pru. You would have the looms torn down and burned to ash. You would have the engines melted into slag. And then what would the people eat? What would those poor creatures wear but rags? By your own account, they must be forced to leave their homes, their dear little village, and journey to Manchester or some other such vile place in search of employment in a mill three times as loud and dirty as Mr. Sherbourne's."

"A landlord worthy of that title provides honest, wholesome labor for his tenants—just as William Sherbourne and his brother ought to do."

"Where? One estate can support only so many gardeners.

One great home can provide positions for a staff of housekeepers and footmen but no more. The mill is a blessing indeed, Pru, and you must stop hounding poor Mr. Sherbourne about it."

"You may take your ease on that account, Mary. I shall never hound Mr. Sherbourne again, for I shall never see him again."

"Oh, Pru, were you rude to the poor man?"

"On the contrary. I was gentility itself. He is the one who kisses me left and right until I can hardly keep my wits."

"Does he truly kiss you? kiss you as a man with genuine love kisses his lady?"

Prudence looked down at her hands, recalling how William had pressed his lips against hers, how he had held her so close she could hardly breathe, how his fingers had threaded through her hair and made her weak with longing. Even now, she could smell the scent of his skin, taste the sweetness of his kisses, feel again the rough brush of his cheek against hers.

William was no Mr. Walker—restrained and respectable even in declaring his love for her. Too aware of the difference in their ages and social class, Walker had held back, trying to protect Prudence from her own passion.

But William had no such compunctions. He made his desires known. He eagerly embraced her whenever possible, and his stolen kisses were given full rein.

"Pru, do you love him?" Mary asked gently.

Prudence lifted her head. "I don't know. I cannot say how I feel, for my mind swims and my heart aches each time he comes near me."

"That is as near a description of love as I have heard in many a year. We must find a way to put you together again."

"No!" Prudence stood. "Heaven forbid! I must not see him! Ever! Indeed, I must return to London with all possible haste."

"And abandon the poor mill children? Really, Pru, I thought you more compassionate than that."

"Do not mock me, Mary! I have had more than enough teasing. You think me silly. He thinks me mad. But I am a grown woman, and I insist on being treated as such. I have great compassion for the mill children. Relieving their suffering is my life's ambition. But how can I stay in Otley when *he* is here? I can hardly think in his presence. And he cannot control his passions in mine."

"Then return to London and write letters to Parliament. Better yet, write to the king."

"The king has lost his faculties and hardly knows where he is. He can do nothing to save the children, nor would he. As for the prince regent—"

"The prince regent is much occupied sorting his mistresses from his wives. I believe we must leave him to his task."

Prudence mustered a faint grin but her heart was too burdened to laugh.

"I shall return to London and speak to Sarah about the mills," she said. "You know as well as I that our sister's wealth and connections give her great influence. She is compassionate, too. Perhaps she will convince Lord Delacroix to take the matter before the House of Lords."

"Sarah would rather convince Lord Delacroix to take you to be his lawful wedded wife." Mary lifted a letter from the table near her chair. "I have heard from Sarah. She writes that Delacroix returned from the Orient as handsome and charming as we all had hoped."

"*I* did not hope him to be handsome or charming," Prudence retorted. "I did not like Delacroix when we first met, and I shall like him even less now. Does Sarah mean to force me into his presence on every occasion?"

"Indeed, and with all possible haste."

"Does she write of Mr. Sherbourne? Has she learned the truth about his character?"

"This letter was written before she received my inquiry. All the same, I am certain she will be distressed by your new avocation as a crusader and wish you safely tucked away at Trenton House, wife to an adoring husband and mother to countless happy children."

"Wife and mother? No, Mary, neither of you will compel me into such a state until I meet a man I can truly love."

"But you may like Delacroix more than you now can believe. Since you last met, he has seen the world and made his mark on it. Come, Prudence, let's pack our trunks and set our hearts toward home."

"But my heart is with the mill children. I cannot leave them." She shook her head. "Nor can I stay here in Otley. Oh, dear!"

While Mary took pen to paper, no doubt informing their sister of the weary travelers she soon could expect to welcome home, Prudence pondered her dire situation. If she returned to London, she would have to endure the efforts of her sisters to marry her off to a suitable husband. Abominable thought!

Her outing on the moors that morning had touched Prudence's heart in more ways than one. She could never deny that William Sherbourne somehow had managed to take her thoughts captive. Though stubborn to a fault, he was witty, clever, and very amiable indeed. Add to that his handsome face and deep brown eyes. Not to mention his kisses . . .

If she were not careful, Prudence might never be able to think of anything else. Or anyone.

Equally distressing, she had discovered a new and even more attractive side to William. He loved the out-of-doors as much as she. Even burdened with an awkward tea basket, he had displayed impeccable horsemanship. If she had seen a finer figure riding anywhere in England, she could not recall it.

But the plight of the child laborers at Thorne Mill troubled her most of all. In the end, the decision was easy.

"I have changed my mind, Mary," she said at last. "You must go to London without me. I cannot leave until I have discovered some means by which I may aid the mill children."

"Stay in Otley?" Mary cried. "By yourself? Inconceivable!"

"No, indeed. I am safe and happy just as I am. The innkeeper and his wife are good, and their staff will see to my needs. Your baby awaits, Mary, and you simply cannot stay here longer. Go home. Take tea with Sarah, and craft schemes to marry me to as many men as you wish. I shall join you when my mission is accomplished."

"If you remain in Otley, Prudence, the family at Thorne Lodge will hear of it at once. You must be asked to dinner again, to balls, indeed to every entertainment they host. You will see Mr. Sherbourne on many occasions. I can only deduce that you have cast your lot with him. Shall I tell our sister that your future happiness lies in Yorkshire?"

"You deduce wrong. My happiness has nothing to do with Mr. Sherbourne or his great estate. I intend to decline all invitations from Thorne Lodge until the family finally surrenders to my polite disinterest in their company."

"And just how do you propose to assist the mill children without making an utter fool of yourself—again?"

Prudence studied the ebb and flow of people on the street below their window. Though she did not know the answer to her sister's question, an idea began to present itself. An irrational idea, but a promising one all the same.

She turned to Mary. "I shall inform you of my method for rescuing the children when the task has been accomplished. Until then, my lips are sealed."

With a rather dramatic sigh, Mary tossed a bonnet into her trunk. "Stay, then. But you know too well that I must send someone to chaperone you in my place. It cannot be Sarah, for she is much occupied. Whoever your chaperone may be, look for her within the week."

Prudence's heart lifted at last. A week . . . if not more . . . alone. She could almost see God smiling on her.

Almost.

◆

"Her sister is gone, yet she remains at the inn? Alone?" Olivia asked, staring at her husband in shock. "Whatever can she mean by such unmannered conduct?"

"I believe the answer to your question stands at the window just there—pondering whether to fling himself from it or surrender to his fate and court the young lady in earnest."

William turned. "Leaping from this window would place me exactly two feet from where I now stand. We are at ground level, as you very well know. You must think of another way to end my bleak existence, Randolph."

"Such nonsense!" Olivia said. "You are both so determined to make light of this situation that you fail to see the truth. Miss Watson remains in Otley without family or friends. We are left with no choice but to invite her to Thorne Lodge again. I like her very well, but, William, you are the object of her fancy. What do you say to this?"

"I say we must not make too much of it. Perhaps Miss Watson has remained in Otley because she wishes to climb to the top of the Chevin and have a look about the countryside. Perhaps she simply enjoys our town and has asked her sister to allow her a brief respite alone."

"Perhaps she has fallen in love with you," Randolph said, "and hopes you will respond in kind."

"Doubtful," William said. "She fled our picnic as though chased by a herd of wild boars."

"Only one *boor*, however, was actually there." Randolph grinned at his brother. "What did you do to the poor woman to frighten her away in such a state?"

William found suddenly that he could not speak. Dare he admit that their kiss had delighted and frightened them both?

"It hardly matters what happened," Olivia declared. "The pertinent issue is whether to invite Miss Watson to our assembly next Saturday. It is no small occasion, for the house will be filled with our family and friends. William, again I plead with you to be serious. Miss Watson has stayed because of you. Will you call on her at the inn? Shall I ask her to Thorne Lodge?"

Pondering the question, William looked out the window at the curls of white mist rising from the bracken and gorse that grew on the moor. He found no answer there. Had Prudence stayed because of him? Or did she hope to renew her attachment to the blacksmith? It was impossible to know.

He reflected on the yellow bonnet even now sitting at the back of his wardrobe. Undecided what to do with it, he had hidden the thing—and then taken it out again and again to drink in the scent of her perfume, run his fingers over ribbons as soft and silken as her skin, imagine her smile and her bright eyes as she gazed at him from beneath its brim.

"I shall call on her tomorrow," he announced before he could give the subject of Miss Prudence Watson yet one more round of tormented speculations and imaginings. "The haberdasher in Otley has just sent a message that my new frock coat is ready to be fitted. On that errand, I shall stop at the inn."

"Fishing for a frock coat but reeling in a wife," Randolph drawled. "Very good, William. You are turning out better than I predicted. I shall write to India and inform Edmund that our little brother is at last becoming a man."

As Randolph and Olivia chatted about plans for the assembly, William turned his brother's words over in his mind. How welcome it would be to label his past misdeeds as little more than the errors of a silly boy. Wrap them tidily and put them away like old toys no longer used.

He might have been young when he went away to sea. But William had become a man too soon. His trespasses could not be so easily undone. And they could never be forgiven.

A wife was not in his future. Most certainly not the lovely Miss Watson, for whom his heart ached day and night.

Eight

Prudence had never been so terrified in her life. Hiding in a barn during the bloody battle at Waterloo was nothing to this, she realized as she stepped into the worsted mill at dawn. Elbowed and shoved forward by the throng of men, women, and children of all ages who were pouring through the door, she prayed for God to guide her steps and protect her.

She touched the arm of a young woman who had been pushed against her. "Excuse me, please. Where may I find the overlookers?"

Dull gray eyes flicked over the stranger in a mobcap and ragged black shawl. "Just there. Along the far wall." The woman pointed toward the shadows that nearly concealed a group of well-muscled men who were conferring in low, guttural voices.

"Thank you," Prudence murmured. But before she could muster the courage to approach them, the woman spoke again.

"Are ye new?"

"Yes. In Otley less than a week."

"No husband or children?" The gray eyes deepened. "You'll want to stay clear of Dick the Devil. He's that big lummox in the gray cap, the piecers' overlooker. You're a pretty one, and he'll set his eye on ye soon enough. There's no way of knowing how many of these wee ones are his."

"His children?" At this news, Prudence's hard-won composure vanished. Her back stiffened as she focused on the wicked man. "Upon my word, such misbehavior should be reported at once!"

The woman drew back in surprise. "Where be ye coming from, lass?"

"The south," Prudence managed, once again aware of her peril should she be discovered as an impostor. Turning quickly, she drew her dusty mobcap farther down on her forehead and stepped away from the other woman.

She must be more careful. Much labor had gone into her scheme, and all could be lost in an instant. The moment Mary's coach had rolled away from the inn the day before, Prudence set to work. She informed the innkeeper that she would be away for a short time, walking the moors. He assumed she intended to climb the Chevin, the granite mount that overlooked Otley, and he wished her well.

Carrying a blue cotton gown, a black shawl, and two plain petticoats in a large bag, Prudence had set off. Once she was out of view of the townsfolk, she spied a patch of boggy ground surrounded by moss and tossed the garments into the mire.

Her kid leather boots, now caked in mud, stamped holes in the fabric.

When they were thoroughly soiled, she retrieved the garments, found a cold stream, and gave them a cursory wash. On returning to the inn, she spread the clothing before the fire to dry. Then she stitched a mobcap from one of her once-white petticoats. She snipped several threads of yarn in her shawl and raveled the wool until its former delicate beauty would never be discerned.

That night, Prudence had slept fitfully, more than once crawling out of the bed and dropping to her knees in earnest prayer. In the half-light before dawn, she rose and dressed in the garments now stained with mud and moss. She tucked her curly golden locks into the mobcap, smudged her cheeks with a dirty scrap, and slipped out of the inn.

Huddled beneath her cap and shawl, she joined the flood of mill workers in their wooden clogs. Now—heart hammering out of her chest—she approached the overlookers.

"What have we here?" Dick the Devil called to his cohorts. At his waist, he carried a whip with leather thongs dangling from it. "Looking for work, are ye, lass?"

Keeping her head low, Prudence nodded. "Aye, sir."

"What can ye do?"

A list of her many accomplishments flashed through Prudence's mind. She could paint landscapes, recite poetry in French, read Latin, dance jigs and waltzes, sing, play the pianoforte, arrange flowers, bead bags, embroider fire screens, and do many other such talents that were completely useless now.

"Well?" Dick growled. "Have ye got a tongue, girl?"

"I am good with a needle," she blurted out.

"But you're too tall to be one of my scavengers or piecers. Bad luck for me, eh?" He laughed along with the other men. "Jimmy, can ye use her at spinning?"

Another man grunted, straightening from his slouch against the wall. "Aye, Dick. Two of my spinners are away sick with the mill fever, and one comes so late I'm obliged to beat her every day."

Prudence stifled a gasp. Jimmy, she noted, had short yellow hair and blue eyes that set him apart from the dark countenance of Dick the Devil. Despite his reference to beating a laborer—and the wicked leather strap hanging from his belt—his tone was not cruel. Prudence began to nurture some hope of fair treatment.

"Ye'll take the place of Moll," Jimmy continued. "I'll be obliged to sack her when she comes—*if* she comes. You'll earn a penny an hour, and don't be asking for more. Be here at sunup, work hard, don't be getting yourself with child, and ye'll have no trouble with me. Come, lass, and I'll show ye to the wheel."

Jimmy led Prudence down an aisle between iron and wooden engines she had never seen before. Men and women were rushing to their places at the carding and weaving machines. Children dropped to their knees and crawled beneath the looms. Then, all at once, a whistle blew and the millworks sprang to life with a deafening clatter, rattle, and bang.

"This here is your billy," Jimmy called over the din as he pointed out a spinning machine. To Prudence, the billy resembled the letter *H*. As the woman who operated it turned a wheel, one side stood motionless, while the other moved back and forth.

"This is the carriage," he said, gesturing to the mobile part of the machine that slid like a drawer into the other. "Some people calls it the spinning frame."

"Aye, sir." With much trepidation, Prudence eyed the whirling spindles as they slid forward several feet, paused, and then slid smoothly away again.

"That's Fanny, there," Jimmy told her, nodding at the woman Prudence had spoken to on entering the mill. "Can ye see how her carriage runs backwards and forwards by means of them six iron wheels on three iron rails? The spindles are inside the carriage. You've got seventy in number, all turned by one wheel. That wheel is in the care of the spinner. And that would be ye, now, your very own self. What name do they call ye, lass?"

"Polly," Prudence replied, thankful she had created a new name and background for herself during the restless night.

He tapped the carriage of the young woman who labored nearby. "Fanny, show Polly how ye work the billy. Lunch is at noon, lass. When the sun sets, we'll shut down the mill, and ye can go home with the others. Take care to follow orders and work quick. I don't take kindly to my spinners coming late or leaving early."

So saying, he turned away and began barking at a man near the far end of the row of spinning machines.

"The master don't like production going down," Fanny confided. "He's a hard one, he is. Now he's back from sea, and we've had word he expects more worsted from us than ever. If ye mean to keep on here, Polly, work fast and clean."

"Indeed I shall."

"Then watch me well," Fanny shouted over the roar of the mill's engines. "The faster and smoother ye work your billy, the better ye'll be treated. See how I bring the carriage close up under the fixed part of the machine?"

Prudence nodded. Though the machine seemed simple, she was concerned. The women and men down the row worked at such a rapid pace she wondered if she could ever match them.

"When the carriage be underneath the billy," Fanny continued, "each spindle will take hold of a length of carding."

She demonstrated, drawing out ten inches of downy white wool that had been cleaned of burrs, dirt, and other imperfections. Now as Fanny pushed the carriage farther away, the carded wool spun into yarn and wound around the spindles.

"It's easy enough, yet it's not hard to go wrong neither." Fanny repeated the action, working faster and faster each time until Prudence could barely follow the blur of movement.

"Can ye do it now, Polly?"

Prudence nodded. "I think so. I shall try, at any rate."

Giving her a curious look, Fanny turned back to the spinning machine and set to work again. Prudence stepped to her new position and took hold of the wheel. She gave it a turn, watched the carriage slide into place, and then turned the wheel in the opposite direction.

As the carriage skimmed back, taking carded wool with it, Prudence noticed a scurrying movement under the machine. Rats! At the very idea, she caught her breath, let go of the wheel, and snatched up her skirts. The carriage spun away, still trailing carded wool. Fanny let out a shriek and raced to the runaway spinning machine.

"What are ye doing?" she cried. "Polly, I told ye to take no more than a hand's length of carding!"

"I saw a . . . a rat!" As Prudence spoke the word, the object under her spinning machine went still. In the dim light, she made out two bright eyes staring back at her in alarm.

"That's no rat!" Fanny snapped at her. "That's your scavenger. What do they call ye, girl?"

"Martha Smith, if ye please, ma'am," she called in a high-pitched voice.

Prudence recognized the name at once. This was the sister of young Tom Smith, the boy who had pushed her into the mud and stolen her reticule.

Fanny explained. "Martha picks up loose wool from under the spinning machine. She takes that brush there and sweeps under the wheels to clean out the oil, dust, and dirt."

"*Under* the wheels?" Prudence had heard of this dangerous work, and seeing it firsthand confirmed her fears. Worse, she was to be the means of any injury the girl should suffer.

"There's my brother," Martha called up to her. "Tom's your piecer, ma'am."

She spotted Tom now, lurking just beneath her billy. Dismayed that he might recognize her despite the disguise, Prudence lifted the black shawl over her mobcap.

"You've got to have a piecer," Fanny said, her mouth breaking into a smile. She was pretty, Prudence saw. Though her teeth had gone bad and her eyes were dull, her gentle face conveyed kindness as she spoke. "Ye didn't suppose the cardings walked themselves over to your spindles, did ye?"

"No, I suppose not," Prudence said.

"Tom takes the cardings in his left hand," Fanny continued, "twenty at a time. He lays the ends of the cardings over each other and rubs them together on that canvas cloth just down there. Ye see it? Sometimes the piecers . . . their fingers bleed.

But Tom is tough by now. He'll keep your spindles well supplied with cardings. If he don't, Dick the Devil will lay him open with the thong."

"Oh, dear," Prudence said under her breath as Fanny hurried back to her own spinning wheel. Prudence could not resist calling to the children below. "Martha, Tom—be careful!"

They gave no answer, so she stepped up to her wheel again and began to turn. She quickly realized she was unequal to the task. Her labor was slow and awkward. The yarn she spun was so uneven—thick in some places and thin in others—that Jimmy was forced to return more than once to admonish her. His thick fingers pointed out the flaws in her work, and he snapped her wool threads with the flick of a hand.

Shoulders aching and her head throbbing, Prudence poured all her strength into the work. On the verge of dropping over in a dead faint, she was never more relieved to hear a whistle blow. The machinery ground to a halt.

"Come, Polly, and be quick! We must eat!" Fanny grabbed her by the hand and dragged her along with the rush of workers pouring toward a large room at the far end of the mill.

Entering, Prudence saw several long, narrow tables and wooden benches. The two women sat, nudging between other workers. Men and boys filled one side of the room, women and girls the other. Prudence searched for signs of tablecloths, napkins, plates, and silverware, but she soon realized these were luxuries the mill workers must never have seen.

Kitchen staff hurried into the dining room bearing heavy, black iron cook pots. Wooden bowls stacked at the end of each table soon held water porridge, lumps of black rye bread, and cooked onions. Diners passed the bowls down both sides of the tables. The moment each received a portion, he tipped it up and drank down the blue-tinged porridge.

"Are there no spoons?" Prudence asked.

Fanny frowned. "Spoons? Nay, but sop the porridge with your bread if ye will."

Prudence looked down at the soggy clump. "What are these bits of white fluff on my bread?"

"Flues—from the wool. Pick them off if ye wish. As for me, I've learned to eat wool same as I've learned to breathe it."

Dipping her fingers into the bowl, Prudence took a piece of bread, pulled away several strands of loose wool, and popped it into her mouth. So soft it stuck to her teeth, the bread was bitter and grainy. She chewed for a moment, then forced herself to swallow.

"Sometimes we have oatcake," one of the other women told Prudence. "The cooks put one in each bowl and pour boiled milk and water over it."

Fanny made a face. "Aye, and remember last Christmas? The master gave us potato pie with boiled bacon in it, a bit here and a bit there. But it was so thick with fat and gristle we scarce could eat it."

"Does the master come here often?" Prudence voiced her question before tipping her bowl to take a sip of water porridge.

"After the mill was first built, he came every day," Fanny said. "This was a good place to work in them days. The over-lookers couldn't beat us often with the master always about. But he was called to war, and off he went. His brother looked in on the mill but rarely, for he supposed it was the same as ever. Now the master is returned, but we have no hope things will go back the way they was."

"He's a changed man," the other woman said under her breath. "Cares only about upping the worsted production. They say he's in debt and wants all the money he can get his hands on—never mind us."

Prudence mulled this information as she regarded her bowl. William Sherbourne could not possibly be in debt. His family owned a vast estate, two great manor houses, sheep beyond number, the worsted mill, and no doubt much more.

"Do ye mean to eat that, Polly?" Fanny asked, eyeing Prudence's bowl with its cold porridge and soggy bread.

"Take it please. I shall fill my stomach at teatime."

"Tea?" Several women exclaimed the word and then began to laugh. One set her hand on Prudence's arm. "We never see tea nor butter nor crumpets. You'll have nothing to eat again until supper, and now Fanny's gone and ate the last of your porridge."

As she spoke, the woman was rising from her bench along with everyone else in the room. The workers had been at their meal for less than half an hour, yet the whistle blew again, setting off another mad rush toward the looms and carding engines.

Stunned, Prudence sat at the table unable to move. She was hungry and tired. Her arms ached from turning the great spinning wheel. The cold stone floor had turned her feet to blocks of ice. No wonder the people wore wooden shoes.

"Oy, ma'am!" A boy's voice rang out. "Hasten to your post, or the overlooker will take his thong to ye!"

She focused on the child and saw it was Tom Smith. He knew her. She could see it written in his face.

"Come, ma'am!" he urged again. "You'll lose your place at the wheel sure enough!"

Without a word, Prudence gathered her skirt and followed Tom back into the work area. The machinery was moving at full speed again, the rattle and roar deafening, and every worker bent to the task. As the boy knelt to crawl beneath the carriage, Prudence resumed her position before the billy.

The hours crept by. She labored over her machine, determined to master it. But her threads broke and tangled. Her spindles snapped. Her carriage jammed. And all the while, the women and men around her produced reel after reel of beautiful white woolen yarn.

Throughout the afternoon, Jimmy patrolled the aisles, watching his crew. Stopping at Prudence's wheel most often, he barked at her to do better or she'd be sacked before the day was out. Nearly in tears from exhaustion and hopelessness, she merely nodded and prayed for strength to endure.

As the sun began to sink, the dim light hindered her work even more. By evening, she could hardly breathe and had coughed until she felt her lungs must burst. Dust and lye drifted in the air, clogging her nose and throat.

The teaseler machine, she learned at the evening meal, was the cause of most of the pollution. Before shearing the sheep, the shepherds washed them in a strong solution of lye. When the animals were sheared, the dried and powdery lye came away with the wool. The teaseler's object was to shake out the lye and dust. This it did—and so well that no one in the mill could breathe with ease.

Dinner had been more brown bread and water porridge.

Prudence was so hungry she ate it without bothering to brush away the flues. Hunched over her bowl, she rubbed at the dust in her eyes as she sopped up every drop of porridge with the soggy bread.

She would die of this, she realized. If God saw her through to the end of the evening, she would surely cough herself to death in her bed that night. Her friend Betsy Fry went into prisons, tended the ill and aged, and brought food and blankets to children who were obliged to live in the cells with their parents. That or be cast into the street.

But Prudence had not lasted a single day in the mill. A voice in her ear taunted her. *You are a sorry thing,* it said. *You are nothing but a pampered, silly girl with golden curls and pink cheeks.*

She had left her billy in a tangled, knotted mess before dinner. As she returned to it now, she saw the overlooker studying her handiwork.

"Well, ye have given me a bit of a surprise," he said, stepping back so she could take her place at the wheel. "I thought ye were good for naught. But this is acceptable work. Ye learn fast, lass, faster than most. Ye will have this same machine on the morrow."

Confused, Prudence peered at the billy she had abandoned in despair a half hour before. Now each spindle stood at attention, its white yarn neatly spun to an even texture and wrapped around it in perfect symmetry.

"Carry on, then," Jimmy said. "We shut down when we can see no more."

Prudence leaned over her carriage, stunned at the workmanship. How had this happened? Was she at the wrong billy?

Bewildered, she glanced to one side and caught Fanny winking at her. The woman held a finger over her lips.

Confused, Prudence bent to turn her wheel. She spotted young Tom below the spinner. One of his hands was filled with cardings, but the other gestured for silence just as Fanny had done.

They knew.

Realization coursing through her, Prudence straightened and looked about the mill. At every position, workers cast glances her way. One man tipped the brim of his cap. Another did the same. Two women gave quick curtsies. Children under the looms and spinners smiled shyly.

They all knew!

Turning quickly to her billy, Prudence began to rotate the wheel. What did this mean? Would the workers reveal her identity to the overlookers? or worse, to the master himself?

Or would they expect something of her that she could not give? Would they expect an avenging crusader who could save them from their misery and woe?

Prudence groaned at the thought. She was, in truth, quite silly. Her sisters and their friends all had termed her so. Though she protested the label with vehemence, she could hardly prove them wrong. She had spent much time flirting with boys, shopping for bonnets and gowns, giggling with her friends, and other such nonsense. In the whole of her life, Prudence acknowledged, she had accomplished nothing intellectually profound, demonstrated no outstanding craftsmanship or skill. Indeed she had done very little beyond singing and embroidering pillows.

Opening her carriage, Prudence cut the yarn on the perfectly executed spindles and set them aside. One of the women had replaced her mess—Fanny, no doubt. Setting empty spindles in their places, Prudence started her wheel again. As the carriage rolled away from her, the white cardings stretched out to their full length, and the spindles began to fill.

She concentrated, wanting to justify the overlooker's confidence. But her mind wanted to wander. How useless her carefully crafted disguise had been. Tom Smith had recognized her at once, and he must have whispered the news. Within minutes, the information must have spread that Miss Watson was inside the mill.

"Watson's workers," these very people had chanted when they spied her carriage on the road. They saw her as a champion, a defender of those who could not defend themselves. And she knew beyond doubt that she would fail them.

The cavernous room was almost pitch-black when the whistle blew to end the day. Prudence heaved a sigh as the waterwheel stopped and the machinery groaned to a halt. She had discarded her shawl in the warm room, but now she wrapped it around her head and shoulders.

"Prudence, why do you do this thing?" The deep voice startled her. "What do you mean by it?"

Her surprise turned to relief. "Mr. Walker," she breathed out. "It is you. Thank God."

"Thank God you have not been found out by the overlookers." He took her elbow and steered her into the crowd flowing toward the mill's door. "Why do you play this game?"

"I want to help these people. I needed to see for myself what they endure. And now I have."

"You have seen, and so what? Will you ride in a carriage to Thorne Lodge and beg the baron and his brother to call off the overlookers? Will you ask them to slow production of the worsted? Will you plead for cleaner air and better food?"

"I could. I might." She stepped out into the road. "They do listen to me."

"Listen? Yes, because you are pretty and charming. Will they make a change here? No. This is their livelihood, Prudence. It is the livelihood of the villagers, too. You must not interfere. Go back to London. Take tea with your sisters; call on your friends; go to the shops."

"Stop it!" she cried, jerking her arm away. "I shall not surrender so easily. You were taken from your people, shipped off to England, paraded before royalty—and you submitted. You resigned yourself to your fate. But I shall do no such thing!"

"Go home, Prudence," he ordered. "Go home tomorrow, and do not return to this place."

"I cannot leave," she told him. "My heart will not allow it."

They were nearing the inn now, and she parted from him without another word. Slipping into an alley beside the brick edifice, she retrieved a dark cape she had stowed behind a stack of firewood. She tugged off the mobcap and gave her head a shake. Curls drifted out onto her shoulders as she tied the cape in place over her ragged dress.

She could think of nothing now but a bath. Warm water would ease the knots in her arms and soothe the swollen ache in her legs. And food. Oh, she must order a late supper—breads and cheeses, oxtail soup, cake . . .

Dear Lord, she lifted up in silent petition, *please let the kitchen have chocolate cake.*

"There you are at last!" The innkeeper's wife rushed toward Prudence when she stepped through the door. "We had all but given you up! Fell down from the Chevin, my husband said. Fell and broke her head. That's what he said, but you are well!"

"Yes," Prudence managed. "Well enough."

"You must hear my news at once!" The woman clasped her hands together in unbridled joy. "He has come to call on you! Come twice! The first time was this morning not long after you had gone away. And then he sent a messenger to ask if you'd returned. And what do you think—but he came again himself!"

"Who? Who called on me?"

"Mr. William Sherbourne, of course! And can you imagine? He has written you a letter!" She presented the white missive as though handing over a treasure. "There! Written in his very own hand, it is. And sealed! Sealed with the family crest—just there in the wax. More to the point, he bade me farewell and said he would hope to see me on the morrow. What do you think of *that*, Miss Watson?"

Prudence thought many things all at once. First, that she would not be at the inn tomorrow, for she fully intended to go to the mill again. Also, she thought that Mr. Sherbourne, despite his protests to the contrary, had become rather persistent in his courtship. Most of all, she thought that it might be quite nice to greet William again—perhaps stroll to the church, take tea together, chat of amiable things.

The memory of his kisses in the glade swelled, nearly enveloping her with their sweetness and passion. She lingered a moment on the wisp of reminiscence. Then she forced her attention elsewhere.

"I have not eaten today," she told the innkeeper's wife. "Would it be possible—"

"A late supper?" The woman took her by the arm and led her

toward the stairs. "Or tea and cake or anything else, my dear. Say the word, and you shall have whatever you desire."

Prudence smiled. "You are kind."

"Anything for the future Mrs. Sherbourne," she whispered, giving Prudence a nudge with her elbow. "Anything for the mistress of the manor!"

Nine

William rode toward the mill as the sun set. Two days now, he had stopped at the inn. Two days, Prudence had been away. He had written to her without receiving any reply. He had asked the innkeeper and the housemaid about the nature of her absences, but none knew where the young lady had ventured.

Where could she be keeping herself from dawn to dusk? William puzzled as his horse passed through the gate in the fence that surrounded the mill and its pond. No doubt the mystery revolved around Walker, the local blacksmith.

Still debating the wisdom of his mission, William reined in his horse and dismounted. One way to satisfy his curiosity would be to catch the woman at her mischief. This meant he would need to confirm that the blacksmith had been absent from his post during the past two days.

Another—and far better—way to resolve the matter would be to ride for home, put the beautiful but troublesome creature out of his head, and resume life as he had known it. Certain of the wisdom of restraint, William nevertheless tied his horse to a post and stepped up to the mill's front door.

Richard Warring, the piecers' overlooker, was the first to spot him. The man whom Prudence had called Dick the Devil now approached. Head low, he swept off his hat and made a bow.

"Sir, 'tis an unexpected pleasure to see ye here."

"Learn to expect it, Warring," William replied, starting down the long aisle between the carding and spinning machines. "I shall visit daily when I am at home, and I expect to stay at home from now until I breathe my last."

"Aye, sir. And glad we are of it."

Glad? Of what? His return home . . . or the moment he breathed his last?

Recalling Prudence's warnings about mutiny brewing in the mill, William wondered if Dick the Devil was among the agitators. Striding across the dusty wood floor, William inspected the massive machinery he had purchased and set into place.

"Three backwashers," he murmured, counting as he passed. "Three gill boxes, three lap boxes, six finishing gill boxes, one scouring machine."

By now the other overlookers had fallen in line behind him. "Sir, I assure you that everything is working very good indeed," Jimmy, the spinners' overlooker, reported.

"I am happy to hear it." William returned to his inventory. "Spindle boxes, spindle dandy frames, spinning frames—"

He halted at a billy halfway down the aisle. The spinner's

carriage, tangled in a spiderweb of unevenly spun wool thread, had stuck fast. As William leaned closer to study the machine, the woman at the wheel gasped and stumbled backward into Dick the Devil. At that, the overlooker shouted an oath and grabbed the woman by the shoulders. She let out a sharp cry as he shoved her to one side away from the others. Crumpling to the floor, she buried her face in her hands.

"Warring, what do you mean by using such force against a female?" William demanded. "From now on, you will keep your hands off my workers."

"Aye, sir." Dick nodded, but his expression conveyed no remorse. "As ye wish, sir."

Disgusted, William turned away. "Madam, are you harmed in any way?" Hearing no answer from the bundle of gray rags, he tried again. "Are you injured?"

"No, sir," came the reply.

"I am glad. And I apologize for Mr. Warring's ill manners. It will not happen again." So saying, he turned his attention to the billy and its mass of snarls and knots. "What is this, Jimmy? Do you expect my weavers to make worsted from such a hopeless tangle?"

"Nay, sir," the man said. "That woman is new to the mill, and the billy be difficult to learn at first. Fanny over there, she be teaching the one on the floor."

William observed the huddled creature once again, and a vague uneasiness crept over him. Was she weeping?

"Yesterday, she done well enough," Jimmy continued. "But today, she ain't done so good. Say the word, sir, and I'll send her packing."

William let out a breath. "What is her name?"

"Polly, sir."

He crossed to the woman. "Polly, have you brothers and sisters? a father and mother?"

"Two sisters, Mr. Sherbourne." She kept her head down. "My parents died."

"And your sisters—do they work in this mill?"

"No, sir. Neither."

"You are their sole support, then. And what did you eat today at my mill?"

"Oatcake and water porridge, sir. Both meals."

William stood over the pitiful little woman in her filthy mobcap and frayed black shawl. Was this the sort of militant rebel who meant to do him in? He could hardly imagine it. Yet, given her destitution and hunger, Polly might be prone to join an uprising.

"Keep her to the end of the week," he told Jimmy. "See how she fares by then. And feed the poor wretch. Give her . . . oh, hang it—give them all cake."

"Cake?" Dick the Devil tilted his head. "Cake, sir?"

"Cake. Have you never heard of it, Mr. Warring? Tomorrow, I shall send cakes down from the kitchens at Thorne Lodge. And see that the labor is given tea to drink. Good, hot tea."

Moving on, he took up his recitation again. "Twelve carding engines. Each of these cost six hundred pounds, I shall have you know. One, two, three . . ."

He spoke to no one, his thoughts absorbed by Prudence Watson and her admonition to treat his workers better. Feed them cake, she had said. Cake! And now, against his better judgment, he had done it.

The girl's opinions were not worth two figs. Yet he had

listened and acted. What was this hold she had over him? Were her warnings a sign of tenderness? Or did she concoct the tale of a rebel plot in an effort to sway him toward reform?

"Looms," he continued trying to drown out his own thoughts. "Stocks. Fulling machines. Have the water pipes been inspected of late?"

"Aye, sir," one of the men behind him called out. "No leaks, sir."

"Very good. I shall inspect the smithy." He started for the stairs, but the object of his visit stood in his path. "Mr. Walker. You are here?"

"As always, sir." The blacksmith extended a hand toward the staircase. "Will you come up?"

William stepped ahead. Had Walker descended to watch his master's path through the mill? Or was there another reason he lurked below his forge?

In five minutes, William made the requisite inspection of the smithy. When asked, Walker explained its operation and listed various implements he was called on to create or repair. The blacksmith was, no doubt, intelligent. Moreover, if a man could be the judge of such things, Walker must be called handsome. It was no wonder, then, that Prudence had lost her heart to him and had stayed in Otley in some vain attempt to win him again.

Silly girl. Silly, empty-headed girl. He descended the stairs and started back down the aisle. As he neared the spinners, he saw a cluster of workers gathered around the woman who had collapsed. One had brought her a ladle of water. Another was helping her to stand.

"No," she was saying. "I am well, quite well. Return to your posts, I beg you."

Spotting William, she struggled to her feet and made for her billy, where Fanny, her teacher, was quickly snipping threads and aligning spindles. The woman . . . was it Polly? . . . now pressed Fanny to step away.

"I can do it," she insisted. "Please, it is all my fault, and I must repair it myself."

William approached, aware that every eye in the mill was on him. He frowned. Something in the woman's air—the way she held herself—compelled him. He had not had a good look at her face, but all the same he felt as if he had seen her before. Perhaps on the street somewhere.

"Madam?" He reached for her arm.

"Fire! Fire!" The shout rang out through the cavernous room. "Run! Everyone run for it!"

Jerking away from the woman, William caught sight of a ball of flame tumbling down the wooden staircase from the smithy. Shrieking in fear, people ran for the doors. Walker hurtled down the stairs, a pail in each hand. As the waterwheel ceased turning and the machines halted with great groans and clangs, the blacksmith tossed water onto the blaze.

William sprinted toward Walker, arriving in time to tear off his greatcoat and beat the smoldering flames. In moments, the fire was out.

And the mill was a shambles.

He looked up to find the place empty, with doors banging in the wind. Jimmy darted back into the hall and paused, silhouetted in the fading light. Walker stomped the last of the ash into the floorboards and started up the stairs.

"Halt," William barked at him. "What was that?"

"Sir?" The smith turned.

"You know very well what I mean. That pile of rags was lit on purpose. Water stood at the ready to put it out. None of my laborers was ever in danger from a fire—were they?"

Walker's eyebrows lifted. "I always keep water at the ready, sir."

"And how often do you toss burning rags among my workers?"

"Do you accuse me, sir?"

"I do indeed."

Jimmy approached warily. "Mr. Sherbourne, the people stand outside awaiting a word from ye. It grows dark, sir, and we normally send them home this time of night."

William gave a snort of disgust. "Tell them to go home. And send in the overlookers to put the machines to rights."

"Yes, sir. To be sure, sir." Jimmy backed away a few steps and then turned and ran for the door.

"I shall require your presence at Thorne Lodge, Walker," William told the blacksmith. "Tomorrow morning at eight sharp."

"Yes, sir."

The smith started up the stairs again. Stifling a groan, William studied the billy that had been a tangled mess only minutes earlier.

He did not like the tension in his mill. He did not trust his blacksmith. And he was reluctantly starting to believe that Miss Prudence Watson had been right to warn him of the potential for mutiny.

Worse yet, it seemed very possible—probable, in fact—that the woman to whom he was losing his heart was also his sworn adversary.

◆

Her cape fluttering and curls bouncing, Prudence flew through the front door of the inn. She ran for the stairs in the earnest hope of eluding the innkeeper's wife.

"Oh, Miss Watson!" The woman herself sallied forth from the kitchen. "Can you imagine? But he came again today! And he has written you a second letter!"

She drew the note from her apron pocket and presented it to her guest.

"Thank you very much indeed." Prudence took the letter and offered a small curtsy before moving away again.

"He was dressed very handsome," the innkeeper's wife said, laying a hand on Prudence's arm to stop her flight. She leaned close to confide. "In my opinion, he is the handsomest of all the Sherbourne brothers. Some say that with a single glance Randolph Sherbourne can drop a woman to the floor in a swoon. Others are partial to Edmund Sherbourne and his upright, pious appearance. But I myself cannot find a handsomer man than William Sherbourne. He is most assuredly the best looking of all three, and today he wore a greatcoat that was cut so well he seemed a foot taller and twice as broad at the shoulder! Can you credit it?"

"No, indeed, I cannot." Prudence smiled. "But I must hurry to my room and read this letter."

"Of course you must! Why do you dawdle? Go, go, child!"

Prudence lifted her skirts and fled up the stairs. She fumbled with her key, burst through her door, and shut it again as quickly as she could. Leaning against it, she tried to catch her breath.

Oh, how very close she had come to exposure! This venture

was not going well. Not well at all! If Mr. Walker had not distracted William's attention, he most surely would have found her out.

And to think that Mr. Walker had risked a fire on her behalf! A fire that could have burned down the mill and caused the death of many people! The very prospect of such a thing was too horrible to contemplate.

Already, Prudence's intrusion at the mill endangered the workers. Mr. Walker had jeopardized his position to defend her masquerade. But she knew he had not done it out of love. He had acted on behalf of all the poor workers at the mill—those kind and gentle souls who had placed misguided hopes on her ability to improve their lot.

A sharp rap on the door startled Prudence. Holding her breath, she swung around and turned the knob.

"Miss Watson!" The innkeeper's wife looked nearly as alarmed as Prudence felt on seeing her in such a state. "He is here; he is here! Just now, he has returned to the inn and asks for you. What shall I tell him?"

"Tell him I cannot go down." Prudence closed her eyes and drew in a gasp of air. "No, wait! Tell him I shall be happy to speak to him."

A grin brightened the woman's face. "I'll make tea!"

As she toddled off to complete her errands, Prudence tore open the letter William had left earlier. She read aloud.

"'Miss Watson, will you please be so good as to join us this Friday evening for an assembly at Thorne Lodge? We should be happy to introduce you to our friends. Only say the word, and my husband will send a carriage for you at eight. Yours sincerely, Olivia, Lady Thorne.'"

Friday? But that was tomorrow evening. Prudence must definitely not go to the assembly. She ought to go home to London, where she would be safe from her own silliness!

But now she hurried to the mirror and gasped at her reflection. Not only were her cheeks smudged with oil and dirt from her spinning wheel, but each eye bore a dark half-moon of exhaustion beneath it. Her curls, untamed by the mobcap, had gone positively wild.

After pouring out a basin of water, Prudence scrubbed her face. Then she pinned up her hair and changed into a clean gown. It was all done in such haste that she felt certain her gentleman caller would wonder how she had spent the day.

Trying to regulate her heart, Prudence hurried down the stairs again. When she stepped into the sitting room, William stood and gave her a bow.

"Miss Watson," he said. "Good evening."

The innkeeper's wife had not exaggerated. He did look handsome in his greatcoat—though Prudence noted a pale splotch on one sleeve that she suspected must be ashes from the fire at the mill.

"Mr. Sherbourne, what a pleasant surprise," she offered after making a curtsy. "I received Lady Thorne's kind letter just now."

"Then you will accept the invitation?"

She forced a smile. "Yes, of course. I can think of nothing I should enjoy more."

"Really? I had thought you were rather partial to riding."

"Indeed, I am." Shaking her head at her inability to play a charade with this man, she sank down onto a settee. "So, Mr. Sherbourne, you returned to the inn for my answer to Lady Thorne's invitation?"

"I returned because I am most bemused and perplexed by you." He took a chair near her. "Miss Watson, where *have* you been?"

"Out. Out and about."

"From dawn until . . ."

"Dusk, yes. Out and about all day."

"May one ask what engrossing activity has usurped all your time?"

"I very much enjoy Yorkshire." She began to pray that the innkeeper's wife would hurry with the tea. "Yorkshire in the spring is . . . well, it is entrancing."

"And wet," he added. "We had ample rain today. But I see you did not find our drizzle a hindrance to your recreation."

Prudence realized belatedly that he was gazing at her mud-caked boots. She tried to tuck them under the settee, but without success.

"Rain has never bothered me," she told him. "I am very fond of a good cloudburst. Or, as you put it, a drizzle."

"Thus, I believe you might like to accompany me tomorrow despite the high likelihood of drizzle. I go out on the dales and fells to speak to our shepherds and inspect our flocks. From thence, I shall show you the hedgerow that caused great dispute between my family and our neighbors. You would enjoy having a look at Chatham Hall too, I think. It is to become my home should I ever wish to depart Thorne Lodge. And of course, we shall stop at the mill."

"The worsted mill?"

"I have none other. Today I ordered cake and tea for those in my employ. I took your suggestion to heart, you see. I am always amenable to new ideas."

"Are you?" She looked down at her hands, realized they were chafed and raw, and made a valiant effort to hide them under her skirt. "I should like to accompany you, Mr. Sherbourne. But as you can imagine—given my great affection for the Yorkshire countryside—I have already made a plan to go out."

"Out and about?" His lip twitched and she suspected he was mocking her.

"Yes." She studied the doorway, willing the innkeeper's wife to appear. "My plan is fixed, you see, and I cannot amend it."

"Ah, but I have just now offered to take you out and about in Yorkshire. Can you tell me whose plan trumps mine?"

"It is my own plan. You can hardly argue with that."

"Can I not? Surely my company is not so odious as to prevent your altering tomorrow's course."

"Tea!" Prudence exclaimed as the innkeeper's wife toddled into the room. "Thank heaven!"

Bearing a tray of teacups and saucers, a steaming pot, and two bowls of gelatinous, creamy strawberry fool, the woman was none too steady on her feet. Prudence almost hoped for catastrophe. Anything to end this dreadful interview.

"How lovely to see you together at last," the innkeeper's wife said, awarding her two guests a sweet smile. "Poor Mr. Sherbourne and I had begun to despair of you, Miss Watson. I told him you went away both days at dawn, just as the streets filled with people bound for the mill. As you can imagine, I lost sight of you in all that great rush. So, as I told Mr. Sherbourne, I could not say which direction you had taken, though my dear husband and I suspected you had gone up the Chevin. If there is a better view of Yorkshire, I do not know it."

"Ah, fell in with the mill labor, did you?" William dropped

two lumps of sugar into his teacup. "Miss Watson, I am of half a mind to suppose you went to the mill yourself."

"La!" the older woman exclaimed. "Why would she do such a thing? Sure everyone knows about her . . . her difficulty . . . of the other day, when she and that rascal Dick Warring had words. But she would not go back again. Not after that."

"There, you see," Prudence chirped, stirring her tea. "Why would I do such a thing?"

"Because you wished to complete what you had only just begun." William set his cup on the table and stood to address the innkeeper's wife. "Thank you, madam, you have been a friend indeed. Your advice and speculations have given me no end of food for thought."

"Well, then!" She beamed. "Thank you, sir. And I shall hope to see you again soon."

"Indeed, I have no doubt of it."

With a fluttering little curtsy, the woman scurried away, looking pleased with herself.

William picked up an iron poker and prodded a burning log on the grate. "You are not well, Miss Watson," he said, his focus on the blaze that had reignited. "You look tired."

"Thank you, I am sure. Such a compliment I have not received in many a day."

His expression remained somber as he faced her. "You should not go out alone. There are gypsies about. And pickpockets."

"And cads, but one cannot be too careful lest all the fun go out of life." She rose. "Thank you for your invitation, sir, but I must respectfully decline."

"Do you think me a cad?"

"*Are* you a cad?"

He regarded her for a moment. "I am. I cannot deny it. My behavior has been reprehensible. You are right to shun me."

"Were I a cad, I should not make so light of it. More than one woman has had her heart broken over the likes of you."

"But you are not such a woman, Prudence. Are you?"

His use of her given name flustered her. She took a step toward the fire, and swaying slightly, she put out her hand to find a mooring. William took it instead, caught it to his chest, and drew her near.

"Woman, you torment me," he said, his voice low. "Tell me why?"

"I cannot say." She looked into his eyes.

"You cannot say . . . or you will not?"

"We are not alike. Perhaps therein lies the torment."

"Do you feel it too? Say you do."

She moistened her lips. "You ask much of me, sir. Please, I must return to my room. You are right—I am tired."

"Have you stayed because of *him*?" William asked. "Does that lost love still impel you?"

She looked away, wishing he would set her free, yet relishing the warmth of his hand on hers. "I am not in love," she told him. "Not with *him* or any other man. My reason for staying has nothing to do with passion."

"And everything to do with compassion."

Surprised, she glanced at him. "Yes. Compassion. How did you know?"

"Do I not know you, Prudence? You say we are not alike. I say we are two of a kind. I see the fire in your eyes. I know what you want."

"Do you? I think not." She swallowed. "But you have given me half of what I want already, William."

"And what is that?"

"Cake. Tea. Kindness to those who labor on your behalf."

"What else would you ask of me, Prudence? Tell me now. Perhaps you have it already."

She longed to speak words that must not be said. Her heart filled with forbidden desire. He smelled of the outdoors, of leather and bracken. She ached to drift into his arms, lay her head against the broad plane of his chest, feel the sweet press of his lips against hers.

But this was not the time for such longings, nor was he the man who could give life to her dreams.

"Hours," she managed. "Shorter hours. That is what I want. Send them all home before dark. Give the children time to play, the parents strength to hold their little ones close. Bring a teacher. Let the children learn to read and count. Give them hope for a better life."

"A better life that would take them from my mill?" He released her hand and took up the poker again. "Do you not understand that these people have served my family for generations? It is all the life they have known. All that *we* have known. The villagers are our tenants. They plow our fields and keep watch over our flocks. They clip and mow our gardens. They polish our silver and shine our windows. And they produce our worsted."

"But have they no right to dream?"

"This is an economy, Prudence!" he barked. "It is a system. A familiar—even comfortable—system. Would you bring it all down with a whispered word of sedition? Would you and your compatriots in revolution topple this great nation by smashing our machines and burning down our mills?"

At his vehemence, her indignation rose. "Did I ask for destruction, sir? Did I speak of an end to England's peerage or the annihilation of her social order? No, indeed. I asked for a shorter workday, better food, cleaner air, and reading lessons for your laborers. It is not so much, William Sherbourne. Not for a man like you."

"A man like me. You know nothing about me." He thrust the poker into the fire again. For a moment, he was absorbed in prodding a log into flame. Then he straightened and turned to her.

"I am not capable of greatness, Prudence. Do not imagine me better than I am. I am a selfish and obstinate man. I have done too much in my life already—too much that is wrong. The fetters I once forged now tighten about my neck. The ball and chain I crafted now prevent my escape. My hands are bound by iron cuffs that constrict every movement. I cannot be good. I cannot be worthy of anything . . . or of anyone who is so much better and more beautiful than the wretch who stands before you now."

The pain written on his face was more than Prudence could bear. "Your heart is not fettered, William," she said, laying her hand on his cheek. "No one can imprison your spirit. No one can lock away your mind. You speak as an old man whose life is nearly at an end. But you are young. Hope cannot be constrained. Nor can faith. And love? Love is beyond the reach of sin and failure."

He took her hand again, held it to his lips. She saw his

struggle, the anguish of words he could not bear to speak. Stepping near, she stood on tiptoe and brushed a kiss on his cheek.

At that, he groaned, took her in his arms, and held her so close she could hardly breathe. His lips found hers, and he kissed her with such passion that the reticence holding back her heart fled at once.

"William, what am I to do?" she murmured against his coat. "What are we to do?"

"Don't speak, my lady. Stay in my embrace forever. Let me hold you and kiss you until every impossibility is erased by our love."

"Our love? Oh, William . . ."

"No," he silenced her. Holding her at arm's length, he shook his head. "No, not love. I cannot . . . I will not imprison you too. Go, Prudence. Go home to London. Leave me here, I beg you. Save your life. Spare your heart for a man more worthy of it."

With a last kiss, he shuddered. His hands laced through her hair, cupped her neck, caressed her face. Then he turned from her and strode out of the room. She heard the door open and shut again. With a sigh, she fell onto the settee, buried her face in her hands, and allowed herself to weep until no more tears would come.

Ten

William sat near the pianoforte and made a gallant effort to listen to a young lady who fumbled every third note. He took some amusement from it, for she carried on playing with great determination despite the discordant notes that echoed through the drawing room. Most of the other guests had moved into the ballroom, where hired musicians played jigs, country dances, and even waltzes with skill. William was half-inclined to join them, but the very thought of dancing with any woman other than Prudence Watson paralyzed him.

"There!" the young lady cried out as the final cacophonous chords quavered across the room. She let out a deep sigh of satisfaction and turned to William with a smile that made her almost pretty.

He observed, with some regret, that he was the only gentleman remaining in the room and that she was awaiting his response. Sitting up, he applauded with as much enthusiasm as he could muster.

"Lovely, Miss . . . ?"

"Miss Madeline Bowden."

"Of the James Bowden family?"

"Yes, sir. I am the youngest daughter but one."

"I am William Sherbourne."

"Yes! Your eldest brother is Lord Thorne and your second brother is a missionary in India."

"Well done, Miss Madeline. You have placed me exactly."

"We are Ivy, Caroline, Madeline—that is me."

"Of course."

"And finally Clementine. She is youngest of all and has not yet come out into society." Her attention returned to the pianoforte. "Would you like to hear another song, Mr. Sherbourne? I have found a concerto here among the music, but I have never played it before. Still, if you wish—"

"Ah, but I should not like to put a lady in distress." At the alarming prospect of listening to her scrabble through an interminable concerto, he leapt to his feet. "Surely you would rather dance on such an evening as this, Miss Madeline?"

"Dance? With you?"

"None other." He held out his hand.

Blushing rather too much, she rose and slipped her arm around his. "You are very kind."

He begged to differ, for his offer to dance was born of self-preservation and nothing else. But he kept his tongue. The evening held little else to divert him, and the young lady was positively trembling at having won his attentions. Sadly, he could not be less interested in her . . . or in anyone else.

Prudence Watson, he had learned from Olivia at tea that afternoon, had been joined by her dear friend Anne. This welcome visitor had lately arrived in Otley with her husband, Ruel Chouteau, the Marquess of Blackthorne. Lord and Lady Blackthorne, it was rumored, had come to retrieve Miss Watson and would depart with her for London the following morning.

As he faced Madeline Bowden across the dance floor now, William tried to be glad about this news. Prudence would tempt him no more. She and her sweet lips, glorious curls, and pert opinions could no longer divert him from his resolve to remain a bachelor—and to be happy about it—for the rest of his life.

The music swelled; he bowed, stepped into the pattern, turned a circle with Madeline Bowden, and found himself face-to-face with the woman herself—Prudence Watson in a golden gown and long white gloves, with silk ribbons woven through the curls in her hair.

His expression of surprise must have been obvious. Prudence audibly caught her breath, her eyes begging him to remain silent. When the formation of the dance moved him away from her, he scanned the couples to determine the identity of her partner.

None other than Ruel Chouteau was escorting the young lady around the room. Chouteau, once a seaman too, had met William on more than one occasion. It was entirely possible that the man knew William's history, had related it to Prudence, and would soon report it to the entire company.

"Good evening, Mr. Sherbourne," Prudence said softly, when the dance brought them together a second time. "You did not expect to see me."

"Indeed I did not. Yesterday I believed you must depart for London very soon."

"And you wished it so," she replied.

Before he could answer, the dance separated them again. He willed his attention to Miss Madeline, who was clearly beyond rapture over the honor of her escort. She smiled, giggled, tittered, missed several steps, winked at her sisters, and otherwise made it quite impossible for William to keep a straight face.

But soon his path crossed the floor toward Prudence again. "Do you mean to remain in Otley?" he asked.

"We leave tomorrow morning." She linked arms with him and turned a circle. "Your cake was well received at the mill. Or so I am told."

They parted again, and he was left to imagine who had informed her about the cake. Walker, of course. The blacksmith must have met Prudence—perhaps this very evening before she departed for Thorne Lodge. His ire at the idea of a secret rendezvous told William she still held his heart. He could not endure the thought of any other man touching her, embracing her, kissing her.

"Thank you, sir." Madeline Bowden gazed at him, her eyes aglow. He realized belatedly that the music had ceased and the dancers were leaving the floor. Her long lashes fluttered as she spoke again. "You dance remarkably well."

"You are too kind. But I fear my years at sea have made me unsteady on my feet. I am grateful for the honor of your hand, Miss Madeline."

"The honor is mine," she replied. William feared they might go on this way for some time, but Randolph stepped in to ask for a moment with his brother.

"Have you seen Miss Watson?" Randolph asked in a low voice as they made their way to the refreshment tables. "She has captured the eye of every unwed man in the room, William. You must ask her to dance."

"*You* ask her, brother, for she will more likely grant you the honor. Miss Watson and I are no longer friends."

"Indeed not, for you are more than that, and you should make plain your claim on her. Leave her no doubt of your intentions, and erase the hopes of any other man who might propose to woo her."

"Randolph, upon my word, I believe you are persuasive tonight. Perchance did Olivia suggest that you advise me thus?"

"What if she did? We both agree you would be wise to form an attachment with a lady so handsome and well connected as Miss Watson. Did you meet her friends? Blackthorne will be duke one day in his father's place. The family owns a grand home in London, a vast country estate, and a flourishing lace industry in France. I believe they are somehow connected to tea."

"Tea? That settles it, then. I shall propose marriage to Miss Watson at once."

"Dash it all, William, can you never be serious?"

"No, Randolph, I cannot. My course is set and my future will never include a—"

"Do excuse me, my dear William." Olivia Sherbourne had appeared at her husband's side. "Miss Watson is hardly lacking in dance partners, but—" and here she prodded Prudence forward—"but I believe I have managed to secure at least one dance in your name."

The younger woman gave Olivia a wan smile. "Thank you,

madam. I am not engaged at present, but surely Mr. Sherbourne prefers to select his own partners."

William stared at Prudence, unable to think beyond the immediate desire to sweep her into his arms and carry her away into a life where they could never be parted. But at his hesitation, her cheeks colored and she gave a little laugh.

"Indeed, I believe Mr. Sherbourne has already asked another lady for this dance. Miss Madeline Bowden is very pretty."

"No," William blurted. "It is you I want."

With that assertion hanging in midair, he took Prudence by the hand and led her to the floor.

◆

Prudence managed the first steps of the dance well enough. But on crossing to William, slipping her arm through his, and turning an intimate circle, she felt her knees go weak.

"You are beautiful this evening," he murmured, his lips near her cheek, his breath warming her ear.

"I am tired," she responded, her eyes meeting his. "I had thought to stay away tonight."

"Then I am to thank your friend for my happiness."

"She insisted we attend—but only after Lady Thorne sent a second invitation. Anne wishes to meet you."

"I am at her service. And yours." He stepped away now, the requirements of the country dance moving the participants into parallel lines, the women facing the men.

Prudence had made every effort to focus her attentions elsewhere that evening. From the moment Anne and Ruel accepted the formal invitation issued from Thorne Hall, Prudence had labored to concoct a truthful reason not to go. Indeed, she was very tired, for she had spent the day at the mill, where her thread continued to be uneven and her spindles a tangle. Yet, as Fanny had assured her, Prudence's efforts were not quite as hopeless as on the previous day.

On learning they must present themselves at the assembly, Prudence decided she would ignore William. If she feigned disinterest in him, perhaps that falsehood would somehow become truth.

But now she had no choice except to gaze on the man who consumed her waking thoughts and sleeping dreams. Though attired as the other gentlemen—in a black suit, damask vest, and white neckcloth—William easily surpassed them all with his form. Broad shoulders, faultless posture, depthless brown eyes, and impeccable dance steps surely made him the object of every woman's hopes and imaginings.

"I think of you day and night," he whispered when they came together again. "I cannot sleep."

"You named yourself a cad," she reminded him. "Perhaps offering such alluring compliments to women is one of your vices."

"I have many vices," he told her. "Deceiving you is not among them."

"Why is that? I am little different from these other lovely ladies who grace the stage of your life."

He was silent for a moment, his hand at her waist as they moved down the line of dancers. "You are in every way different," he said finally. "I love you."

At that declaration, the steps of the dance parted them again. Prudence tried to believe she had misheard William. The music was loud and the chatter of onlookers pervasive. But he *had* said the words. Said them with reluctance, as though loath to admit the truth of his own feelings.

And how might she respond? More men than she could count had pronounced themselves violently in love with her. She could not recall the number of marriage proposals offered to her on bent knee. How many had sworn they could not go on living without her? that they must surely perish in the barren desert of her rejection? that their existence would no longer have meaning without the daily, hourly vision of her smile?

But which of those vaguely remembered suitors moved her heart as William Sherbourne did? Only one. And that man had spoken to her on this day—as on every other since their reunion—of his engagement, his fond attachment, his deep desire to wed another. He loved Bettie, a little widow with pretty dimples and threads of white hair woven through the brown. He would unite himself to this woman who could give him what Prudence could not—a simple life, a warm cottage, food prepared by her own hands, the peace of knowing he at last had come home.

As Prudence struggled to answer William's avowal with anything but the truth—that she loved him too—the music came to an end. The couples bowed and curtsied, joined hand in hand to depart the dance floor, and made polite conversation.

"Lord Blackthorne's carriage will depart for London tomorrow at first light," she told William when he led her to a quiet corner of the room. "My sisters insist on my return."

"You go because you are commanded? or because you wish to leave?"

She knew the real question behind his queries. "I cannot stay. Perhaps I am admired here, but I am not wanted."

"I will not deny that. I cannot wish your life to become attached to mine in any way. You deserve better, and you should go to London in search of it."

"But who are you to tell me what I should do?" She took out her fan to cool her neck and cheeks. "I am not a child to be ordered about. How I choose to live my life is neither my sisters' affair nor yours. Believe me, I do not go to London in search of a husband."

"But you came here on that quest."

"Did I? How so?"

"Your blacksmith."

She bristled. "Mr. Walker is my friend. Nothing more."

"You stayed in Otley because you wanted to see him. You went to the mill on that pursuit. You meet him at night under cover of darkness."

At this, she drew herself up with indignation. "I beg your pardon, sir! Your accusation is wholly without merit. Mr. Walker is engaged to be married. I am an honorable woman. How dare you charge me with such wickedness?"

"I saw you," he retorted. "Some nights ago, I desired to speak with you and rode down to the inn. I discovered you there—outside, near the door. With him. You kissed his hand."

Mortified, Prudence snapped her fan shut and pushed it into her reticule. "You *spied* on me?"

"Which of us is the spy, madam?"

At his intimations and accusations—all of which were true—she could formulate no response.

"Never mind," she sputtered, "for tomorrow I shall be carried away from this place in Lord Blackthorne's carriage. Your path and mine will never cross again. I assure you, I shall trouble you no longer."

"But you *will* continue to trouble me," he growled, blocking her attempted exit and taking her hand in his. "Teach me how to hate you, Prudence."

She was trembling now, half in fury and half in desire. But desire for what? She could not say, and so she tarried.

"Hate me because I hated you first," she suggested. "Hate me because my every purpose is to bring about the downfall of your enterprise. Hate me because you were not mistaken in what you saw that night. I did meet the man in question, and I kissed his hand. I loved him once. I love him still. Hate me for that. Hate me because even now I shall walk away from you and never speak to you again."

"I can hate you only if you say you do not love me." His hand tightened on hers. "Say I am nothing to you. I am never in your thoughts. I am of little consequence and no importance. Then perhaps I can learn to hate you, Prudence."

"Shall I add untruthfulness to the other sins of which you accuse me?" She snatched her hand away. "Do you wish to make me a liar too?"

He stared at her. "What is your meaning?"

"You annoy and vex me day and night. You infuriate me. Thoughts of you torment me until I fear I shall go mad. How can a man who causes me such distress never leave my consciousness? You ask to be assured that you are of little consequence and no importance to me. I should be the greatest liar in the kingdom if I said such things. I rue the day Tom Smith pushed me into a puddle. I regret every moment I have spent in your company. Every touch . . . every kiss . . ."

Clenching her hands into fists, she struck him once on the chest. "Do not love me!" she cried. "Do not make me love you! I cannot endure it. My heart cannot bear the weight of it another moment. You must release me, I beg you."

Tears welled, and she saw him turn to one side as her friend stepped into their company. The tension of the moment snapped.

"Prudence, you have not introduced me to this gentleman," Anne said, her lovely smile and warm brown eyes comforting as she slipped an arm around her friend. "It is rumored that he is brother to our host and heir to Chatham Hall. My husband and I passed that charming home as we came into Otley this morning."

"Forgive me," Prudence stammered. "My lady, I should like to present William Sherbourne. Sir, I am pleased for you to know my dearest friend, Anne Chouteau, Lady Blackthorne."

"The pleasure is mine, I am sure," she said with a curtsy that answered William's bow. "I have not seen much of Yorkshire in my life, Mr. Sherbourne, but I am compelled to tell you how very pleasant I find this countryside."

"You were brought up in London?" he asked.

"I was born in Nottingham, and there I lived until sad circumstances sent me to London. My father is a minister, a man who inspires his family not only by his words but also by his deeds."

"An ideal father, then," William observed. "I have visited Nottingham on more than one occasion. It is a lovely town."

"I am sure you know it has been home to much of England's lace manufacture. I am very interested in the production of fine goods."

"You are connected to the lace industry in France, I am told."

"Indeed, for Prudence and I became quite enamored of handmade bobbin lace during our tenure in Calais. We founded a lace school, you know, and we made many improvements to the efficiency of that much-admired craft."

"A lace school?" William's eyes widened as he turned to Prudence. "A lace school?"

"Dear Mr. Sherbourne," Anne continued, "you must not fall into the trap of underestimating the talents and determination of my beautiful friend. Men so often do."

"My offenses against Miss Watson are legion, I assure you. I can only beg forgiveness if I have committed this crime so recently brought to my attention."

Anne laughed. "You cannot be as bad as that, Mr. Sherbourne, for if so, my friend would not like you half so well as she does. But of course you are absolved at once."

Still speaking, Anne drew Prudence closer to her side. Though Prudence would have chosen any other conversant than William Sherbourne and any other topic than this, she was glad of Anne's companionship. But now her friend ran on, introducing the very topic that Prudence had cautioned her against on their way to Thorne Lodge.

"My friend tells me that some years ago your family constructed a worsted mill. I understand you intend to make many improvements there now that you are returned from sea."

William glanced at Prudence. She coughed a little and began an arduous search for a handkerchief in her reticule.

"Your information is correct, Lady Blackthorne," he replied. "Today we enjoyed cakes and tea at the mill. If Miss Watson has her way, we shall soon build a school, reduce working hours to ten per day, and ruin ourselves as swiftly as we can."

Anne chuckled. "But perhaps your weavers will be more productive if they are not quite so tired."

"There is a delicate balance, I begin to see. One must continue production at such a rate and quality as to remain competitive with other mills. Yet one cannot enslave the labor to such a degree that they revolt—as did the Luddites in your own town. I assure you, I should be most displeased to discover anyone smashing my looms and carding engines. Those who fostered and engaged in such an uprising in Nottingham were rightly tried, imprisoned, and banished from England."

"Oh, dear!" Prudence interjected as loudly as possible. "I fear I have forgotten my handkerchief and must return to the inn as soon as may be. Anne, you must be weary after your long journey. Let us retire to the carriage, for I find suddenly that I am simply undone."

"My father," Anne informed William as she handed Prudence her own lace-trimmed handkerchief, "was imprisoned for supporting his parishioners in the Luddite rebellion. They were right to defend their livelihood—the manufacture of handcrafted lace. My father was justified in his actions, as well, and he endured his detention with more good cheer than could be expected. Had God not chosen to bless me with a husband both wealthy and well connected, my father would have faced trial and exile as did so many of his beloved flock."

The moment of discomfiting silence that followed this discourse gave Prudence the opportunity to consider her options. She could faint. This would draw attention to herself, however, and she knew she would not fare well under scrutiny. She could flee. An appealing idea, but one unlikely to resolve the issue at hand. She could introduce another subject, but she could not imagine what it might be.

William cleared his throat. "Lady Blackthorne, you have successfully played me for the fool, and I congratulate you most heartily. It is not easily done, for I have learned to shame and confound everyone around me with all possible haste. You were right to escort me into your trap. I spoke without thinking, an action that invariably leads to disgrace. Now I have only to throw myself on your mercy and beg your forgiveness. But before I do, I must assure you of my happiness at your success in winning such an esteemed husband and at your pleasure in the liberty of your beloved father. Moreover, should my own weavers choose to smash my looms and burn down my mill, I shall know it is done for all the right reasons. Indeed, if I am aware of it in time, I shall issue invitations to you and Miss Watson."

He concluded his speech with a congenial smile, as if they had been discussing the pleasure of fresh strawberries in the springtime. Anne looked to Prudence, who forced a laugh.

"Dear me! I nearly forgot we had come here to dance. Mr. Sherbourne, I see Miss Madeline stands near the door without a partner. I feel certain she would—"

"Ah, but I have reserved this dance for you." So saying, he took her by the hand, wrapped his arm about her, and all but pushed her onto the dance floor.

Unable to resist casting a look of despair at her dearest friend, Prudence moved alongside her escort and quickly found her place in the roundel. She was grateful to discover they were dancing a jig, which ruled out the possibility of serious conversation.

The moment the music ended, Prudence detached herself from William and hurried toward the hall. She would don her cloak and *walk* to the inn if no other means of transport could be found. The night had begun badly and ended worse.

So much for her sad career as a crusader. Prudence could think of nothing she wanted more than to drink five cups of tea in a row while seated by a fire with her dear sisters. She would join Sarah and Mary in eating buttered crumpets, speculating on the latest fashion in pelisses, and reading Miss Pickworth's most recent report on the scandals and passions currently *en vogue* among London's *ton*.

It would be heaven!

"If you leave me now, I shall never sleep again." William appeared alongside Prudence in her headlong dash toward escape. He caught her arm. "I must know if the feelings and sentiments you expressed to me a few minutes ago remain, or if my unfortunate conversation with your friend has altered them."

"Too much has been said between us already," she told him, still pressing toward the foyer with all the force she could muster. "I want to go home."

"'Do not make me love you,'" he quoted. "'My heart cannot bear the weight of it.' Those were your words, Prudence. Now I cannot rest until I know the truth—have I made you love me? Has God somehow looked down upon me with favor and permitted me such a gift?"

"What does it matter?" She paused in a long corridor and sagged against the wall. "I go home tomorrow. Home where I belong. At last my heart will be my own again."

"Then it is true. For now, for this instant, you love me."

"Yes." She heaved a deep sigh. "Yes, but I have always been silly. I drift hither and yon with droves of suitors at my heels. I torment men with my beauty and make them mad with desire. So I am told again and again by everyone I hold most dear. Give no consequence to my words, William, for I am . . . I am . . . I am silly."

"You are anything but that." He stood beside her, his back rigid and his arms at his sides. "You are wise and spirited and good. You are beautiful. You are kind. You are honest. But you are *not* silly."

She looked into his eyes, searching for the spark of mockery and ridicule that so often marked his discourse. She saw none.

He let out a breath. "Prudence, if you go to London, I must go there too. But you should not go. You will never be at home in town. Your heart is here, on the moorlands, in the glades, in the rushing streams of the country. Stay a little longer. Let us learn what it is that binds us."

"I cannot. If I stay, I may find that I am hopelessly in love with you. That must never be, for I have determined that my future is a life without husband, hearth, home, children."

"I am unworthy of you, of that there can be no doubt. But if you love me at all, may there not be something of God in it?"

"God?" She turned to him. "What has God to do with anything so unholy as my dreams of you, my thoughts of you, my heedless desire . . . my wanton, willful longing for you? God is purity and light. But every moment I am with you, William, my mind is torn between right and wrong, good and evil."

"God is love, Prudence. There can be no evil in that."

She reached for him, touched her fingertips to his cheek, drew them down the plane of his face and over the squared line of his jaw to his neck. William once had told her that nothing in life was truly black or truly white. But could there be something of God in the tumult that filled her heart?

"There you are, Pru!" Anne waved as she and Ruel approached their friend down the long hallway.

"We are relieved to find you well," Ruel called out. "Anne feared you were stolen away by the gentleman she endeavored so mightily to insult this evening. And this must be the hapless fellow himself. William Sherbourne, I believe our paths crossed in Plymouth."

"Once or twice, perhaps."

Ruel and William discussed the prospects for rain on the morrow. They congratulated each other for their fortune in escorting two women so lovely on this evening. They made promises to visit one another at a future date.

And then Anne was drawing Prudence into the foyer and down the steps of Thorne Lodge. As she ascended into the carriage, Prudence glanced behind in search of William. But he had remained inside the house.

Prudence fell back into her seat and closed her eyes, praying she could erase everything that had happened on this day. But Anne took her hand and squeezed it tight.

"Such a man you have found!" she whispered in Prudence's ear. "Ruel and I are in full agreement that you must stay in Otley and continue your clandestine visits to the mill. You will bring about a revolution, my dearest Pru. A change for the better at that horrid workplace. And a transformation in the soul of a man so very much in love with a woman who adores him, too."

Eleven

Her wooden shoes clattering on the stone steps, Prudence left the mill through the front door along with all the other laborers. She had worked at her spinning machine two full weeks now, and each night she felt more weary than the one before. Her narrow bed with its thin blanket and straw mattress beckoned, though she knew morning would come far too soon.

Moving into the small cottage that Bettie Barns and her children called home had been Anne's idea. Prudence must *appear* to depart the inn with her friends, Anne explained, but she must be given safe lodging in the town.

With this aim, Lord and Lady Blackthorne had called on Mr. Walker the morning after the assembly at Thorne Lodge. Ruel and the American-born blacksmith had been the closest of companions for many years. It was natural, therefore, for the men to meet again, and their intimate association caused only the mildest ripple of surprise in town.

After discussing the conditions at the mill with Ruel and Anne, Mr. Walker had suggested that Bettie, his intended wife, would welcome the disguised spinner. Prudence's identity must be kept secret from the overlookers as well as their master. Once she had gathered enough inflammatory information to force improvements at the mill, Prudence would return to London and rejoin her family.

Now, as she and the other laborers made their way down the dirt road toward Otley, Prudence recalled how vehemently she had rejected the scheme. The risks were too great, and she longed to see her sisters. Worse, she disliked the idea of meeting Mr. Walker so often—as she surely would while living in the home of his future wife. Worst of all, William Sherbourne might find her out. Since their final encounter in the hallway of his home, Prudence could not bear the thought of the disappointment and displeasure he would feel if he discovered her duplicity.

But Anne had persuaded her friend to reconsider the high calling God had laid out. Had Prudence not vowed that she had heard His voice in her heart? Prudence was to be a reformer, Anne reminded her. A crusader. A woman whose labors would impact the needy for decades to come. And think of the poor mill children. How they suffered!

Moreover, Mr. Sherbourne must be given due consideration. Despite their disagreement at the assembly, Anne was convinced that the man was ultimately good-hearted. True, the situation at the mill was deplorable. And perhaps Sherbourne once had been something of a rake. But what was God if not a divine reformer? No one must underestimate the power and plans of the Almighty, for look what He had done in Anne's life.

Letting out yet another sigh of resignation, Prudence now trudged toward the tiny moonlit cottage at the edge of Otley. Though the throng pressed close, a touch on her elbow startled her, and she looked over to find young Tom Smith at her side.

Supporting his lame brother as always, Tom tipped his cap at her. Prudence smiled through her exhaustion. Though she constantly dreaded the exposure of her charade, she understood that the entire company of laborers had conspired to keep her presence at the mill a secret, even the children. The overlookers and their master suspected nothing—or so she was assured again and again.

"Ye done good today, ma'am," Tom declared. "Davy says so too, don't ye, Davy?"

"Aye," the child agreed. "Not near so many tangles today as when ye first began."

"Thank you," Prudence murmured. "But I am still very slow."

"Jimmy don't mind," Tom assured her. "I heard him tell Dick the Devil that the very day you came to the mill, his spinners began to work twice as fast. And along with you came the master's order for tea and cakes too. Jimmy thinks you're good luck."

"Me?" Prudence shook her head.

"Ye mean to help us, ma'am," Tom said. "If our lot goes better, it won't do Jimmy no harm neither."

Prudence groaned. Struggling to put one foot in front of the other, she could hardly imagine doing anything to improve the workers' lives. Though the tea and cakes were a feast to the others at the mill, they hardly touched the hunger that gnawed at her stomach day and night. The swiftly spinning wool threads had blistered her fingers. Her palms had become callused. Her shoulders ached, and her feet felt like blocks of ice on the unheated floor. Each night she dropped into her bed, only to be shaken awake before the first light of dawn.

Bettie was kind and cheerful, even though her houseguest had once been attached to Mr. Walker, the man she most dearly loved and intended to marry. It pained Prudence to see the two of them together, sharing meals, laughing over incidents from the day, enjoying the antics of the children. But it was best. Let Mr. Walker have a wife and a family of his own, she told herself again and again. He deserved only happiness.

"I had treacle on my cake today," Davy piped up. His high-pitched voice carried through the chill night wind. "Did you, ma'am?"

"Treacle?" Prudence realized she had been nearly asleep as she stumbled along the road. "I suppose I did have treacle, but I—"

"Whisht!" Tom placed a warning finger over his lips as he caught her arm. "'Tis him! 'Tis the master!"

And now Prudence saw what those around her had already discovered. In total silence, William Sherbourne had been riding alongside the river of people moving down the trampled roadway. His dark steed was almost invisible in the night, only the tapping hooves and the snuffle of the horse giving him away.

Stifling a gasp, Prudence tugged the mobcap lower on her forehead and wrapped her black shawl more closely around her shoulders and neck. William had visited the mill several times in the past fortnight—more often, she was told, than he had done before she came. Each time, she found reason to be absent from her post. Her fellow spinners made excuses for her to Jimmy.

But it was whispered and feared that Mr. Sherbourne *knew*. That someone had divulged the great and wonderful secret. That a turncoat had betrayed Prudence, their champion of hope, and that her identity could be revealed at any time.

Head down, she shivered as the horse slowed, now moving at an even pace with her stride. "Good evening to you all," William called out.

"Good evening, sir," a chorus of voices responded.

"And how were your cakes today?"

"Lovely, thank you, sir," people shouted.

"My cake had treacle!" Young Davy's squeaky voice cut through the threads of tension woven across Prudence's spine. She sagged, suddenly longing to fall at William's feet and confess her deception, then beg to be taken to Thorne Lodge, poured a hot bath, given a cup of tea—

"Treacle?" William's horse stepped toward the boy. "Did everyone have treacle?"

"Yes, sir," the refrain rang out.

The river of humanity had ceased its flow. Now William dismounted, his focus on the child who had spoken out of turn. Prudence debated whether to try to sink further into the shadows of the nearby public house or step into William's path and declare her presence.

"Is that you, Tom Smith?" William approached the two boys who stood beside Prudence. "I believe we have met before. This must be your brother?"

"Yes, sir," Tom said. "Davy Smith."

Though Prudence kept her head bent low, she cast a side-ways glance to find William standing but an arm's length away.

"I am pleased to meet you, Master Davy," he said, giving the boy a bow.

To Prudence's consternation, Davy giggled. His twisted legs almost buckling beneath him, the child tried to copy his master's bow. "And me too. Pleased to meet ye, sir."

"But who is this lady, Davy?" William asked, taking another step nearer to Prudence. "Madam, may I know your name?"

"Polly," Tom put in. "'Tis Polly, sir. She is . . . she is my . . . my cousin."

"Ah, your *cousin*. Miss Polly, what is it that you do at my mill?"

"She's a spinner," Tom responded. "She spins very well indeed, sir."

"And you answer for her, Tom? Is your cousin mute?"

"I am not mute." Prudence stared at her feet as she spoke. "My cake had treacle too. I thank you."

"I believe I remember you, madam," he said. "You are new at the mill."

"Two weeks, sir."

"You had quite a tangle near the beginning of your employ-ment, I think. But you worked it out quite swiftly."

"Yes, sir."

William stood in silence before Prudence. She felt his eyes on her, and it was all she could do not to look up at him. Her heart ached to see the man's familiar face again, to set aside this dreadful drama and return to her former life.

"Did you have tea today?" he asked her at last. "With the others?"

"I did."

"Was it to your liking?"

"It was . . . hot." She wrestled for a moment. "But the milk was not fresh. It had curdled."

"Had it? And you found that distasteful?"

"Anyone would."

"Was the sugar pleasing?"

"Lumpy," she said. "But sweet."

He chuckled. "I am glad to hear my sugar was sweet. At least in that I may take comfort."

Prudence knotted her fingers together, praying that William would leave without discovering her identity and at the same time hoping he would. He had not moved since speaking to her. The crowd around them hovered in expectant silence.

"Miss Polly, may I inquire what you like best about your work at the mill?" William asked now.

Prudence stiffened, mentally grasping for anything good to say about the endless torturous hours, the dry oatcake and water porridge, the chill that numbed her feet, and the bits of lint she inhaled each time she took a breath.

"Polly is pleased to earn her wages," Tom Smith spoke up. "We are all glad of that."

"Indeed," Prudence concurred. "I am most grateful for my wages."

"But what do you dislike about your work?" William asked. "The long hours? The noise?"

"Yes, sir. All of it."

"*All* of it?"

"Except the wages."

"Miss Polly, I should very much like to hear more about

these dissatisfactions that plague you. You remind me of some-one I knew once—a lady who was slow to praise and swift to find fault. Tell me where you live. I shall send a carriage for you and your two young cousins tomorrow morning. We shall meet for tea at Thorne Lodge and discuss the conditions in my mill."

Prudence quaked. "Tea at Thorne Lodge—no, I couldn't possibly," she blurted out. "I'm needed elsewhere. Wages, you know. I must earn my wages. Under such circumstances, one can hardly think of tea and a chat."

"*Tea and a chat?* Upon my word, you speak very well for a woman in such a station in life. You have attended school, have you not? Perhaps you were brought up in a condition unlike the one in which you now find yourself."

"I was . . . not always so humbly situated, sir. But I . . . I—"

"Never mind," William said over her stuttering speech. "I accept your rejection of my invitation to tea, Miss Polly, and it is probably for the best. I go to London tomorrow. Several matters of business demand my attention, and I mean to call on friends. Young Tom will remember two ladies who recently kept rooms at the inn in Otley. I mean to visit them and discover how they have fared since departing Yorkshire."

At this news, Prudence stifled a yelp of dismay. But before she could find her tongue to make a response, he continued.

"Thank you, Miss Polly, the young Masters Smith, and all those in my employ—I have kept you from your hearths long enough. Good evening."

"Good evening, sir," came the chorus from the throng.

As William mounted his horse and rode away, people crowded around Prudence.

"He's going to London to look for her!" one cried.

"He knows who she is!"

"He has uncovered the truth!"

"We're doomed!"

Fully awake now, Prudence pushed ahead until she caught up to Mr. Walker. He was walking with Bettie. When Prudence called his name, he paused. She reached for his hand, but noting the eyes watching her, she drew back.

"I must return to London this very night," she told him. "I have not a moment to lose. My sisters know almost nothing of my activities here, and they will betray me to Mr. Sherbourne with no intention of harm. You must engage a coach. Or find me a carriage. I shall pay any amount. We must—"

"I have a wagon and two good horses," he cut in. "We can leave within the hour."

"A wagon? But a wagon is too slow. He will pass us on the road."

Her protests went unanswered as the blacksmith turned from her and spoke a few low words to Bettie. Then he strode away to make arrangements.

In an agony of dread, Prudence allowed herself to be led into Bettie's cottage and plied with a cup of warm milk and a slice of black bread. As she swallowed the last bitter bite and rose to pack her trunk, the truth of the situation finally made itself known. For the next two days she would be alone in the company of Mr. Walker. Mr. Walker and none else.

◆

"It was she," William said, pacing before the fire in the drawing room that evening. "Of that I have no doubt whatsoever."

Seated nearby, his brother was enjoying little success in his effort to read the thin volume of Shakespeare's sonnets his wife had given him for Christmas some three months earlier. Olivia was miffed that he had ignored the book so long, and William had taken much delight in sabotaging Randolph's efforts to make amends.

Now William's focus lay in another direction. Frowning, he shook his head. "Prudence Watson feigned a departure from the inn and took lodgings elsewhere in Otley. She secured a position among the spinners at my mill for the express purpose of fomenting rebellion. I have suspected her duplicity for some time, but now I am certain the pitiable creature to whom I spoke this evening was none other than Miss Watson. She pretends to be someone she is not, and all the while she plots my downfall."

"Miss Watson should save herself the trouble. You have nearly managed the deed all by yourself."

"Thank you, Randolph. Your sympathy for my dilemma is remarkably true to form."

"Oh, bosh." Randolph tossed the book of sonnets onto a table. "I met the lady, and I have little doubt that she is too accustomed to luxury and comfort to surrender it in favor of such a wild scheme. But what if Miss Watson truly has done all these preposterous things? Any effort to rally a revolt at the mill will have no consequence, for you now maintain iron control of the place through its overlookers. Furthermore, Miss Watson can have no effect on your heart, for you continually declare it sealed, locked, and hidden away from any passion that might threaten your blissful state as a bachelor."

"Do not make light of this, Randolph. You know too well how that lady has tangled my well-ordered plans. I love her.

I cannot deny my feelings, and I will no longer attempt to stifle them. But Prudence Watson is no ordinary woman."

"They never are, William. Because we love them, they become unattainable angels hovering at a maddening distance. They appear too far beyond our grasp, and we cannot rest until we have found a way to conquer their hearts."

"You speak from your own experience, but you do not know Prudence. She truly is beyond me in every way. Yet why has she done this deceitful thing? Why would she toy with me? She professed to love me, Randolph, and I believed her—yet all the while she was plotting to undo my single means of financial gain."

"Perhaps she was only plotting to help the mill workers. Her scheme might have nothing to do with you personally at all."

"You are saying she may truly love me—yet wear the disguise of a peasant to foment mutiny among my employees? That makes no sense."

"Women are not known for making sense, dear brother. They are known for changing their minds. For wavering. For dillydallying. For displaying humors first hot and then cold within the space of a single minute. Women are mysterious and beguiling, but you must know they more often follow their hearts than their brains."

"Randolph?" Olivia, who had entered the room unnoticed by the men, crossed toward her husband. "Did my ears deceive me, or were you disparaging the sisterhood to which I belong?"

"Your ears deceived you, dearest, for I was merely enlightening my brother on the wonders of womankind. But you must settle the question before us. Is it possible that Miss Watson loves William but hates his mill?"

"Of course."

"There you have it," Randolph said to his brother. "Irrefutable truth." Holding out a hand to his wife, he beckoned. "Come to me, sweet goddess of all that is most delightful. Sit here beside me, and let me whisper my love in your ear."

"Honestly, Randolph!" she protested. "First you speak ill of women; then you attempt to cover your malicious assertions with beguiling folderol. Do you suppose you can simply charm me out of my current resentment and black humor?"

"I do, my darling. For in the words of the great bard:

'Let me not to the marriage of true minds
Admit impediments. Love is not love
Which alters when it alteration finds,
Or bends with the remover to remove:
O no! it is an ever-fixed mark
That looks on tempests and is never shaken.'"

"Well recited, brother," William spoke up, clapping. "But, Olivia, I beg you not to let your indignation be overthrown by Randolph's display of poetic facility. I assure you that your husband might just as easily have quoted Hamlet's famous aside: 'To be, or not to be: that is the question.' He learned both verses at the feet of our tutor and understands the meaning of neither."

"All the same," she replied, awarding Randolph a pretty smile, "I confess I am utterly charmed. You are reading the book I gave you, and you quote sonnets to me from it. William, when you marry Miss Watson, I hope you will be as good and kind to her as my husband is to me. As Shakespeare expressed so well, Randolph and I have endured tempests, but we are not shaken."

William watched in befuddlement as Olivia sank down onto the settee beside Randolph, nestled against his shoulder, and set a light kiss on his cheek. Randolph, meanwhile, wrapped his arm about his wife's shoulders and gave his brother the most insolent and victorious smirk in the entirety of their kinship.

Barely holding in a groan of dismay, William stalked out of the room and started up the staircase toward his rooms. He would leave for London at dawn, ride directly to the row of elegant homes on Cranleigh Crescent in Belgravia, present himself at Trenton House, and ask to speak to Miss Prudence Watson. She would not be there, and his suspicions about her would be confirmed.

It was a good plan, one that could not go awry. His only hesitation was its outcome. Did he really want to know that Prudence was playing the role of Polly the bashful wool spinner? that her purpose was to fuel an uprising among the mill workers? that each word she had spoken to him, every kiss, every longing gaze . . . that everything about her was false?

◆

The jolt of the wagon's wheels crossing a rut in the road startled Prudence from her sleep. With a start, she realized she had been resting her head on Mr. Walker's shoulder. He had kept the rough wood cart moving toward London all night, but try as she might to stay awake, Prudence had been unable to keep him company.

Streaks of lavender-hued clouds now stretched across the orange sky as the sun crept into view. Trees, dusted with pale green buds and pink blossoms, lined the roadway. Rabbits dotted the new grass that had risen from the ground at the first signs of spring. Hungry and heedless, the small creatures hardly looked up as the wagon rattled by. Overhead, robins, wrens, sparrows, and titmice swooped and chittered as they gathered twigs for their nests or fussed at other birds invading their territory.

"You were tired," Mr. Walker said as Prudence covered a yawn. "Now you understand the lives of the poor laborers who supply the aristocracy with their luxuries."

Despite her drowsiness, Prudence bristled. "You forget that I was not born into wealth, nor do I revel in the opulence that my father's fortune might afford me. Moreover, I worked with Anne to build the lace school in France, and I labored alongside the women as they pinned patterns to lace pillows and wove threaded bobbins among the pins."

"I had forgotten," Walker confessed. "The months we were apart brought me a numbing agony. I could not think of you except to imagine you dead. And so I taught myself not to think of you at all."

"Did you forget me?"

His dark brown eyes met hers. "I could never forget you. Why do you think I left Tiverton? Why did I refuse to stay in London with Ruel? You were there. You were everywhere. I needed to escape you before it was too late."

At his confession, Prudence's eyes misted. "After you went away, I thought I would never love again."

"You were wrong. I see the way Sherbourne looks at you . . . and you at him. It will be a good match between the two of you."

"There can be no serious attachment between us. You know that as well as I." She studied a small flock of sheep grazing near the road. "I like your Bettie very much. That is the better match."

"You approve, then?"

"Do you need my approval?"

"No. But I would welcome it. You are a woman of insight and wisdom. You saw something in me to love, even though I was an old blacksmith with a stolen youth and a bitter heart."

She shook her head. "You had a broken heart, not a bitter one."

"It was broken, but you mended it. Your love healed me, Prudence. I will never be able to thank you enough."

"I want no thanks. My joy will be found in seeing you happily wed. The father of children. The master of a home."

Walker fell silent for some time, letting the horses amble along the road to tug mouthfuls of grass and startle the rabbits. At last, he spoke.

"Sherbourne's life will be blessed by you. He is not a bad man . . . nor is he a good man. Instead, he is a lost sheep, and the Good Shepherd has not yet found him."

Prudence reflected on Walker's reference to one of Jesus' many parables. He had told His followers about a shepherd who owned a flock of one hundred sheep. When the shepherd realized that one had gone missing, he left the ninety-nine and searched for the lost lamb until he found it. Jesus had gone on to explain that in the same way, God—whose love for mankind is greater than the mind can understand—pursues those who go astray. Prudence had always liked the thought of a loving shepherd, but she never imagined that the poor lost lamb had gone willfully astray.

"How can William be both good and bad?" she asked the

man at her side. "Jesus said we cannot serve two masters. We will love the one and hate the other."

"Sherbourne serves no master. He is like so many—serving only himself. A man who honors his own desires above all else will one day discover that he is nothing more than bones, skin, flesh—a small worm that has little strength and will soon die."

"I know what you say is true." As she spoke, Prudence reflected on her father, a man who had given away his heart in the pursuit of money and power. Was William Sherbourne like that?

"The god of self is powerless and imperfect," Walker was saying. "He is like a badly forged iron rim on a carriage wheel. When the road is rough, the weak rim snaps, the wheel breaks apart, and the carriage falls to the ground in pieces. Sherbourne makes this discovery now, and this is why he needs you."

Prudence considered Walker's words. As always, his wisdom and insight touched her deeply. But in this case, his argument was flawed.

"You speak as if Mr. Sherbourne and I already have formed an attachment," she pointed out. "I assure you, we are not engaged. A marriage between us would be a disaster from start to finish. I cannot save him, and certainly he can never make me a happy woman."

Walker chuckled. "Miss Prudence Watson, you know so much about everyone—and so little about yourself. Let me tell you what I have observed. You are happiest when the man you truly love is near. And though I have struggled to understand it, that man is William Sherbourne."

Twelve

Mary squealed, leapt to her feet, and threw out her arms as her sister stepped into the drawing room at Delacroix House. "Prudence! You are here! You are here at last!"

With equal ardor, she clapped her hands to her cheeks and shrieked at the appearance of her younger sibling. "Good heavens, what has happened to you? You look like a guttersnipe!"

"Pru?" Now Sarah, the eldest of the three sisters, rose from her chair near the fire. "Is it truly you?"

"It is I," Prudence confirmed, hurrying forward, unable to think beyond the anxieties that plagued her. "I am so glad both of you are here. I remembered only moments ago that today is Friday, and therefore the two of you would be joining Henry for tea. Or at least I hoped that was still your custom."

"But of course," replied the man in question. "It has been

my delight to host my aunt every Friday since my return from sea several weeks ago. When Mrs. Heathhill returned from the north country, she began to join us as well. And today our joy is made complete by your unexpected arrival."

Prudence cast a glance at Henry Carlyle, Lord Delacroix. A tall, well-built gentleman with a mop of curly gold hair and the brightest of blue eyes, he stood near the hearth, his expression one of amused surprise.

But there was no time for formal greetings. Prudence caught Mary's hands. "I speak of Mr. Sherbourne. He is on his way to London even now, sister, and he must not learn that I have been staying in Otley."

"William Sherbourne sent a message to Delacroix House this morning," Henry spoke up. "Though I have never met the gentleman, he stated that he wished to confer with me about an urgent matter of some import. He hoped also that I might include in the party my aunt, Mrs. Locke, and her family. As I expected them today for tea, I invited him to join us. We expect him momentarily. Indeed, we believed your knock on the door was his."

"Mr. Sherbourne is coming here? Momentarily?" Prudence stifled a gasp.

"We hoped that you might be in his company," Mary said. "Sarah and I were certain the reason Mr. Sherbourne requested to meet the entire family was that the two of you had reached an understanding and were coming to London to give us your happy news."

"Were we correct in our thinking?" Sarah asked. "Have you become engaged to William Sherbourne?"

"Upon my honor, no!" Agitated, Prudence shook her hands. "Of course not. Do I look like a woman newly engaged?"

"Truthfully, no," Henry replied.

All three sisters turned to him, their expressions conveying varying degrees of annoyance. But Mary was quick to regain her footing and address her sister again.

"If you did not come to London with Mr. Sherbourne," she began, "how are you here? How is he here without you—yet both arriving on the same day? And why are you garbed in these . . . these rags? Your fingers, sister! They are turned to leather knobs!"

"I have been working in the mill," Prudence explained. "In disguise."

Before her sisters could make further exclamations of shock and horror, she went on. "Mr. Sherbourne knows of neither my masquerade nor my purpose in it. Praying that I might anticipate his arrival, I engaged Mr. Walker to drive me here by horse cart, and I—"

"Horse cart?" Mary cut in. "You came to London on a wagon?"

"Mr. Walker?" Sarah cried. "Mr. Walker of Tiverton? The blacksmith? *He* brought you by horse cart?"

"It is too much to explain," Prudence said. "If Mr. Sherbourne is expected at any minute, I must—"

"*Ahem.*" A footman stepped into the room, a silver tray resting on his open palm. "My lord, a gentleman calls on you, wishing to present his card. He awaits your pleasure in the foyer. May I show him in?"

"Who is it?" Henry asked, reaching for the small white name card lying on the footman's tray.

"Oh, it must be William!" Prudence wailed, turning to her sisters. "He will see me! I am ruined!"

"Indeed, it is Mr. Sherbourne," Henry announced as he studied the card. "His family's crest is very noble."

"Hang his crest—we must leave the room at once!" Mary grabbed Prudence by the arm and began dragging her to the far end of the drawing room. "Sarah, why do you dawdle? Help me wash our sister and try to restore her appearance to some semblance of normalcy. Dear Henry, do your business with Mr. Sherbourne—and take your time about it!"

"Of course," the young man replied, the hint of a grin tugging at his mouth. "I am most eager to see the washed version of my dear cousin."

The three women hurried through a side door, rushed down a corridor, and scampered up a flight of steps to the suite of rooms once inhabited by Sarah and her late first husband. She told her sisters she felt certain she had abandoned several items of clothing there after she wed Charles Locke and moved away.

"Bring us a pitcher of water," Mary ordered one of three maids who had been summoned along the way. "Warm water, but not too warm, for we must make haste. Go to it at once, I beg you! And you, young lady, what is your name?"

"Eliza, madam. And she is Jane."

"Eliza, please search the drawers and chests for gloves. Anything will do, for we must cover my sister's woefully spoiled hands. Jane, if you cannot find slippers, clean her shoes as swiftly as may be."

"Oh, dear, my memory has failed me!" Sarah's voice echoed as she peered into an enormous mahogany armoire. "The wardrobe is empty. No, wait—I see a gown near the back. But this is a ball gown. It will never do."

"Give it to me," Mary ordered, snatching the filmy blue-green garment from her sister's hands. "Do something with her hair, Sarah. Have you a comb? Oh, horrors—these sleeves are wildly out of style. Whatever are we to do?"

"William will never notice the sleeves," Prudence avowed. "He's not that sort of man. He likes the out-of-doors and riding in the country far more than appraising the fashion of ladies' dancing gowns."

"*William?* Do you call him that?" Sarah was attempting to untangle her sister's flaxen curls and pin them up again into a semblance of ladylike mode. Pulling pins from her own hair, she inadvertently dislodged an artful coil near the top of her head. But after a momentary groan of dismay, she returned to her charge.

"You *must* be Mr. Sherbourne's intimate friend, Pru," she insisted, "for you would not address him so informally if you were mere acquaintances."

"Acquaintances?" Mary huffed. "Had you seen them together as I did, you would harbor no doubts about their undying passion."

"Please, Mary, we are not at all passionate—oh!" Prudence yelped in pain as her sister began scrubbing away the dirt on her cheeks. "You will tear my skin off! Sarah, you have poked my head three times with that pin!"

"I have never seen your hair in such snarls," Sarah declared. "You cannot have washed it in weeks. Whatever were you thinking?"

"She was thinking of saving mill children," Mary groused

as she went to work on Prudence's neck. "Our sister would rather eat black bread and wear rags than earn the affections of a man who is handsome, wealthy, and well connected. She prefers a horse cart to a grand carriage. She enjoys laboring fourteen hours a day over a loom more than painting landscapes, playing the pianoforte, and eating petits fours."

"I was not working at a loom," Prudence protested. "I am a spinner. And I shall have you know that when I departed Thorne Mill, my threads were nearly all evenly spun and my spindles were well ordered in the carriage. Even the scavengers and piecers are pleased with my progress."

"Our youngest sister prefers the company of scavengers to that of lords and ladies of the realm," Mary continued. "She has forgotten that our father labored all his life to raise us from association with such riffraff and provide us a better future."

Sarah shook her head. "I am sorry, Mary, but I cannot disapprove of Pru's efforts at reform or her interest in the lot of those whose society is beneath her own. We must not think of ourselves more highly than we ought. Our father was a tradesman, and his wealth was purchased at a terrible price to himself and his daughters. I admire our sister, though I do wish she had gone about her crusade in a manner more forthright."

"But I was very plainspoken in the beginning," Prudence protested. "I told William exactly how I feel about his mill. He mocked me."

"Mocked you? That is unacceptable," Sarah pronounced as she stepped back to study her efforts at creating a satisfactory coiffure.

Mary had finished scrubbing and was attempting to tug off her sister's ragged gown.

"What was Mr. Sherbourne to do but make light of our sister's heedless behavior and assertions?" Mary asked. "Do you believe he should have agreed with Pru's condemnations, torn down his mill, set all his workers out on their ears with no livelihood, and conceded his worsted trade to competitors? Of course not! Thorne Mill sits on the estate of a great family with a rich ancestry. The water that powers the looms is theirs, as are the stones that built it. To destroy such a thing would be a sacrilege. Now stand up straight, Pru, and I shall try to tie this ribbon in place. Good heavens, Sarah, did you really wear this gown? I hope not. It is tragically horrid. Indeed, I am tempted to pity the poor thing for its utter hideousness."

"I must have abandoned it here for that very reason," Sarah said. "It is truly awful. The neck is too low and the sleeves too short. The fabric is . . . oh, dear . . . very thin."

Mary crossed her arms and sighed as she joined Sarah in regarding their younger sister.

"Pru, you look terrible," Mary concluded. "Your hair has gone utterly mad, and the gown could not be worse. But I fear nothing else can be done to redeem you."

"Wear my pelisse," Sarah suggested. "I do not need it, for I shall be warm enough if I sit near the fire."

But before she could shrug out of the lightweight plum-hued jacket, Prudence shook her head. "Keep your pelisse, Sarah. Its color would make the gown appear even more dreadful. No, indeed, I have brought this moment upon myself, and I must face the consequences. Let us go down and greet Mr. Sherbourne. But if I may beg your mercy, dearest sisters, please make every effort to conceal my recent activities in Otley. William must be told, but I am the one who should confess."

"Very well," Mary agreed. "Sarah, lead the way."

As Sarah's younger sisters assumed their positions behind her, Prudence lifted up a prayer for mercy. She had sinned against William. No one could doubt that. Soon she must pay the price for her transgressions. The very thought of disappointing and angering him inflicted a pang of pain in her heart. But the anticipation of seeing him again, speaking with him, losing herself in his deep brown eyes brought a lighter spirit, a warmth that could only be ascribed to love.

◆

William decided at once that he liked Henry Carlyle, Lord Delacroix. As the two men sat across from each other near the fire, their conversation took amiable and pleasant turns. Henry had recently undertaken a sea journey to China in an effort to establish a profitable tea trade. His partners in the fledgling enterprise included Charles Locke, the husband of Prudence Watson's eldest sister, Sarah.

Henry must know Prudence well, William deduced. Perhaps the man had set his hopes on making her his wife. It certainly would be an agreeable arrangement for both families. But she could not possibly return Henry's affections. William remained convinced that her ardent avowals of love for him alone precluded the success of any other suitor.

"How did you find your late uncle's widow and her sisters upon your return?" William asked as a maid entered the room bearing a laden tea tray. "I trust they were all well."

"Mrs. Heathhill and Miss Watson had ventured away on a tour of the northern counties. But Mrs. Locke greeted me with as much pleasure as did her husband—especially on learning the success of my journey. The tea trade, you must know, is . . ."

His words drifted off as something near the door captured his attention. William turned to look. The sight that met his eyes took every thought from his head, every word from his tongue, every movement from his limbs. Henry was rising to offer greetings, but William found he could not move as three lovely women glided across the carpet toward the tea table.

"Ah, you have come at last," Henry intoned. "Welcome."

With supreme effort, William managed to force his frozen legs to stand. But when Prudence Watson's eyes met his, the endeavor was nearly undone.

He had never seen her so beautiful. Never seen *anyone* so glorious, magnificent, stunning—

"Mr. Sherbourne, I should like to introduce my guests," Henry was saying, words barely heard through the numbing, swirling mists in William's head. "As you may know, my late uncle wed Miss Sarah Watson not long before his untimely death. That union gave her the title of Lady Delacroix and a most awkward kinship as my aunt—for as you see, she is younger and certainly more handsome than I."

Hearing the polite laughter of the others in the room, William attempted a smile. But Henry continued.

"Lady Delacroix was soon widowed, and she might have remained in that mournful state had Mr. Charles Locke not stepped in to make her the happiest of women. She willingly surrendered her title and estate to me—a most generous gesture, I assure you. Mrs. Locke and I were always great friends, and now we are business partners as well."

"I am pleased to meet you, Mr. Sherbourne," Sarah said,

favoring William with a graceful curtsy. "I hear much pleasant news of you from my sisters. I believe Mary and Prudence were guests in your ancestral home on several occasions."

"Indeed," William responded with a bow. "Mrs. Heathhill and Miss Watson will always be welcome at Thorne Lodge. And now . . . now you and your husband must find an occasion to make a tour of the northern counties. My brother and his wife would enjoy nothing better than to make your acquaintance."

Realizing he had woefully fumbled the words, William made every effort to focus his attention on the matters at hand: tea and convivial conversation. But it was hopeless. He could do nothing except stare at Prudence—just as she, in turn, fastened her eyes on him.

He had been wrong about her, William realized. Utterly mistaken. Just as she had assured him before their final fare-well, Prudence had returned to London with her friend Anne. All his qualms about Polly the spinner were nothing more than the work of a suspicious mind. Prudence had not been labor-ing to foment a rebellion at the mill. Malicious subterfuge and deviousness had not occupied her these weeks since they parted company.

No, indeed. Yet something about her had been altered. If possible, Prudence Watson was more beautiful than ever. Like blossoms on porcelain, her cheeks were suffused with pink. Never had William seen her hair so deliriously riotous. Golden curls tumbled here and there, framing her glowing eyes and dancing against her ivory neck.

The gown she wore, a delicious confection in some mysteri-ous shade of blue tinged with green, clung to her form, high-lighting the narrow waist and curved hips he had imagined in his dreams. The ethereal sleeves of her gown exposed her slender arms . . . arms that he ached to feel wrapped about him once again.

"Is she well? Mr. Sherbourne?" The strident question drew William's attention, and he realized belatedly that Mary had been speaking to him.

"I beg your pardon," he said. "Is who well?"

"Our dearest Olivia, of course. No great estate could boast a more gracious mistress."

"My brother's wife is well," William said quickly. "She expects to welcome a second child in the autumn."

"Delightful!" Mary exclaimed. "A baby. How very agreeable."

"It is happy news indeed. The continuing addition of children will make Thorne Lodge truly a family home again. So much so, in fact, that I have decided to remove myself to another lodging on our estate."

"Chatham Hall?" Prudence spoke up. "You are to live there?"

He studied her face for a moment, attempting to read any possible message in those green eyes. Did Prudence now wish she had agreed to view the grand home that day when they had ridden together across the moors? Could it be possible that she cherished the hope of becoming his wife and building a family of their own?

But he could not grant himself the luxury to speculate further. All eyes were on him.

"Chatham," William answered, "is indeed to become my home, Miss Watson. Until recently, Lady Thorne's brother lived there. The young man suffers a vast deal from a malady of the mind, and at Chatham he was cared for by a staff of tutors, apothecaries, and others charged with improving his health.

I am happy to say that he continues to recover very well, far better than anyone expected or hoped. So well, in fact, that his sister has elected to situate him in a school near Canterbury. There he will continue his progress under the care of doctors and teachers who specialize in such cases. Chatham Hall is empty, therefore, and I have been invited to make use of it."

"But to live in a great house all alone cannot be pleasant," Mary remarked. "Perhaps you have reconsidered your position against matrimony, Mr. Sherbourne. Are you are not eager to wed and to begin a dynasty of your own?"

It took every fiber of William's strength not to glance at Prudence. Reading her response to her sister's comments would tell him so much. But that moment of revelation must wait until they were alone together.

The thought of holding Prudence in his arms as he proposed such a union filled William with a warm gratitude and joy. The hope that she might accept him despite his flaws was almost too much to bear. But such a rendezvous must take place in the perfect setting. For this reason, he was eager to advance the idea he had concocted on his journey to London, and he determined to turn the present conversation toward it.

"When the time is right," he told Mary, "I shall reflect on my future and what it may hold. Until then, I have more than enough to fill my plate. I am in London to accomplish an aim I hope might improve the fortunes of my mill."

"Your letter to me hinted of some such business," Henry said, as if on cue. "May I ask your purpose in wishing to meet with me and these fair ladies?"

"Of course," William said. "My request is a bold one, sir. I presume to make such an audacious appeal on your generosity only because of my high regard for you—a regard fostered by Mrs. Heathhill and Miss Watson."

"I am glad to know I merit their commendation of my character. I believe I have not always been so favored. Indeed, more than one member of my extended family has called me a cad."

William chuckled. "That label, I believe, is too easily given out. I myself have been regarded as such on occasion."

"Excuse me," Prudence said, "but I believe no one would call a decent, honorable gentleman by that name. A true cad earns his own reputation."

Both men turned to her. Mary gave a small squeak. Sarah cleared her throat.

"But the character of these two dear friends," Prudence went on, "must be considered above reproach, for we know them too well to doubt they are both true gentlemen. I am most eager to hear Mr. Sherbourne's proposal."

"And you shall have it," he replied. "As you know, my family has deep roots in Yorkshire, and from thence we have never traveled far. We are happiest in the country, you see, and through the centuries we have seen no reason to establish a permanent residence in London."

"Ah, the picture begins to clear already," Henry said. "I presume you wish to make some use of Delacroix House."

"Very astute, sir. I do indeed, though with all possible humility. Having built a worsted mill a short time ago, the Thorne family are involved in trade."

"I cannot disparage you for that, my good man. The aristocracy is not what it once was. As we discussed before the ladies arrived, I myself have taken partnership in a tea enterprise."

William tipped his head. "That is my very reason for being

so bold as to approach you with the request I now make. In an effort to court the merchants and brokers with whom I hope to do business, I wish to hold a somewhat intimate reception."

"But why not a ball?" Mary asked. "I long for a ball."

"As you wish, madam. If my hopes are fulfilled, you and your sisters will agree to accept the task of preparing for the occasion."

"Of course!" Mary beamed at Sarah and Prudence. "We shall be delighted to assist you in every way."

"But first I must obtain Lord Delacroix's permission to make use of his home."

"Without hesitation, sir." Henry awarded William a warm smile. "Name your day, and we shall dispatch the invitations."

They discussed the details of the event, sipped their tea, inquired after the health of various friends and acquaintances they had in common, speculated on the weather, and at last William stood to leave.

He knew he ought to depart the house after a brief but heartfelt farewell. Yet he could not resist posing a question.

"I wonder, Miss Watson, if I might have a word with you in the foyer," he asked. "If your family does not object, I should like to resolve a matter left pending at our last meeting."

"Of course you may take her," Mary said. "Go, Prudence. Show Mr. Sherbourne to the door."

The color heightened in the younger woman's cheeks as she looked to her older sister.

Sarah nodded. "We shall await your return."

Prudence cast a glance at Delacroix, then stepped away from the fire. William caught up to her, offered his arm, and escorted her from the room. The foyer was but paces away, and he knew he had too much to say.

"Dear lady," he began, "I cannot express my surprise and delight in finding you here today."

"Really?" she asked. "But where else would I be? Did you not request the attendance of both Mrs. Locke's sisters?"

"I did, of course. Yet, I thought . . . I feared you might not come."

"Why not? We are friends, and I am happy to see you again."

"Friends?" He paused and took her hand. "Prudence, on our last meeting we professed our mutual love. Have you forgotten?"

"As I said, sir, I am very silly—"

"No! No, you are not the least bit silly. You are beautiful and good, so good that I am wholly unworthy—"

"I am not good," she cut in. "No one is truly good. You said so yourself. We are all painted in shades of gray. Right and wrong—who can tell one from the other these days? A very bad man might perform kind and genteel acts now and then. A very good woman might do something . . . something . . ."

"Prudence?" He tilted her chin with his fingertip. "Are you weeping?"

"No . . . perhaps a little. . . . You must admit things are all at sixes and sevens."

"Are they?"

"Indeed, for I had no idea you would come to Delacroix House today. And things are so much changed since last we met."

"What has changed? You? Indeed you have, for you look more beautiful to me than ever. Your hair, your eyes. You are radiant. What has altered you? Dare I hope that I am the cause of it?"

She looked away, struggling again to control some emotion he could not interpret. But at last she faced him.

"If I am altered," she said, "it is due to events I have experienced recently. Mr. Sherbourne, I regret to confess that I have not been fully honest with you."

"In what way?" He gripped her gloved hand, alarm coursing through him. "How recently have these events occurred? Who has changed you? Prudence, are you in love with someone?"

"Yes!" she exclaimed the word, then clapped her hand over her mouth. "Oh, dear, I should not have said that. But it is true. And despite this great love, I have . . . I have . . ."

"Who is he? What man has captured your heart?" He took her shoulders. "You have been gone from me no more than two weeks. In such a short time, who has usurped your heart?"

"I cannot say." She pulled away from him. "I must not say. I have to go. My sisters will wonder what has become of me, and Henry will have questions."

"*Henry?*" William barked the word. "*Henry?* Do you mean Henry Carlyle? Lord Delacroix has captured you?"

"Truly I must go." Tears spilled freely now, tumbling down her cheeks as she backed away from him. "I am sorry, William. So sorry."

He stood rigid, unable to move, powerless even to draw breath as she turned and fled through the house toward the drawing room. Toward her sisters. And toward the man who had stolen away her love.

Thirteen

"I cannot go to the ball," Prudence announced for the third time that afternoon.

Her sisters had insisted on forcing her into the bedroom at Mary's home where she had been staying the past two weeks. With the express purpose of making her as miserable as possible, they began opening her trunks and sorting through her bonnets, slippers, gowns, pelisses, and jewels in anticipation of the ball to be held three evenings hence at Delacroix House.

"I shall *not* go," Prudence reiterated. "He will be there, and I shall be obliged to dance with him, and I shall wish for a life I cannot have, and everything will be worse than it is already."

"Do you prefer the pink brocade, Sarah, or the pale yellow silk?" Mary held two gowns aloft for her elder sister's evaluation. "The pink will heighten the color of her complexion, making her appear more lively than ever. The yellow favors her hair so well, yet I confess I do prefer the pink."

"Our sister has been lively enough to make at least a dozen men fall violently in love with her," Sarah remarked. "Perhaps wearing pink she will capture several more beaux, and one of them will charm her into abandoning poor Mr. Sherbourne's mill and letting him get on with his life."

"I beg your pardon," Prudence retorted. "I do not intend to abandon the mill workers. In fact, I mean to return to Otley and take up my quest as soon as this dreadful ball is ended."

"Then you ought to put Mr. Sherbourne out of his misery and try not to love him so dearly." Reclining on a settee near the fire, Sarah was perusing the latest issue of *The Tattler*. Periodically she read bits of news aloud to her sisters.

But she had not yet finished meting out advice to Prudence. "You must make a sincere effort to find Henry Carlyle irresistible," she instructed, "for he is as handsome as any other man, is richer and better titled than most, and is laboring to quell his former reputation as a cad."

"Former?" Mary asked. "How do you know Henry's days as a cad are ended, Sarah? Although he claims to have reformed, Henry may be as much a rake as ever. Perhaps more so, for he has been to sea, and you know the havoc island girls can play with a young man's morals. I have decided on pink. This gown is so lovely. Besides, we have nothing but the yellow one to replace it. Yellow may make her appear sickly. We cannot have Pru looking ill if she is to win Henry's heart and cast off poor Mr. Sherbourne."

"Dear sisters, I must remind you that I am in this room too, in case you have forgotten!" Prudence exclaimed. "You will no more dictate my future husband than my ball gown. I am old enough to choose the direction of my life, and I have decided neither to go to the ball nor to marry anyone. I certainly will never relinquish my position as a crusader against injustice."

"Flowers would be lovely in her hair, do you not agree, Sarah?" Mary examined a pink ribbon adorned with tiny silk roses. "This would look charming woven into a small braid near the top of her head. Have you found Miss Pickworth yet? I am eager to hear what she says about the Delacroix ball."

As Prudence fumed, Sarah turned another page and scanned the newspaper. "No, it is largely news of Napoleon," she told her sisters. "America is causing no end of trouble, as always. And of course our honored prince regent can be relied upon to concoct one scandal after another—as if we had nothing else to keep us entertained."

"Oh, dear." Mary laid the ribbon on a table near the bed. "Has he forgotten he is to be king one day? Why must he always keep England in peril of losing her last shred of decency? It is not bad enough that he has *two* wives, for he must insist on siring sons by any number of mistresses. I am truly *quite* put out!"

As her sisters chatted about nothing, Prudence drew back the curtain over a window near the fire and studied the busy street below. Sarah and Mary had little to do but fuss over gowns, beaux, the *haute ton*, and the antics of the prince regent. Once upon a time, she had been no different.

But her journey across the moors had altered everything. When God had commissioned her to save the mill children from their plight, Prudence had been transformed into a different woman. Such an undertaking required persistence and an ardent determination to overcome all obstacles—the current most pressing of which were named Mrs. Charles Locke and Mrs. John Heathhill, better known to her as Sarah and Mary. Surely the Lord, in all His sovereign wisdom, had not intended sisters to be so incredibly annoying.

As Prudence scanned the large semicircle of grand homes that formed Cranleigh Crescent, memories of Bettie's small, thatch-roofed cottage on the outskirts of Otley filled her thoughts. The occupants of these residences enjoyed a vast difference in rank, wealth, and the expectation of a happy future.

Prudence had little doubt that despite Mr. Walker's love and protection, Bettie would die too young. No one could breathe the lint-filled air inside the mill without developing one or more illnesses of the lungs. Bettie often endured fits of unabated coughing, and nothing Prudence tried could ease her condition.

Her children, Bettie had lamented, would never learn to read or write. Their mother could do neither, and with no school nearby, what hope had they for education? Furthermore, why should they bother to learn at all, when their destinies lay within the ear-shattering din of Mr. Sherbourne's mill?

Prudence's stomach tightened into knots as she thought of the stone edifice, its churning waterwheel, its clanging carding machines, its whirring looms. What were young Tom, Martha, and Davy Smith doing even now as the sun set over England?

No doubt some other woman already had taken her place at the billy, a woman who would look down at the scrawny children scuttling back and forth beneath the dangerous metal contraption. Davy would never grow up straight and tall like William Sherbourne, Henry Carlyle, Ruel Chouteau, or the other gentlemen of the *beau monde*. Tom would help his brother hobble to and from the mill day after day until the child's crippled limbs could no longer bear his weight at all.

"I have found her!" Sarah cried out, waving the newspaper in the air. "You were right, Mary—Miss Pickworth's first matter of discussion is the Delacroix ball."

"Let me see!" Mary abandoned the pink gown and raced to take a place beside her sister on the settee. "Oh, indeed, it is! Read it to us, Sarah. Dearest Pru, leave your gloomy thoughts and join us for a moment of fun."

Fun? Prudence let the curtain fall back into place and settled onto a chair. "If Miss Pickworth is going to alliterate her way through the society gossip," she told her sisters, "I shall be unable to abide it."

"Miss Pickworth always alliterates, Pru," Mary reminded her. "Steady yourself, for our sister is now prepared to enchant us."

Sarah began with the headline. "'Dancing at Delacroix Destined to be Delightful.'"

At this, Prudence emitted a loud groan. "Oh, this is too agonizing to endure. Truly I must go."

"Stay and listen," Mary said, catching her sister's arm. "Perhaps you will learn something useful."

"'Friday's festivities,'" Sarah continued, "'will feature fortunate friends and fine fashion. Delacroix House, Cranleigh Crescent's most coveted abode—'"

"That is untrue," Mary cut in. "Trenton House is equally sumptuous."

"Do you mind not interrupting? And I refer to both of you," Sarah intoned, sternly regarding her sisters over the top of the newspaper before beginning again.

"'Cranleigh Crescent's most coveted abode will warmly

welcome the *haute ton*. A celebration of Lord Delacroix's deliverance from stormy seas and weary wanderings awaits. Miss Pickworth presumes to propose the guest list. Mr. and Mrs. Charles Locke will likely attend—'"

"Oh, Sarah, you are named first!" Mary cried. "Such an honor."

"'Mrs. Mary Heathhill, widow to the esteemed late John Heathhill—'"

"That is I. How kindly she words the mention of my dear departed husband."

Sarah continued reading. "'Miss Prudence Watson, sister to the aforementioned belles of the ball, will be ardently admired as always.'"

"There!" Mary said. "How esteemed you are, Pru."

"Indeed," Sarah agreed. "You cannot fail to attend now, Prudence, for everyone in town will be waiting for you to make an entrance."

"If you avoid an appearance," Mary added, "you will humiliate Henry and sadden your sisters, all of whom hold high hopes for your success in society."

Prudence stared at her sister in astonishment. "Mary . . . you are alliterating."

An infusion of bright pink bloomed across the young widow's cheeks. "Am I really?" Mary asked. "How odd. Perhaps I have been perusing Miss Pickworth too punctually."

Openmouthed, Prudence turned to Sarah, whose eyes had gone wide. Then both sisters faced Mary.

"Are *you* Miss Pickworth?" Sarah voiced the very question on Prudence's tongue. "You must confess at once, Mary. Is Miss Pickworth your *nom de plume*?"

The silence following the question went on too long.

"You *are*!" Prudence gasped. "I can see the evidence written across your face, Mary. You have been penning society news for *The Tattler* these many years, and none of us has guessed the truth until this moment!"

"Do not be absurd." Mary rose from the settee and bent to warm her hands over the fire. "How could I possibly be Miss Pickworth? I am a faithful reader of her column, and I often find my name there. Would I indulge vanity and write about myself?"

"Indeed you would!" Prudence said with a laugh. "You would most delightedly write about yourself and all of us. How could I have missed it? This is really too amusing—my very own sister is Miss Pickworth!"

"No, I believe we are in error," Sarah murmured, touching Prudence's arm. "If you recall, Mary was as eager as we to hear Miss Pickworth's news."

"I did not care to hear her news at all," Prudence declared.

"But Mary did. Besides, she was recently traveling with you in the north for nearly a month. How could she have detailed society's most intimate schemes and assignations without observing them firsthand?"

"Not to mention the death of my dear husband," Mary added. "Do not forget that I am in mourning. I could hardly attend assemblies and balls in such a situation. No, sister, you must surrender your suspicions."

"Very well," Prudence said, "though you alliterated your way right through that last avowal. If you are not Miss Pickworth, Mary, you are certainly like her in every way."

"Prudence, you will wear the pink," Mary decreed, turning

from the fire. "You will dance first with Mr. Sherbourne and then with Henry Carlyle. After that, you will fill your dance card with as many different men as possible. Mr. Sherbourne will understand that his hopes are in vain and hasten back to his worsted mill in Yorkshire. Henry will consider you a challenge and do all in his power to win your heart. By the end of the evening, if all goes according to plan, you will select Henry or some other eligible gentleman, agree to wed him, and relieve your poor sisters of the constant headache they suffer in attempting to settle you."

Ending her pronouncement, Mary snatched the newspaper from Sarah's fingers and stepped toward the door. "I do not alliterate," she concluded. "And my silly sisters should surrender their speculations . . . oh! Hang it all, Pru, now I really am doing it!"

As Mary bustled from the room, Prudence relaxed in her chair. *"If all goes according to plan,"* Mary had stated. But whose plan? Sarah and Mary, dear though they were, did not control their sister's destiny. Only God held Prudence's life in His hands. To Him—and only Him—would she submit her future.

"I am all astonishment," Sarah announced, casting Prudence a look of total bewilderment. "I think our sister is Miss Pickworth. Somehow, without anyone the wiser, she has been observing us and all our friends, penning her scandalous and rumor-filled missives, and sending them to *The Tattler* in complete anonymity."

"An investigation is in order," Prudence stated. "It cannot be difficult to find her out."

"No, indeed." Sarah stood and shook out the folds of her gown. "Do you know, Pru, lately I seem to have become quite the sleuth. I have written to friends in Plymouth asking for the history of your Mr. Sherbourne. I have gone down to the wharf and inquired about the character of Henry Carlyle—who is my husband's business partner and must not be allowed to ruin him. And now I am determined to ferret out the truth about our sister's secret life as Miss Pickworth."

"I can think of none more discerning than you," Prudence said as her sister stepped through the open doorway. "You must send me word at once when you have any intelligence on these matters."

"*Send* you word? You are not seriously planning to return to Yorkshire, are you?" Sarah shook her head. "I see that you are, and I cannot dissuade you. I understand you better than you suppose, for I once felt the urgency of a godly mission myself. Only my darling Charles was able to help me see reason and learn to balance my pious ambitions with good sense. Do go to the ball, Pru. If only to please Mary. She must have something scandalous to write about, must she not?"

Both women were giggling as Sarah shut the door.

◆

William stepped out of his carriage onto the street outside Delacroix House. The intimate gathering he had suggested a fortnight ago obviously had taken on a life of its own, rising and swelling with pomp, grandeur, and a magnificence far beyond the paltry sum he had offered Henry Carlyle in compensation for the use of his home.

As he watched lords and ladies clad in their finest silks, satins, diamonds, and gold ascend the massive staircase to the home's double front door, William sincerely hoped he would not be expected to produce further funding for the event. His own guest list had been short—a few shipping barons, the financial patrons of several noted haberdasheries in London, and a collection of well-heeled gentlemen who might be inclined to invest in his worsted mill. Thirty attendees at the most. The current count of guests filing into Delacroix House must exceed a hundred.

He joined them—climbing the stairs, stepping into the grand foyer, removing his top hat and cloak, handing them to a footman, and shouldering his way through the crowd in search of the object of his quest.

But he was soon waylaid.

"Aha, there you are, Mr. Sherbourne!" Henry Carlyle clapped William on the back. "I began to fear you had changed your mind and returned to Yorkshire. How do you find London these days?"

"Busy, as always, Lord Delacroix," William replied, forcing a smile.

He saw at once that his host had outdone him in a grandly ruffled neckcloth, a red brocade vest embroidered with game birds, and a suit of fine gray wool featuring a faint checked pattern. William had worn nothing more elegant than a black worsted suit with tails, a white shirt with a simply tied white muslin neckcloth, and a vest of dark sapphire silk.

Had they been peacocks in pursuit of a mate, William would have been forced to bow in surrender to the grand plumage of his rival. As it was, he elected to judge himself a worthy competitor for the affections of Miss Prudence Watson.

"London is busy indeed," Henry agreed. "Though I suspect its lively pace might make one long for the sedate charms of a country life."

"One might suppose we bumpkins have little to do but loll about, napping under haystacks. But I challenge you to visit my family's estate, Lord Delacroix, for I shall keep you occupied enough."

"Milking cows and shearing sheep?" Henry guffawed at his own humor. "I should like that very well indeed. But let us dispense with formalities. I am Delacroix to you, and you must be Sherbourne to me. After all, we are friends and colleagues now—each of us having added *tradesman* to our résumé, and each, I daresay, rather pleased with the outcome."

"Your tea trade thrives, I take it?"

"Indeed it does, and here is the very reason why." He moved them toward a tall, good-looking gentleman who appeared perfectly at ease in the crowded room. Henry singled him out with a tap on the shoulder and then made the introduction. "William Sherbourne, I should like you to know my business partner and boon companion, Charles Locke."

They exchanged niceties and made brief mention of their respective trades. From Sarah Locke's husband onward, Henry compelled William to make the rounds of the ballroom, meeting everyone and discovering that he was "the finest of men."

Henry, it became obvious, was given to superlatives. "Lord Blackthorne!" he exclaimed as they neared the marquess. "You must meet my dearest friend, William Sherbourne, a man whose character and lineage surpass all but your own."

Ruel Chouteau bowed upon encountering William again. "But Mr. Sherbourne and I are acquainted already," he informed Henry. "My wife and I were recently compelled to make a hasty journey northward. Our aim was to rescue a certain young lady whom everyone feared had lost her heart to this gentleman."

"You must now congratulate yourselves on a successful undertaking," William suggested. "For I am told that the lady in question retrieved her missing heart, departed Yorkshire posthaste, and promptly lost the fickle organ once again the moment she arrived in London."

"Do you refer to Miss Prudence Watson? I cannot believe she has fallen in love again so soon. What would Anne say to that?" Ruel turned to search for his wife, who stood at the edge of a cluster of young women. "No, Mr. Sherbourne, Anne did not tell me her friend had cast you off in favor of another. Indeed, if I heard her recitation of the report aright, Miss Watson's affections for you have now grown to colossal proportions."

"Really?" William frowned in confusion. "But I fear you have developed a husband's most heinous flaw—failure to give adequate attention to his wife's chatter."

Henry and Ruel chuckled at this.

"No, Mr. Sherbourne, I believe I have learned to avoid that matrimonial pitfall," Ruel assured him. "Besides which, my wife's conversation usually contains much sense. I discovered early the peril of failing to heed it."

"But, Sherbourne, which man did you believe had captured Miss Watson's heart?" Henry asked. "I am mystified."

"Are you?" William studied his rival. "If you have not been told by the lady herself, perhaps she does not wish it known."

"Want what known?" Mary Heathhill stepped up to the group. "Gentlemen, it is very rude to keep gossip to yourselves. You must announce the topic of this conversation to one and all, that we too may revel in its intricacies and thrills."

While the men protested and the petite brown-haired woman entertained them with witty quips, William made an effort to decipher the information given him by Ruel and Henry. Was it possible he had been mistaken in his assumption that Prudence now loved Lord Delacroix?

If they had formed an attachment, surely the man himself would know about it. And what of Lord Blackthorne's assertion that Prudence not only loved William but that her love had been growing since their separation in Yorkshire?

As Mary wandered away to seek further amusement, William could dally no longer. Where was Prudence? He had searched the ballroom countless times—sorting through any number of ostrich-plumed, silk-gowned, pink-cheeked ladies without success. Was it possible she would not attend the ball? Her tears upon their last parting told him her emotions ran deep. He had assumed she wept for the pain of hurting him as she confessed her love for another. Now he wondered what the real truth could be.

"Shall we ask Miss Watson to give us the unmitigated facts?" Henry was saying. "I see her there—dancing in the arms of a single man of large fortune. Sirs, we must set ourselves in place to capture the lovely creature the moment this tune is ended, or we are doomed to languish in ignorance."

William caught his breath as he finally saw Prudence. In a gown of pale blue that floated about her feet, she stepped and turned across the floor. Her partner was an older man—far too old for her. But William knew Prudence gave such differences little heed. She had once loved the American blacksmith, a man of mature years and little education, wealth, or standing.

Not only immune to the dictates of society, the woman was beautiful. She knew it. Every man in the room knew it. Every lady, too. There were none to compare, though they tried.

As William watched, she turned her head, and he noted a silver chain clasped about her long neck. A pearl pendant lay at her throat, a creamy white orb against her velvet skin. Gold ringlets were caught in a knot atop her head, blue ribbons wove their way through tiny braids, and gossamer curls danced at her cheeks. Her form was perfect in every aspect, and he ached at the fear that she would never be his.

"Worry, indeed!" Charles Locke was saying with a laugh. "That man is my father, and I would wager my fortune that he views Miss Watson as nothing more than a pretty child. She is perfectly safe with her present partner, gentlemen. Safe for the moment. James Locke has captured her, but soon he must set her free. Which of you will be next to beg a dance?"

William and Henry looked at each other, the competition between them finally surfacing.

"I am the better man," Henry announced, "and I shall prove it by generously offering the next dance to Sherbourne."

"Why?" Ruel asked. "Because you have already filled the lady's dance card for the remainder of the evening?"

The men were chuckling as the music died and the couples drifted across the floor in search of refreshment or the night air. Prudence stepped away in the direction of her sisters, who were laughing with a group of friends over some small amusement. William could endure the suspense no longer.

"I shall take your offer, Delacroix," he said, "and endeavor to usurp your reign as the king of hearts as swiftly as possible."

"Best of luck," Henry replied. "You know the knave never wins."

The men's eyes met again, and for the first time that evening,

William sensed hostility behind Henry's smile. He gave his rival a curt bow and strode off in search of the lady.

Prudence did not move from the cluster of women as he neared. He was forced to approach them, capture their attention, and endure an endless round of introductions. Finally, he focused on the one he sought.

"Miss Watson, I wonder if I might have the honor of the next dance." He assessed her reaction but could make nothing of it. "Unless you have promised it already?"

"I am not engaged," she told him. Without bidding her friends farewell, she linked her arm through his and moved toward the dance floor. "I had not planned to attend tonight. You must believe me."

"I do believe you, though I cannot understand why you would absent yourself. You are the most beautiful woman in the room, and every man who dances with you must consider himself fortunate indeed."

As he turned her into the dance, his hand rested for a moment at her waist. At the intimate touch, her green eyes darted up, meeting his. They circled the floor together, each unable to look away.

"You danced with Mr. Locke," he said in a foundering effort to initiate conversation. "I met his son. Your sister's husband is an amiable man."

"Sarah is blessed to have married Charles Locke. He is very good to her."

"And you? Are you blessed as well?"

"Indeed. But not as Sarah is. She and Mary have known true love—its beauty and its agony. I have known only its heartache."

As the dance parted them, William struggled to understand her meaning. Did her heartache arise from the loss of Walker the blacksmith? Had it something to do with Henry Carlyle? Or might it be a reference to William himself—to the many obstacles that seemed determined to part them?

"Are your efforts to enhance the worsted trade rewarded tonight?" she asked him when they came together again and joined a line of dancers moving down the floor. "Do you find your aims achieved?"

"My true aim for this evening had little to do with the trade and much to do with you. Prudence, I beg you to speak plainly. Do you and Delacroix have an understanding?"

"What is your meaning, sir?"

"Do you love him?"

"He is more nearly my brother than any other man. In that way, I love him well."

"How can you tease me?" he demanded. "You know my feelings for you are unchanged. Once you loved me too. I doubted you; I distrusted my own heart; I did all in my power to convince myself we could have no future together. Even now, when I consider the facts, I know it must not be. Yet I cannot rest."

She drew away from him, circled with another man, and returned. When she spoke again, her voice was tinged with despair. "If you know it must not be, why do you persist in your effort to make me love you? Stop at once, I beg you, or I shall come undone!"

"Prudence, nothing I say or do can *make* you love me. But if you do, only say the words and bring me some relief."

"Relief for you and increasing agony for me? Is that your desire?"

"No, indeed. My agony must always be the greater, for I hang suspended like a spider over a flame. If we cannot speak the truth, Prudence, I—"

"Truth about love? No, I cannot. I must do as God leads me. That is all there is, and it is enough. Do not ask for more, William."

The music died; the dancers bowed and clapped. He took her hand and led her from the floor. "Will you give me the next dance?" he asked. "Or accompany me outside onto the portico, where we might find a place to speak privately?"

She hung her head for a moment, pain written across her face. When she looked at him again, her eyes were rimmed in tears. "I have promised this dance to Henry. I do not wish to speak to you further. I find I cannot confess the truth about my feelings or my actions. I am all confusion. You must understand that I am not set against you, William. Far from it. If the situation were different, if our paths had not been laid out in such contrary fashion, perhaps this moment would not be so difficult. But we are not intended to walk through life together, and we must accept it."

"How can you know that? We have hardly given love room to flourish. Do not dismiss me, Prudence. I will not be so easily shed."

"I shall never cast you off, William. You must leave of your own accord. Henry comes now. We cannot meet again."

She made him the briefest of curtsies and hurried away. Smiling as she neared, Henry caught her about the waist and spun her into the dance. She did not look back.

Fourteen

Outside the ballroom, William stood on the long portico that opened into the garden. At least an hour had passed since his dance with Prudence. Henry Carlyle and other suitors vied to fill her card, but William made no effort to add his own name to the list.

Instead, he had used the evening to good advantage. Speaking to guests he had invited personally, he singled out the men most interested in investing in his worsted enterprise. Most had agreed to make the northward journey to inspect the mill and then to speak with their stewards about a financial stake.

Now, one shoulder leaning against a marble pillar, William surveyed the moonlit lawn that swept downward, away from the house. Near a gravel path, roses budded on thorny branches.

Daffodils, their golden petals folded away for the night, filled a pair of garden beds. Intricate knots and twists formed a hedge maze in the distance.

William sighed as he studied the complex pattern. The roads he had taken in life had been no less contorted. He had blundered his way through the years, crashing now and again into a wall or a blind alley. His mistakes nearly fatal, he had wandered aimlessly, brushing often against death, financial ruin, depravity. Lost in the maze, he had at last stumbled upon the awful truth.

He did not know where he was going.

Aware of no destination, he might have continued staggering through the labyrinth. What he had known of right and wrong would have continued to blend, their edges blurring until he had little sense of honesty, ethics, justice, or integrity. But one monumental transgression had stopped him cold, split the gray into black and white, and pointed his way out of the maze.

As he stood staring at another one now, William saw suddenly that Prudence had been right. Good and evil were diametrically opposite. Benevolence could never be mistaken for malevolence. They were too different. God had neatly divided light from darkness. William understood this now, but what was he to do with his newfound awareness?

A breeze sifted through his hair as he started down the wide steps leading from the ballroom into the garden. Compelled by the maze, he pondered the very real peril of becoming hopelessly lost in it. But the soupy fog that so often blanketed London had lifted. The scent of new roses and sweet jasmine hung in the air. Hope lifted his spirits.

And then he saw Prudence. Skirts lifted from her ankles,

she was skipping down the steps at some distance from him. Seemingly unaware of the couples strolling the alleyways or chatting on the portico, she bounded onto the path and hurried around a large conifer that had been snipped into the shape of a conch shell.

Without considering consequences, William changed course and started after her. A sense of dread told him Prudence was on a mission—and he knew what it must be. Crossing the path at the foot of the steps, he spotted her beneath a large oak tree. Adorned with the pale green leaves of spring, the sweeping boughs nearly concealed her . . . and the man she had run to meet.

His heart heavy, William elected to alter his path once again. He stepped to the entrance of the maze and paused to give the pair a last look. Her blue gown drifting in the breeze, Prudence clasped her hands at her chin, almost as if she were praying. The man pushed his hands into the pockets of his greatcoat. He turned and looked up at the moon, and William saw his face. It was not Henry Carlyle, Lord Delacroix.

Prudence's midnight suitor was Walker the blacksmith.

⬥

"What do you mean *Gag Acts*? I have never heard of such a thing." Prudence shivered from the chill wind and from her shock at the summons she had received in a curt message delivered moments before by a footman. "I do not understand. You must speak plainly and swiftly, for it cannot be long until I am missed."

Walker shifted his weight from one foot to the other. "Did you know that in January a mob attacked the regent's carriage?"

She searched her memory. "January . . . that month my sister and I began our journey to the northern counties. We read about the incident in *The Tattler*, I am sure. But I fear we were more . . ." She hated to admit that she and Mary had been far more interested in Miss Pickworth's society reports than in the distressing news of revolts and protests.

"We read only the briefest account of it," she concluded.

"Almost immediately after the attack on the regent," Walker told her, "Parliament took action to prevent a widespread revolution like the one in France. They passed three bills—the Gag Acts, people call them now. First, they suspended the right of *habeas corpus*. Without it, any man can be cast into gaol and imprisoned indefinitely—given no reason, afforded no trial, permitted no opportunity to defend himself."

"But that is abominable," Prudence protested. "It is utterly unfair."

"Unfair but they have done it," Walker continued. "Next, they prohibited large meetings. No more than fifty men may gather together at any time. Last, they ordered the lords lieutenant to apprehend all printers and writers responsible for seditious material."

Prudence frowned. "Surely such measures are a threat to liberty, but why do you bring this information tonight? Parliament's posturing cannot affect me."

"Can it not? Prudence, you were the first to press for better treatment of the workers at Thorne Mill. Your voice was heard. Your protests took root. Do you suppose the laborers know nothing of the rebellion that led to the Gag Acts?"

"I doubt they have heard even a whisper of that news.

Yorkshire is far from London, and your Bettie told me how few of Mr. Sherbourne's workers can read."

"Do not underestimate the power of rumors and hearsay." He pushed his hand into his pocket and took out a sheet of folded paper. "Not half an hour ago, I received this letter from Bettie. She paid the lamplighter in Otley to set out her message to me in pen and ink."

"The lamplighter?"

"He is the only one among them who can write." Walker held out the missive. "Bettie tells me that the cotton mill laborers in Manchester are starving. New machines are replacing the spinners, and the people have no food. They have decided to march."

"March? But they will all be tossed into gaol at once!"

"Perhaps not. It is to be a peaceful march in protest of the Gag Acts. They will carry a petition to the prince regent, asking him to relieve the plight of the poor."

Prudence took the letter and scanned the scrawled penmanship and badly spelled words. "Bettie says that the workers at Thorne Mill intend to leave Otley, journey to Manchester, and join the march. Oh no!"

"Read on," Walker said.

She turned slightly to let the moonlight illuminate the page. "The cotton mill workers propose to set out on March 10 from St. Peter's Fields in Manchester. The worsted mill workers from Otley will accompany them. But this is terrible! They must be stopped."

"Who will stop them?" His dark gaze pinned her. "You set this in motion, Prudence. You stop them."

"Me?" She caught her breath as the awful consequences of her heedless actions suddenly unfolded before her. Men and women would be arrested and tossed into gaol. Children would have no parents to tend and guide them. William's mill would cease to operate. Everyone would go hungry.

Such calamity. And she had been the cause of it!

"I did not intend for this to happen," she told Walker. "I meant to make their lives better."

"How? Tea and cakes? Dreams of health, wealth, and happiness? You began this, Prudence, and then you fled to London—to your sisters and the arms of your new love. Did you think you could set the wheels of rebellion in motion and then escape the results?"

"I did not think at all." She clasped her hands together, praying for answers that would not come. "I am so sorry. I gave the future no thought, for I wanted only to help the present circumstances of the workers."

"But there is always a future. Life goes on."

"*You* went on. You left me and never thought of those consequences. Now you have no right to presume you understand the situation of my heart. I have made no attachment to William Sherbourne."

"But you love him."

"What I may feel has no bearing on how I must act. When I came to London, I had every intention of returning to Otley, and I am not one to run from a pledge. I shall depart tomorrow morning. The moment I arrive in Otley, I shall do all in my power to put a stop to this reckless march."

"The horse cart is waiting on the street, and I leave tonight. I have tarried far too long in this wretched city."

"Then you go alone. I must first bid my sisters farewell and set my affairs in order. Then I shall dress in disguise and take the post coach. None will be the wiser."

"You suppose he does not know your trickery? William Sherbourne may be a reckless man, but he is not a stupid one. Perhaps your deceit eludes him now, but he will go back to Otley and he will find you out."

"Meanwhile, I shall have stopped the workers from marching and returned them to their former state."

"Starving, ignorant, crippled, poor. Well done, Prudence."

"Chastise me if you wish. I deserve it. But I did what I believed was right. Good evening, sir."

Afraid Walker would see the anguish in her face, Prudence turned on her heel and strode across the grass. *I am not only silly,* she told herself. *I am bad. I harm those I mean to help. I cause trouble instead of resolving it. Can I do nothing right? Am I destined to fail at everything I try?*

Brushing away tears as fast as they tumbled down her cheeks, Prudence snatched the ribbons from her hair and started down the path that led toward the drive. Trenton House was only a short walk across Cranleigh Crescent from Delacroix House. She had not wanted to attend the ball anyway. Sarah and Mary had begged and cajoled her until she could see no way out. At least she had not worn the pink gown!

She would go back to Otley and tell everyone the terrible truth that just like she, they were destined to do what they had always done. They would continue to be who they had been born to be. Nothing would ever change.

Prudence hurried along the path, gravel crunching beneath her slippers and the breeze whipping her hair from its pins. She reflected on her friend Betsy Fry, who had taken blankets into the gaols and workhouses. But Betsy had freed no prisoners. She had changed no laws. Indeed, the Gag Acts had been ratified right under her nose! Just as Betsy had ultimately failed, so must Prudence. William had insisted she was not silly. How little he knew her.

Rounding the gate that opened onto the drive, she nearly walked straight into the man himself. Catching herself, she gasped as he reached to steady her.

"Excuse me," she breathed out and stepped aside. "So sorry. I did not mean to startle you. I am going home."

He assessed her, his dark brown eyes depthless. When he spoke, his voice was hard. "You have been in a tussle, I see."

"I beg your pardon?"

"Your hair. You were engaged in a scuffle with someone. Or perhaps the two of you were simply sporting about."

She reached up to the tangle of wind-whipped curls. "What is your meaning?"

"I speak as I see, madam."

"But what you see is not what you think. I took down my hair because I am going home, and I should never have gone to the ball but my sisters forced me and I had to dance with everyone—and I hardly even like most of those brainless men! Everyone supposes I enjoy having pink cheeks and green eyes and curls, but they have never had to endure them, for if they did, they soon would learn that no one believes them the least bit sensible! And as for you, I hope you stay in London and find yourself a lady to marry—some straw-headed ninny who does not care that your workers eat water porridge and oatcake and labor from sunrise to sunset and never learn to read or write so that if they want to send a message, they have to engage the lamplighter to write it for them! That is all I have to say to you, because I am very tired and out of sorts and I wish everyone would just leave me alone!"

Before he could answer, she stepped off the curb and started across the great crescent-shaped park fronting the elegant homes. So much for William Sherbourne. He had all but accused her of dallying in the dark with a suitor. As if she had nothing but feathers and fluff for a brain!

"You should know one thing at least." William caught up to her and now matched her pace. "I did love you, Prudence. I loved you, and I thought you were beautiful and perfect. That was before I knew the depths of your deception."

"My deception?" She glanced at him askance, wondering if he knew of her clandestine activities in Otley. But perhaps he referred to some imagined lover for whom she might have cast him aside. Either way, she hardly cared, for William Sherbourne's good opinion could mean nothing to her now.

"You speak your opinions of me most decidedly," she told him. "Do you presume to understand everything about me?"

"I understand very little about you, but I have observed your behavior. You are more than able and willing to beguile a man. You captivate and then betray your victims."

"I have victims, do I? Are you one of them? I hope so!" She continued her headlong march across the park. "You make me out to be a spider luring men to their doom. But in the ballroom tonight you claimed to be the spider—hanging by a thread. Perhaps you are the deceitful one, William. Is that possible?"

"It is . . . possible."

"But difficult to admit. At the least you are fickle, for you claim to love me, then you chide me, then you love me again, then you accuse me of betrayal, and so it goes. Have you ever lied, sir? Or is your every action impeccable and without flaw or blemish?"

"No one is perfect," he answered.

She stepped onto the gravel path in front of Trenton House. "Then I hope you will allow me some imperfections. I never claimed the labels of goodness and excellence you attached to me. You taught me that the world was gray, William. I disputed that, but for some time now, I have known that you were correct in your assessment. I am nothing but gray from head to toe and inside out. In every way, I have failed—"

"No, Prudence." He put his fingers to her lips to stop the flow of words. "Say nothing more, I beg you. I have only just learned to accept that *you* were right—that the world is all black-and-white. Gray does not exist. Right and wrong are opposites, and nothing may muddy them. Good cannot be bad. Bad can never be good. Do not tell me now that you have slipped into the sea of gray from which I have just escaped."

"Oh, William!" She took his fingers and pressed her lips to his hand. "How I wish we had met at another time and in another place. But God set our courses, and He knew how it was to be. I admit my many wrongs, yet I fear there is just enough good left in me to prevent my disputing with the Lord."

"And there is enough bad left in me to argue against Him. I have asked—and I shall continue to ask—that He will redirect my path and align it with yours. I ask Him to take what is left of me and do something of value with it. Perhaps there are not enough crumbs worth saving. Yet I cannot help but pray."

At this, she looked up into his face and knew he was the man she loved most in all the world.

"I see the butler has noted your arrival," he said. "He awaits at the door."

Prudence glanced behind for a moment. Then she turned back to him. "Good evening, Mr. Sherbourne."

"Good evening, Miss Watson." He tipped his hat as she fled toward the house.

◆

"Oh, Pru!" Mary burst into the room where Prudence was packing her trunks. "You must go downstairs at once, for Sarah has come to see us and she will not speak a word to me until she has talked to you! She has brought a letter, a message of great import, and it has given her such a fright that I am tempted to call for smelling salts!"

Prudence glanced to the window, where the morning sun had already begun to slant through the open curtain. A carriage awaited outside—a gift from Anne, who could not bear to think of her dearest friend returning to Otley by the post coach. Farewells to Sarah and Mary had been made already, and Prudence had no patience for extending them.

"Bid Sarah come up to me here," she told Mary. "I have still to put away my bonnets and gloves. If she is so eager to see me, let her hasten to my side."

"Wicked girl! She is your elder sister, and you will do as she asks!"

"Very well, Mary, then you shall stay and pack my things."

"I shall do nothing of the sort! I am as eager to learn Sarah's news as you are."

"More eager, I should wager," Prudence grumbled as she and Mary stepped into the corridor. "I am sure all of London will know Sarah's news once our dear Miss Pickworth has heard it."

"Will you stop making these unfounded accusations?" Mary cried. "I cannot possibly be Miss Pickworth!"

"Pretty Prudence persistently presumes Mary is Miss Pickworth," she teased as she scampered just ahead down the staircase. "Sister Sarah surely supposes the same!"

"Stop it!" Mary swatted Prudence on the arm as they entered the drawing room. "Stop saying such silly—"

"Aha! Aha! You are at it again, Miss Pickworth!" Prudence darted toward the fire but halted at the sight of Sarah's face. Drawn and pale, the eldest of the three sisters rose.

"What is it?" Prudence asked in a low voice. "Sarah, what has happened?"

"You must sit down, Prudence. You too Mary." Sarah indicated the settee across from her chair. "I have received some sobering news."

Anxiety and dread coursing through her, Prudence settled on the edge of the settee. "Tell us at once, Sarah. Has someone died?"

"It is not as bad as that, but nearly so." Sarah seated herself again and unfolded a letter. The broken seal indicated a correspondent of some prominence, though Prudence could not distinguish whose crest had been imprinted in the wax.

"A letter came to me this morning," Sarah continued. "It was written by my dear friend, Charlotte Ross, who lives in Plymouth. I once mentioned her to you, Pru, for I felt she might be able to provide us some account of your Mr. Sherbourne."

"He is not *my* Mr. Sherbourne," Prudence corrected, though

her heart quaked with alarm that anything regarding him might be amiss.

Their parting the night before had left many questions unanswered and the future undecided. Yet she now had no doubt of his attachment to her, and she knew at last the truth of her own feeling for him. She loved William. Loved him deeply and desperately. It was clear to both of them that little could come of their devotion, yet they knew it could not be denied.

"You insist he is not yours," Sarah was saying, "and I pray you have not confessed your true feelings to him or made him any pledges."

"No," Prudence whispered. "We have no formal understanding."

Sarah nodded. "I am glad, for I fear he is not at all the man we hoped he might be. His character, I regret to report, must be irredeemably bad."

"Bad?" Prudence recalled William's revelation to her—that just as she had accepted life's moral grayness, he had come to believe in its absolute clarity. *"Good cannot be bad,"* he had declared. *"Bad can never be good."*

"But surely no one can be irredeemably bad," she told Sarah. "Redemption is God's gift to even the worst of sinners."

"I cannot imagine anyone worse than Mr. Sherbourne has turned out to be."

"Has he killed someone?" Mary asked. "Sarah, I beg you to enlighten us at once. This delay is distressing our poor sister no end."

Sarah looked down at her letter for a moment before speaking. "Charlotte writes that she has made discreet inquiries regarding Mr. Sherbourne's standing in the Royal Navy and his reputation in Plymouth society. Of the first, she can find nothing amiss. He was, in fact, a respected officer and proved himself valiant in battle on more than one occasion of armed conflict."

"There!" Mary said. "It is not as dreadful as we feared, Prudence. You may take comfort in his bravery. Mr. Sherbourne is both courageous and gallant."

"I should not go so far as that," Sarah said. "Courageous, perhaps, but if gallantry implies anything of chivalry, he is dismally lacking. I believe you described him once, Prudence, as a cad. You could not have been more correct."

"Oh, dear," Mary murmured. "I fear we are in for shocking news."

"While living in Plymouth," Sarah went on with a sigh, "Mr. Sherbourne displayed behavior that was morally reprehensible. None can dispute the fact that he dallied with every eligible young lady in the town."

"No!" Mary cried aloud. "Impossible."

"I thought so myself, but Charlotte has been so kind as to supply names and details that leave no room for doubt."

"Do you call that kind?" Prudence snapped. She leapt up and snatched the letter from Sarah's hand. "Your friend is nothing but a gossiping rumormonger! William's behavior may have been less than prudent, but we must allow that in those years he was very young and his character could not have been fully formed. He is no longer that sort of man!"

She flung the letter into the fire and watched the flames lick at the paper, ignite the wax, and crumple it into ash.

"That is what I think of your dear friend Charlotte and her precious news," she cried. "I hope I may never see the woman in the whole of my life, for I should not be responsible for what

I might say or do! She has maliciously sucked up every sala-cious tidbit—no doubt mingling truth with falsehood—and conveyed it to you in utter triumph. I hate her, and I do not believe one word of what she has written."

"Prudence, sit down!" Sarah commanded. "Sit down at once."

"I shall not! My carriage awaits, and I am needed at the mill."

"You will sit down now!" Sarah stood, pointing at the set-tee. "I shall not permit you to leave this house until you have understood the possible consequences of your actions in regard to that man."

"I do not go to Otley because of *that man*. I go because of the mill workers. I have no plan ever to meet with Mr. Sherbourne again."

"No plan, perhaps, but it may occur nonetheless. After all, you met him first by accident."

"That is true, Prudence," Mary put in. "You fell into the puddle and he rescued you."

"Was that an accident? I think not. My faith assures me that God knows the number of hairs on my head, and He certainly knew that Tom Smith would take my bag and knock me into the mud. He knew Mr. Sherbourne would rescue me, and He knew how our friendship would grow."

"What God *knows* and what He *approves* may be two very different things," Sarah said. "I have not told you the worst of Charlotte's account, and your rash outburst will forever prohibit my reading it to you."

"I do not want to hear Charlotte's account of anything, espe-cially of a man she knows so little!"

"But you must learn what he has done. You must be told facts that cannot be disputed." Sarah gestured again to the settee. "Dearest Pru, no one in this room desires anything but your happiness. Mary and I love you and pray daily that you will find God's best purpose and His truest companion for your life. What His purpose is, we do not yet know. But His chosen companion for you cannot possibly be William Sherbourne. As much as it pains me to tell you why, I cannot release you until you know the truth."

Prudence stood, hovering between all-out flight through the door, into the carriage, and away from this place—and hearing the worst information about the man she loved most in all the world. As the battle raged within her, she took a deep breath and sat down.

"If you say he killed someone," she whispered, "I shall know it is a lie. William would never do such a thing."

"No, indeed," Sarah said, returning to her place in the chair by the fire. "I am sure he would not intend to kill anyone. Yet someone did die, Prudence . . . a woman who had given herself to him . . . in every way."

Fifteen

Catching her breath, Prudence covered her face with her hands. "No. Please tell me this is not true."

"It is true, for Charlotte is the aunt of the lady who lost her life. Her name was Caroline Bryse, a young woman of good standing in society and sufficient means to make her an appealing match. Mr. Sherbourne, however, was not the sort of man her family would approve of. His habits of gaming, drinking, and consorting with fallen women were well-known."

"Oh, this is very bad indeed!" Mary exclaimed as she took a fan from a nearby table and opened it to cool her flushed face.

"According to Charlotte," Sarah continued, "Miss Bryse's father flatly forbade any attachment between his daughter and Mr. Sherbourne. Yet that man displayed no respect for the wishes of Miss Bryse's family. Indeed, he continued to court her in secret. Before they could wed, she gave birth to his son."

"Worse and worse!" Mary cried, fanning at an ever-increasing speed.

Despite both her sisters' obvious distress, Sarah carried on with her report. "I am sad to tell you that only minutes after the child was born, his mother died. Mr. Sherbourne made neither apology nor recompense to the family. His tenure in the Royal Navy was at an end, and he wasted no time in returning to his home in Yorkshire."

"Heaven help us," Mary moaned. "Dearest Pru, you will recall that when we first met Mr. Sherbourne, he was only just back from sea. No more than a month could have passed since the tragic circumstances our sister has related."

"A month is hardly enough time for the redemption of Mr. Sherbourne's character," Sarah observed. "Even a year might not be sufficient."

"Mr. Sherbourne's brother always did speak disparagingly of him," Mary recalled. "We supposed it was done in jest, but now I see how serious were the overtones."

Prudence clasped her hands together, unable to move or speak. Her mind reeled with memories of moments she had spent in William's company. His rescue of her from the puddle, their ride across the moorlands, those precious minutes they had enjoyed dancing and kissing and whispering avowals of love.

But she was nothing to him. Another conquest among many. A pretty trifle to whom he had offered false assurances of his admiration, desire, and commitment. She had believed him. She had entrusted him with her heart. Yet she had been nothing more to him than a game of chance on which he had wagered very little.

"I must go," she declared, lifting her focus to her sisters. "I cannot delay a moment longer. As I have told you, the mill workers intend a desperate act, and Mr. Walker insists that I am the only one who can stop them. Please forgive the anguish I have caused both of you. I never meant to make you worry."

"Dearest Pru," Sarah replied gently. "Our only concern is your happiness. You have been dealt a great blow by this news of your friend, and I beg you to stay in London, where Mary and I may look after you. Can you not send a message to Mr. Walker? Surely his influence will put a stop to whatever rash and foolish actions the workers might plan to undertake."

Prudence considered Sarah's request. She heard the love and compassion in her sister's voice. Yet God's voice was far stronger. He had sent her on a mission to improve the lives of the worsted mill workers. The day of their march was at hand, and she must make all possible haste to prevent them from joining the protesters in Manchester.

Prudence shook her head. "I cannot stay here. Mr. Walker rightly accused me of fomenting rebellion at Thorne Mill. I am the one who now must put it down."

"Sarah, you must forbid Prudence's departure at once!" Mary insisted. "I have seen how Mr. Sherbourne looks at her, and her feelings for him may reignite! Make her stay in London."

"Mary, our sister is not a child. We cannot force her to do anything."

"Thank you, Sarah," Prudence said. "And, Mary, you may make yourself easy. I have seen the truth about William Sherbourne at last. My heart is no longer in danger."

"So she says!" Mary cried out, addressing their elder sister. "But his wiles are skillful indeed. If he has taken in one woman, you may be sure he will take in as many as he can. Shall we allow Prudence to become one of the poor souls he uses and then casts aside? Sarah, you cannot let Pru go back to him."

"I do not go back to *him*, Mary," Prudence assured her as she stood. "I go back to them—to Tom and Davy, to Fanny and Bettie and Mr. Walker, to all those in whom I planted false hope for a better future. If they are clapped in irons on my account, I assure you my agony will be far worse than it is upon hearing the dreadful account of Mr. Sherbourne's wicked character."

"Very well, Prudence." Sarah rose, drew her sister into a warm embrace, and kissed her cheek. "Accomplish your mission swiftly, and return to us as soon as may be."

"You will see me at home again in less than a fortnight." Prudence smiled at Mary. "Do not look so glum, sister. I am not quite as silly as you suppose."

Wildly fanning herself, Mary stepped to Sarah's side. The three embraced again, murmuring endearments and best wishes for success and Godspeed. Prudence walked to the door, but as she started into the corridor, she turned back.

"Sarah . . . what became of the baby?"

"Baby?" Sarah frowned.

"Mr. Sherbourne's child. Did the baby die too?"

Sarah cast a glance at the fire flickering on the hearth. "Charlotte did not say. I shall write to her again and ask what she can tell me."

Prudence dipped her sisters a brief curtsy. Then she fled up the stairs to finish her packing and make a diligent search for some way to ease the terrible ache in her heart.

⬦

"What do you mean by interrupting my family like this?" Randolph Sherbourne rose from the breakfast table to face the burly man who had burst into the dining room at Thorne Lodge. Now Randolph turned to his brother. "William, is this man as he claims to be—one of your overlookers?"

Already on his feet, William addressed the intruder. "Warring, you are out of line. If you wish to speak to me, make application at the door. Jones, see him out."

Richard Warring brushed off the footman who reached for his arm. "Nay, man, I'll not be sent away until I've had my say. Mr. Sherbourne, sir, I am come to inform you that your mill be empty of labor this morning. They've gone off, all of 'em. Gone to Manchester."

"Manchester? You're telling me—"

"Every one of 'em, sir. At dawn this morning, only two women and a handful of boys arrived at the mill to take their rightful places. Straightaway, me and the other overlookers seen something was amiss. At first the women would say nothing, but when we took it on ourselves to beat it out of the children, they began jabbering like a flock of magpies."

"You beat the children?" William asked. "Against my orders?"

"Aye," Warring said. "For we knew the women would soon confess—as they did. They told us that last night under cover of dark, all the spinners, carders, weavers—the lot of 'em!—set off walking toward Manchester."

"But why would they go to Manchester?"

"To join the cotton workers of that town in protesting the ill treatment they claim their employers be giving 'em. They writ

out a petition for the king, asking the poor mad wretch to give
'em a better life. Your labor will add to the mass marching along
the roads and byways. You got no one working inside your mill,
sir, and no way of knowing when they'll be back—if ever."

William glanced at his brother. "I sensed this was coming,
Randolph. I felt it."

"So much for your fancy reforms, eh?" Warring crowed. "Me
and the other overlookers knew something was afoot, and there
weren't naught could be done to stop it. Not even them reforms
done the trick."

"Of which reforms does this man speak, William?" Randolph
asked.

William heaved a deep sigh. "No more than two days ago,
I met with the overlookers and outlined a list of improvements
I expected them to put into place. In fact, I had initiated one
aspect of the plan before I left for London—adding tea and cake
to the day's repast. My next step is more drastic. I have decided
to shorten the workday by two hours."

"Two hours? William, is that practical?"

"In light of Warring's news, perhaps not. My efforts apparently had no effect."

"None," Warring confirmed.

"What were the other reforms?" Randolph asked.

"I engaged a teacher from Leeds to help the children learn
to read and write. And I ordered the kitchen to begin serving
meat, potatoes, good bread, and tea."

"You will ruin yourself," Randolph predicted. "With such
measures, there can be no margin for profit."

"I am pleased with William's reforms," Olivia spoke up.
"I have always said the workers would do well with more

sleep and better food. As for the school, that is a great kindness, William, and you will be rewarded with loyal labor from the parents whose children benefit."

"Your wife is not only lovely, but she is right," William told his brother. "At least . . . I believed so until this moment. My sojourn in London had served me well in more ways than one. While there, I took time to consider the possible effects of the reforms I was pondering, and I set out to undergird them. Seven financiers have agreed to visit the mill. I held great hope that what they observed would encourage them to invest in its future."

"Maybe yesterday they'd have wanted to," a smirking Richard Warring said. "But if they come today, they'll see naught but an empty building."

"Did you and the other overlookers obey my order to inform the workers about my plans?" William asked him. "All but the lessons are to begin on Monday."

"We told 'em but none believed us. To my way of thinking, they had already made up their minds to march." He lowered his voice. "That woman came back, if you catch my meaning, and we seen how she stirred up the crowd with her whispering and secrets."

"Which woman do you mean, Warring?"

"Her . . . that Miss Watson. Polly, who works as a spinner."

"Miss Watson?" William's heartbeat faltered. "*Polly* Watson?"

"Aye, sir. She'd been away a fortnight or more, but when she come back, the workers started all their muttering again. None of your high-sounding promises could keep 'em from marching."

"I fully intend to make good on those promises."

Warring shrugged. "Them people don't have the brains God gave a goose. To be honest, sir, I didn't credit you neither. I been a mill overlooker these twenty years, and most workers don't lift a finger lest they be threatened with a beating. Like I said at the meeting, reforms won't last a week afore you see the ill effects of treating the labor good."

Unwilling to hear another word, William turned to his footman. "Jones, tell my man to ready a good horse. See that my greatcoat and boots are laid out."

"Yes, sir," the servant replied with a bow. "At once, sir."

"Warring, you have done your duty. Return to the mill and ensure that it is kept secure. I shall not have Luddites destroying my worsted looms as they did the stocking machines in Nottingham."

"Aye, sir. Good day, sir."

William watched him go. He knew Richard Warring was referred to as Dick the Devil, a man who would rather administer a beating than give instruction. While the brute's report had been of benefit, William now had more than enough reason to dismiss him for insubordination. Had Warring and the other overlookers followed their master's orders to the letter, the workers certainly would have expected the reforms to benefit them. If they had believed that a school would be started and the workday shortened, surely they would not have dreamed up this half-cocked scheme to march with the Manchester cotton mill workers.

And what of Warring's mention of Polly, the spinner who had been absent, yet recently had returned to the mill? Polly Watson. Surely it could not be . . .

"Randolph, Olivia," he addressed the two remaining in the

room. "I go to Manchester at once. If the workers marched through the night, they may be in the city already."

"You have my full support," Randolph said. "I would accompany you, but the lambing season has begun."

"It is no matter," William told him. "I shall return shortly. Pray for me, if you will."

Olivia's eyebrows lifted. "We shall, dear William. Of course!"

Taking some solace in her glad smile, he made his farewells and left the dining room.

◆

"Miss Watson, wake up! 'Tis time to march!" The urgency in Bettie's voice roused Prudence from uneasy slumber. Like the other worsted mill laborers who had walked to Manchester from Otley, she had slept the remainder of the night on a rough wool blanket. And she had rested poorly—roused often by carousers bent on making the rally an opportunity to drink too much, by groups of men bursting into song, by babies crying, by her own troubled heart.

"Drink this," Bettie ordered, handing Prudence a mug of hot water sprinkled with a few tea leaves. "Mr. Walker says the rain is just over the hill and coming at us quickly. We must roll up our blankets and hurry to St. Peter's Fields."

With a sigh of despair, Prudence sat up and took a sip of the weak brew. Frowning at its bitter taste, she set the mug aside and began tucking wayward curls into her muslin mobcap. During the night, a pale gray mist had rolled across the moors, blanketing the gathered crowd in a cool and murky cloak. As she stood, the first droplets began to fall.

"At least I may take some hope that this rain will put an end to the march," Prudence told Bettie as she rolled her blanket. "How long did I talk at the meeting yesterday? It felt like hours—and all for naught."

"Take no worry about it, Miss Watson," Bettie said. "No one wanted to listen to warnings of disaster while setting out on a journey of hope."

Prudence shook her head. From the moment she had arrived back in Otley two days before, she had done her best to discourage people from joining the march to Manchester. Though the worsted mill workers had seemed pleased at her return, she soon realized they would not heed her admonitions.

She had warned them that the authorities in Manchester would never permit the moving assembly of such a great crowd. The journey from Manchester to London was long, she reminded the mill workers, and they could not carry enough food and water to sustain them. The cold and damp would likely cause sickness, she pointed out more than once. People already weakened by hunger and exhaustion might even perish during such a difficult expedition. But all her cautions fell on deaf ears.

Bettie felt that she must join the marchers to avoid the shame of failing to support her friends, and Walker would not let her go without his protection. Prudence decided she had no choice but to go too and continue in her effort to turn back the surging tide of dissenters.

"No one along the way will welcome us," she muttered. "Certainly we shall be neither fed nor sheltered. Why would people risk supporting a mob marching to London with petitions for the king?"

A deep voice entered the conversation. "It is not the lack

of encouragement and help that worries me." Walker joined the women in rolling blankets. He had slept at some distance from them, but now he helped gather up the few supplies they had brought. "I fear some might join the march who are not reformers. Among us there may already be men bent on evil."

"I hold John Johnson, John Bagguley, and Samuel Drummond to blame in this," Prudence said, naming the three men who had rallied the opposition to the Gag Acts and organized the Manchester march. "I fear they have led us like lambs to the slaughter."

The planners had urged protesters to carry wool or cotton blankets with them on the journey—as a symbol of their craft as well as a means of keeping warm. Whispered from man to woman to child, the journey had quickly come to be known as the March of the Blanketeers.

"I wonder now if the mill owners may have anticipated this undertaking," Walker was saying. "Perhaps they hired false supporters to bring the marchers and their cause into disgrace."

"What mischief could they do that has not been done already?" Prudence asked. "The mills are abandoned, the fields are trampled, the roadways are spread with vagabonds, and soon the town of Manchester will swarm with people bent on a reckless quest."

"If scoundrels planted in the crowd begin to plunder cottages and farms along the road, the punishment and disgrace will fall on all of us."

Prudence clutched her blanket to her empty stomach as she joined the others on the muddy track. "If immorality and wickedness ensue, it will hardly matter who is at fault, for we shall all be denounced as robbers and miscreants. I should not be the least surprised if an armed force comes to cut us down or take us prisoner. Oh, what can I say to stop this nightmare? I am beyond despair."

"You should go back, Miss Watson," Bettie told her gently. "Go back to Otley and take refuge at the great manor house. Neither you nor Mr. Sherbourne can stop the march now, but he would welcome you into his home and put you back to your rightful place."

"What is my rightful place, Bettie? I am the one who caused this folly. I have no choice but to walk alongside these people and keep trying to dissuade them from their foolhardy crusade."

"No offense, Miss Watson," the small woman offered, "but your place is with them that God saw fit to make well-off and easy. Leave us be. We'll take our grievances to the king, and if any good comes of it, we'll rejoice. If not, we can only pray that Mr. Sherbourne will hire us back at his mill. Let that be your mission, madam, if you must have one. Soften his heart to us."

"That task would be ten times more difficult than stopping this march." Prudence paused, reflecting on the past before bringing herself to speak again. "Mr. Sherbourne, I have learned, has no heart."

At that, all in the group fell silent. Slogging through the mud, Prudence heard only the sound of shoes sucking and sloshing. Rain that had begun as a mist and then a dribble soon fell in sheets. Prudence draped her blanket over her shoulders for protection, but the wool quickly grew so heavy with water that she could barely put one foot in front of the other.

"We approach Manchester," Walker said at length, pointing to the left of the roadway at a steepled building and the outlined roofs of a small town. "There is the church. You can see houses along Windmill Street and Peter Street. St. Peter's Fields lie just beyond."

"Dear God, help us," Prudence prayed aloud as she witnessed the mass of people coming from every direction to gather in the open meadow. The rain had eased, and the size of the multitude stunned her. "How many can there be?"

"Five thousand at least," Walker muttered. "Perhaps closer to ten. The men reported to me last night that Johnson has told the weavers if the leaders can get them as far as Birmingham, all their aims will be accomplished. By then, Johnson said, the crowd will be grown to a hundred thousand, and it will be impossible for anyone to resist them."

"Blanketeers!" someone cried out from a distance. "Begin the March of the Blanketeers!"

"Hail the Blanketeers!" Another voice took up the cry. Soon the chant swelled across the field. "The March of the Blanketeers! The March of the Blanketeers! Begin the March of the Blanketeers!"

"Look," Bettie said. "They've set up a platform near that horse chestnut tree. Who is talking?"

"'Tis Samuel Drummond," an elderly, gap-toothed man told Walker's group as they pressed closer in an attempt to hear the discourse over the patter of rain. "Drummond says we're to behave with decorum. Whatever that is!"

"*Decorum* means respectability," Prudence informed him. "Good manners. Mr. Drummond is urging us to be polite."

His attention riveted to the speaker on the dais, the man paid her little heed. But in a moment, he turned to address Walker. "Johnson was arrested yesterday. Did ye know?"

Walker shook his head. "What became of him?"

"Tossed into gaol."

"Are the other leaders here?"

"John Bagguley stands just there beneath the tree. Afore Drummond spoke, Bagguley warned that if any of us causes trouble, he'll be handed over to the magistrates."

"Exactly as it should be," Prudence tried again. "Indeed, the best thing would be for everyone to go home and put this nonsense out of—"

A cry cut short her words as uniformed men on horseback rode through the crowd, dismounted, and swarmed onto the platform. At once Prudence recognized their uniform of red coats, white trousers, and plumed black helmets.

"It is the King's Dragoon Guards!" she told the others.

Within moments the dragoons had apprehended Drummond and Bagguley. With the crowd shouting and hissing at them, the soldiers seized the most aggressive among the throng and dragged them away.

Amid the chaos, a magistrate in a wig and black robe mounted the stage and opened a large book. Protected by armed dragoons, he began to read.

"'The Riot Act,'" he called out. "'An act for preventing tumults and riotous assemblies, and for the more speedy and effectual punishing the rioters.'"

"What's he talking about?" the gap-toothed man asked Prudence. "I don't take no meaning from it."

But the magistrate continued: "'Our sovereign Lord the King chargeth and commandeth all persons, being assembled, immediately to disperse themselves, and peaceably to depart to their habitations, or to their lawful business, upon the pains contained in the act made in the first year of King George, for preventing tumults and riotous assemblies. God save the King!'"

Prudence strained to hear through the grumbling of the crowd and the drumming of rain. "'Unlawfully, riotously, and tumultuously assembled together . . . ,'" the magistrate cried out. "Offenders therein shall be adjudged felons . . . shall suffer death . . . without benefit of clergy.'"

"He is reading the Riot Act," Prudence told the others. "Any group of more than twelve people unlawfully assembled is to disperse or face punitive action."

"Disperse?" Bettie asked. "What is that?"

"Twelve?" the other man said. "We've got more than that here, don't we?"

Prudence shook her head in frustration. "Indeed there are many more than twelve. I assure you—"

Her words were drowned as another cry arose. "Begin the march! Blanketeers—march!"

At that, the crowd heaved and swelled, moving like molten honey across the field in the direction of Lancashire Hill and the town of Stockport. Swept along with the mass, Prudence saw Bettie stumble and go down. As Prudence screamed for Walker, she realized she had lost sight of him.

While she struggled to keep her own footing in the thick mud, the dragoons waded into the marchers with sabres drawn and muskets at the ready. Shrieks of terror rose. A bolt of lightning flashed across the gray sky. Thunder boomed over the moors, echoing and drowning the cries of mayhem in the crowd.

Pushed along, Prudence searched for a way through the panicked throng. Behind her, a shot rang out. Another sounded nearby. The scent of black powder drifted in the air. Horses whinnied and sabres hissed. People began to run—as much to begin the march as to escape the dragoons. Gasping for air, Prudence could do nothing but move forward with the surge.

Now the rain rushed down in chilly cascades. A woman running near Prudence slipped in the mud and tumbled onto the road. Prudence reached for the woman but missed the open hand as the crowd pushed her onward.

Forever, it seemed, she ran. Up Lancashire Hill and down again toward Stockport. Now the clot of people loosened and began to break apart. But a scream from the rear sent them into a mad dash once again.

"Dragoons! Dragoons! Run for your lives!"

Prudence picked up the pace again. Looking over her shoulder, she saw a white horse bearing down. The soldier's eyes fastened on her. His saber cut through the rain as he dismounted. A hand grasped her shoulder, an arm hooked around her waist. She cried out as he dragged her across the muddy road and out onto the wet bracken.

Brushing rain from her eyes, she struggled to stand. But a dark cloak fell across her face, blocking the light. Screaming for help, she fought and scratched the dragoon as he bundled the cloak around her head. Then he rolled her into the cloak so tightly that her arms could no longer move. She felt herself heaved into the air and tossed across something so hard it crushed every last breath from her lungs.

Stars sparkled before her eyes. Pain in her stomach made her gag. The object across which she lay began to move, rocking her and jarring her spine. A horse! Her senses reeled with the smell of damp woolen blanket and polished leather saddle.

Choking out a sob, she laid her cheek against the horse's flank. Trying to pray, she fought the fears of what might lie ahead. *"Offenders therein shall be adjudged felons . . . ,"* the Riot Act declared, *"shall suffer death."* Her future might hold nothing more than a dark prison cell, a trial before a magistrate, or worse.

Even now, her peril was great, for the dragoon had her in custody. She could do little to protect herself against him.

Forcing herself to think of other things—Sarah and Mary, tea at Delacroix House, Miss Pickworth's silly alliterations in *The Tattler*—Prudence was unprepared when the horse suddenly halted. A rough hand grasped the cloak that covered her head and gave a yank.

She looked up into the face of the man who had captured her. It was the face of William Sherbourne.

Sixteen

"William?" Prudence gasped. "But what are you doing here?"

"I might ask the same." Though boiling with anger at the woman's trickery and deception, William was shocked at her appearance. Prudence's face had gone pasty white. Her hair was a sodden tangle, her boots and skirt up to the knees in mud.

Still unwilling to show even the smallest spark of tenderness, William lifted her down from the horse and set her upright. Taking Prudence by the arm, he propelled her through the door of an inn he had noted on his mad dash through the small town.

Though Prudence trailed a long muddy path across the wood floor, William pressed her onward toward the brick fireplace. Coming at last to an empty table, he pulled out a chair and deposited her into it.

"Do not move," he enunciated firmly. "If you are not here on my return, I shall send the commander of the King's Dragoons to hunt you down, arrest you, and throw you into the darkest gaol in England. Do you understand?"

Looking at him with luminous green eyes, Prudence nodded. "I am so sorry to have troubled you."

"*Troubled* me? Is that how you think of it?" Loath to demean himself by expressing aloud the full measure of his wrath, William turned on his heel and strode back across the room. He beckoned the innkeeper and ordered a meal of thick potato soup, fresh bread, strawberries, and tea. Then he ascended a narrow staircase and knocked on the nearest door.

Walker opened it, emerged into the corridor, and greeted his employer. "Did you find her, sir?" the blacksmith asked in a low voice.

"I did. She sits below."

"I am relieved." Walker nodded toward the door. "Come in, if you will. Bettie wishes to thank you for saving her life."

"I did nothing of the sort," William retorted. "Tell Bettie if she wishes to thank me, she will recover her good health, return to Otley, and marry you at once."

Walker's craggy features softened into a smile. "Thank you, Mr. Sherbourne. You may be sure that is our plan."

William was not sure at all. Had he not discovered Prudence Watson consorting privately with the blacksmith on two occasions? Clearly, whatever love once existed between the two had not died.

No matter the blacksmith's plans to marry the little weaver, nor the young lady's professions of passion for William himself. Truth won out too often, just as it had an hour ago when he rode into town and spotted Walker carrying Bettie—limp and unconscious—in his arms.

The blacksmith had called out, begging William to follow the throng of marchers and rescue Prudence Watson. Even as he rode through the rain, William had struggled to accept the truth. Prudence had lied to him and misled him in every possible way, for Polly Watson the spinner was indeed none other than Prudence Watson.

"I shall cover your expenses here," William said. "Stay as long as necessary."

"Thank you, sir." Walker rubbed his brow for a moment before continuing. "Mr. Sherbourne, I know you rode to Manchester in the hope of halting disaster. You must understand that Miss Watson accompanied the worsted mill workers for the same reason."

"She intended to halt the very disaster she provoked? That is nonsense, man."

"But I speak the truth."

"I am sorry to inform you that I have lost faith in such an avowal. Truth, it seems, is an elusive and malleable quantity."

"Whether you believe me or not, I must attempt to assure you that Miss Watson's aims were pure and her activities innocent."

"Innocent!" William laughed. "Spare me this discourse, Walker, I pray you."

Lest the blacksmith make further effort to defend the woman he loved, William held up a hand. Chuckling in bitter disbelief, he turned away and descended the stair.

As he neared the fire, he saw that the meal had been brought and laid out on the table. But Prudence sat huddled inside his sopping cloak, her head bent and eyes closed. Was she asleep? or praying? It hardly mattered.

"Eat," he commanded, seating himself across from her. "Eat, for the coach I ordered will arrive shortly."

Her eyes fluttered open and she stared at him. "I am not hungry," she murmured.

"Yet you *will* eat." He lifted the lid on the tureen and dipped a ladleful of soup into her bowl. "I should not like for you to die just yet, Miss Watson. I must return you to Thorne Hall, set you in a carriage for London, and assure myself that you are gone from Yorkshire forever. Then, if you wish, you may perish with my full blessing."

"You *want* me to die?"

"Certainly—if that is your aim."

He stirred sugar and milk into his tea and took a sip. Though the woman's face had drifted nightly through his dreams, now he found he could not bring himself to look at her. Instead, he took a slice of bread, buttered it, and set it beside his empty bowl.

"I prefer you to die of pneumonia rather than hunger," he told her. "Then you will be faulted for it and not I."

"I see how much you loathe me."

"On the contrary. You cannot possibly understand the depth and breadth of my revulsion."

"Nor do you know the full measure of my disgust and abhorrence toward you."

At this, he looked up. She was gazing at him, unblinking. He set his teacup on the table.

"Am I to know the cause of such profound hatred?" he asked.

"I believe I have done nothing but rescue you from various and sundry muddy thoroughfares, escort you to picnics and dances, court you with far more passion than was wise, and generally behave the besotted fool. Is it for these reasons you choose to revile me?"

"No, indeed," she said. "You have done everything by the book."

"By the book? And which book is that? I believe you once asked me to read the book of St. John. I did so and made a great attempt to transform myself accordingly."

"If, as you claim, you did read that Gospel, you would know that a man can do nothing to transform himself. Change is wrought only by faith in God."

"And you claim to be a woman of faith? a bondservant of Jesus Christ Himself?"

She looked away. "I am far from perfect, as you well know. Yet, I do try to live in accordance with His teachings."

"I have no recollection of Christ instructing His followers to travel about in disguise and create mischief wherever possible while deceiving and betraying those who love them most. In which chapter and verse might I read such a holy command?"

"You are angry with me, and I accept your wrath. I must assume my sister Mary wrote to you, informing you of my activities and begging you to put a stop to them. Mary was not happy at my leaving London, and I cannot fault her for divulging my secret. Her worry was justified, as is your hostility. Yet, I may defend myself with one claim. My deeds arose from pure motives. Can you say the same of all your conduct?"

He studied the crackling fire. A log shifted and fell, shooting a spray of bright red sparks. He reflected on the happy family he had left behind at Thorne Hall. How easy Randolph and Olivia were together. How well they blended, each admiring and honoring the other.

Such serenity would never belong to William. Prudence was correct in her assessment. He had rarely acted from pure motives. His life until now was lived for one purpose only—self-pleasure.

"Eat your soup," he said finally. "It grows cold."

She shook her bent head. In a moment, he heard a sniffle. He turned to her, startled to find that a tear had trickled down her cheek and now hung from the tip of her nose.

Dear God, do not let her weep, he prayed in silence. *Anything but that. You cannot expect me to forgive her any more than I have forgiven myself.*

"God will forgive me," she said in a soft voice.

"What?" He barked the word, startled that her statement was a direct response to his plea.

Her thin hand slipped out from the cloak and brushed away the tear. "God will forgive me," she repeated, "but I know you never will. I am guilty of everything you suppose about me."

His thoughts flashed back in time to the night he had witnessed her kissing Walker's hand as they stood outside the inn at Otley. Again at Delacroix House, she and Walker had met in secret, hiding in the shadow of a tree.

"So you admit that all my accusations and charges against you are true?" he asked.

"Indeed. In fact, it is possible that you do not know the half of my wickedness."

"I suppose I might ask you to enlighten me further. But I fear I have heard and witnessed enough already."

"Thank you," she whispered. "I have already given my

account to God, and I shall be compelled to give it again to my sisters. Twice is quite enough to dampen any defense I might wish to make on my own behalf."

So saying, she dipped her spoon into the soup and brought it to her lips. William ate his buttered bread, enjoying it not at all.

Why did he feel so very bad when Prudence was the one who had lied to him and betrayed him? He sipped at his tea, wishing its warmth would comfort his heart as well as his stomach.

"I have decided I must tell you one thing that is very bad," Prudence said as she set her spoon on the table. She dabbed her napkin beneath her eyes. "I fear you do not yet know that you have lost all your employees."

William did know, of course. Richard Warring had announced it, and the mass of marching peasants had confirmed his report. Yet he felt his bitterness toward her rise again.

"Really?" he asked. "I have *lost* my employees? Can you tell me where I might have misplaced them?"

To his dismay, she smiled. "They journey toward London to take a petition to the king. A petition about the Gag Acts."

This he did not know. "The suspension of *habeas corpus*? The arrest of men who publish seditious treatises? This is why they march?"

"The mill laborers want the freedom to assemble in groups larger than twelve. That wish arises from the desire to force employers to pay better wages, provide a safer and cleaner workplace—"

"And tea and cakes? Is that inscribed on the petition they take before the king?"

Now she giggled. To his consternation, her cheeks had turned pink from the warmth of the fire. Her curls, brought to life by the damp air, framed her face in a golden halo. The cloak had fallen from her shoulders, and he could see the beautiful neck that had so entranced him.

"The workers at Thorne Mill cannot complain on that account," she said. "I am told they enjoy tea and cakes every day."

He wondered if she knew about the other reforms he planned to make. Had his overlookers bothered to inform the workers, or had Warring lied about this?

"I should think a ten-hour day, a school for the children, and better food might have kept them from their march," he said. "Or were they so determined to gather in groups of more than twelve that they disregarded such improvements altogether?"

"Had they been offered this sort of hope, sir, I am sure any illusions about appearing before the king would have vanished. I did all I could to dissuade them from their course, for I feared it would come to naught. Now they are attacked, arrested, even killed for a dream that could never come true. Worse, they have disgraced themselves and forfeited their positions at the mills."

"Indeed they have."

She stirred her tea. "I had no success in convincing them not to march," she said after a moment. "Perhaps I will have no success in begging you to take them back. Yet I must plead for them."

"Spare me your entreaties," he said. "I shall manage my laborers as I see fit."

"Yet your management caused them to flee the mill and unite with the Blanketeers."

"Excuse me, but I believe it was *your* inflammatory and seditious troublemaking that caused them to flee the mill."

"You flatter me, sir. I may have some small influence upon

those I meet, but I am hardly the sort of woman to command their obedience."

"Too silly, are you?"

Her green eyes flashed. "Perhaps I am silly," she said. "At least I am not evil."

"Evil? By the expression of distaste on your face, I must presume you think of me so."

"'Wherefore by their fruits ye shall know them.' Matthew 7:20. You will find it in the Bible."

At that, he stood. "You may quote the Bible, Miss Watson, when you begin to live by its teachings. Until then, please forgive me for ignoring you."

Unwilling to allow her another moment to castigate him, William strode across the room to the door. He must see to his horse—at this moment, the only creature alive he felt certain he could abide.

◆

"Will you join us in the drawing room, Miss Watson?" As she spoke, Olivia gently touched Prudence's arm. "The chill air here in the garden cannot be good for your fragile health."

"It is nothing but a cold, Lady Thorne, I assure you." Prudence dabbed her nose with a lace-trimmed handkerchief. In the two days since returning from Manchester, her voice had grown hoarse and her nose began to drip. She was mortified at the idea of sniffling her way through tea while William Sherbourne glared at her across the table.

"Truly, I am well enough," she reiterated. "I enjoy watching the mists curl across the moor."

"Yet more than one young lady has been undone by a trifling

cold. Do come inside and warm yourself by the fire. I am sure we should all welcome your presence at tea."

"Thank you, madam, but I am quite sure of the opposite. I have made a fool of myself and caused your family no end of trouble. I cannot think of any way to apologize that might bring an end to this torment."

"My dear Prudence, you judge yourself too harshly. You intended your involvement with the mill to bring about nothing but good. How can you be faulted for that?"

"Very easily, I assure you. Your husband's brother will help you count the ways."

Chuckling, Olivia shook her head. "You must not think ill of William. He chastises you because it is much easier to be angry than to be in love."

Prudence gave a short, humorless laugh. "Love? Lady Thorne, you are mistaken indeed on that account. William hates me. I deceived him. I led the mill workers astray. I have been nothing but trouble to him from the moment he saw me tumble into a muddy puddle."

"You have troubled him, indeed, but I wager it is his heart that aches far more than his vanity. His mill will soon be serviceable again. I have no doubt that William intends to employ those workers who return to the mill, and all will be well. Better, in fact. Despite my dear husband's qualms, William's reforms can do nothing but increase productivity, build loyalty, and lure the very best of Yorkshire's weavers to his mill."

"Reforms?" Prudence shivered as she spoke the word.

Olivia slipped off her own shawl and wrapped it around Prudence's shoulders. "Did he not tell you? Well, you must ask him yourself, for see how he comes even now? William—how happy I am to find you in the garden! Perhaps you can persuade Miss Watson to join us for tea, where I have been utterly unsuccessful. And you must tell her about your reforms, for I have just learned that she knows nothing at all about them. But do not tarry long. Tea waits for no one!"

With a brief wave, Olivia hurried off toward the great house and the warmth of its massive fireplaces.

William turned a stony gaze on Prudence. "I wish to inform you that your sister has sent a message to me by courier. I received it just now in the library. Mrs. Heathhill writes that she will arrive at Thorne Lodge tomorrow morning. She asks me to tell you that she intends to depart the same afternoon, taking you with her and intending never to return to Yorkshire lest her family incite further calamity upon mine."

Though Prudence had been at Thorne Lodge for the better part of two days, this was her first encounter with William. Sequestered in her room, she had been nursing her cold with ample rest and much reading. His sister-in-law had informed Prudence that William was meeting with his overlookers in the effort to put his mill back to rights. Now she saw by his glowering expression that his wrath had not abated.

"Thank you for relaying the message," she said, dipping him the slightest of curtsies. "I am sure Mary cannot come too soon."

"I assume your sisters knew of your ruse."

"They did—and tried to steer me from it. You must not blame them."

"No, indeed. I am content to lay all the fault upon you."

Though she felt sure she should shrink into herself with humiliation, Prudence discovered that her own ire prevented it.

"You enjoy my misery," she stated. "This does not surprise me. I believe your greatest happiness arises from abusing others and making them feel as wretched as possible."

The brown eyes sparked. "Do you speak only of yourself, or do you include the entire human race in your catalog of those whom I have abused?"

"Not everyone," she replied. "Yet you have caused more than enough pain and despair to those whose lives you have tainted."

Prudence read the flicker of guilt that crossed his face. William knew he had been the cause of much agony. He was well aware of his grave sins—not only in regard to the late Miss Bryse, but also toward his own child, abandoned by the father he would never know.

"You are a wicked man, William Sherbourne," she declared. "But I cannot hate you. Rather, I pity you the joy and satisfaction you might feel had you behaved in a more gentlemanlike manner throughout your life."

"Wicked. Evil. These are the labels you paste on me. Not long ago, you told me you had ceased to see the world in black and white. You confessed that your own sins had made you aware of the gray morass into which most of us fall. Yet now I see you have reverted to your former position. You call me evil, and by that pronouncement, you elevate yourself to the opposite character. You are good. Perfect, in fact."

"I am hardly faultless, sir," she snapped back, turning her shoulder on him. "You know that only too well. I am guilty of many things, yet your wrongs are far graver than mine."

"Are they? And how is that?"

"You ruin lives."

"By operating a worsted mill?"

At this preposterous response, she whirled on him. "Do you think I speak of the mill? No, indeed! You are a bad man where *women* are concerned, and I have no doubt you will suffer greatly for your iniquities."

"And you are a good woman where *men* are concerned? Spare me your self-righteous indignation, madam. I am the witless buffoon who has succumbed to your wiles so often as to realize at last your duplicitous nature. You, Prudence Watson, are the wicked one."

"Wicked?" She covered her mouth with her hand, recalling suddenly the endless line of men with whom she had toyed, her secret trysts with Mr. Walker, and her dalliances with William even as she plotted to bring about the downfall of his mill.

"Oh, you are right," she blurted. "I am bad. Perhaps as bad as you but . . . but . . ."

"Who is good, Prudence? Who is truly good but God Himself? And which of us is good enough to please Him? Who may stand before Him guiltless? None. I cannot rattle off Scripture so easily as you, yet my reading of the Epistle to the Romans taught me that all have sinned, and St. John's Gospel assured me that Jesus Christ provides our only path to God. No one approaches the Father apart from Him."

"Yes, Christ makes us clean," she agreed, humbled at the recognition of her many failings. "You have read more of the Bible than I supposed, and you are quite right about our sin. All the same, God loves us. He did not go to the trouble of sending us His Son merely to point out our transgressions. I am convinced that Christ came to save us, to die in our place. Anyone who trusts in Him is acquitted."

"Acquitted? Do you believe that, Prudence? Do you truly believe it?"

The somber tone of William's voice took her by surprise. "Of course I do," she said softly. "If we but ask, God forgives all our sins."

"All?"

She thought of the abandoned baby. "Forgiveness is an odd thing. God pardons us if we ask, yet He rarely removes the earthly consequences of our wrongdoing. For some, the penalty spreads, afflicting everyone around us with pain and sorrow."

"I imagine God must find it rather easy to forgive. It is far more difficult for others to pardon us and for us to pardon others. Forgiving ourselves is hardest of all."

"Yet not impossible."

With that, he bowed. "I wish you good afternoon, Miss Watson. I am to be away from home on business all day tomorrow. It is unlikely we shall meet again."

As he turned to walk away, Prudence called out. "William!"

He halted. When he faced her again, she saw agony written in his eyes and suffering in the turn of his mouth. "What is it, Prudence?"

"Reforms. Olivia spoke of reforms at your mill. She said I must ask you."

"I described the reforms to you already. A ten-hour workday. A school for the children. Better food. My employees' rebellion had nothing to do with my instituting reform. They have you to thank for the improvements. I was swayed more by the petitions of a pretty girl. My laborers' seditious march threatened my resolve, but I concluded that the changes are for the best. Good day."

Stunned, Prudence watched him walk away. A ten-hour day. Better food. A *school* for the children!

"Upon my word," she murmured. "I succeeded after all."

❖

William made every effort to be out when Prudence and her sister left Thorne Lodge. Early the next morning, he rode to the mill alongside his brother. Randolph was in a jolly humor, eager to tease William and joke about one thing after another—though his mood was little appreciated by the younger Sherbourne.

Both men were gratified to find most of the looms, carding engines, spinners, and other machinery back in operation. Shamefaced, none of the laborers dared to look up from their work as their masters inspected the building from the smithy upstairs to the waterwheel below.

"She will be gone when you return to the house," Randolph observed as he and William sat on a low stone wall beneath the mill to watch the massive wooden wheel turn. "Did you not wish to bid her farewell?"

His brother was speaking of Prudence Watson, of course. Despite the woman's treasonous deceptions, both Randolph and Olivia persisted in making references to her beauty, her keen wit, her good intentions toward the needy, her happy financial situation, and her family's beneficial connections in society. In short, they did everything but insist that William propose marriage to the young lady at once.

"I bade her farewell yesterday," he told Randolph. "It was a weighty conversation for two people so prone to being frivolous. We discussed the Bible."

Randolph shot him a look of disbelief. "And how did you find it?"

"Mysterious but true."

With a laugh, Randolph elbowed his brother. "Come, man, enough of your nonsense. When do you plan to see her again?"

"I have uncompromising plans *never* to see her again."

"But you love her. More to the point, she loves you. You witnessed the mighty battle I fought to win my dear Olivia from the clutches of those who tried to part us. Will you let Miss Watson escape without putting up the smallest effort to keep her?"

"She does not want to be kept, nor do I wish to keep her."

"Because she upended your tidy little world of mill, moor, and hearth?"

"My world has never been tidy, brother. You know that better than most."

Randolph fell silent for a moment before speaking again. "William, you are not the same man you were before this last outing with the Royal Navy. Did something unpleasant happen that you have not told me?"

"At sea? No, indeed. I am a fine officer. I make my king proud at every opportunity."

Randolph laughed. "I am sure you do. But what about ashore? I met the two Bryse sisters—both of whom admired you—and I heard rumors of other women who esteemed you greatly. I begin to wonder if you lost your heart to one of them."

William reflected on the face of Caroline Bryse as she lay dying. It was not his heart that had been lost at that moment. It was his youth, his naiveté, his careless immorality, his swaggering love of himself above all others.

"If you will allow me to keep one or two secrets from my elder brother," he told Randolph, "then I shall be much obliged. Have no fear on behalf of my good humor. I assure you, it is quite intact."

"But you will talk to me if the need arises? As the eldest of three, I am not accustomed to taking lightly anything amiss with my brothers."

"Be assured—"

The clattering of wooden clogs on the iron stairs near the waterwheel halted William's words. He turned to find Richard Warring bearing down on them.

"Sirs, I beg you to come above!" the overlooker cried out. "She is returned! That woman is returned even now!"

"Who is returned?" Randolph asked.

William already had guessed. "Miss Watson, I believe, pays a final visit to the scene of her great insurrection."

"Indeed she do, sir!" Warring was breathing hard. "She allowed as she came to bid the others farewell, but I don't believe a word of it. No, sirs, I think she is come to inflame the labor again and make them run off to London with her!"

"Thank you, Warring," William said as he stood. "I shall see to it that our guest minds her manners. You are dismissed."

As the man pounded back up the stairs, Randolph shook his head. "You must see Miss Watson again in spite of your good intentions to avoid her."

"She avoids me as much as I avoid her. Contrary to the assertions made by you and your dear wife, Miss Watson and I do not like each other."

Starting for the stairs, William heard his brother chuckling behind him.

"That, my dear man," Randolph said, "is a bald-faced lie."

"Half of it at least is true," William called back over his shoulder. "We do avoid each other."

"And how very well you succeed at it!" Randolph replied, laughing as his brother vanished from view.

Seventeen

"Good morning, Miss Watson."

Startled at the sound of William's voice, Prudence swung around. "Mr. Sherbourne! You are here."

"It is my mill—should I not be here?"

"Of course you should be here, but I did not expect you." She fumbled out the words while searching vainly in her bag for a handkerchief. "I have been here but a few minutes."

"Jimmy?" William called over her shoulder. "Have you a spare billy for Miss Watson? She has returned to her position, and I daresay we shall be glad of the help."

Prudence gasped. "But I—"

"Do not trouble yourself to apologize," William went on. "I am well aware of your tendency to tangle and snarl the thread on your spindles. Fanny, please make an effort to be patient with Miss Watson as you continue to train her. She is not as quick to learn as some, but keep at it, and she may be taught in time."

"Sir!" Prudence said, cutting in lest poor Fanny swoon from the shock of her master's orders. "I have not come here to—"

"Dear Miss Watson, spare your breath," he interrupted, holding up a hand. "I am well aware of your concern for your fellow spinners. I understand your reluctance to take the place of another who may need the income more than one so prosperous and favorably connected among London's *haute ton* as you. But I am certain Jimmy can make use of you at the billy. I have been told it is quite possible that some of my laborers may reach the king and never come back."

This remark took her by surprise. "Some are marching still?"

"Indeed. Several Blanketeers reached the bridge at Stockport, while a very few have struggled on as far as Macclesfield and even Ashbourne in Derbyshire. I admire their fortitude."

"I am sure you do, Mr. Sherbourne," she agreed. "One who lacks certain qualities usually admires them in others. But let me assure Jimmy and my other acquaintances that I would do nothing to hinder their progress toward the production of your fine worsted. I stopped by the mill, in fact, to express my joy over the many beneficial reforms you have instituted and to bid my friends a fond farewell."

She found her handkerchief at last, drew it from her bag, and waved it at the workers, who stood gawking at her and their master.

"Mr. Sherbourne," she continued, dabbing her nose with one hand and taking his arm with the other, "I beg you to accompany me to my carriage, for I am sure my sister would wish to greet you, as would our dear friend Henry Carlyle, Lord Delacroix, who accompanied her to Yorkshire. Henry finds it difficult to be away from me, you know, and I am loath to be parted long from such an amiable man. He is never rude or impolite, as some men are, but always warm and witty. The perfect gentleman, in fact."

By now Prudence had steered William across the mill to the door. As they stepped outside and began to descend the steps, she lowered her voice.

"You have had your revenge on me, sir," she told him, "and I am as ashamed as you ever wished me to be."

"I hardly think so." He paused, drawing her closer. "You rarely do anything I wish."

"You wish me to be quiet and pretty and amiable. I wish you to be moral and well-mannered. We are neither good enough to please the other."

She looked into his eyes—a mistake, she realized as soon as she had done it. He was gazing at her with the fondest and most tender expression she had ever seen on his face. A smile tilted the corners of his mouth and warmed his eyes into pools of melted chocolate.

At that moment, she became aware of her hand—which had somehow been taken by his. His fingers tightened as he leaned against her.

"Prudence," he whispered, "I like you very much the way you are. If you were quiet, pretty, and amiable, I should not like you half so well."

"Am I not pretty?"

"No, indeed. You are beautiful, and you know it."

"Still, it is nice to hear, even from my sworn enemy. Though

I will say that, of late, both your morals and your manners seem to be improving."

"Not too much so, I hope."

"Just enough. I am glad you read St. John. It gives me hope."

"That I will be spared the flames of hell?"

"That I may learn to forgive the bad you have done."

His smile faded. "That, I fear, is impossible. And so, Miss Watson, we are back to our beginning again. I recall that we agreed to be friends."

"Chums," she reminded him.

"As comfortable as a pair of old shoes." His eyes softened again. "But I am not quite moral enough to send you off with just a handshake, one chum to another. I pray you may forgive me one last indiscretion."

Before she could respond, he pulled her into his arms and kissed her cheek. And then her lips. And then she slipped her arms around his neck and kissed him back with all the pent-up fervor and anguish that roiled inside her.

"Excuse me!" Mary's voice splashed cold water down Prudence's spine. "Mr. Sherbourne, how unexpected it is to see you again, for we were assured you had gone away on business. But here you are!"

Prudence broke away from William in time to see that Henry and her sister had stepped down from the carriage and were fast approaching.

"Mrs. Heathhill, delighted," William said, offering a bow. "And Lord Delacroix. How nice to see you again. The tea trade is flourishing, I hope?"

"It is indeed." Henry took Prudence's arm and tucked it

under his own. "And how fares your worsted mill? We are told there was an unexpected exodus of your labor."

William glanced at Prudence. "A brief bump in the otherwise smooth operation of the mill," he replied. "It seems my workers were inspired to play out a French Revolution in miniature. A lovely Napoleon led the revolt, and the poor king narrowly escaped a beheading."

"Reformation swept through the kingdom," Prudence added, detaching herself gracefully from Henry. "'Liberty, equality, and fraternity' may not have been achieved in full, but I am quite sure the insurgency accomplished its aims."

"And I am quite sure we should be on our way again," Mary spoke up. "My dear sister is the one who has nearly lost her head. Before it is completely gone, we must hurry to London and its more genteel pursuits."

"I wish you Godspeed, then," William said.

Now his brother had emerged from the mill and was moving toward the group. But as Mary and Henry stepped into the carriage, William set his hand at Prudence's waist and drew her near.

"Despite my best intent," he murmured against her ear, "I love you still."

At words she had longed to hear, Prudence trembled. A curl of longing settled in her chest. "I love you, William," she whispered, knowing she would regret it.

"I shall never forget you," he vowed.

He helped her up into the carriage and shut the door. His brother clapped a hand on William's shoulder as both men stood back. The carriage started with a jerk, and the horses began their long journey. Prudence leaned back into the leather seat and closed her eyes.

"Take this," Mary ordered, nudging her and holding out a clean handkerchief. "I shall pray that what I witnessed just now was the result of a fevered brain and its unstable thoughts. I shall pray, in fact, that your head cold grows exceedingly worse and that eventually we may all agree you were not in your right mind as you departed Yorkshire."

"I cannot believe your younger sister will concur with that, Mrs. Heathhill," Henry said. "Miss Watson appears quite lucid, in fact. I suspect she will not wish it spread about that she ever lost her reason."

Prudence blew her nose and dropped her head back on the seat. She did feel ill. Very ill. But she could not pinpoint the source of her condition. Head or heart?

Chums, she thought and sneezed.

◆

"Pru, are you awake?" Sarah slipped into the room and stood in the shadows. "I did not wish to disturb you, but you have a most persistent caller."

"A caller?" Prudence rose from the bed, her spirits lifting. "Who is he? Tell me at once!"

"Lie down, dearest." Sarah pressed her onto the pillow where she had spent the past week. "Calm yourself, I pray. Your caller is not a man. Elizabeth Fry wishes to pay you a visit."

"Betsy is here?" Though this was not the visitor she had hoped for, Prudence was delighted to hear the name. She endured a short spell of coughing before demanding more information from Sarah. "Does she know I am ill? Would she mind coming to me?"

"Mrs. Fry informed me in no uncertain terms that she longs to speak with you. I tried to dissuade her, but to no avail. She vows she spends most of her time in the company of ill prisoners or ill children, and you will be no threat to her health whatsoever. She is determined to talk to you—if you will have her."

"Of course," Prudence said, rubbing her temples as though that might somehow ease the pounding in her head. "I should love to see her."

Sarah frowned as she gazed at her younger sister. "I am very worried about you, Pru. You are not at all well."

"Yet I am content in my punishment."

"Punishment? Whatever can you mean? Surely you do not believe God is chastising you by making you ill."

Prudence looked toward the curtained window. "I told William that God forgives our sins, yet He allows us to endure their earthly consequences. This is my penalty for rousing the mill workers and then accompanying them vainly to Manchester in the driving rain. I should have a cold—or worse."

"Nonsense. You are certainly not being punished for your efforts at reform—which were successful, in case you have forgotten. And you must not wish worse upon yourself than this dreadful cold, which I fear grows more violent by the day."

"Thank you, Sarah. You have always believed the best of me."

"I shall send in Mrs. Fry. And do try very hard to get well, dearest. Mary is fretting wildly and predicting that you will perish, for her beloved Mr. Heathhill's final illness progressed in the same manner as yours. You must not prove her right."

Sarah left the room and was gone only moments, it seemed, before a knock fell on the door. Elizabeth Fry stepped inside, cast her gaze on the large bed where Prudence lay, and hurried to the younger woman's side.

"Oh, my dear child!" she exclaimed. "You are not at all well. Has a doctor seen you?"

"Daily," Prudence said, motioning her friend to a nearby chair. "Please make yourself comfortable, Betsy. I am not so ill as I might seem."

At thirty-six, Mrs. Fry was many years older than Prudence. Yet the two women had formed a strong bond of friendship, begun when they met during a reception for tea merchants at Delacroix House. Her husband was a banker who had invested heavily in tea—some of which belonged to the firm established by Henry Carlyle and Charles Locke.

Henry enjoyed Mr. Fry's company, though he and his wife were plain Friends who spoke to each other in a quaintly antique style. The Frys addressed their acquaintances in proper English, however, and this set all who met with them at ease.

In the drawing room after dinner that first evening, Mrs. Fry had told the enraptured Prudence about her efforts to better the lives of female prisoners. Their unlikely alliance continued primarily through letters, though they had taken tea together on several occasions.

"I fear you are very ill," Betsy said now, the sharp features of her face softening as she studied Prudence. "From the anteroom downstairs, I could hear your coughing. Your sister tells me that you believe God is punishing you for assisting the mill workers in the effort to improve their lot. I must assure you, my dear, that you are utterly mistaken in this."

"Thank you, Betsy. But I have not told my sisters a detail which I must now admit to you: this illness began during my clandestine labors at Thorne Mill. While working at the spinner, I was afflicted with a cough. Bits of dust and lint float about in the air, you see, and everyone working there breathes it in. What began as 'mill fever' continues now as this vile illness."

Betsy smiled tenderly. "You share the plight of your dear friends."

"Yet they have no money for doctors and cannot afford to lie abed day and night until they are healthy again."

"You feel guilty that your life is better than theirs. But do you not know that God created you just as you are for a reason? You have accomplished your purpose at the worsted mill—which is more than I can say of my own efforts at reform."

"If my task is done, then perhaps God will take me. Yet I should very much like to stay and . . ."

She looked down, realizing what she had nearly confessed aloud—that she longed to see William Sherbourne again and could not bear the thought of dying before she had.

"Did you know I have ten children now?" Betsy's clear voice filled in the silence. "A new one arrives every eighteen months or thereabouts. My seventh, sweet baby Elizabeth, died two years ago at age four, yet I count her among the rest. Mr. Fry and I have been married sixteen years, most of them happy ones. I have a grand home in East Ham, an enviable place in society, a husband whose reputation as a banker and a tea merchant are exemplary, and more than enough leisurely distractions to occupy my time. God has greatly blessed me. I assure you, my dear Prudence, there is nothing wrong with longing for a husband, a home, and children of your own."

"You see into my heart, Betsy."

"It is not difficult. You have the heart of a woman."

"Yet your effort to improve the lives of prisoners defines you as well. Mary told me that you have created a union to that effect."

"Indeed I have. It is called the Association for the Reformation of the Female Prisoners in Newgate. We conduct a prison school for children who must be locked away in the gaol with their parents. We provide materials so the ladies can sew, knit, and make other goods to sell. Our members take turns visiting the prison and reading the Bible to them."

"Perhaps I should join your cause."

"But you have your own! Do children still labor at mills all over England? Are they injured day after day? Does lint still float about? Do women perish of mill fever? You have improved *one* worsted mill, my dear, but this sacred isle is filled with them."

"How can one woman really do anything to better the lives of mill children? It is impossible. Only a law handed down from Parliament could . . ."

Her eyes on Betsy, Prudence's words described a vision as it unfolded before her. "A law . . . an act as powerful and far-reaching as the Riot Act . . . regulations and edicts regarding every aspect of the mills. There should be a law limiting the number of hours a child may work."

"Indeed there should," Betsy agreed. "Better yet, a law prohibiting children from such work at all. And why not?"

"The owner of Thorne Mill would tell you quickly why such legislation would be devastating. How would families earn enough to feed themselves? What would mills do without the labor of children? On and on he would rattle until finally you would begin to believe him. Yet it might be possible, Betsy. If Parliament passed such a law, people would find a way to comply with it."

"Good laws will always be obeyed."

"Oh, Betsy, I can see the regulations now! There must be a law ensuring that the air inside the mills is clean. A law requiring that the laborers have good, hot meals. A law limiting the number of hours a man or woman could work. Can you imagine?"

"Indeed I can. It is too bad women have neither the authority to sit in Parliament nor the privilege of casting votes. If we had, I am sure we should shortly set the kingdom to rights."

Prudence laughed at such a preposterous idea. Her laughter set off a bout of coughing, and Sarah hurried into the room bearing a clean spoon and a bottle of tonic.

"I am so sorry, Mrs. Locke," Betsy said. "I fear I am unable to go anywhere without rallying the masses—or inflaming the heart of one woman at a time. Your sister has a mighty spirit. God has endowed her with will, wit, and wisdom. She is a treasure indeed."

"Mrs. Fry," Sarah said as Prudence's coughing eased and the syrup's sedative compound began to take effect, "your work inspires us to do all we can to make the world a better place. What do you foresee for your own future?"

"I am no prophet, but when I was about Prudence's age, a woman in our Friends meeting prophesied about me. She said, 'You are born to be a light to the blind, speech to the dumb and feet to the lame.' I am sure my future holds the arrival of more children to keep me busy. Nevertheless, in addition to prison reform, I have decided to take up the cause of abolishing capital punishment. My brother joins me in this effort. We hope soon to put our appeal before the Home Secretary."

"I am told," Sarah said, "that Friends oppose war along with any sort of activity that might lead to death."

"Our aim is to prevent untimely death, Mrs. Locke, and I am deeply distressed by the plight of the homeless, who so often perish in winter's chill. I should like to establish a shelter where they might take nightly refuge. The predicament of the poor, as well, causes me no end of concern. I am praying that God may reveal a way to gather volunteers who would visit in the homes of the needy to provide assistance and comfort. Now, as for my interest in nursing—"

"Enough!" Sarah said with a laugh. "You have quite exhausted me already. My efforts to support the establishment of mission schools abroad are pitiable in comparison."

"I don't believe God compares His people, do you? He has awarded certain gifts and tasks to you, Mrs. Locke, and He has given others to me. With His mercy, you will accomplish yours to the best of your ability. As will I. And one day we shall hear Him say to each of us, 'Well done, thou good and faithful servant.'"

As Sarah escorted Betsy out of the bedroom, Prudence drifted in a peaceful ocean where everything had gone blurry about the edges. She saw Tom Smith's face and the dark fringe of his eyelashes. Now poor Davy Smith hobbled before her, his freckled cheeks marred by a layer of grime. Bettie, Fanny, Mr. Walker, Dick the Devil, Jimmy the spinners' overlooker . . . all floated in and out of her vision.

William, too, hovered just beyond reach. He held one hand out to her, calling her name, speaking words she could not understand. As her eyelids drifted shut, she thought she heard his voice.

"*I love you still,*" he whispered. "*I love you still.*"

"William, how long has it been since Miss Watson bade us farewell?" Olivia had stepped into the library at Chatham House, where coats of creamy new paint now covered every wall. William would take residence in her ancestral home within the month, and efforts to clean and brighten the place were well under way.

"Six weeks," William called down to Olivia from a rolling ladder that permitted access to the top shelves. "And five days. And . . ." He took out his pocket watch, opened the gold casing, and studied it. "And seven hours. Do you require minutes and seconds, as well?"

She chuckled. "No, indeed. But I now see that memories of the young lady cross your mind even more often than they do mine."

"Possibly. I think of her every five minutes. Three on Sundays. You?"

"At least daily."

"Aha—then I am the champion in this contest. But if you can tell me whether John Milton's *Paradise Lost* should be shelved with poetry or religion, I shall surrender my laurel wreath to you."

Tucking the dusty volume under his arm, William descended the ladder and leapt past the final three rungs to the floor, landing neatly at Olivia's feet.

"There you are," he said, holding out the book. "Study it at your leisure. When you have determined its proper place in the library, I shall put it there."

"It is poetry," she said, pushing away the proffered tome. "Weighty, inscrutable, depressing poetry. I began it three times, and I was never able to read past Mr. Milton's description of the great serpent."

"Then you cannot know the outcome of the tale. I shall enlighten you. While the serpent plays the villain, the woman is a scoundrel too by the name of Eve. The only other player in the drama is a feckless fellow known as Adam. In the end . . . well, let me just say that keeping one or two handkerchiefs might serve you well whilst reading the ending."

With a pretty tinkling laugh, Olivia took the book from him and tossed it onto a settee. "Without doubt, William, you are the very image of a naughty little brother. Of course I know the ending, as does anyone who has happened to sit still for five minutes in church. But perhaps that eliminates you."

"It did until Miss Watson worked her wiles on me. You may have noticed how eagerly I set my sails for Otley's church each Sunday. Reverend Berridge and I confer often about matters of great doctrinal import. Of late, I have even been known to read the Bible for hours at a time."

"Shocking!" She looped her arm through his. "But walk outside with me now, William dear, for I have news that requires fresh air and a clear mind."

William did not like the sound of that. He and Olivia strolled onto the wide stairs leading from the house down to the stretch of green lawn upon which she had played as a girl. Olivia had endured a difficult childhood and might have followed the path her mother took to an early grave. But she and Randolph met one day in church, and the course of true love was set.

William admired the couple. Envied them too.

"Am I to continue in suspense for some time?" he asked Olivia. "Perhaps you plan to walk about with me for a good while and then deliver your news after tea."

"You may have it now, though I should have preferred never to deliver it." She took a letter from her pocket and gave it to him. "This came today from Miss Watson's friend, Anne Chouteau, Lady Blackthorne. She addressed it to me, but I am convinced the message was intended for you."

Opening the letter, William tried to regulate his stumbling heartbeat. This would be news of Prudence, he felt sure.

"'Dear Olivia,'" he read aloud. "'My husband and I were delighted to pass so many happy hours with your family during our recent visit to Yorkshire. Your kindness and courtesy were immeasurable, and we reflect often on our memories of that delightful sojourn.'"

"She goes on this way for quite some time, William," Olivia inserted. "She already had written to thank me, but now she does so again—perhaps as a way of delaying the information which follows."

William scanned to the end of the letter. "'I regret to inform you that our mutual friend, Miss Prudence Watson, lies very ill. Her doctors say she is unlikely to recover her full health, though they hold fond hope of preserving her life. May I ask you, dear friend, to pray for her? And will you also please convey this information to her other acquaintances in Yorkshire? She was particularly attached to . . .'"

William could not continue reading. The image of Caroline Bryse's face as she lay dying swirled before his eyes. But now the image transformed and shifted until he saw Prudence there, pale and gasping for breath as she endured her final moments.

"I must go," he told Olivia. "I must ride for London at once."

"Of course," she said. "But are you steady enough to ride? I fear this news has shocked you. Let me order a carriage—"

"No. I thank you, but a carriage will not be quick enough." He folded the letter. "May I keep this?"

"It was meant for you."

"You will tell Randolph?"

"He knows already."

William looked at her. "Olivia, what shall I do?"

"Love her. That is all you can do. And it is all she wants." She squeezed his hand. "Go, William. Do not tarry a moment longer."

With a nod, he left her and made for his horse. The ride to London would clear his head and fuel his resolution to do all in his power to return Prudence to her former vigor—though he had no idea how he might accomplish such a thing when doctors had failed.

He barely glanced at the house as he strode through it toward the drive. Of what use was a grand new home, fresh paint, and a flourishing flower garden? Meaningless. Nothing mattered but the woman he loved.

He untied his horse and spoke a few words of calm as he stroked the animal's neck. Then he mounted and set off down the drive.

Nearing the road between Chatham House and Thorne Lodge, he spied a figure walking toward him at a fast pace. He soon recognized the man as Mr. Walker . . . the mill's blacksmith and Prudence's first love.

"Mr. Sherbourne, sir!" Walker hailed him from a distance.

"I must speak with you at once. Please grant me a few moments of your time."

The men regarded each other in silence. Then William reined in his horse. "What is it, Walker?" he asked. Even as he said the words, he felt sure he knew the answer.

"I have information, sir. Information you must hear before the day is out."

"Regarding?"

Walker let out a breath. "Mr. Sherbourne, I beg you to walk along with me in order to hear me out. The news must be kept private. Indeed, none may know of it but you."

Certain Olivia and Randolph already knew, William dismounted. The blacksmith must have had word of Prudence's illness. This fact in itself gave the attachment between Walker and Prudence precedence over William's own feelings for her.

"Very well, Walker," he said. "I am listening."

Eighteen

Exhausted, dusty, worn from riding all night, William pulled the bell cord outside Trenton House. He was surprised that a footman had not been stationed outside to await callers. Perhaps this foretold news he dreaded to hear—that the family was in mourning and not to be disturbed.

But the door soon opened and a maid put out her rose-cheeked face. "I'm sorry, sir, but the house has been closed up," she informed him. "My mistress is not in."

"Miss Watson? But where has she gone?"

"I am not at liberty to say, sir."

"Excuse me—what is your name?"

"Jane, sir."

He doffed his hat. "Jane, I am your mistress's dearest friend.

She will wish me to know where she has gone, and you will be glad you told me."

Her cheeks flushed a brighter pink. "Lord Delacroix's country estate," she blurted out. "In Derbyshire."

"Thank you, Jane." He put a coin in her hand. "You are a good, steady girl, and I believe you will go far in the world. Perhaps one day you will be housekeeper in this very home."

At this she laughed. "Me? Housekeeper?"

"And why not? Anything is possible these days, is it not?" He set his hat again and gave her a wink. "Good day, Miss Jane. I am sure we shall meet again."

Walking toward his horse, William pondered the information. He could not guess why the family would take Prudence to the country, but at least she was still alive. He prayed the clean air would serve as a healing balm. On the other hand, perhaps her sisters had done as many families did, removing their ill loved one to a remote place where her final days might be spent in privacy and silence.

◆

Reclining on a lawn chair plumped with cushions, Prudence tilted her face toward the sun. She had been trying with little success to sketch a yellow cat lying in the shade of a nearby clump of blossoming lavender. On the porch, Mary was playing with her baby daughter, their coos and giggles drifting on the light breeze. Sarah had gone to the market at Pentrich in search of Spanish oranges. Henry had been attempting to set up a white tent next to the rose garden—while the tent had enjoyed regularly toppling Henry into the thorny branches and making him yelp.

It was a pleasant enough afternoon, Prudence admitted,

though she felt restless and a little hungry. She glanced at Henry, who was now attempting to extricate his trousers from a pink rosebush.

"Shall we enjoy tea beneath your tent today, Lord Delacroix?" she called out.

"In time, yes," he muttered. "But first I must put this stake into the . . ."

His guttural curses faded, and Prudence smiled. She had learned to like Henry rather well. Sarah and Mary had declared that if their younger sister was well enough, a wedding must take place before the year was out. Even Charles had put in a good word for his tea-trading colleague.

Prudence had thought a good bit about marriage but settled against it. Her doctors had warned that even if she was ever well enough to take a husband, her fragile constitution might prevent her from successfully bearing children. In an effort to put this dire news out of her mind, Prudence had decided that any good health she regained must be seen as a gift from God—a gift that would permit her to resume her high calling to improve the lives of mill families.

Though she could not remember Betsy Fry's visits well, Prudence did recall an idea that had played endlessly through her fevered mind like a singsong chant—*a law, a law, a very good law*. She had even begun to hear a little tune, a jingling cadence that never failed to brighten her spirits.

"A law, a law, a very good law," she sang now in a low voice. Eyes closed, she drummed the rhythm on the arm of the wooden chair. "A law, a law, a very good law . . . The very best law that I ever saw . . . Take it away to Parliament . . . The very best law that ever was sent."

At someone applauding behind her, Prudence opened her eyes and tilted back her head. "William!" she gasped, nearly tumbling out of her chair. "Upon my word, you frightened me!"

"I beg your pardon," he said, stepping onto a rug spread out across the grass. "If I startled you, it was unintentional. I meant to startle Lord Delacroix. His antics are far more amusing."

Her heart hammering, Prudence glanced at the man who now sat beside her. He was as handsome as she remembered—brown hair curling at his neck, dark eyes studying her. His lean, athletic form stretched with ease on the rug, one knee crooked and an arm resting on it.

Did he know how very striking he was? Surely he did, and he had used his manly allure to woo the poor creature who eventually lost her life bearing his illegitimate child. As she gazed at him, Prudence reminded herself that she must try to abhor William for the awful things he had done. She had taught herself to think about that unfortunate woman as often as possible—and not to recall William's warm charm, tender words, strong embrace, and extremely . . . exceptionally . . . impossibly delightful kisses.

"How did you find me?" she asked him, breaking into her own forbidden thoughts. "I expected never to see you again and certainly not in Derbyshire."

"I apologize for failing to meet your expectations," he said, "but this visit could not be helped."

Despite herself, Prudence smiled at his familiar silly banter. "My *expectations* must not be equated with my *hopes*. You did not fail to meet the latter."

"That is happy news indeed." He studied her for a moment—

long enough that she became uncomfortable and reached for her fan.

"We had word from your friend," he continued. "She said you have been ill."

"Anne wrote to you?"

"To Olivia. Her message alarmed us all. As soon as I read the letter, I departed Chatham at once."

"Chatham? Do you live at Chatham Hall now?" She reflected on the grand manor house she had seen across the rolling moors. "Are you . . . alone?"

"No, no. My home is filled with laughter and song, people bustling about from attic to cellar. A jolly place indeed."

Prudence lowered her fan as she tried to imagine who might have moved into the home with William. Had he suddenly wed a widow with many children? Was he visited by friends who enjoyed revelries at all hours?

"But," he continued, "when the painters, window washers, silver polishers, and carpet beaters have thoroughly transformed the place, I shall move into it at last and rattle about on my own."

"Oh," she sighed. "I am relieved . . . that is, I am comforted to know you are not overwhelmed with visitors . . . and that sort of thing."

"Visitors can be a great nuisance," he concurred. "For some time now, I have been of the firm opinion that visitors and every other sort of caller should be outlawed."

"But then you would not be allowed to sit here and tease me, and I should miss that very much indeed."

His smile warmed her to the tips of her toes. "I should miss it too. I have missed *you*, Prudence."

"We did not part on happy terms. Have you yet forgiven me for my dismal charade as a spinner?"

"Forgiven you? Certainly not. Had you not become Polly the spinner, I should never have known how essential it was to sack Dick the Devil."

"You have dismissed him? Oh, I am very glad to hear it. I know Davy Smith's injuries were caused by his labor beneath the billy, yet I cannot help but think that Dick the Devil played a part in the poor child's suffering."

"Dick is gone, as is Polly. I say good riddance to them both. Polly, as you well know, was forever raveling her threads and tangling her spindles."

"But she was improving day by day," Prudence said. "Jimmy will tell you that."

"He did indeed. You are greatly missed at the mill. The workers always ask about you."

"Do they? I brought a great deal of havoc into their lives. The decision to join the ill-fated March of the Blanketeers was a direct result of my futile efforts at reform. Such a catastrophe."

"More than you know. I am told most of the aristocracy believes that the poison of the American and French revolutions led to the protest at Manchester. There is great fear that a similar revolution may be afoot in England."

"Good heavens. Have I been ill so long as to miss this news?"

"Have you not been reading Miss Pickworth? She is full of information on the inanities and idiosyncrasies of our artful aristocrats."

Laughing, she shook her head. "You certainly alliterate as well as Miss Pickworth. I shall have to begin suspecting she is your *nom de plume* and spare poor Mary from my accusations.

But you are right about my activities of late. I have been unable to muster interest in society's comings and goings. My chief focus has been the restoration of my health."

His eyes warmed to dark pools. "Prudence, I cannot bear to think of your suffering. Please tell me you are greatly improved."

"I believe I shall not expire just yet." She tried to read his expression. "But, William . . . I must ask if you know Bettie Barns. She is a weaver at your mill."

"Perhaps you refer to Bettie Walker?"

Prudence sucked down a breath as this revelation penetrated. So Mr. Walker and Bettie had married at last. It was done now, and she realized she was glad. Very glad for him, for his new wife, for their children, and even for herself. She could close the door on that chapter of her life forever.

"I know Bettie well," William was saying. "She has been employed at the mill from the start."

"Did you know she is ill? She suffers from mill fever." Prudence looked away, and her gaze fell on the cat. It had yawned and stretched and was now lying in an impossibly contorted pose beneath the lavender. "I, too, contracted mill fever. The journey to Manchester in the rain hastened its progress. My persistent cough became a trifling cold. My cold grew worse and led to a violent pneumonia that has rendered me little more than a helpless rag doll."

Prudence fell silent when William made no response. Rather than listening to her, he seemed to be watching Henry, who had just set the central tent pole into place—only to have the whole thing collapse on his head. Amusing though it was, William did not smile when he turned to Prudence again.

"Anne wrote that you nearly died. I understood at that

moment how much I love you." He looked away again. "I am sorry if my words of affection distress you. We are not meant for each other. Still, I thought you should know. I have never taken my feelings for you lightly."

"As you have for other women?"

He glanced at her, his eyes flashing. But in an instant his face sobered. "Yes, actually. Very lightly. I have been something of a rounder. A cad. And more. I was a gamer, risking everything to win at cards. I won often. I lost more often. I drank too much—at first to join the revelry, then to numb myself to my own failures. Finally, because I could not stop."

Her breath growing shallow as his words poured out, Prudence feared she might swoon. If she collapsed, she could blame it on her poor health. She was stunned—more by William's brutal honesty than by the facts he related.

"Midway through my last military mission," he continued, "we put out to sea. Our ship engaged in several skirmishes with the French. Responsibilities to my men ended my drinking. As you may imagine, there was no choice in the matter. On my return to Plymouth, I was clearheaded enough to comprehend the havoc I had caused there. Far more havoc, dear lady, than your well-intentioned protest march."

Prudence set down her fan, praying that William had concluded his declaration of guilt. If he went further, if he spoke of the poor dead woman, she did not know how she might bear it.

"Why are you telling me this?" she asked. "I cannot absolve you, and thoughts of such behaviors as you describe render me faint. I see now that you have been as licentious and wicked as ever I feared. I cannot imagine how I am to reconcile this information with my former good opinion of you."

"You held a good opinion of me?"

"I loved you, William, and I told you so."

"You told me more often how you despised my mill, my treatment of the workers, the very essence of my character. I believed you hated me far more than you loved me."

"I tried very hard to dislike you."

"Did you succeed?"

She closed her eyes, willing away any tenderness she felt for him. "I did succeed," she answered. Then she sighed. "And I also failed."

"Upon my word!" Mary's loud voice cut off William's response. "I am beyond astonishment. Mr. Sherbourne, such a surprise!"

He clambered to his feet and bowed. "Mrs. Heathhill, how delighted I am to see you again."

"And you are here with my dear sister. . . . How very . . . very unexpected!"

"I was commissioned by the Royal Art Society of Otley and Thereabouts," he quipped, "to judge the merits of Miss Watson's sketch of a . . . a cow."

"A cow?" Prudence cried, holding up her notebook. "It is not a cow."

"It is a dog," Mary opined. "One of our sweet corgis."

"I am sorry to disagree with you, Mrs. Heathhill," William said, "but I see it now. It is very clearly an elephant."

"An elephant!" Laughing, Prudence struggled to her feet. She pointed to the feline stretched out near the lavender. "It is a cat. *That* cat, to be exact."

"Aha, just as I suspected," William said, taking the sketch and studying it. "It is an elephant disguised as a cat—exactly the sort of clever artistry most admired by the Royal Art Society of Otley."

"And Thereabouts," Mary added.

Henry strolled over and took the sketch from William. "Very nice rendering of a fox," he pronounced. "Though it wants a sharper nose, I think."

"Give me that!" Prudence snatched the paper. "Go away, all of you. I must be left in peace, or I shall have no choice but to perish on the spot and make you rue your biting commentaries."

"That is a threat not to be taken lightly," William said, scooping Prudence up in his arms. "We must not allow you to perish, Miss Watson. Rather we must fortify you with the tea and cake that is even now being set out under Lord Delacroix's fine white tent."

"Oh!" Mary cried as William started across the lawn toward the tent. "Put her down! Put down my sister!"

Prudence's own exclamation of shock quickly transformed into giggles as she wrapped her arms around William's neck and laid her head on his shoulder. They entered the cool shade of the tent and he settled her into a chair. But not before brushing a soft kiss on her cheek.

"I am grateful you ever loved me at all," he murmured. "It is a treasured gift."

"Scones!" Mary squealed as she stepped under the canopy and observed the tea spread out on a table. "Thank heaven for scones. Without them I should simply fall to pieces."

"I am in pieces already," Henry declared. "I have never met a tent more determined to defeat me nor a rosebush more eager to tear me to shreds."

As the others chatted back and forth, Prudence quietly

sipped her tea. Now and again, she cast a glance at William, who—she soon discovered—was always gazing at her. It was, she decided, the most delightful tea she had enjoyed in many weeks.

Six, to be exact.

⬦

Seated near an open window, William listened to Mary Heathhill playing the pianoforte while her elder sister sang. Sarah Locke had a high, clear voice so sweet and lulling that it might easily charm a man into peaceful slumber. Henry Carlyle, in fact, had succumbed almost the moment he sat down.

William was far too restless. Filled with such anxiety that he could hardly endure lyrics about lost love and dashed dreams, he finally got to his feet. The song was in the midst of its second verse, and his unmannered movement caused Mary to fumble the keys. Yet he could do nothing but pace the carpeted floor.

Prudence had retired to her room after tea, and William had not seen her since. Her place at the dinner table had been empty. The chatter of her family and friends omitted any mention of the young woman—almost as if they had grown accustomed to her absence. He asked Sarah about her sister once, and she reminded him that Prudence was yet unwell and kept to her room.

Was that true? William raked a hand through his hair as he paused before the fireplace. Could it be possible that Prudence was so weak she could not come down to the dinner table? Was her health so fragile that anything more than a brief excursion in the garden might overwhelm her?

He recalled their ride across the moors—how easily her

horse had overtaken his, leapt a low rock wall, threaded its way through the woods. How beautiful and vibrant Prudence had been as she sat by the brook and coyly teased him until he was weak with desire. Had that woman vanished? Had Prudence suffered such infirmity that she could never recover her zest for life?

Not for his own sake did he lament the possibility. True, he had fallen in love with the vivacious golden-haired beauty. But his passion for her had deepened far beyond physical longing. He admired her noble ambitions, enjoyed her wit, took delight in her lively opinions, respected her intellect—

"I feared you might have grown lonely for the moors and returned to Yorkshire."

At the sound of her voice, William swung around and almost caught her up in an embrace. Only the sight of her pale face and tentative steps prevented him.

"Have I rendered you speechless?" she asked. "If so, I must count it as my greatest achievement."

"Prudence, I . . . I thought . . . I feared . . ." He shook his head. "I am glad to see you."

"I am gladder to see you," she countered as she gingerly sank into a chair near the fire. Her sisters continued playing and singing while Henry dozed. She studied them for a moment before returning her attention to William.

"If you had gone back to Yorkshire," she said, "I should not be able to share with you my theories regarding the American and French revolutions and their effects on England's restless working class. I should like to know if my effort at fomenting revolt inside your mill has had a similar far-reaching impact, for I am eager to take the credit for it."

Greatly relieved to find Prudence well enough to chirp away with her usual provocative views, William dropped into the chair beside hers.

"Discuss away, dear lady," he invited. "I shall neither challenge your declarations nor deny you credit for your successful crusade against injustice. Instead I shall simply gaze at you, thanking God you are alive and praying that He will heal you fully."

Her eyebrows rose. "What changes are these? How am I to speak unless I can be sure you will spar with me and dispute all my opinions? And what am I to make of this newfound respect for your Creator?"

He held his tongue for a moment, studying her beloved face, her green eyes, her sweet lips. "You may wish to speculate on political upheavals, but I have experienced a revolution more far-reaching. Mine is a revolution of the heart. You have the credit for this transformation, Prudence. Had you not dared me to read the Gospel of St. John, I might never have learned of Nicodemus. When Jesus told Nicodemus he must be born anew—not as a child from a womb, but as a man whose spirit is reborn—I began to wish that I might start my own life anew. My past, as you now know, is filled with many regrets."

As he finished speaking, William realized that Prudence had gone perfectly still. His concern for her well-being flared again, but she reached out and laid her hand on his.

"It is possible to be reborn, William," she said. "One can begin again."

"Yet you told me that many of us—certainly a man as vile as I—must endure the earthly consequences of wrongdoing."

"Sometimes."

"In my case, always." Unable to meet her unwavering eyes, he looked at the fire. "I accept this. My sin can be forgiven, but it cannot be undone. A revolution of the heart cannot wipe clean the slate."

"William . . ." She seemed to hover on the brink of a question she did not know how to ask. He surmised her curiosity had been piqued, and she wanted a more thorough account of his trespasses.

He leaned back in his chair, took her hand, fondled it gently. "I can speak of the past no longer. Let us talk of the future instead."

"You declared we can have none. What is left to say?"

"I shall speak of what I may. Mr. Walker came to me as I was riding out for London. My blacksmith wanted to report that restlessness still brews at the mill."

"Oh, dear."

"Walker has heard rumors that Sidmouth, the home secretary, has sent spies and informers to crisscross the land and investigate centers of discontent—among them, my mill. These scouts, Walker says, are paid by results."

"That cannot be wise," she said. "They may be tempted to become *agents provocateurs*."

"Indeed, it now appears these spies have begun fomenting rebellion in order to be rewarded. Walker fears these men have stirred to life the dying embers of the March of the Blanketeers."

"He has proof there are spies at your mill? He has seen them and heard them urge the people to mutiny?"

"He has not. The center of discontent, according to Walker, is at Pentrich."

"In Derbyshire!" She let out a breath. "Pentrich is not far

from the Delacroix estate. Barely two miles. Sarah went to the market there today in search of oranges. Is it possible the laborers are unaware that the very man who brews trouble among them is a spy who will report their discontent to the authorities?"

"Possible—I think not. It is probable."

"Then we must go into the town tomorrow. The people must be warned. I have to remind them that the Riot Act will doom them to expulsion or worse. They may be hanged."

"*We* shall go nowhere." William hardly knew whether to rejoice at the sudden color in Prudence's cheeks or to fear for her life. "You will stay here, and I shall stay with you until I am convinced that you are no longer in danger."

"But, William—"

"Shh!" he declared, laying a finger across her lips. "If you were in good health, I should happily beg you on bended knee to don your clever disguise, wander among the people, and flush out any agitators inciting them to rebel. But such a transgression would stain my newly washed heart with a very large blot. You inspired me to discard my gray world and begin to see it in black and white. I have decided I much prefer the white."

"I believed I was correct about the absence of gray," Prudence said, "and I am very certain gray can never be good. But, William, exposing a troublemaker can only be a noble deed."

"For one who is healthy, hale, hearty, and—"

"You, sir, have been reading far too much Miss Pickworth."

"I object!"

"An argument? A lovers' spat?" Henry, speaking through a yawn, stepped nearer the fire and bent to warm his hands. "Sherbourne, I hope you know that Miss Watson is quite attached to me. Her sisters prepare our wedding even now—for if you listen carefully, you will notice they are selecting music for the ceremony."

"What?" Prudence leapt to her feet. "Upon my word, Mary, I told you I am not going to marry Henry!"

Striding across the floor toward the pianoforte, she snatched up a sheaf of music that her sister had been following. The ensuing spat was observed with amusement by the two men near the fire.

"Miss Watson is suddenly quite energetic," Henry observed. "I believe you have wrought something of a miracle, Sherbourne."

"I did cherish the fond hope of restoring her to good health," William responded. "But I believe you, Delacroix, have the credit for this swift and unexpected display of vigor. The mere *thought* of uniting with you in the bonds of matrimony produced such horror and revulsion that she was instantly healed of all her maladies."

Henry threw back his head and laughed. "Quite right you are, Sherbourne! Well, you may have her with my blessing. I have set my eye upon another lady whose beauty and virtues trounce the attractions of any other."

"Ah," William said. "Is the fortunate lady someone you know by way of the tea trade? or via your illustrious position in society? Or perhaps she is some exotic creature who lured you whilst you circumnavigated the globe."

"The apple of my eye is a lady neither exotic nor particularly elevated in the *ton*. She is, in fact, quite well known to you."

"To me?"

"Indeed, for I believe you once rescued her younger sister from a mud puddle."

At that, both men looked across the room to where the woman in question was engaged in delivering a stream of eloquent admonitions to both her siblings. And William understood all at once that Henry intended to wed Mary Heathhill.

Nineteen

Hesitating, Prudence hung in the silence of the long dark corridor. She should not do this. A hundred reasons had presented themselves—all of them well-founded and sensible. Yet her heart spoke louder, urging and commanding her to act.

Swallowing hard, she knotted her hand into a fist and knocked. Nothing. She waited for almost a minute. Knocking again, she leaned closer to the door and listened.

The sounds of a grumbling voice and staggering footfalls made her smile. Relief poured through her as the muttering and thuds approached. The door opened.

"What?" William looked out, eyes squinting and hair tousled. "Who are you? What do you mean by waking me at this . . . Wait—is something wrong with Miss Watson? Is she ill?"

"No, I—"

He grabbed Prudence by the shoulders. "Take me to her. I must be allowed to see her. At once!"

"William, it is I—Prudence Watson."

His grip on her relaxed. "But you . . . ? You look like a maid."

"That is good news indeed, for I am going to Pentrich as a scullery maid. Dare you come with me?"

"No," he barked. "No, you are not going to Pentrich. Not tonight. Not ever."

She took a step back. "I *am* going, and I should very much like for you to join me. Look!"

Holding up a basket, she showed him a pair of ragged trousers, a patched shirt, and wooden clogs. "I took these from the line outside the kitchen. They are still a bit damp, but—"

"You are wearing damp clothes? In your condition! Prudence, are you mad?"

"Madly happy, for, you see, I have finally found good reason to live. As long as I tortured myself with accusations about my part in causing the march to Manchester and tormented myself for having turned you away, I could barely summon the strength to walk from one room to the next. But now look at me!"

"I see you—and you are still unwell, and you must go back to bed." He reached for her, but she danced away. He growled, "Prudence, do not make me shout. I shall wake the whole house."

"Do not shout," she sang out in a soft voice. "Follow me!"

As she started down the stairs, she heard him coming—muttering about damp gowns and wooden shoes and impossible women. Suppressing a laugh, she tiptoed past the wing of the house that Mary and her daughter had taken during

Prudence's convalescence. Now she was at the front door, but she thought better of it and made for the parlor to one side.

"Wait."

A hand clamped over hers as she reached for the handle of the long glassed door. From behind, William folded her into his arms and held her close. His breath warmed her hair and the back of her neck. His cheek pressed against hers.

How could it be, she wondered, that a man who had done so much wrong was so perfectly right . . . for her? How had she, who always tried to tread the good and moral and decent path, so easily forgiven a man who had walked the treacherous path to destruction for much of his life?

But was this not exactly what God did again and again? He so loved Prudence—and every other fallible wretch—that when any of them begged His forgiveness, He gave it. Gave it willingly. Gave it gladly. Gave with compassion and mercy.

"I love you, Prudence," William said. "If I lose you . . . if anything happens to you . . . if your health is endangered in any way—"

"Shh," she said, turning within his embrace and placing her finger on his lips as he had done hers not many hours before. "Let us trust God with our lives. Let us grant Him our faith."

"And your sisters? When they find us both gone, they will assume we have eloped to Gretna Green."

"Never fear. I left a note." She stood on tiptoe and kissed his lips. "Come, Will the stableman, for the moon is rising."

"Stableman?" he asked, linking arms with her as they slipped out through the side door and set off down the road. "I should at least like to be inside the house. A footman, perhaps."

"No, indeed. You will never make a good footman, for

you are too well formed to stand about in liveried silks while waiting to deliver messages or open carriage doors. You must work outside in the stables, lifting buckets of oats and shoveling—"

"I draw the line there, Polly the scullery maid. I shall be happy to carry oats, curry horses, or polish saddles, but I will not muck out the stalls."

She laughed. "You must do as I say, sir."

"Indeed, I must." He caught her around the waist and tugged off her mobcap. As her curls spilled onto her shoulders, she cried out and grabbed for the scrap of gathered cotton.

"Oh, William, you are very bad! It took me half an hour to hide all my hair inside that cap."

"I could not go on until I had seen your ringlets. Only they can assure me that you are you."

"Of course I am me! Who else would I be?" She snatched the mobcap from his hands. "Help me, William, for you are the cause of this calamity."

"With pleasure, my dear," he said, cupping a mound of glossy curls in his hand. But instead of continuing to tease her, he spoke in a low voice. "I never thought to have this privilege, Prudence. I never imagined that—"

A fit of coughing seized her all at once, stopping his words and nearly collapsing her onto the road. William caught her in his arms and held her until the spell subsided.

"Dear God," he murmured. "Dear God, do not let this illness go on, I beg You. I beg You!"

Prudence clung to William, drawing hope from his prayer and strength from his embrace. God would be with them, she knew. He was with them now. Even now.

⟡

Pentrich's market square was coming to life as Prudence left William for their separate missions. Hooking her basket over one arm, she began perusing the stalls. Fishmongers laid out salted eel, pickled herring, and dried mackerel. Dairymen arranged wheels of yellow cheese and stacked rounds of butter. The meat market occupied one entire side of the square, and Prudence glanced there now and again to reassure herself of William's presence.

He was examining the legs of mutton hanging from hooks, an array of plump ox tongues, a pig's head, a row of live chickens suspended by their feet, and several ham hocks. Greeting the butchers and poultrymen, he engaged them in amiable conversation. One, he slapped on the back as they laughed at some joke. Another seemed eager for a lengthy discourse.

"Mornin' to ye," an egg seller called out as Prudence passed by her makeshift stall. "These are fresh—still warm from the hen, in fact. See for yourself!"

Prudence hefted a couple of eggs, paid for them, and set them gingerly in her basket. A young woman nearby was assembling a display of vegetables—green beans, peas, tomatoes, leeks, and potatoes. Prudence picked up a bean.

"You must have planted early," she commented. "These look small but tasty."

"They are very sweet, I assure you. Try one, if you will."

"Thanks, but I am looking for cheese today."

"Yet, take a few beans, will you? I must sell them all, or my husband will join . . ." She fell silent and nervously began lining up her leeks. "He was a stockinger, you know."

"Ah," Prudence said, clucking in sympathy. She did not know what had happened to the woman's husband, but she could imagine. "So many are unwaged these days. I cannot blame the men for what they do."

"Nay, yet I wish they could find another way."

"A law," Prudence said. "A very good law or two should do it."

The woman laughed without mirth. "Next time I'm sitting in Parliament, I'll pass one for you."

"You are right—the idea is far-fetched. Still, a law must be better than a revolt."

"Without doubt. My sixth is unwell, and if aught becomes of her father, I cannot imagine but it will kill her straight out."

"Give me a measure of beans, then. Perhaps you can buy a tincture to ease her distress." She held out a few coins.

The woman had just taken them when another bout of coughing wracked Prudence.

"You're ill too," the woman said. "Wicked sick, by the sound of it."

"Mill fever," Prudence explained. "I was a spinner in Yorkshire."

"You're new here, I see, but you understand how we suffer." She dropped her voice. "Oliver has ordered the rising to begin tonight, and I wager my husband will be among the men."

Prudence was surprised at how swiftly the secret plans were revealed. If it was so easy for her to get information, surely the government must know too.

"I have never met Oliver," she said. "Do you know him well?"

"Does anyone?" The woman set the beans in Prudence's

basket. "He stands just over there with the Nottingham captain. In the mackerel."

Looking toward the fishmongers' stalls, Prudence spotted a cluster of men discussing something with great animation. Among them stood William, looking for all the world like a stableman.

"That sallow, ill-looking chap?" Prudence asked. "Is he the Nottingham captain?"

"Aye, Jeremiah Brandreth he calls himself. Like my husband, he were a stockinger once. He come from Sutton-in-Ashfield to lead the rising." She clucked as she rearranged her beans. "Thomas Bacon used to direct the reform meetings. He went about the Midlands and the North visiting one meeting and another. He's the one who first told us about the insurrection plans."

At that, Prudence had to stifle a gasp. "An insurrection?"

"Aye, lass. Men from Yorkshire, Nottingham, and who-knows-where plan to march on London and overthrow the government."

"Oh, heavens. They can never win."

"And Thomas Bacon agrees with you. He feared he'd been found out and would be arrested. So he went to ground at Booth's Hovel."

"I cannot blame him. But which man is Oliver?"

The vegetable seller pointed him out. "The captain leads the meetings at Asherfield's Barn and the White Horse pub, but Oliver is the one who set the date for the rising and prodded everyone to agree."

"I must go," Prudence murmured, starting away. "This is dreadful. Simply dreadful. They will all be killed."

"But what about your cheese?"

Unable to delay a moment longer, Prudence left the woman and hurried across to the meat market. To her dismay, the promise of morning sun had quickly given way to a rolling fog. As she neared the stall where William stood inspecting dressed geese, rain began to fall.

"William, we must talk," she said, holding his arm for support. She lowered her voice to a whisper. "The rising will be tonight."

With a nod, he led her through the meat market toward the flower stalls. "Jeremiah Brandreth leads the seditious meetings," he said. "But it is this chap Oliver who prods the men to revolt. Did you learn where they have been gathering?"

"Asherfield's Barn and the White Horse public house," she said.

"Oliver told me the men will depart for Nottingham at ten tonight. They'll gather at Hunt's Barn in South Wingfield and march out from there. Prudence, they are well armed."

"But what can they have? Sticks and stones?"

"Brandreth has assured everyone that they will collect more men and arms en route. When they reach Nottingham, he has promised, each will get one hundred guineas, bread, beef, and ale."

"Reason enough to join the march."

William hurried her out of the rain and into the dimly lit recesses of a small inn. He settled her before the fire and went to order tea. A contingent of soldiers occupied several tables nearby, and Prudence prayed they soon would leave. She could feel a chill creeping up her back and spreading into her chest, and it worried her. Of late, the doctors had begun to give her hope for a return to normal life, but they cautioned against exposure to the elements or vigorous exercise.

"Tonight," one of the soldiers was saying, his voice muffled by the drumming rain on the windowpanes. "That's what he told us. Tonight at a barn in South Wingfield."

"Whose barn?" another asked.

"He'll give us the name soon enough."

Stiffening, Prudence realized at once that the soldiers were discussing the rising she had learned of in the vegetable market. She ducked to hide her face as she continued to listen.

"Where do they go?" a soldier asked.

"Nottingham. And thence to London to overthrow Parliament and banish the king."

This was met with hearty laughter and a call for more ale. As a serving maid arrived with a pitcher, William returned to the table where Prudence awaited him.

Laying her hand over his, she leaned forward. Speaking in the barest of whispers, she began to relate the information she had overheard.

William glanced at the soldiers now and again, his brow furrowed. "If they know of the rising already," he murmured, "then a turncoat has given them the information. Someone who meets with Brandreth and the other men must be ferrying details to the troops."

"We must tell the men at once," she said. "Lest they be ambushed."

"They will not listen. I did everything but give Brandreth my true name in an effort to caution him, but he ignored my warnings."

"Perhaps Brandreth himself has betrayed the rebels. Might he be working for the king as a spy?"

"Fomenting an uprising so he will be able to report

insurrection and be well rewarded? An *agent provocateur*—indeed, it is possible. If Brandreth is urging the rebels and betraying them to the troops, he will be protected."

"Then what can be done? It will be another March of the Blanketeers—but worse. If the insurgents are armed, the soldiers will have an excuse to fire on them."

"What we can do and must do is return you to Delacroix's home and the care of your sisters. Prudence, you must know that these marches and protests can accomplish very little. America succeeded in throwing off the king. Another monarch was conquered in France. But you can be very sure that in England, the Crown will continue."

"I cannot deny what you say is true, William. But the ill treatment of children and their parents who labor in the mills and factories must end."

"The aristocracy knows the people are restless. But they will not listen to revolutionary rhetoric."

"Then they should be prodded in another way. Change must occur."

"What were you singing yesterday when I found you? Something about a law in Parliament?"

She smiled in discomfiture at her silly ditty. "I think laws should be brought before Parliament. Good laws that will ensure the safety and welfare of the labor force."

"Sing it, Prudence."

Aware her cheeks were flushed, she nevertheless sang softly. "A law, a law, a very good law. The very best law that I ever saw. Take it away to Parliament . . . the very best law that ever was sent."

William laughed. "I like it far better than the rallying cry of the French."

"*Liberté, égalité, fraternité.* My verse is not quite so eloquently spoken though." She glanced at the soldiers. "William, what are we to do? We cannot simply pretend to ourselves that we know nothing of the coming debacle. No, we shall not sit idly by. We must learn the name of the traitor and reveal his identity to those poor men lest they are slaughtered."

William studied the diamond-paned window before speaking. "Prudence, can you trust me to resolve this? Will you allow me to put you into a carriage and send you home? I shall do all in my power to halt the revolt. If I can learn the name of the *agent provocateur*, I will expose him. Please grant me that measure of your confidence, and my heart will press me on."

She considered his request. It hardly seemed wise to place her faith in a man who trailed behind him a life of debauchery and waste. William had very few good deeds to boast about and mountains of evil to try to overcome.

Yet he looked at her now with his deep brown eyes, begging her to give him what he did not deserve—her trust, her understanding, her love. She had forgiven him already, even for wrongs he had not confessed. And so her choice was made.

"I shall return to Henry and my sisters," she said. "Do what you can, William. Their lives are in your hands."

"As is your hope that I may rise above my reputation."

She smiled. "You read me well."

"And why not? We are chums, after all."

A maid brought a tray of tea and cake. Prudence drew off the tattered shawl she had worn over her gown, tugged the mobcap from her head, and arranged her curls. As William slipped out of the inn, she heard one of the soldiers give a muffled cry of surprise.

"Look over there," he whispered far too loudly. "When did *she* come in?"

"Another sip of ale to fortify me," another requested, "and I shall make so bold as to pay a visit to the lady's tea table."

With a sigh, Prudence leaned back in her chair, closed her eyes, and waited for the accustomed response to her golden curls and pretty face. It was not long in coming.

◆

"I have news! I have news!"

Waving a copy of the London *Star*, Mary ran across the grass toward Prudence, who was seated on a swing reading *Samson Agonistes* and wishing not to be disturbed.

"If it is Miss Pickworth of whom you speak," Prudence told her sister, "I shall thank you to take it away. I am in no humor to hear her thoughts on the latest fashion in necklines."

"I shall have you know that Miss Pickworth writes about far more than necklines," a breathless Mary said on arriving at the giant oak tree that supported the swing. "Her advice to young ladies is very useful and well considered. But this is not about Miss Pickworth. It is about the Pentrich Revolution."

"Does the press call that ill-fated rising a revolution?" Prudence stepped away from the swing and snatched the paper—but she soon passed it back again. "What does it say about Mr. Sherbourne? Oh, Mary, please read it to me, for I am all atremble. It has been nearly a week, and I have heard nothing from him. Where can he be? Why has he not returned to us? What has become of him?"

"'Six Men Will Hang,'" Mary announced.

Prudence fell back against the oak tree. "Oh, dear God, please not that!"

"My word, Prudence," Mary exclaimed. "William Sherbourne is not among them, of course. How could you think such a thing?"

"How am I to know what to think when you blurt out such news willy-nilly?"

"It was not willy-nilly. It was the headline. Now listen and you will soon know what to think." Mary resumed reading. "'For their roles as traitors in the Pentrich Revolution, Jeremiah Brandreth, Isaac Ludlam, and William Turner were today sentenced to be hanged, drawn, and quartered.'"

Prudence gasped. "So severe a punishment?"

"The men will not actually hang until they are dead, you know," Mary explained. "They will remain alive to be cut open and their intestines drawn out—"

"Mary, stop! For heaven's sake, spare me!" Prudence grabbed the paper away again. "'Fourteen men will be transported to Australia. Six more will be jailed.' This is harsh justice indeed."

"If you think the sentence cruel," Mary said, "you must read what they did."

"And I shall, if you will stop interrupting." Prudence cleared her throat. "'On the night of June 9, two groups of armed insurgents set out from Pentrich to knock on farm doors and force other men to join their march. They met with resistance at once. During a dispute with the Widow Hepworth, her servant Robert Walters was fatally shot.'"

Mary let out a squeak. "Shot? I had not read that far when I brought you the paper. How many others died?"

"'Walters was the only man to die that night,'" Prudence

read. "'The two groups gathered again at Pentrich Lane End and marched to Butterley Ironworks. Brandreth demanded weapons from the Butterley men. But they stood their ground, and the marchers departed empty-handed.'"

"The Butterley men should have captured the rebels at that very moment," Mary said.

"'In pouring rain,'" Prudence continued, "'the marchers stopped at three public houses, promising to pay for their drinks after they had toppled the British government. Soon drunk, dispirited, and wet, many defected. The small party remaining crossed into Nottinghamshire, where they faced a detachment of the King's Hussars. After a brief scuffle, most of the revolutionaries fled. Those who did not were taken into custody.'"

"With such a pitiful display of force, they can hardly be called revolutionaries," Mary said. "Their punishment does seem brutal—though one must never take treason lightly."

"No, indeed." Prudence sighed. Six days had passed since she departed the inn at Pentrich, leaving William alone to quell the rising. Clearly he had not succeeded in preventing the marchers from setting off. But perhaps the end result would have been worse without his intervention. If the revolution had ended that same night, she asked herself for the thousandth time, where was William?

Despite her anxiety, Prudence had felt her health returning as the days warmed and the mists rolled back. She took long walks about the grounds of the Delacroix estate. Henry and Mary often accompanied her on these excursions, though Sarah had chosen to return to London. Eating more, sleeping better, coughing less, Prudence began to hope that she had rounded a corner and was on the road to complete recovery.

But what use was robust health without William to tease and cajole her? A life dedicated to labor reform had begun to look rather empty. Despite her regularly announced determination never to marry, Prudence often thought about Chatham Hall and William's warm embrace and children.

But no. She must focus on current events and not on hazy dreams.

"I wonder what became of Oliver?" she now asked Mary, while scanning the article again. "Why is he not mentioned?"

"Who is Oliver?"

"The man who spurred the rising. I saw him myself, along with Brandreth and the others. If Oliver had been captured, he would have faced the gallows with Brandreth, for he was equally guilty."

"Perhaps he got drunk and deserted. Perhaps he did not like the rain."

Prudence rolled her eyes. "Honestly, Mary, what do you think causes men to revolt? Insurrection is not a lark. These people long for a better life—a healthy workplace, reasonable hours, good food, safety—"

"Oh, here is Henry! Thank goodness you have come!" Mary skipped across the grass to loop her arm around his. "You must make Pru laugh, Henry, for she has grown very dull again. She cannot say a single word lest it is bleak and full of foreboding."

"I have hope that I may accommodate your wishes in that arena, my dear lady," he told Mary. "For I am sure you will smile when you hear my news."

"I hope it is better than what we have just been reading," Mary chirped. "Pru and I are overcome with distress. Indeed, we are both quite dispirited."

From her perch on the swing, Prudence watched the pair of them tittering and teasing like two lovebirds.

Lovebirds?

She sat up straight.

"I cannot allow you to be dismayed in any way," Henry was saying as he gazed at Mary. "Your happiness is my only desire."

"Then I shall be happy," she cooed, "for fulfilling your desires is my greatest joy."

What was this? Prudence gawked at her sister and Lord Delacroix—who were paying not the slightest attention to her. How had this happened right under her nose? The truth was blatant. Mary and Henry were in love.

In love!

"Excuse me," Prudence said. "I am loath to disturb your tête-à-tête, but I should very much like to know Henry's news."

He glanced at her as if noticing for the first time that there was another woman in the garden. "Ah, Prudence, of course. My news is happy indeed. We are all wanted in London as soon as possible. The regent gives a ball—a masquerade!"

"Oh!" Mary shrieked and clasped her hands together. "And we are invited? Dearest Henry, this is due to you! Poor Pru and I would never be invited were we not so favorably connected to the house of Delacroix. A masquerade! Who shall I be? Oh, Henry, how will you dress? No—do not tell me! Say not a word! I must spend the evening searching for you—"

"And I, for you!"

At this utter silliness, Prudence slipped away from the oak tree, her volume of *Samson Agonistes* tucked under her arm. Milton, she felt, was just the dose of gloom required to offset the gleeful hysterics of Mary Heathhill and her newfound love.

Twenty

William Sherbourne stepped into the offices of the *Leeds Mercury*, a respected newspaper published in that quickly growing West Yorkshire town. Letting the door fall shut behind him, he scanned the room in search of a particular gentleman with whom he hoped to converse.

Though the office hummed with workers—any of whom might be Edward Baines—William's attention was quickly drawn to the printing press. The massive machine had a cast-iron frame and various levers, a wheel, and an iron carriage. Bending down to study the movements of the press as it cranked out one printed page after another, William pondered whether small changes to his looms, spinners, and carding machines might increase productivity. The action of the carriage was particularly unusual and—

"Invented by Charles, third Earl of Stanhope. Do you like it?"

At the unexpected question, William straightened. Beside him stood a middle-aged gentleman sporting large black side-burns, a high forehead, and thinning hair.

"I like the press very much," William responded. "May I assume you are Edward Baines, owner and publisher of the *Leeds Mercury*?"

"If you are a friend to dissenters, textile mill owners, and abolitionists, then I am indeed Edward Baines and your newest friend. If you oppose them, then I am still Edward Baines but now your staunchest foe."

"Then I am pleased to meet a friend," William said, shaking the man's proffered hand. Baines, he saw at once, could become a valuable ally if their aims and purposes were aligned.

"My name is William Sherbourne of Otley—owner of Thorne Mill, producer of the finest worsted in the realm."

"Ah, I have heard much of you, Mr. Sherbourne. Like me, you are something of an agitator. The reforms recently insti-tuted at your mill are quite the sensation of the moment."

"Indeed? I am surprised to hear it, though I can hardly doubt the veracity of a man whose sole profession is to gather and publish the news."

Baines chuckled. "I pay close attention to Yorkshire's textile mills. Some twenty years ago, I purchased carding and roving machines and started a small enterprise in the village of Brindle. Do you know it?"

"Near Preston?"

"The very same. But I abandoned the production of yard goods in favor of journalism. I have owned this newspaper since the turn of the century. 1801 was a stellar year, was it not?"

William reflected for a moment, realized he had been but a boy of nine at the time, and could recall nothing of it. "If you purchased the *Mercury* in that year," he said finally, "then it was indeed momentous."

Laughing, Baines beckoned. "Come with me, young William Sherbourne. We must take tea and speculate on Parliament."

"Parliament?" William queried as they stepped into a smaller room at the rear of the office.

"I believe," Baines said, "that such manufacturing towns as Leeds, Manchester, and even your little Otley should be well represented in government. What say you?"

"We shall have to disagree there, sir. If Leeds and Otley are represented in Parliament, then Parliament will make every attempt to exert its authority over our mills. Governmental regulations and strictures would overwhelm us."

"Not necessarily." Baines settled into a large leather-upholstered chair and urged William to do the same. As the two men enjoyed an animated discussion of the role of government in private business, a tea girl entered and set out cups, saucers, spoons, raisin cake, and a pot of steaming tea. Baines poured, waved at William to drink, and began slicing cake.

"But you did not come to the *Mercury* today to discuss Parliament," Baines said. "I must know your purpose, and then we shall proceed with our discourse."

"The workings of Parliament are not so very far from my chosen subject," William replied, recalling Prudence's tune about laws that would benefit the labor class. "But my first order of business is to make a report on the Pentrich Revolution."

Baines's face fell into lines of disappointment. "I am sorry to say, Mr. Sherbourne, that your news is already too old to be of use to me. Two weeks ago, the *Mercury* reported every aspect of that rising."

William excused himself, stood, and walked to the door.

"Now, do not take me so much to heart!" Baines called out. "At least drink your tea, young man. Let us discuss worsted, for I am very partial to wool suits."

Shutting the door, William turned the key in the lock and returned to his chair. Baines watched with eyes narrowed. William seated himself again, then took a slip of paper from his pocket and handed it to the publisher.

"Agent provocateur?" Baines scowled at the paper on which William had written the two weighty words. "Who?"

"Oliver." William lowered his voice. "I do not have the man's full name, but I know without doubt that Oliver led the rising at Pentrich. On government orders, he went to that town disguised as an unemployed mill worker. He then sought out the most disgruntled and restless among the villagers."

"Jeremiah Brandreth, Isaac Ludlam, and William Turner." Baines recited the names while running a finger around his collar, as if to ensure that his own neck was still intact.

"Those men and many others. Once accepted among the general public of Pentrich, Oliver orchestrated seditious meetings. It was he who provoked the men to revolt."

Baines rubbed his hands together. "You are certain of this?"

"Absolutely. Oliver planned the armed march to London. He encouraged the people to believe they could successfully take their petitions to the king. If the monarch refused to hear their complaints, Oliver told them, then they must overthrow the government. When the rising was set and the men were preparing to march, Oliver informed the local militia."

Baines caught his breath and then began to cough. "Upon my word, I have not been so astonished in my life! The same man who stirred the embers of revolt was employed by the prime minister?"

"And acting under the authority of the home secretary. Oliver was hired by Sidmouth as a spy to report on seditious meetings and treasonous plots."

"But how are you so certain he was assigned and sent out by the government?"

"After the meeting during which the final details for the rising were put into place, I followed Oliver. He went directly to the militia and informed them of the very plans he himself had prepared."

Looking down at the scrap of paper that William had given him earlier, Baines shook his head. Snatching up the message, he crumpled it and pushed it into his pocket.

"You *do* know, young man," he said, "that this report—were it published—could end the career of Robert Banks Jenkinson, second Earl of Liverpool and prime minister of England."

"And embarrass the king, the regent, Parliament . . . and, as a matter of fact, me."

"Quite right, quite right." Baines sat back in his chair. "Tell me how you have this information."

"I was in Pentrich the night of the rising. I, too, was disguised as a disgruntled worker. I met Oliver and the other men, and I learned their plans."

"But is your elder brother not Lord Thorne? What in the name of all that is sane were you doing dressed as a peasant in Pentrich?"

William shrugged. "I was following a pretty girl."

"Good heavens."

"Heaven has been very good indeed, sir. God, in His mercy, brought a golden-haired, green-eyed, impassioned young crusader into my life, and she woke me from my dark musings. From her, I learned that the welfare of my labor force must be uppermost in my mind."

"Labor reform is not normally the occupation of the landed gentry."

"No, indeed. Most of my peers are of the opinion that the lower classes will work harder if they are beaten regularly, compelled to labor from daylight to dusk, and given water porridge and black bread to eat. I have discovered, however, that my workers will produce better quality goods in greater quantity if they are treated well, educated, fed properly, and allowed occasional free time to enjoy their families and friends."

"Astounding."

"My reforms? Or my decision to follow the lady to Pentrich?"

"Both. Do I understand that you went to Pentrich to learn what the workers were plotting?"

"Yes, and to try to dissuade them from it."

"But you are an advocate of reform. Why would you wish to halt a rising that had the stated aim of bringing about reform?"

"Reform can come in many guises," William explained. "A law, a very good law, is what I believe can effect real change. This law must be drafted, taken before Parliament, and ratified. A revolution in manufacturing is inevitable, Mr. Baines. How much better if it could happen without marches and shootings and hangings."

Baines took a sip of tea. Then another. Finally he focused on William. "Mr. Sherbourne, your story is implausible and preposterous. But I believe it. What I do not understand is why you have brought this information to me."

"Because Oliver is here."

"In *Leeds*!" Baines gave a violent jerk. His cup teetered on its saucer for a moment, then toppled over. As tea spilled across the white tablecloth, Baines leapt to his feet. "You have seen the man here, in this very town? Is he rousing the rabble?"

"You will have to determine that for yourself, Mr. Baines," William said, standing. "I now consider my mission complete."

"And you return to your lovely green-eyed crusader?"

William studied the floor, unable to speak. When he found his voice, he murmured an answer. "The woman I love challenged me to reform more than my mill. My entire life must be altered, I understand now. With that reformation comes responsibility that must part me from her forever."

"You are a better man than I." Baines rose and held out his hand. As William shook it, the newspaperman continued. "Thank you for information that will benefit not only the people of England, but . . . I hesitate to confess . . . may greatly benefit me, as well."

"I am glad for you if it does, sir."

"Will you come to Leeds again, Mr. Sherbourne? I should very much like to continue our discussions. The abolition of slavery—"

"I must stop you there," William said, chuckling as he held up a hand. "I am in full agreement with those who advocate the abolition of slavery. But I have had quite enough of crusades for the time being. You will forgive me."

"Then you must do nothing more ambitious than come to

my home for dinner. I vow to refrain from all topics of contro-versy or sensation while you are my guest."

"And a very dull time we shall have." William smiled. "When I am recovered from my brief career as a spy, I shall visit you again, Mr. Baines, and we shall debate to our hearts' content."

The two men walked together across the outer office and bade farewell. As William left the building, he settled his hat on his head and stepped out into the street. It was time . . . past time . . . to complete the task before him.

◆

"I have never had such a lovely evening in my life!" Mary declared as she descended the steps of Carlton House to await a carriage. "Prinnie looked marvelous, I thought."

"Is it right to call the prince regent by such a familiar name, my dear?" Henry queried. Escorting Mary, he followed Sarah and Charles into the portico.

"Prinnie?" Mary asked. "And why not? We are among his acquaintances, and that is how he is known to his closest friends. Did you see Beau Brummell, Sarah? What can one think to say about such a man?"

"He has his own sense of fashion," Sarah replied. "And an odd one it is."

Prudence, trailing her sisters and their escorts, lifted her skirts and took the last few steps. Thank goodness she had man-aged to escape the growing number of eligible young men who were vying for her attention. Anonymity, she felt, was the only real benefit to a masquerade ball.

At her sisters' insistence, she had gone as Helen of Troy—the face that launched a thousand ships. Her unspoken reason for accepting this guise was that she could wear one of her own gowns as her costume—a soft muslin in a pretty pink shade.

Mary dressed as Hera, the Greek goddess of marriage, women, and childbirth. Carrying a glittering scepter, she had arrayed herself in a gown covered with peacock feathers. Henry was Zeus, husband to Hera. In one hand he carried a painted wooden thunderbolt—which he had twice inadvertently poked into the portly abdomen of the prince regent and once into Mary's peacock-garbed posterior.

Charles and Sarah were Romeo and Juliet. Their obvious pleasure in each other's company overruled the tragic aspects of Shakespeare's star-crossed lovers.

Standing at the edge of the portico, Prudence tried to shake the sense of disquietude and unhappiness that had weighed on her for many weeks. She knew its source. William Sherbourne had not returned to her at the Delacroix estate in Derbyshire. No letter or message from him had been delivered. And since her return to London, she had neither seen nor heard from him.

Other than the aching sense of loss, Prudence thanked God that her health had been restored and her family were all well. Sarah and Charles delighted in each other, and their tea enterprise prospered. Mary and Henry, she felt sure, would announce their engagement within the year. Prudence was so glad they had found each other. Though she liked Henry very much, she had never loved him. Now and again, he had attempted to play the attentive beau, but his heart was not in it.

Looking down the street, Prudence wondered what was keeping their carriage. She was eager to return to Trenton House, sit by the fire and read for a while, and then drift off to sleep, lulled by thoughts of—

William?

Prudence stiffened with shock at the silhouette of a tall gentleman standing alone at the far end of the street. The profile of his face could not be mistaken. The curl of his hair. The bearing and demeanor she had admired so many times.

Unable to stop herself, Prudence started down the street. She could hear Mary and Henry guffawing about something or other. Sarah and Charles were laughing too. And now the gentleman tipped his hat at a passing couple. Prudence had seen that tilt of the head, that jaunty bow, far too many times to remain in doubt.

"William!" She called out to him in as hushed a voice as she could manage. "William Sherbourne."

He turned. "Prudence?"

"William, is it really you?"

He squared his shoulders and made her a stiff bow. "It is I. Good evening, Miss Watson. I hope you are well."

"I shall know how I am when you tell me why you are here, in London, at Carlton House, on this street."

"I am . . . I have . . ." He took off his hat and raked his fingers through his hair. "Business. I am in London on business."

"How long?"

"I have been here only two days. I leave tomorrow for Otley. And you?"

"We returned to town no more than a week after Pentrich." She could hardly believe she was actually seeing this man who had so often occupied her thoughts. Yet, where was the teasing, mocking wit she had loved? Where was the dashing air of confidence? the warm brown eyes? the eager lips?

"I hope . . . I hope you are recovered from your illness,"

he stammered. "I have wished to know that you are in good health."

"I am well enough. Much better than when you saw me last."

"Happy news," he replied without the glimmer of a smile. "You must know already that I was unable to stop the rising in Pentrich. Brandreth and the others will hang for it."

"Surely you do not blame yourself."

"No. But I should have liked to prevent it."

"Oliver was exposed," she said. "The *Leeds Mercury* had it first, though *The Tattler*'s story was more entertaining."

"Miss Pickworth?"

Prudence glanced over her shoulder at Mary. "Miss Pickworth enjoyed the scandal very much indeed. The home secretary and the prime minister were publicly shamed—a much-deserved censure, I thought. I am glad to know that at least one *agent provocateur* can no longer practice his deceits."

"Ah, I see that your carriage has arrived," William said. He made another stilted bow. "I wish you very well, Miss Watson."

"William, wait—" She held out a hand. "Why do you speak to me in such a way? Are we not still friends? If you have been in London, why have you never called on us?"

"I was much occupied."

"I see." She noticed her sisters beckoning. Mary soon would set out to retrieve her. "Your brother and his wife? Are they well?"

"Very well."

"Please give them my greetings."

"Of course." He rubbed his brow a moment before speaking again. "Prudence, please understand that I cannot . . . I am not at liberty to . . . I must not see you."

"But why?" She paused as the truth rushed in like a sudden slap. "Is it because of that woman? the woman who died? Miss Bryse?"

His mouth fell open. "You *know*? You know about—"

"Prudence, for heaven's sake," Mary called out. "What on earth is keeping you?"

"Oh, William, can you please take tea with me tomorrow? We must talk. Will you come to Trenton House at ten?"

"I am sorry, Prudence. I . . . I cannot. I am . . . I am much engaged."

"Engaged? To be married? You are—"

"Oh, Mr. Sherbourne!" Mary joined them.

"Mrs. Heathhill." He bowed. "You are looking very . . . bird-like . . . this evening."

Mary tittered. "Indeed, I am! We have just enjoyed the love-liest masquerade, and we are in high spirits. And how happy we are to find you here with us! Will you join us this evening? We go to Delacroix House to play at cards and eat far too many puddings."

"You will not want me, madam. I always win at cards. And when I do not, I am not at all inclined toward puddings."

"Oh, Mr. Sherbourne, how we have missed you. You always make us laugh!" She linked her arm through Prudence's. "But we must away. If not this evening, do call on us when you can!"

"Excuse me, Mary." Prudence removed her sister's arm. "I shall join you in a moment."

She glared until Mary gave a little shrug and hurried off.

"I have known about Miss Bryse for some time," Prudence told William in a low voice. "Sarah learned the news from a friend. I have been alternately angry, sad, fearful, worried."

"Your family cannot be pleased at our friendship."

"No, indeed." She moistened her lips. "Your reputation is . . ."

"Reduced to rubble. I tried to tell you several times about my past."

"You did. You were as honest as you could be without revealing all."

"Perhaps I should have revealed more than I did. You must understand now why I am not at ease in London. The assembly at Lord Delacroix's house was difficult, for I had not expected it to be so well attended. I confess, my sole aim in proposing it was to see you. But I managed somehow to elude my own ill repute and to acquire the patronage of several gentleman who were in attendance there."

"Their support must have made your reforms easier to implement. I am sure the expense to you has been substantial."

"Not so much as one might think. In fact, today I spoke to a number of my elder brother's colleagues about the monetary benefits of reform. The men are all members of the peerage. I believe it will not be long before a law—a very good law—will be proposed in Parliament."

"The very best law that ever was sent?"

He chuckled. "Or nearly so." The muscle in his jaw flickered as he gazed at the sparkling flame of a streetlamp. "Guilt plagues me, Prudence. I bear the blame for Miss Bryse's death. I have lived a life of vice and dissipation. My gaming habits and my dependence on drink caused me to owe a great sum. My debts threaten to keep me at the brink of financial ruin. That is what prevented me from reforming the mill sooner."

"But you did reform it, and God has rewarded you. William,

do you recall the words Jesus spoke to Nicodemus? New birth can happen to any man—any man who entrusts his life into the hands of a merciful Savior."

"I live by those words. I have repented, and in my heart, I know I am reborn. But a wise young lady once told me that though our sins can be forgiven, the consequences of past wickedness often live on. I can never escape what I have done, Prudence. And I would never ask you to join your own life to another so encumbered."

"Join my life . . . to yours?" She tried to breathe. "William, I—"

"You should go. Your family is waiting. I am sorry, Prudence. I did not intend to trouble you."

He made her a crisp bow, then turned away, walking quickly. Standing at the edge of the street, she watched him round a corner and vanish. She heard the rattle of wheels and the clatter of hooves only moments before the carriage rolled to a stop beside her.

"Come inside with us, Pru," Sarah called softly. "It is time to move on."

◆

"I had an appointment with Mrs. Norris," William told the footman outside the front door of a grand home. He set a calling card on the silver tray in the servant's hand. "Please deliver my sincerest apologies and inform her that I shall call again tomorrow."

"Of course, Mr. Sherbourne," the footman replied. "But she told me to bring you in. She wishes to see you—no matter the hour."

"Ah, how very like her."

The imposing edifice, just across from St. James's Park, stood near Pall Mall and was uncomfortably close to the prince regent's residence at Carlton House—as William had discovered only minutes before. Still shaken from the unexpected meeting with Prudence Watson, he stepped into the chilly foyer.

She had looked like an angel coming to him through the foggy London night. Her pink gown glowed as she materialized into view. Golden hair piled on her head and trailing down her neck in soft ringlets had entranced him. Unable to move, unable to think, he most certainly had been unable to elude her.

Dear God, why did You allow such a thing? William lifted up in silent prayer. *Why did I have to see her? hear her voice? remember again how much I love her?*

It was hardly a punishment worthy of Job, but William nonetheless felt betrayed. He had come to London in such a way as to avoid Prudence completely, along with anything that might remind him of her. Carrying out his business, he had managed to stay far from Cranleigh Crescent and its semicircle of fine homes, where resided her closest society of family and friends. He had occupied himself from early morning to late at night, all in the vain hope of preventing a single thought of her to cross his mind.

"William! At this hour? We were all abed!" Hands outstretched, dressing gown billowing, Eugenie Norris floated toward him across the carpeted floor. His aunt, nearing her seventieth year, was as elegantly beautiful as ever. "Do come into the drawing room, my dear boy. We shall stir the fire and put on tea."

She embraced him, enveloping the air around them in the

scent of heliotrope and roses. Taking his hand, she led him into a vast room filled with too many settees and chairs to count.

"Aunt Norris, I must apologize for my late arrival." William took a place near the fire. "I had hoped to come much earlier in the day."

"I received the message you sent regarding your delay, dearest, and I am not at all put out." Seated in a large chair, she smiled at William while her servants hastened to rekindle the fire. "And how do you like your new name?"

"New name?" He always enjoyed sitting with his aunt. Not only was she often amusing, but she reminded him very much of her sister—the mother he had loved so well. "I believe my name remains as it always has been."

"Oh no, certainly not. You are no longer William Sherbourne," she declared, availing herself of a sweet from a tray offered by one of her maids. "You are now and forever to be known as 'Father.'"

"Ah, yes. Of course." Immediately uncomfortable, William leaned back in his chair and hoped that the retinue of servants would dissipate before his aunt took the conversation any further.

"I am mother to five," she continued as the tea table was laid out with cups, saucers, spoons, and other accoutrements. "I much prefer that title to any other. They are all grown, you know, but I cannot think of them in any way other than as my children. They still call me Mummy—all of them."

William found it difficult to imagine Rupert Norris, the eldest son and a renowned financier, referring to anyone as "Mummy." Furthermore, her eldest daughter, Lady Broughton, seemed unlikely to let such a familiar word escape her lips.

"At home," Aunt Norris was saying, "among our family, we never change. You will always be little Will, to me. And now you, blessed man, will always be 'Father.' Are you ready?"

"Ready to be a father? I believe I became one several months ago."

"Eight months, to be exact." She took a sip of tea. "Oh, my dear little Will, I am very pleased with you."

"Pleased? I should hardly think my behavior worthy of any praise whatsoever."

"Nonsense! You are exactly as I had hoped you would be. A courteous cad. A reformed rake. A moral, upright gentleman of the first order."

"Thank you, aunt. But I am sure there are many who would disagree with your assessment."

"Reform, we must agree, is a lovely thing. If one has never been anything but good, kind, even tempered, and pious, what sort of character can one have built? No, as odd as it may seem, I think a man who has been a little *bad* can be much more interesting, and certainly much more intensely *good*, than those simpering fops one can hardly abide."

William could not hold in a laugh. "Dear Aunt Norris, surely you jest. Your sons have all turned out very well indeed, and you would not have it any other way."

"And you have turned out well too," she pronounced. "Now, shall we introduce you?"

"Introduce me . . . to whom?"

"To your son, of course." She gave her footman a little wave. "Please send Matilda in."

"I—I thought tomorrow might be—" William began.

But he fell silent as a woman entered the room bearing in her arms a bundle of laces, blankets, and trailing gossamer fabric. For a moment, he could not move. His fingers clenched the arms of the chair in which he sat. The blood drained from his cheeks. He feared he might never breathe again.

"Ah, here is little Timothy!" Aunt Norris rose and laid her hand on William's. "Stand up, dearest, and meet your son."

William pushed himself from the chair. His legs felt like they were hinged with rusted metal. His mouth was dry and his heart thundered. He managed a single step.

The bundle of lace and fabric squirmed. A pink arm emerged—an arm ending in a hand with five of the tiniest fingers he had ever seen.

He took another step.

Large brown eyes—exactly like those that looked back at him in the mirror each morning—gazed up at him. And he saw the small nose, no more than a tiny pink button. Lips, soft and formed into a perfect O. Hair, brown hair, just like his own.

He stared . . . stared until tears blurred his vision . . . and at that moment knew he loved with a love deeper and fuller and more painfully exquisite than any love had ever been or ever would be.

"Hello, Timothy," he whispered. "I am your father."

Twenty-one

Prudence stood at the window and gazed across the rolling purple moors. At the sound of footsteps, she turned. A beautiful woman entered the parlor and caught her breath.

"Miss Watson?" Olivia Sherbourne lifted a hand to her throat. "This is an unexpected pleasure!"

"Lady Thorne," Prudence said. Taking a step, she made a deep curtsy. "Forgive me for not sending word ahead. I have come on a delicate matter."

"Won't you sit down?"

"Thank you, but I cannot stay long."

"You are passing through Yorkshire?" Olivia approached her guest. "Or have you come to inspect the mill again?"

Mortified, Prudence looked away. "I am so sorry for all the trouble I—"

"Oh, my question was not a condemnation!" Olivia cut in. "On the contrary. I have been among your most ardent supporters. I merely wondered if you had come to see the astonishing changes you brought to the mill."

"Truly I brought no changes. Indeed, it is my fault your laborers joined the March of the Blanketeers. I am to blame for their unrest and rebellion. If any alterations occurred, they were at Mr. Sherbourne's hand."

"He is very grateful to you, as are we all. A ten-hour day. A new school—the teacher arrived two weeks ago. And kitchens refurbished to provide good hot meals for the labor. Did you know William is attempting to improve the air inside the mill? He has a great interest in machines and engines. My husband cannot believe his brother's efforts to invent an air-cleaning machine will succeed. But I say anything is possible."

Both humbled and amazed, Prudence crossed the carpet until she stood near Olivia. "Is he well?" Prudence asked. "Mr. Sherbourne?"

"In the best of health. It is you about whom we worry most."

"I am much recovered from my illness, though . . . though it is quite possible that I may suffer the effects of it throughout my life."

"I hope it will not prevent your riding. William said he had never seen a finer figure on a horse."

"Did he?" Prudence took another step closer and lowered her voice. "I have come to you today to learn if Mr. Sherbourne is at home. I should also like to know whether my unexpected visit would be accepted."

"William is at Chatham Hall today, meeting with his

steward. I am certain he would like nothing better than to see you, Miss Watson. He often speaks very fondly of you."

"Thank you, Lady Thorne."

"You must call me Olivia." She put her arm about Prudence's shoulders as they walked toward the foyer. "William's situation, you must understand, is somewhat altered since you saw him last."

"Altered? In what way?" A secret fear she had harbored came tumbling out. "Has he formed an attachment? I see by your face that he has. I suspected such might have been the reason for his recent trip to London. He did not call on us, and I supposed he wished to sever all contact."

"Yet you came here anyway?" Olivia tilted her head as she appraised her guest. "I can see why he likes you so well. You have a spirit as determined and resolute as his own."

The two women stood at the door as Prudence prepared for the words she dreaded to hear. Yet Olivia smiled tenderly as she spoke.

"William has indeed formed an attachment. He is quite smitten. One might even call him besotted. Go to him now, Miss Watson, for I am sure you will soon share our great happiness."

Fighting a sudden lump in her throat, Prudence managed a curtsy. "Thank you, Olivia. But I believe I shall return to London instead."

"Oh, nonsense. You must go to Chatham Hall. It is not far, and William will wonder why you did not call on him when you came so near. Here, you must take our footman in your carriage. Steeves, please guide Miss Watson's driver to Chatham."

Stunned, Prudence made her farewell and hurried down the steps, eager to hide the tears that rose unbidden. She could not possibly go to Chatham Hall. Seeing William so blissfully happy in the anticipation of marriage to another woman would destroy her.

But even as Prudence determined never to go near William's home, the footman helped her into the carriage and took his seat. The driver started the horses, and she could do nothing to forestall the results of yet another of her disastrous schemes.

Sarah and Mary had warned her not to go to Otley. Her own heart had cautioned her time and again. But she had never been as obedient as she should, and so even now she was drawing near the grand home perched majestically amid meadows of gorse, heather, and bracken.

"Thank you," she said as the footman helped her down onto the drive that bordered the home. "I shall only be a moment. If you wait here, you may ride back to Thorne Lodge in my carriage."

"As you wish, madam," he replied.

Her heart beating nearly out of her breast, Prudence lifted her skirts and ascended the impressive stone stairway to the front door. A footman received her and led her into the house.

"I am Miss Watson," she whispered as she set a card on his silver tray. "If Mr. Sherbourne is busy, please do not disturb him. I should not wish to bother him in any way. Indeed, I believe I shall—"

"Miss Watson?"

Sucking down a breath, she turned to find William striding toward her across the marbled floor. He had been outside, she saw, for his sleeves were rolled to the elbow and his leather boots bore a coating of dust. His brown hair had been tousled by the wind, but his eyes were steady as they met hers.

"I did not expect you," he said.

She curtsied. "Forgive me. I did not have time to send word ahead."

"You are distressed. Come, please sit down. Is something amiss? Your sisters?"

"No, no, they are well. Very well. Mary is to wed Henry at Christmas."

His face broke into a smile. "Happy news indeed. At one time, I had thought Lord Delacroix intended another bride."

"No. He is very happy, as is my sister. Though I believe the illustrious career of Miss Pickworth may be at an end."

"Miss Pickworth?" Cupping her elbow, he led Prudence to a chair near an open glass door that faced out onto the gardens.

"Mary, we have learned, kept many secrets well hidden."

Chuckling, he sat across from her and studied the scene beyond. "Would you agree it is a fair prospect?" he asked, indicating the expanse of meadows dotted with sheep. "Our lands give me great pleasure. I have never been happier."

Prudence nodded. "You are certainly more at ease than on our last encounter. I believe you have many reasons for joy."

"I do indeed. My mill now produces the finest worsted in Yorkshire. I cannot employ all those who come to my door seeking work. I am settled at Chatham Hall. No, I cannot complain about my situation in any way."

Prudence swallowed. "I spoke to Lady Thorne this morning. I understand you are to be congratulated."

He looked at her with a quizzical expression. "On the success of the mill?"

Prudence closed her eyes and gritted her teeth. Must he

make her say it all aloud? Must she be the one to introduce this most devastating news?

Suddenly, she stood. "I recall your enjoyment of jests and teasing, Mr. Sherbourne, but I am in no humor to be mocked. Lady Thorne informed me that you are engaged to be married. I wish you much happiness, and now I shall see myself out."

She stepped out onto the portico that ran the length of the house. Her carriage could not be far. In three strides he caught her arm and swung her around to face him.

"I am not engaged to be married," he said. "Why did Olivia tell you as much? It is not like her to dissemble."

Her lips parting in shock, Prudence looked into his brown eyes. "You are not engaged? But . . . but she told me that you have formed an attachment. You are quite smitten, she said, even besotted."

"Ah!" His lips tilted at the corners until he could not hold in a laugh. "I *am* attached. But not to be married. My attachment is of another sort. Come with me, Prudence."

He looped her arm around his and stepped down from the portico. Feeling as if she might swoon at any moment, Prudence could neither speak nor think beyond the certainty that this man . . . this man she so dearly loved . . . was not to be married.

They rounded the corner of the house, and Prudence spied in the distance a white blanket spread across the grass beneath a large oak tree. Near the blanket stood a chair, and in it sat a somewhat large woman with gray hair and spectacles. More disconcerting was the tiny creature who lay perfectly still on the blanket.

"It is a baby," she breathed out, coming to a sudden stop. "A baby."

"My son." William's face was unreadable as he faced her. "I thought you might not know the whole of the news you related to me in London. I felt it imprudent to tell you that the woman who died—"

"She died in childbirth. Yes, I knew. But I assumed . . . I thought . . . When did you—?"

"I met Timothy Charles Sherbourne the night of the masquerade. When you and I spoke, I had just departed a meeting of members of Parliament interested in labor reform. I was on my way to my aunt's home in Pall Mall."

"Your aunt had kept the child?"

"Yes. The family of Miss Bryse had rejected the baby and, quite naturally, me as well. In my former state of selfishness and debauchery, I, too, wanted nothing to do with the baby. My Aunt Norris, who had brought up five very successful children and was now widowed and lonely, declared that she would take him. And so Timothy's first months were spent in the care of my aunt and the nursemaid."

They had resumed moving forward, and now Prudence could see the baby's face, perfectly round, with pink cheeks and long dark lashes. Her heart ached at the sweet beauty of tiny fingers and toes, soft lips, a dusting of brown hair.

"If I may be excused," the nursemaid murmured, after greeting her master and his guest, "I should be glad of a cup of tea."

"Of course, Matilda. Thank you very much."

William held out his hand, indicating the blanket on which the child lay. Prudence sank with relief onto the soft cotton fabric. William took a place so close she could smell the scent of the open meadows on his white shirt.

"He is beautiful," Prudence said. "I am happy for you."

William gazed at the sleeping baby. "I love him. I love him with such passion."

"*Besotted*," Olivia said."

He laughed. "Quite right. I only regret I missed the first months of his life. He is always a delight—alternately a clown, a screech owl, a mouse, a burbling brook. He talks, you know. I am very sure he begins to say words."

Now Prudence laughed. "You will have him reading the Gospel of St. John in another month."

William focused on her. "Why did you come? I was certain I should never see you again. I comforted myself that you were happy and well and, most of all, unencumbered by a reformed rake and his wee son."

"I came because you left me no choice. I had to understand you. As we stood outside Carlton House, you said that you would never ask me to join my life to another so encumbered."

"Indeed I did. You could not have known—nor dared I tell you—that I referred to my son. He is no encumbrance to me, but to another . . . to a wife . . ." He let out a hot breath. "Forgive me. God has altered me greatly, but He has not yet succeeded in controlling my tongue."

She reached out and smoothed the baby's blanket, tucking it more closely around him. "I am the one encumbered now," she said. "I stayed in London—away from you—so long because of it. When you spoke of our lives united, I knew it must never be. My long illness . . . the severity of it . . . the doctors have declared it unlikely that I shall bear children."

He looked at her. "Indeed? But you are well."

"It is possible I may recover all my former fortitude. But it is equally likely that I shall not."

"Then . . . you may have lost the ability to bring a child into the world . . . while I have managed—through carelessness and immorality—to bring about . . . *him.*"

They both turned to the tiny boy. Prudence shivered as she spoke. "As for me, I am not so unfeeling as to allow only a child of my own into my heart. I believe it is possible that I myself might become quite besotted by *him.*"

"But he . . . this son . . . is my heir. I will give him—and none other—my legacy."

"As is only right."

She dared lift her focus to his. William's brown eyes had gone as dark as midnight. "I am not the sort of man," he said, "who would be welcome in some circles of society. I might be considered more than a liability to any woman who might closely associate her life to mine."

"Perhaps you are right," Prudence said, her heart welling. "Or perhaps . . . with the love and esteem of the brightest ornament of English society, the genuine admiration of the prettiest young lady in court all season, the steadfast loyalty of a woman whose reputation is beyond reproach . . . with such a woman at your side, perhaps your past will not appear quite so black nor your future so bleak."

At this, William laughed. "Miss Watson," he said, "do my ears deceive me, or have you just proposed a marriage between us?"

"Of course not," she replied archly. "If you wish to take my hand and go down on one knee, however, I might give serious consideration to such a proposal."

"For such an action to occur, you would have to stand up," he pointed out, extending a hand to her. "Like this."

They both rose.

"Miss Watson," he began.

"Down on one knee," she repeated.

He obeyed. "Dear Miss Watson, you have revolutionized my mill, transformed my black soul, and converted all my views of the world and my place in it. If you would willingly surrender your heart to me, I could want nothing more than to yield my own to you. My life, my fortune, my future, my dreams, in short, all that I am, I would gladly give you if you would consent to become my wife."

"Come here, you ninny," she said, tugging his hands. As he rose, he drew her into his arms and held her close. Wrapped in his warm embrace, she could not prevent the tears that filled her eyes and spilled down her cheeks.

"Of course I shall marry you," she murmured into his neck. "I could want nothing more in all my life."

"Mill reform?"

"A hobby."

"One you must continue." He groaned as he drew her closer. "I love you, Prudence. I have loved you from the moment we met."

"William, you cannot possibly know how deeply I love you and long to—"

A very loud wail cut through her words. Startled, she stepped back as William bent and scooped up the suddenly squalling, red-faced, very unhappy baby. In the same motion, he held out the miserable creature and deposited him into Prudence's arms.

"I should like to introduce you to Timothy," he called out. "Our son."

Giggling, she held the baby out and peered into his wretched little face. "Good afternoon, Timothy," she shouted over his screams. "I am your mother!"

"He does this often," William said loudly as they started across the lawn toward the house. "He is frequently rather unhappy."

"Are you a bother, Timothy?" Carrying the baby on one shoulder, she skipped up onto the portico and into the house. At the movement, the baby's cries subsided.

"Are you a difficult and contentious fellow just like your father?" she asked. "Very well, I shall simply have to reform you too. Because, Timothy, you must know that I cannot help but reform those I love. And I love you . . . very, very much."

Matilda scurried into the room, out of breath and mortified. "Oh, I am so sorry, Miss . . . Miss . . . Miss . . ."

"Mrs. Sherbourne," William said. "Very soon she is to become Mrs. Sherbourne."

As the surprised nursemaid carried the baby away to be fed, William pulled Prudence into his arms and kissed her lips. "I am," he said, "the most blessed of men."

She looked into his eyes and knew that she had at last found her home.

⬦

Summer was just ending as wedding bells rang out across the town of Otley. Mill workers lined the streets to wave at the handsome couple emerging from the church. Prudence Watson, Miss Pickworth reported in *The Tattler*, was as bright and beautiful a bride as ever had been seen. Her new husband, though once considered a cad, displayed the courtesy of the true gentleman he had become.

Like the finest silk threads twisted and crossed to form a net of gossamer lace, Anne Webster's plan had to be executed perfectly or it would unravel into a thousand strands. The seedcake must be steaming, the ripe quinces baked to perfection, the tea piping hot. The Limoges cup and saucer must gleam in shades of blue and gold on the black lacquer tray. Every facet of the silver teapot must reflect the fire crackling on the grate. Nothing could be out of order, for this afternoon Alexander Chouteau, son of the Duke of Marston, was taking tea alone.

A shaky breath clouded the creamer Anne took down from the Welsh cupboard at the back of the large, dimly lit kitchen. Lifting the hem of her apron, she buffed the silver vessel. She must not tremble when she poured Sir Alexander's milk. Her voice must not quaver when she offered the sugar. Above all, she must remember to shut the door behind her when she went in. If anyone heard her speaking to him . . . if anyone knew what she had planned . . .

"Anne, do stop your dawdling." Mrs. Smythe slid a dish of baked fruit down the slick boards of the scrubbed pine worktable. The glass clinked as it hit the tea tray. "Sugar those quinces, and be quick about it. I shall not have Mr. Errand screeching at me because the tea was late and His Grace complained at its being tepid. The duchess cannot bear cold toast, and you certainly know how their son demands punctuality."

"Of course, Mrs. Smythe." Anne glanced at the pink-cheeked cook and wondered what the portly woman would do if she knew about the roll of delicate Honiton lace tucked into the pocket of her housemaid's dress.

Mrs. Smythe must never know. If she found out, Anne would be forced to sell her work to the laceman who came out in his chaise every month from London. The long, narrow panel of lace had taken her three months to design, its pattern two months to prick onto parchment, and its silk threads another ten months to weave with her pillow and bobbins.

In France, where it was illegal to own lace, such a panel would be worth a king's ransom. Even in London, the laceman could sell her work for a small fortune, though he would pay her only a fraction of its value. Thus she had designed the pattern for the Chouteau family alone, praying that her plan would succeed. Into this bit of lace she had woven her future.

Quickly Anne took the nippers and broke several lumps from the hard sugar cone. She slipped one lump into her pocket as a treat for Theseus, the duke's mastiff; then she sprinkled a spoonful of sugar crystals across the peeled quinces.

Dear God, she lifted up in a swift and silent prayer, *please let these satisfy Sir Alexander's exacting tastes.*

As she carried the dish across the kitchen, the chill of the black-and-white-tiled floor crept through her thin slippers and around her ankles. Her toes ached. She had been on her feet since before dawn, and she would work at Slocombe House until the last dinner plate was cleared and washed that evening. In between, she must pray that the duke's son would have the temper to listen to an impertinent, headstrong housemaid, that he would have the patience to inspect her length of Honiton, and that he would have the wit to realize the value of the lace.

As she set the dish of quinces on the tea tray, Anne squeezed her eyes shut. *Lord and Father above, this is my only hope*, she reminded Him. God already knew her dire predicament, of course, but she felt it behooved her to call it to His divine attention one more time. If Sir Alexander paid her even half the market value of the Honiton, she would have enough money to quit her position at Slocombe House and return to her family's home in Nottingham. She could hire a barrister to secure her father's release from prison and save her sisters from the mills.

Satan's workshops, her father called the drafty, machine-filled buildings with their deafening clatter and sooty windows. The mills, he had preached in more than one sermon, caused women to sicken and children to die early deaths. As the eldest child in the Webster family, Anne knew that what her father said was true, and she had supported his association with the Luddites even though their activities had landed him in prison.

Now the family's only hope rested in her hands. Could a length of lace, more air than thread, be their salvation? Anne swallowed at the gritty lump in her throat. It had to.

"Head in the clouds, as usual," the cook huffed as she bustled past with a plate of steaming cinnamon and currant scones. "Have you remembered to put tea in the pot, Anne?"

"Yes, Mrs. Smythe."

"She probably put in coffee." Sally Pimm, the first kitchen-maid, eyed Anne as she sifted salt into a copper pot of soup on the stove. In the scullery a cluster of maids giggled at the notion while they scoured stewpans, colanders, and utensils.

"Will not Sir Alexander be surprised," Sally continued, "if

he sips up a mouthful of coffee when he is expecting his afternoon oolong?"

"No more than when his oxtail soup tastes as though it were made with water from the English Channel," Anne returned.

Mrs. Smythe's wooden spoon cracked across Sally's knuckles, and she let out a shriek.

"Have mercy!" Sally cried.

"Then stop your chatter and pay heed to the supper, girl! Shall we all be tossed out on our ears thanks to your heavy hand with the salt? Have this as a reminder!"

Forcing herself to turn a deaf ear on Sally's wails as the cook added another whack for good measure, Anne laid a starched cloth over the tray and set the tea things on it. She knew the kitchenmaid was envious of her position. Under normal circumstances, Anne would have joined the staff as a scullery maid. After several years, she might have worked her way up to second kitchenmaid, first kitchenmaid, and then, possibly, cook.

Circumstances were not normal. After the Luddite riots and her father's subsequent imprisonment in Nottingham, Anne had journeyed by coach to the south of England. In London, she had found a position at Trenton House on Cranleigh Crescent in the tony Belgravia district. Hired as a housemaid, she displayed a wit and propriety that soon elevated her to the station of lady's maid to the widowed homeowner's sister, Miss Prudence Watson. Not long afterward, Lady Delacroix had returned from a sea voyage to the Far East. When the young, wealthy baroness took up residence in Trenton House once more, Anne became her trusted assistant and companion.

In that position, Anne had hoped she might earn enough money to pay for a legal defense for her father. But it was not to be. To the shock of London society, Lady Delacroix fell deeply in love with a common tea tradesman. Their winter wedding stripped her of her title—though not her immense fortune—and she was now known simply as Mrs. Charles Locke. Sadly, she had informed Anne that their association could not continue, for she intended to travel with her husband. He had formed a partnership with two men, one of whom was Sir Alexander. Because of this relationship between the two families, Mrs. Locke had penned a glowing referral that led to Anne's joining the staff of Marston House, also on Cranleigh Crescent.

Despite Mrs. Locke's commendation of the clergyman's daughter, the housekeeper at Marston had intended to put Anne into the kitchen, until Mr. Errand intervened.

"Look at the girl, Mrs. Davies," the butler had intoned, one bushy white eyebrow arching as he inspected the newcomer. "With that face she will be wasted in the kitchen. She has kept all her teeth, her eyes are clear, and though she is no great beauty, she has a certain grace to her carriage. The letter from Mrs. Locke indicates she may have a measure of wit, as well. Put her in the house, and you will please His Grace, for you know the duke despises the fishermen's daughters we normally get."

Anne had been given a position in the grand home, though she was once again a housemaid and earning very little. While most of the *ton* went to London for the spring social season and thence to the beach for the summer, the Duke of Marston preferred Slocombe, his country house in Devon. And in March, he went there with his wife, his younger son, and most of his staff, Anne included.

Not long after their arrival, however, word came that Miss Prudence Watson had fallen prey to a nervous malady and would benefit from a sojourn away from the city. The duke and his wife insisted she be brought to them at Slocombe, and once again, Anne had the pleasure of waiting upon her as a lady's maid. Anne attended solely to Miss Watson's needs except on Saturday afternoons. On that day, Miss Watson kept to her rooms to write letters, the footmen took their leave, and Anne was given the honor of serving tea to Sir Alexander.

A knock sounded on the door. "Now what?" Mrs. Smythe mopped her forehead. "More charity? Sally, see to them."

"I beg your pardon, mum, but I am in the midst of beating eggs." The kitchenmaid shot a glance at Anne. "Perhaps Anne will do it, if she is not too proud."

"I should be happy to feed the poor if I had the time," Anne said, surveying the hungry men, women, and children who had gathered around the door that led from the kitchen. She could so easily be one of them, and yet she had worked hard to improve her lot. Now she must press forward with her plan.

Touching the lump that was the roll of lace hidden in her pocket, she lifted her chin. "Sir Alexander—"

"Do it now, Anne, and quickly," the cook cut in. "We cannot have them loitering about and gawking at us. The leavings are in a stewpot by the back door."

"But the tea. The duke's son—"

"Ooh, she is in a hurry to be off," Sally Pimm taunted. "Have you an assignation with Sir Alexander today, Miss Webster?"

Anne's cheeks went hot. "He is awaiting his tea."

The cook gave a snort. "Tend the charity first. His Grace's tea has just gone up to the library, where he is meeting with the vicar. The duchess is in the drawing room with two ladies from church, and I am sending theirs now. Sir Alexander's scones will not be ready for five minutes." She pointed her spoon at the door. "See to them or I shall have to tell Mrs. Davies of your impertinence."

Anne grabbed a ladle. "Yes, Mrs. Smythe."

As she hurried past Sally Pimm, the kitchenmaid smirked. "Do not dirty your apron now, Anne. They say Sir Alexander likes his girls pretty, unsullied, and clean. You must try to please him on at least one count."

"Sir Alexander admires respectful manners and silence," Anne retorted. "That is why his attendant at tea today is I and not some other."

In the scullery, Anne stacked clean bowls and spoons in which to ladle the leavings. She must ignore Sally and hurry. Trying to steady her fingers, she loaded a tray with the dishware and carried it back into the kitchen.

The poor of Tiverton village watched her, eyes shining with hope in their dirt-darkened faces. How could she think only of her own plans when such people were starving around her? Yet she must not let her father go on languishing in prison. And what of her sisters?

"Thank ye kindly, miss." An elderly man tipped his battered hat as she filled a bowl with leavings and handed it to him.

"God bless the duke." A man with no teeth gave her a smile. "And God bless the duchess."

Hurrying down the row of outstretched hands, Anne ladled meat and other scraps from the large pot. *Quickly now, quickly.* In all the months she had served Sir Alexander, this would be his first Saturday to take tea alone. Her only chance to speak with him! If she was late with the tea, he would be in a foul mood and would send her away at once.

"Thanks." A little girl looked up, her tiny face pinched and white as she wrapped one arm around her full bowl. "Be ye an angel from heaven, then?"

"I am but a housemaid, my dear." Unable to resist the child's sweet expression, Anne dug from her pocket the lump of sugar she had saved for Theseus and tucked it into the little one's hand. "There you are. A gift from the duke himself."

The girl turned the lump one way and another. "What is it?"

Anne could hardly imagine she had never seen sugar. "Put it into your mouth."

The child eyed the gift for a moment; then she gingerly placed the small lump on her tongue. "Mmm." Her eyes drifted shut. Long lashes fanned her cheeks. A smile spread across her lips.

The door blew open in the March wind as yet another of Tiverton's needy slipped into the kitchen. Anne took little notice. She knelt before the ragged girl and grasped her sparrow-thin hands.

"For this moment, you are a duchess," she said softly. "In your mouth is the taste of Christmas plum pudding, black currant ice cream, treacle, and Turkish delight. You are dressed in a gown of fine green silk caught up with rosettes of pink ribbon. At your neck is gathered a length of the most exquisite *Point d'Angleterre* lace. Your hair is braided, looped, and curled. Your skin is scented with fragrant heliotrope."

"Now that is a good 'un," a man said with a laugh. "She smells more like coal dust, I should think."

"Hush!" A woman gave him a sharp elbow. "Do not spoil it."

Anne watched the little girl drift in the vision she had created. "White gloves slide up your fingers and over your arms, all the way to your elbows. You have in your possession a lace fan figured with tiny Chinamen trotting across a footbridge. On your feet you wear thin slippers of emerald green kidskin. Pale mint ribbons wind around your ankles. You dance like the wind; your voice sings as high and clear as a bird's; you can draw and stitch and play the pianoforte better than anyone in the realm. In short, my little one, you are the most enchanting duchess in all of England. That is the taste in your mouth. It is dreams."

"Coo!" The little girl's eyes popped open, and everyone chuckled as she threw her grimy arms around Anne's neck. "I almost thought it was true!"

"And well it should be." The man who had just tramped in from the street swept off his dusty hat and gave the child an elegant bow. "The Marquess of Blackthorne, dear little duchess." Then he turned to Anne and repeated the bow. "I am at your service, madam."

Though heavily bearded and scruffy, he possessed a pair of gray eyes that sparkled with fun. What could she do but curtsy in return? "Queen Anne, of course."

"Your Majesty, the pleasure is all mine." Before she could react, he took her hand and lifted her bare fingers to his lips. Warm in spite of the chill outside air, his mouth brushed across her knuckles, lighting a tingle that skittered up her arm. His mustache surprised her in its softness, and she jerked her hand away.

"I beg your pardon!"

"Lavender," he pronounced, straightening. "A clean scent, slightly astringent, with all the promise of spring. Very appropriate."

"I was putting up . . . putting up the linens this afternoon." She shoved her hand beneath her apron. "Tucking lavender among the sheets."

Disconcerted more by her reaction than by the stranger

himself, Anne filled a bowl with leavings and handed it to him. Never mind. She must put him aside. He was the last of the charity, and she had not yet heard Sir Alexander's bell. There was still hope. She started down the row again, this time collecting spoons and bowls.

"If yer going to play at peerage, ye will not want to be Blackthorne," the toothless man said to the tall newcomer. "They say the poor man be dead."

"Dead? Good heavens, how did it happen?"

"Met with an accident while traveling in America. Scalped by them red savages."

"Better him than Sir Alexander," a woman uttered in a low voice. "The marquess was nothing but a rogue, he was. Roved about the country, spent money like water through a sieve, sired babes everywhere he stopped, but could not be bothered to marry here at home and give the duke an heir."

"Good riddance to the blackguard," Anne affirmed. Then she added, "God rest his soul."

"Abominable, was he?" the stranger asked. "Well, the devil take him."

"I should never wish the forces of darkness upon anyone." She set a handful of spoons on her tray. "But an heir apparent has his duties. The Marquess of Blackthorne rightly should have seen to his father's duchy. He was said to wager large sums at cards, and he engaged in more than one duel. He was even known to attend glove matches."

"And bare-knuckle boxing, too," the toothless man confirmed. "If yer bound to play at royalty, man, be the duke. He is well loved by everyone."

"Ah, the Duke of Marston." The tall man turned to the

housemaid. "Your Majesty, Queen Anne, be so good as to acquaint me with the health of the master of Slocombe House."

Stacking the used bowls on her tray, Anne tried to suppress her growing irritation with the dusty intruder. She had no time for games. "His Grace is well. He is taking tea in the library."

"And the duchess?"

"With friends in the drawing room." As she approached the man, she realized he was still lounging by the door, his bowl untouched. "You must eat, please. I am to serve Sir Alexander his tea at any moment."

"Is that a royal command, Your Highness?"

Unamused, Anne stared into the man's deep-set gray eyes. In his brown tweed coat with its tarnished brass buttons, though clearly no better off than his companions, he had a demeanor that spoke of some wit. His features were all of angles and planes, and his nose slashed down the middle of his face like an arrow, straight and determined, nostrils flared slightly. Beneath that uncompromising nose, his mouth tilted upward at one corner. Perhaps he was entertained.

"If you will not eat," she told him, "please give me your bowl."

"My dear queen, I have not finished my inquiry. How fare the duke's daughters, the ladies Claire, Lucy, Elizabeth, Charlotte, and Rebecca?"

"I could lose my position at the house," she shot back, her voice low. "Will you eat or not?"

He took a mouthful of mush and grimaced as he chewed. "The ladies?"

"They are fine, of course, all of them married and gone away."

"Even Lady Rebecca?" He raked a hand through his hair.

Coal black, it was a rumple of uncombed curls. "She is young to be wed. What of Alexander, the duke's son?"

"He is to marry in six months' time."

"Is he now? And who is the lucky lady? Not Miss Mary Clark, I hope. She may be a beauty, but she is only the daughter of a baronet. He can do much better."

Anne stared. How did such a beggar know the names and ranks of Society? With his heavy beard, unruly hair, and dark eyebrows, there was an air of wildness about the man. His large hands in their tattered knit gloves appeared so strong as to make him dangerous.

He dipped his spoon into the leavings. "This supper actually grows on one. Not bad at all, in fact. Alexander is not still dallying with Mrs. Kinnard, the actress, is he?"

"Sir Alexander's fiancée is Gabrielle Duchesne, the daughter of the Comte de la Roche."

"Blast! Has he no better sense than to choose a Frenchwoman? With Napoleon restless and France in a muddle, there is no guarantee she can hold on to her fortune."

Anne pressed the tray into her stomach as Sir Alexander's bell began to jangle on the far wall. Absorbed in his own musings, the stranger tapped his spoon against the rim of the bowl. She had to go. But this last of Tiverton's needy was clearly odd, perhaps even a lunatic, and she did not want to irk him. The others began to file out the door as he straightened, focused on Anne's eyes, and gave her a brief nod.

"Is Smythe in?" he asked.

Surprised at his common use of the formidable cook's name, Anne glanced behind her. "She is seeing to the seedcake and—"

"What of Errand? Is he still butler at Slocombe?"

"Excuse me, but please may I have your bowl?" She tried to grab it as he walked past her into the center of the kitchen. "Sir! You must go out the back way! Please, sir!"

"Mrs. Smythe," he called.

The cook lifted her head from sniffing the seedcake and swung around.

"Mrs. Smythe, have you any gingerbread nuts for my tea today?"

"Awwk!" At the first sight of the man, she dropped the plate of seedcake and threw up her hands. "It is . . . it is . . . it is—"

"Ruel Edward Chouteau, Marquess of Blackthorne." He winked at her as he gave his thick beard a tug. "Not quite as hairless as the red savages might have wished me. In fact, I am a little on the bristly side, I fear."

"Lord Blackthorne!" Mrs. Smythe shrieked, her tongue loose at last. "Great ghosts, you are dead!"

"On the contrary. I am quite alive and eager for a cup of your finest oolong. And do send for a barber, will you? I shall speak to Errand on my way up. Perhaps he ought to prepare my father with the news that his elder son has arisen from the grave."

"The marquess is in my kitchen!" As Sir Alexander's bell jangled, the cook stepped over the shattered dish of seedcake and shouted at her kitchenmaids as if they might have some explanation for what had just occurred. "He walked into the kitchen from the back! Where is his carriage? Where are his footmen? Where is the valet? Oh, how could we have known it was Lord Blackthorne? He came in with the charity!"

"Calm yourself, Mrs. Smythe. You know, I always believed the only place to learn the truth about life at Slocombe House was in the kitchen. Besides, I must have my gingerbread nuts."

"Gingerbread," the cook repeated. "Gingerbread nuts. It is you! Oh, my stars! Oh, help! Mary and Lissy, run to the larder for ginger and treacle! Sally, find Mr. Errand at once. Anne, see to Sir Alexander's tea, for pity's sake. Gingerbread. We must have gingerbread nuts."

Sucking air back into her lungs, Anne slid the tray of used bowls and spoons onto a kitchen table and picked up her skirts. She edged around the room to avoid the tall man in its center, swept up the tea things, and made for the curtained doorway that led into the hall. Her legs felt as though they had been jellied.

That ragged, dusty specimen of charity was the marquess? But the marquess was dead, scalped, and buried in America. And she'd only just wished him good riddance. She had called him a blackguard. Straight to his face!

"Your Majesty," he called out. "Good Queen Anne."

She paused, every limb suddenly rigid. She could not bring herself to look at him. "Yes, my lord?"

"Would Your Royal Highness be so kind as to extend Sir Alexander cordial greetings from his brother?"

"Yes, my lord," she whispered. "Of course, my lord."

The Marquess of Blackthorne was chuckling behind her as she brushed past the green baize curtain and fled into the hall.

A Note from the Author

Dear Friend,

Thank you for your patience as you awaited the tale of William Sherbourne and Prudence Watson. I hope you've been along for all six books that feature characters you have met again in this novel. If not, you'll meet my "country" folk (the Sherbourne family and their friends) in *English Ivy*, *Wild Heather*, and *Sweet Violet*. Some of them also appear in the novella *A Victorian Christmas Rose*. And my "city" aristocrats (Prudence and her family and friends) appear in *The Affectionate Adversary* and *The Bachelor's Bargain*. It was such fun for me to bring them all together in *The Courteous Cad*.

And what lessons our courteous cad has learned. Facing our wrongdoings, and learning to view them as God views them, is a challenge for all of us. Both William and Prudence have strong views about morality when they meet, but it isn't long before they completely reverse themselves. And most important, William learns that no sin is beyond God's forgiving grace.

If you haven't taken a close look at yourself lately, give it a try. We all need to remember that—like William and Prudence—we are works in progress. We may reverse our opinions, make serious mistakes, commit outright sin, and try to cope with a guilty conscience. But the Holy Spirit waits to transform each of us into a new creature. Pray now that His work in your heart will be profoundly life changing.

Blessings,

Catherine Palmer

Acknowledgments

My thanks to everyone at Tyndale who helped bring Miss Pickworth and her friends to life: Kathy Olson, Ron Beers, and Karen Watson. Also I thank those in design, sales, marketing, public relations, author relations, and all who see my books from manuscript to bookshelf. My gratitude also to Becky Nesbitt and Anne Goldsmith Horch, who now work elsewhere but are certainly not forgotten.

I also thank my husband, Tim Palmer, whose guiding pen is always the first to cross the pages I write. Thank you, honey. Bless you, Andrei and Geoffrey, for loving and supporting good ol' mom. May God richly bless you all.

And most of all, thank You, Lord, for holding me by the hand.

Miss Pickworth's Ponderings

After reading the tale of the courteous cad, please peruse Miss Pickworth's ponderings. She has a quantity of questions, and she wonders if you, dear reader, may come to any clever conclusions.

1. Prudence Watson was waiting to hear God's call. When she received her mission to save the mill children, how did God speak to her? Has He spoken to you? In what ways?

2. Mary chastises Prudence about her crusade, saying, "You would do better to marry a rich man and redeem the world by bringing up moral, godly, well-behaved children." Can this kind of work be a valid call from God?

3. Mary and Sarah waver wildly in their advice to Prudence about William Sherbourne. Why do they want her to

pursue and marry him? Why do they urge her never to marry such a man?

4. How do you feel about the way Prudence managed her deep love for Mr. Walker? How did she succeed in letting him go—to a more appropriate woman and a better life?

5. Jealousy rears its ugly head throughout the book. Of whom is Prudence jealous? Who does William fear may take his place in Prudence's heart? How can a Christian manage feelings of jealousy and suspicion?

6. Prudence and William are quick to act on their physical attraction to each other. How does this affect their relationship as time passes? Might they have handled this better? How?

7. Describe William's relationship with his brother Randolph. How does each rely on the other?

8. What was Prudence's view of morality at the beginning of the book? When William speaks of "gray" shades, what does he mean? How do their positions change and shift? How do you view the world?

9. Does God truly love people who make such terrible mistakes as William made? What if these wrong things are not mere mistakes but are outright, intentional sins? Can

God forgive them? How does reading Jesus' discussion with Nicodemus in John 3 affect William and Prudence?

10. Here are several Bible passages that speak about sin, forgiveness, and new life in Jesus Christ. Read them and decide what you believe God is trying to say to you about this subject.

The human heart is the most deceitful of all things, and desperately wicked. Who really knows how bad it is? (Jeremiah 17:9)

If we claim we have no sin, we are only fooling ourselves and not living in the truth. But if we confess our sins to him, he is faithful and just to forgive us our sins and to cleanse us from all wickedness. (1 John 1:8-9)

For the wages of sin is death, but the free gift of God is eternal life through Christ Jesus our Lord. (Romans 6:23)

If you confess with your mouth that Jesus is Lord and believe in your heart that God raised him from the dead, you will be saved. (Romans 10:9)

Now repent of your sins and turn to God, so that your sins may be wiped away. (Acts 3:19)

We are made right with God by placing our faith in Jesus Christ. And this is true for everyone who believes, no matter who we are. (Romans 3:22)

This means that anyone who belongs to Christ has become a new person. The old life is gone; a new life has begun! (2 Corinthians 5:17)

Therefore, since we have been made right in God's sight by faith, we have peace with God because of what Jesus Christ our Lord has done for us. Because of our faith, Christ has brought us into this place of undeserved privilege where we now stand, and we confidently and joyfully look forward to sharing God's glory. (Romans 5:1-2)

We know that God's children do not make a practice of sinning, for God's Son holds them securely, and the evil one cannot touch them. (1 John 5:18)

So now there is no condemnation for those who belong to Christ Jesus. And because you belong to him, the power of the life-giving Spirit has freed you from the power of sin that leads to death. (Romans 8:1-2)

Do you think you are perfect—or in need of forgiveness and new life? Why don't you ask God to forgive you right now—and then help you to follow Him more closely? You'll be amazed at the changes!

About the Author

Catherine Palmer has published more than fifty novels, many of them national bestsellers. She is a graduate of Southwest Baptist University and holds a master's degree in English from Baylor University. She has won numerous awards for her writing, including the Christy Award—the highest honor in Christian fiction—and the Romantic Times Career Achievement Award for inspirational fiction. Her many collections include A Town Called Hope, Treasures of the Heart, Finders Keepers, English Ivy, and the Miss Pickworth series. She also coauthored the Four Seasons fiction series with Gary Chapman, the *New York Times* bestselling author of *The Five Love Languages*. Catherine and her husband, Tim, have two grown sons and live in Vero Beach, Florida, where they serve as missionaries.

By purchasing this book from Tyndale, you have

helped us meet the spiritual and physical needs of

people all around the world.